MESSINA

CRIME

FAMILY

BOOK THREE

Twisted

PROMISES

LILIAN HARRIS

This is a work of fiction. Names, characters, organizations, places, events, and incidences are either products of the author's imagination or used fictitiously.

Editing/Interior Formatting: CPR Editing

Proofreader: Judy's Proofreading

Cover Design: Kate Decided to Design

This book is dedicated to Jackie Walker, author and friend. It's thanks to you Iseult had the time of her life with Mr. Tongue. This is what friendships are made of.

Names and Phrases

Dear Reader,
I hope this helps, especially for the fun names I chose. (LOL.)

- Iseult – "Ee-salt"
- Eriu – "Air-ooh"
- Tynan – "Tie-nan"
- Cillian – "KILL-ee-in"
- Fionn – "Fee-yun"
- Bratva – Russian organized crime or Russian Mafia
- Pakhan – Head of the Russian Mafia
- "Kak zhal', chto ya dolzhen ubit' takuyu krasivuyu zhenshchinu" – It's too bad I have to kill such a beautiful woman
- "Nu da, moya dorogaya." – That's right, my dear.
- "Zatknis', malen'kaya suka!" – Shut up, bitch!
- "Oni zdes.'" – They're here.
- "Khorosho" – Okay
- "Boodym zdarovy" – To health
- "On kak sobaka." – He's like a dog.
- "Privet, moya dorogoya. Ya skuchal po tebe. Ne mogu dozhdat'sya, kogda my snova budem vmeste." – Hello, my dear. I've missed you. Can't wait until we're re-united again.
- "Zamalshi, suka!" – Quiet, bitch!
- "Malinkiya suka" – Little bitch
- "Privet, dorogaya." – Hello, darling.

- "Ya ih ubyu." – I will kill them.
- "Krasavitsa" – Gorgeous
- "Idi prover." – Go check it out.
- "Lodna" – Okay
- "Vazmi yeyo." – Take her.

Part One

ONE YEAR AGO

One

GIO

Two weeks ago, I lost my best friend, Bryce. He was gunned down in some dark alley like an animal. The man they arrested, Donny, confessed to the whole thing. The gun was retrieved from the nearby dumpster. His fingerprints were on the weapon, him on the scene. It was all perfect.

Too perfect.

So much so that neither my other friend, Grant, nor I believed Donny had actually done it. Didn't stop me from putting out a hit on him in prison, though. Just in case. He's still awaiting trial, but a lot can happen between now and then.

Stepping into my Bugatti Chiron, I hit the road and head toward Grant's company, Westfield Enterprises—named after his grandfather, who started it. Grant makes a shitload producing the most popular cell phone and memory chip that's currently on the market. He's got his hands in AI tech too.

The most impressive thing about Grant, though, is his ability to hack anything and find anyone.

Grant, Bryce, and I met in business school. We were pretty close, knew all the fucked-up shit each other did. There were no secrets between us…as far as I knew.

But I still don't know why Bryce was in that alley near some exclusive dance club. He was supposed to meet Grant and I at one of the bars my family owns, but he never showed and never returned our calls. Several hours later, I got a message from one of our police contacts, telling me they'd found his body and arrested someone.

There was nothing to go on other than the confession and the evidence, which was all the detectives cared about. There were no cameras in the area to catch what happened, either. At least none that we've found so far.

It could've been just about anyone who did it. Anyone Donny is covering for. Bryce's family has plenty of enemies. They're oil tycoons or whatever the hell you call those people. I know we're missing something. So when Grant called telling me to come to his office to look at some evidence he found on Bryce, I dropped everything.

A car honks when I veer into the right lane at an accelerated speed. This is me going slow. They don't want to see this car do the max at 273 miles an hour.

Rolling off the highway, I make it to Grant's office building and ease my car into one of the reserved spots.

The elevator ride is quick to the thirtieth floor, and I greet his secretary, Tamila, whose rosy cheeks get even rosier when I pass her by with a grin. She flicks her shoulder-length auburn hair back and answers the ringing phone as I head to Grant's office.

The only reason I haven't fucked her yet is so I don't mess shit up for Grant. Otherwise, I'd have her on her knees sucking my dick by now.

I don't even knock when I enter, finding Grant leaning back in his chair talking to someone on the phone. The view of the city is brightly lit behind him, visible through the floor-to-ceiling glass windows.

"I don't deal with pussies, Tyson," Grant chides. "If he can't handle a twenty million investment, then I don't want him."

There's a long pause.

"That's right. You can tell him that." He zeroes his gaze on me and gestures toward the chair in front of his desk. "You tell him that if I don't have the money in my account by sundown, he's out."

The shouting of another man's voice echoes as he pulls the cell away from his ear and ends the call while I settle down.

He presses two fingers into his temple, closing his eyes as he takes a deep breath.

"That sounded fun."

His attention wanders over to me as he draws himself closer to the desk. "Some of these assholes think they can run in the big leagues when they haven't even graduated from the minors." He shakes out of his black suit jacket and fits it over the back of his chair.

"So, what do you have on Bryce?" I ask.

He gives me a tight look, his crystal blue eyes darkening right before he opens his laptop and presses a few keys. "Take a look at this."

My pulse quickens as I drag my chair closer, just as he turns the screen toward me.

"I managed to borrow a recording from a satellite camera. This was taken the night he was killed."

"By borrow, you mean…"

He nods with a satisfied look on his face and runs his fingers through his jet-black hair.

He hacked it. Of course he did. The rumor about him getting into the CIA database when he was in high school? All true.

The video begins to play, and my eyes zero in on the slightly blurry aerial image. I squint at it, unable to make out the setting. It's damn dark and the video isn't very zoomed in, but I can easily tell there's no one there.

But a minute later, two figures appear, a third running after them in a hurry. I can only make out the tops of their heads.

I drop my face even closer, trying to catch their faces, anything at all to give me an indication as to who was there with him that evening. One of the individuals is holding a woman, I think, her long hair fluttering while the third keeps running after them. Could be a man or woman.

"What the fuck is this?" I glance up at Grant momentarily.

"Keep watching." His features grow tense.

The one running approaches the two others.

"Is Bryce holding a woman?"

"Has to be him." He nods once. "This was exactly where he was killed, around the time he was killed."

Fuck.

My temples throb. "What the hell was he doing?"

"I don't know. But whatever it was, it got him killed."

I grind my molars, my eyes still on the screen.

The person continues to argue with the man we think is Bryce, hands flinging in the air, feet getting nearer. But he walks away a short distance and drops the woman he's holding like dead weight.

I stare at the imagery before me, trying like hell to make sense of it all. Bryce was never violent with women. Not around me, at least. There has to be more to this.

Shadows cover their faces, and there's no real indication that this is even Bryce, except that the person moves exactly like he did. Bryce was a big dude. Tall. Solid. And from the small glimpse, so is the person on the video.

While Bryce argues with the stranger, his arms slowly rise, and he collapses seconds later and the video suddenly cuts off.

"What the hell? What happened to the rest?"

"That's all I was able to get."

I ball a fist. Dead end again. No face means no ID.

"Now we know for certain Donny didn't kill him. I mean…" I lean back into the chair. "Donny is over six feet, around Bryce's height, and whoever shot Bryce looked smaller."

"I know. It's exactly what we thought. He's covering for someone."

Someone else killed Bryce. A single bullet struck him in the chest, and he bled out to death while whoever actually did it is living scot-free.

What the hell was he up to? What could've gotten him killed?

Was he saving the woman he was holding from that other person? Was he gambling again? Did that have something to do with it?

If it did, I would've helped him, if only he'd come to me. He told us he wasn't doing that anymore, not since his family swore they'd cut him off.

"We need to find out who those people were and how they knew him," I tell Grant, who nods in agreement.

His thick brows drag inward. "We will, even if it takes our entire life. We'll get to the bottom of it."

"I need to go see Donny," I tell him.

"You can't. I already told you. He's in solitary because of that fight. They won't let you anywhere near him, Gio. And we don't have an in with that prison."

"Fuck!"

I slam a fist on his desk, sending pens scattering everywhere. He doesn't bother to collect them.

It's my fault Donny is in solitary. The hit on him didn't work out so well. The man I paid ended up dead.

"We can't assume Bryce was doing something wrong," I say, feeling the need to defend him.

He was our friend. We owe it to him not to think the worst. He may have not been a Boy Scout, but he wouldn't have hurt a woman. Something had to have been going on.

"Never assumed he was guilty of anything." Grant pauses, pulling in a heavy breath. "Don't mention this to anyone. Not even his family."

"You think it's them?"

"Could be. We don't know who is behind it." He rocks back and forth, thoughtfully covering his mouth with a hand. "They were pretty mad at him when he stole money from the company to pay off the loan sharks."

"Yeah." I nod slowly. "I remember that. But it's been years. Why now?"

He shrugs. "Who the hell knows? But I want this to stay between us just in case."

"Okay."

His intercom beeps.

"Sir," Tamila's voice comes through. "You have an urgent call from Taiwan on line three."

"I'll go, and you get that," I tell him, getting to my feet.

"I'll keep you posted on anything else I find," he replies as he picks up the phone and hits a key.

I head back out toward the elevator, needing to go meet with Michael. And the whole way there, I keep wondering if we're deluding ourselves into thinking we'll ever find Bryce's true killer.

Two

GIO

The world is filled with people you can't trust. They're out there right now, waiting to screw you over.

And being who we are—the kings of the underworld, the ones they warn you about—those people are all around us. But the flip side is, if we catch wind of their disloyalty, they pay the price.

With their life.

"I know where he's going to be tonight," my brother Michael informs me, taking the glass of whiskey to his mouth and downing the contents.

He slams it back down with a heavy clank, his elbows hitting his desk. As he leans in, his dark eyes fill with contempt for the one man we haven't been able to locate for the past three years.

"Where?" I settle back comfortably into the leather chair, staring right back with the same indignation.

Carl Nelson was one of our bankers. He was good at laundering for us overseas. Except little old Carl decided to play with our money…a little too much. Hookers, drugs, yachts. That's what he did with the ten million he stole from us.

I don't know if most people are fucking stupid or just the ones we encounter, but did he not think we'd eventually find him?

Maybe he thought we'd high-five him for eluding us for this long.

Yeah, Carl, thanks for stealing that money from us. Can't wait to take a ride on that yacht we bought.

May as well have bought it. It's our fucking money.

Maybe he even thought we'd eventually forget about the dough. I mean, we have plenty of it, but that's not the point. He took what's ours, and that equals death. It's that simple.

Michael has been working hard to grow our legitimate enterprise. The money from our underground casino businesses from around the globe, on top of the online gambling we run, has allowed us to grow our legal businesses tenfold. That, of course, allows us to hide the dirty money so the feds can't find it. And believe me they've tried.

To the outside world, we're just your average billionaires in suits, working from a desk most of the time. But they don't see our real side—and if they do, it's because we're probably about to end their life.

"He's going to be at the Titans' fundraiser tonight," Michael explains. "It'll be at their hotel on the Upper East Side. Invite only." My brother's face turns with a cold, calculating grin, the scar on his right cheek jerking. "And it so happens, you're on the list."

"Lucky me."

I can't wait to get my hands on him. I won't need weapons—

not that I'll go empty-handed. But I'll enjoy choking him to death a lot more. It's a good thing Carl never met me, or his untimely end would be a lot harder to accomplish.

The Titans are friends of ours. They're philanthropic as fuck on the outside and as dirty as us on the inside. It's funny; the rich think they're better than us, but in actuality, they're their own version of organized crime. Corruption, greed, murder. They know it all well, even though they hire others to do their dirty work. I'd imagine it's easier to pretend. To fool themselves into believing they're clean. As though their soul gets an automatic pass in hell just because they think they're superior.

"Some of our guys will be working the event." Michael's arms fold across his chest. "They'll let you pass without checking if you're strapped. But don't make a scene," he warns through a narrowed gaze. "We can't afford to rock the boat with the law. Don't want to push our luck so soon."

"Is Captain Jared still pissed about the dead guys in that office building?" I chuckle under my breath.

"Oh yeah." He nods with a bemused twist of his mouth.

"Guess he didn't appreciate the evidence of wiretapping I left him either?"

"He did thank us for that. But he had a lot of cleanup to do." He laughs dryly, probably recalling the phone call he got because of it.

Last week, when I took some of our foot soldiers to gather intel on where Carl might be, we met some of his friends…and let's just say it didn't go well. Lots of blood. And limbs. It wasn't pretty. Can't really blame the captain for being pissy. He may be in our pocket, but he's still a damn cop.

But nothing will stop us from finding and killing Carl. He's done well hiding from coast to coast around the globe, and every time we got close, he'd vanish again. Must've gotten cocky to return to the States. But more than three years have passed since we discovered what he'd been doing, so he probably thinks we got tired of searching.

"I'll be ready tonight. He won't leave that hotel alive."

Michael pours more amber gold into his glass, lowering the decanter back down beside him. "I know you'll get the job done. Not worried about that."

"What's the fundraiser for?" I wonder curiously.

I don't like those damn events. Too many people to shake hands with. But I do my fair share of donating to various causes, especially if they're related to kids or animals.

"Children's cancer hospital," Michael replies. "It's going to be an auction."

"Ah, fuck. It's ugly fucking art again, isn't it?"

The last time I was forced to attend one of these types of events, I ended up with three paintings that looked like something a kid made in art class. I donated them to a museum. But I couldn't resist when they were raising money for domestic violence shelters.

"They're not auctioning off art." My brother snickers when he registers my unsavory expression.

"What, then?"

"Women," he remarks pointedly.

I jerk my head back. "Say that again?"

His chuckling rumbles through the room. "You heard right. Rich women auctioning themselves as dates for rich, old fucks."

Great…

If I win, I have to take some uptight princess on a date? Not happening. I don't date. I fuck. But I guess we can do that too…

Well, now this evening is looking a tad more interesting.

"I know that face." Michael's stern voice is hard to miss.

I swear sometimes he thinks he's my damn father, even though

I'm twenty-eight and he's only six years older than me.

He's not even the oldest. I've got another brother, Raph, who's thirty-seven and not exactly around anymore. Had a lot to do with him starting a war with the Irish Mob over the recent death of his wife, Bianca.

He blamed them. They denied it. So, of course, he went in guns blazing and ended up killing the nephew of the head of the Mob. Patrick obviously isn't that impressed that his nephew is dead, and now he wants to kill Raph. So Michael forced Raph into hiding until he can resolve the conflict.

Michael's the next in line to lead the Messina crime family, which our father is currently the head of. He's planning on retiring, though, and is pressuring Michael to find a wife so he can do just that. It's just how it's done in our circle. The men want a family man to lead them, someone who has stakes in the game. Someone who can show them he can keep his own family well protected.

Except a wife is the last thing Michael wants. But he knows it's what he must do if he wants to take my father's place.

It should've been Raph taking over, but our father would never let that happen. He and Raph have always despised one another. As the years have passed, it has only gotten uglier between the two of them. I don't know what my father's problem is. Raph has never done a damn thing except try to make that man proud. He's never succeeded, though, and he never will. We all know that.

I'm just glad I was born the youngest. The last thing I'd ever want is to get married. What the fuck for? Do people end up happier when they're stuck with one person? And if they claim they're happy, I'd like a sit-down. I bet by the end of it, I'd have them divorced.

Look at my parents, for example. My father fucks anything under thirty, and Ma just stays there and takes it. I'd probably end up just like him. Why would having a wife stop me from fucking around?

Never met a woman I wanted to marry anyway.

"Alright, I've gotta go," I tell Michael and rise to my feet.

"Where are you off to in such a hurry?" He cocks his head with a curious gaze. "And what's her name?"

I do admit I have a bit of a reputation. Usually in the form of a long-legged brunette. Or a blonde. I'm not picky.

I roll up the cuffs of my baby-blue dress shirt and smirk. "Wouldn't you like to know?"

He shakes his head. "Better not be someone who works for us."

"You worry too much." I start for the door. "Have a little fun."

"I'll leave that up to you," he scoffs. "Don't get anyone pregnant this time." He reminds me of the time I got a bartender from one of our bars knocked up.

Or so I thought. Ended up being someone else's baby.

"And end up with a kid like you?" I joke. "Never."

"You shut your mouth." He cants his chin up with a hard stare. "Sophia is the best thing that ever happened to me." He inhales, emotions overtaking him.

"She's the best thing that ever happened to all of us," I confidently reply.

We're all crazy about my five-year-old niece. When Michael brought her home, none of us had any idea how we'd be able to live the life we did with a kid around. But leave it to my brother to make it work. Protecting her is our number one priority. She will always come first.

It's another reason I don't want to get married. My wife is definitely going to want kids, and I don't need to worry about keeping her and the kids alive. Too many people to be responsible for. It's better not to have anyone's death on your conscience.

Bianca's death taught us all that.

"Alright, I'm out of here." My mouth turns up. "For real this time."

Michael gives me a tense look before he says, "Keep me informed about tonight."

"Of course." Tugging the door open, I make it out of his office and head toward the garage.

Three

GIO

Hours later, and I'm at the Titans' hotel, making myself comfortable at the bar, where I have eyes on Carl. But he's been too busy drinking too much champagne to even notice me following his every move.

The dimly lit ballroom is scattered with round tables and simple white tablecloths that cost more than they're worth.

I grab a bacon-wrapped shrimp from a waitress, who offers me one as she passes. My attention, though? It's on Carl as he laughs with two younger women, both in expensive-looking black gowns.

I wonder how many people Carl actually stole from. Definitely not from anyone here, or he wouldn't have come. But I bet we're not the only ones he's pissed off.

Carl was the go-to banker for the underworld. He knew how to hide money better than anyone. But little old Carl got too cocky, and now little old Carl is going to die.

"Hi there," a woman's voice drifts from my left.

I turn to find golden eyes sparkling, but not as bright as the large studs that accent her ears. Her ivory dress hugs her tight, the length sweeping the floor as she moves to settle on the empty chair beside me.

"I'm Vivian Trout." She holds out her hand. "And who may you be?" A flirtatious smile widens across her face.

She's pretty enough. Maybe forty. Blonde hair pinned up into some intricate-looking web. Her ring finger, though? It's not bare.

And that just proves my point about marriage. It's bullshit.

"I'm Giovanni." I lift her hand to my mouth and lower my lips across the top of it before letting it go.

"What a beautiful name." Her face lights up. "Will you be staying for the auction? It should start shortly."

"I intend to."

"Good, then." She begins to leave, coming to stand between my spread knees. "I do hope you bid on me, Giovanni." A single finger slinks out and rolls up my thigh while I stare at her indifferently. "I'd *love* to get to know you better."

Wicked intent lines her gaze, and it does nothing to impress me. My dick just about shrivels. If these are the kinds of women they're auctioning off, I may as well donate some cash and be done with it.

She doesn't wait for me to respond, strutting away with a sway of her hips, a little too obnoxiously for my taste. And I'm even less interested in fucking her now than I was a moment ago.

A whole thirty minutes passes, and I'm still seated in the same spot, watching Carl talking to the same women.

This shit is boring the hell out of me, and I force myself to glance around the room, eyeing people I never had any desire to be at the same event with. Some of them know who I am and are staying as far away from me as possible.

My gaze darts to a woman at the far end of the room. One I failed to notice earlier…but fuck, am I noticing her now.

My pulse instantly kicks up and I straighten my back, completely transfixed. I've never seen her before. Because believe me, if I had, I'd remember.

Her bright red lips match the crimson dress she wears, her tits spilling out from the deep V-cut. She's on the tall side, maybe five-eight, and she's got those curves men would go to hell just to see bare. And her hair… My God, I've never seen hair so flaming red, as though she's walked through fire and lived to tell about it.

She throws on a radiating smile as she speaks to two men who appear as though they may blow a load from merely being in her presence. She places a palm on the shorter man's arm—about a head shorter than her—and nods, right before she gives them her back and walks off. As she does, she rolls her eyes, and I just about burst into a laugh.

Her whole demeanor shifts when she thinks no one is looking. With a tight grimace, she quickly fixes the top of her dress discreetly, pulling it up like she doesn't want to show much skin. But that would be kinda hard when that ruby-red material clings to her like a second skin, accentuating every bend on her sinful body.

She turns, giving me more of a side view, while she gives her gown one more gentle tug, and as she turns to face the room, her lips jerk into a forced grin.

Her gaze scatters around the space as though she's looking for someone, and then it instantly hits mine.

For a few aching seconds, she stares at me intently. My heart races, the noise of the room reducing to a buzz as though she lowered the volume. My mouth lifts at the corner, and instantly, she scowls. But her eyes…they remain gripped to mine.

Who the hell is she, and why do I want to know everything about her?

Those long, fiery strands shimmer in the light as she runs a finger through them, pushing the waves off her cheek. I bet all that hair would be soft in my fist. I bet she's a screamer too.

My dick throbs at the thought.

Hopefully, she's part of the auction. In either case, I will find her after I get rid of Carl, and I *will* get to know her.

I grind my molars, getting myself to focus on the task. Carl is why I'm here. Hopefully that sexy little redhead isn't going anywhere.

As though sharing my thoughts, she breaks our connection and slowly strides out of the room, and my face instantly falls.

Fuck. If I didn't have to watch Carl, I could've followed her out. What if she leaves and I never see her again?

Why do I even care?

With a flick of my finger, I get the bartender's attention, order a whiskey neat, and drown in the scorching liquid pooling in my gut, trying to get that woman out of my head. Then I order another.

I need Carl to head up to his hotel room. That is where I plan to end him. One of the security guys at the event informed me that Carl's got himself a suite upstairs. All I have to do is get rid of his bodyguard, who stands not too far from Carl. Pretty stupid to hire just one man to keep him safe. But I can't say Carl is all that smart to begin with, or he'd never have stolen from people like us.

"Hello, everyone," a gray-haired emcee announces, tapping on the microphone from the stage to my right.

Shifting, I face him as he looks on with a grin, bright lights bathing his face. Laughter and whistles explode.

"You guys are a rowdy crowd," he chuckles. "Thank you, thank you."

He waves down a hand, and the noise begins to die until it's quiet.

"I hope you're all ready to open up those wallets for a worthy cause."

The room breaks with a round of claps, and the host grins as he goes on.

"Shortly, we'll have ten beautiful ladies who were gracious enough to volunteer to be auctioned off as dates to help us raise money for St. Augustus Hospital."

More cheers echo through the room.

"That's right." He nods, fixing his black bowtie with his free hand. "Are you all ready to get the ball rolling?"

The response is filled with excitement while I swallow my whiskey and slam the glass back down on the bar, my eyes scanning the room for my redhead.

But she's nowhere to be seen.

Fuck. She left. Of course she did. She didn't even want to be here. Wasn't that difficult to tell. Was she roped in like I was?

"The first woman up is a board-certified plastic surgeon," the emcee announces, and I stare as that woman Vivian walks onto the stage. "She graduated first in her class at Harvard Medical School and…"

The rest blurs. I'm not going to be bidding on anyone, so it makes no difference who these women are. I'll make the Titans real happy with a check for five million before I leave.

Woman after woman climbs up on the stage. Some younger, some older.

I focus on Carl, though, who's settled at one of the tables in the middle of the room. He hasn't bid on anyone either, which is good. Wouldn't want any witnesses when I take him out.

"Are we ready to start the bid on our last contestant?"

Thank fucking God.

Hopefully after this, Carl goes up to his suite.

"Help me welcome Izzy onto the stage!"

People whistle, and I force myself to look at the woman, expecting anyone else.

Anyone but *her*.

My chest swells.

Same gorgeous fake smile.

Hair as bright as the sun at dusk.

Ruby-red dress clinging to her hips.

Fuck me. I'm in trouble now. So is my wallet.

Because I'm not going home until that redhead is mine.

The ends of her lips curl even deeper for the crowd, like she knows she has them in her pocket. Because she sure as hell owns me in this very moment.

My feet are moving of their own volition, marching closer until I'm taking a seat at the first table, right by the stage, not giving a shit if this chair belongs to someone else. Because right now it belongs to me, like she will by the end of tonight.

Her gaze immediately locks with mine like it did earlier, and I don't dare look away. I cross my arms over my chest and lean back, welcoming the challenging glint in her turquoise gaze. And the more she stares, the more my heartbeats go haywire.

She's the most beautiful woman I've ever seen in my goddamn life, a sophisticated and refined kind of beauty. She carries confidence in her posture, like it's a secret strength, and it causes my attraction to her to turn insatiable.

A few men whistle provocatively, and I'm about to rush over there and break their fucking necks.

From over my shoulder, my eyes connect with one of them. The rage must be evident on my features, because the prick instantly shuts up.

Her lips jerk when I look back at her, in what one could only describe as her version of an authentic smile.

I return it, the small crawl of my lips deepening into a smirk. As I do, her face hardens and she looks past me, like I've offended her.

"Izzy here is a pianist," the man continues, and she laughs flirtatiously. "She speaks five languages and, according to her, she can cook better than anyone here."

Laughter erupts.

"Let's start the bid at one hundred thousand dollars. Do I hear one hundred?"

"One hundred," someone calls out.

I violently peer back, finding an older man with an arm across a woman's shoulder who looks to be his age, both of them grinning.

The numbers keep growing, and in all this time, I stare at her, waiting for my chance to win. I'm gonna have that woman smile at me like she means it if it's the last thing I do. But I have to get her alone first.

"Three million dollars," says someone in a thick English accent, and it belongs to only one person.

Carl. Fucking Carl.

My pulse surges.

First he took our money.

Now he wants to take my girl.

Not gonna happen.

Except she's not your girl.

She can be for one night, though.

I raise a finger in the air. "Five million."

Her eyes pop wide.

"Eight million," Carl counters.

I don't have to look at him to hear the smugness in his voice. He really wants to die tonight.

Izzy's lips quirk.

"Ten million," I reply, a fist curling at my side, barely containing my simmering wrath.

Her chest twitches with a quick breath, and her face turns tight. She dares me a look, and I find irritation clouding over her gaze, wondering why it's there.

She shakes her head, but just barely, and I slant my head curiously. She wants him to win. Now I'm really intrigued about this little redhead.

I'll let that asshole win if that's what she wants, but only to find out why.

"Twenty million dollars," Carl throws out.

I snicker to myself. Probably stole that too.

From the far left, I look at him and nod graciously.

We'll see each other real soon.

I turn my attention back to her, finding her glistening gaze raking me with deep concentration.

"Congratulations to the gentleman in the back," the emcee announces.

And she instantly perks up, looking over at Carl and grinning.

Well, Red, seems I've lost. But don't worry, we'll be getting to know each other real soon.

And then you'll tell me exactly what you're up to.

four

ISEULT

Who the hell was that stranger, and why can't I stop thinking about him? He just kept staring at me, like he couldn't stand the thought of doing anything else.

I felt his eyes the whole time I stood on that stage, being auctioned off like a piece of goddamn meat.

Unfortunately, I had no choice in the matter.

When he practically ripped some guy's throat off for whistling at me, I felt a tiny bit vindicated, though I'm pretty capable of ripping throats myself.

The intensity behind those deep, dark eyes had me forgetting for a moment why I was at this event in the first place. I have a mission to accomplish, or Daddy Dearest will be quite pissed off, and I only piss him off in small doses at a time.

It was easy to fake an identity, and it was even easier to get an invite to this event. Flash some cleavage, throw on a pretty smile, and these men eat right out of your palm.

One of the tech guys who works for my father got a copy of the guest list. So I followed one of the attendees—some bigshot surgeon—to a bar last night, and when I passed his table, I "accidentally" knocked off his drink and spilled it all over his lap. And by accidentally, I mean completely on purpose.

I offered to buy him another, and instead he was buying one for me. Five drinks later, and I was getting an invitation to this event. I made him believe I was a trust-fund baby, and that's all he heard before he asked me to join him. These people are so easy to con.

Once I got here, he got a call about an emergency surgery, so I was left to entertain myself, which is exactly what I wanted.

I knew about the auction before I followed him, and I knew that to get what I wanted, I had to participate. And they were more than thrilled to accept my offer. It was the best way to get Carl alone. He has a thing for redheads, and I knew he'd want me.

Then I kill him.

It's simple, really. Lure the sucker into his room, let him grab my ass once or twice, and when we're on his bed and he thinks I'll let him fuck me, I'll stab him with my lipstick.

Well, it's not a lipstick, exactly. More like a tiny needle that'll shoot him with enough sleeping meds to put him out for days. Can't really kill him while he's conscious. Last thing I need is for him to scream and have his bodyguard find me with a knife to his master's throat.

Can't just stick him with a lethal dose of something, either. Wouldn't want to risk a toxicology report picking something up. But that wouldn't be an option anyway. Daddy wants to make this personal, and that means blood. That way all his friends know he died brutally for what he'd done, and that'll make them think twice about ever doing the same.

I do enjoy getting my hands dirty. It's kinda my toxic trait. And I'm perfectly okay with it.

Carl snakes his grimy arm around my lower back, his fingers deepening into my hip like he owns me, while I wonder how fast I can murder the man.

I throw on a fabricated smile while he talks to some hedge-fund guy, treating me like his personal arm candy.

It's okay, though. I'm used to being underestimated by men. My goal tonight isn't to impress this rat of a man.

The faster we can be done here, the faster I can leave New York City behind and return home to Massachusetts. Where I can easily forget that attractive man from earlier who's presently poking holes into my back. I can practically feel his eyes following me everywhere I go.

Just to see if I'm right, I discreetly glance over my shoulder. And sure enough, there he is, thick black hair perfectly styled back, eyes as dark as the midnight sky, yet glistening like two stars. The muscle in his sculpted jaw tics as his eyes sink into mine, and I hold them for long, breathtaking seconds, wondering why I haven't turned back around.

His black tux fits him like a glove, and I bet all the hidden muscles beneath would feel firm under my fingertips.

My eyes rove down his body, and his mouth curves up deliciously on one side.

Geez, does he have to smile at me like he's already thinking about all the different ways he wants to fuck me?

Quickly, I whirl back around. What the hell am I doing? I really shouldn't be staring or thinking about riding him like a dirty cowgirl.

Yep. I've gotta get laid. It's been a while since I got some, not that it really does anything for me. For some pathetic reason, the men I seem to attract don't know how to fuck for shit. It's why I don't have orgasms with any of them. Don't even know why I bother sleeping with men anymore. Most of the time, I'm lying there thinking about the logistics for my next kill.

My work is a lot more exciting. I go where I'm sent. It's the job of an enforcer. Never imagined that I'd not only be the first female enforcer in the Irish Mob, but also the first female instructor at Caellach Academy. But here I am, paving the way for women everywhere. Real fucking trailblazer.

Took some time to convince my father to give me a shot, but it was pity. He blamed himself for what happened to me all those years ago. So, of course, when I begged to join the academy at eighteen, he couldn't refuse. It's where kids turn into killers, and I'm one of the people who help them get there.

My father would give me almost anything to atone for what I went through. But after I graduated from the academy, he admitted that he didn't think I'd ever pass. See, my father runs our underground assassin school, which is what the trainees like to call it, and the last thing he wanted was his daughter joining it. Sexism and all.

He thought I'd give it a shot, fail out, and that'd be that. He never actually thought he'd have a daughter who kills people for a living. Well, it's the family business after all, and I'm quite good at it.

And if I'm being honest, it's the one thing in my life that helps me forget. All that ugliness I endured is still there, hiding behind the shadows, waiting, hoping to take me back there every chance it gets.

What *he* did to me? It's imprinted in the marrow of my bones, branding me with an unending hit of poison. His poison. Every day, I wonder if I'll see him again. If I'll get the chance to end him.

Until then, I imagine that every single man I kill wears his face.

I don't fear death. I don't fear anything except solitude. When I'm alone with my own thoughts. With the nightmares that come. With the panic that seeps into my waking days, infecting me with the past.

And every time it comes, every single moment I'm taken there, I fight those thoughts like it's my greatest threat. But sometimes I lose. It's the only time I ever do.

My three brothers—Tynan, Fionn, and Cillian—are just like me. Fighters. Killers. But my baby sister, Eriu, on the other hand, isn't. Which is a good thing. She's far too innocent and sweet to ever do what we do. She couldn't even hurt a fly.

Unless that fly was trying to hurt someone she loves. Then she'd do what she had to. It's in our blood, whether we want it to be or not.

I'd do anything for that girl. The nine-year age difference didn't stop us from being close. She may only be seventeen, but we've always had a great relationship. I practically raised her when our mother died.

I was fourteen when it happened, and I was forced to grow up fast. Our father was too busy blaming himself to worry about a five-year-old girl. He was hungry for revenge against the Russians for killing our mom, and it consumed him until he got his vengeance.

Then tragedy hit once more, and this time it came for me. Once again, his blame ate him up, and I don't think he ever recovered. Not fully. Years have gone by, and we all pretend it never happened.

Including me.

But how long can you pretend before it eats you alive?

It doesn't matter. It's in the past. No one can take me back there.

But he can. He's still out there. He can find you, and he can make you pay for what you did.

Do you remember how loud you screamed? How much you cried?

My heart races.

My vision grows out of focus.

No. Not here. This can't be happening here.

Breathe. Just breathe.

In. Out. Repeat.

I inhale slowly, trying to still my climbing pulse.

He can't scare me. Not anymore. I'm not that little girl he remembers.

"So, Izzy, are you enjoying yourself?" Carl drawls, his voice like an echo.

I bite down, forcing myself to concentrate on his face, even as my heartbeats pound in my ears.

He hands me a glass of something red, his accent even thicker now that he's had more to drink.

I take a pretend sip and smile. It's what men like him enjoy. Pretty women who grin at them politely, while keeping their opinions to a minimum.

"Oh, yes, it's so lovely to be here to support such a worthy cause." I finger my hair, grinning from ear to ear like a fool.

"I couldn't agree more." His eyes snake down my curves, not missing an inch.

God, I hate this dress. It's too tight. I can barely move. Why did my friend Kora make me wear it? I feel like a high-priced escort.

I can just hear her voice.

It makes your ass and tits look like you paid good money for them. He'll want to eat you alive. He won't even see you coming.

"Thank you for my drink," I tell him just as his fingers slide out and run down my shoulders.

The crinkles lining his hazel eyes deepen as he stares at my tits like he's about to make a meal out of them. Too bad for Carl, he won't be eating much of anything after tonight.

"I have quite the collection of the finest wine in my suite," he tells me. "And since it appears as though the party has come to an unfortunate end, let's continue upstairs, shall we?"

He gestures toward the exit with an outstretched arm. Doesn't seem like he's offering me much of a choice. I guess no one taught Carl not to open the door for strangers.

"You've read my mind." My mouth tilts up as I lower my glass on a nearby table, the drink still full.

But Carl doesn't care. He just wants me naked.

Sorry, Carl. Not tonight. Or ever, for that matter.

He hooks his arm through mine, and his bodyguard follows close behind. He's tall, built like a linebacker, and looks at me like I'm Satan. I guess he has to look at everyone like he hates them. Part of the job.

As we start to slip out of the ballroom, I pivot to find that handsome stranger still staring at me, glued to the bar.

A chill scurries up my spine.

He isn't even checking me out like most men do. They look right at my tits or my ass, but not him. Not from where I stand. He's gazing right into my eyes like he's wondering who I am. He did the same when I was up on that stage, when he was bidding on me. I swear if he won and ruined all my plans, I was going to kill him.

I'm unable to peel my eyes off of him, even as my feet force me further away. The man has this aura about him like he knows how to have a good time, but mess with him and he'll show you just how fun things can really get.

Maybe that's what drew me in. The danger lurking in those obsidian eyes. It's what I'm addicted to, isn't it? Danger?

Doesn't matter, anyway. After tonight, I'll never see him again.

Men are not to be trusted. Especially good-looking ones.

His gaze lowers to Carl's arm, still perched around the small of my back, and the intensity brewing in his eyes would scare any other woman.

But not me.

Men don't scare me.

Least of all him.

GIO

As soon as she looked at me right before she walked out with that prick, everything in me said to follow her. Killing Carl wasn't even on my mind in that moment. It was the fact that she was leaving with him, probably going up to his room.

I know what men like Carl do to women. He's going to hurt her, and I won't stay on the sidelines while he does. He won't get to touch her. I don't care what her reason was for wanting him to win. It's irrelevant now.

They went up seconds ago, and I'm inside the other elevator riding up to the fifteenth floor, the penthouse. His is the only room up there.

I plan to take out his bodyguard as quietly as possible, then throw him in the janitor's closet. Our friends working security told me there's one up there. All the cameras have been shut off until after I've taken care of him. By the time the cleaning staff finds Carl tomorrow morning, I'll be gone, with no trace that I was even here.

Grumbling, I start to sway once the elevator doors part, pretending I'm drunk. As soon as that jerkoff bodyguard sees me, he turns.

"Hey, m-man," I slur. "C-can you show me…firteen n-nineteen?"

I wobble, my head lolling. He stands there, back against the wall, and completely ignores me.

Thanks for your help, jerkoff.

I groan, my body swinging toward him, a hand in my pocket, getting ready to take out that syringe I've been saving for him.

He starts toward me, clenching his jaw.

As soon as I fall into him, he tries to push me off.

"Hey, asshole," he clips out. "Get the fuck off—"

The needle punctures his thigh before he even realizes it's happened.

"Have a nice sleep," I whisper into his ear as he starts to collapse on me. "Can't say you'll be waking up, though."

Quickly, I grab his arms and drag him all the way to the end of the floor. With one hand, I pop open the closet and shove him inside. It's roomy in there. He fits just fine.

Taking out my nine, the silencer on, I put a bullet between his eyes. He could ID me. Can't keep him alive. I'll have Michael send someone to clean this up.

Reaching into his pocket, I take his keycard for Carl's room and proceed toward it, slipping the weapon back in the holster at my waist and making sure my jacket covers it.

When I'm right beside the door, I lean in, listening for voices, but not hearing any. Fuck, what if he hurt her already? Or drugged her. I wouldn't put that past him. I can't wait to get my damn hands on him.

And then it hits me.

She'll be a witness too. I'm going to have to kill her. Shit. Why the hell did she have to get involved with him? There's no way I can end her life. I don't kill women, especially innocent ones. Or hot ones.

Fucking hate how hot she was. And who can forget the way she was staring at me? Like she wanted to stab my eye out with a fork while wanting my hands all over her body.

I especially enjoyed the feisty glimmer in her gaze. Bet she'd hate me once she finds out what kind of man I truly am.

Maybe I can drug her and leave her here long enough to wake up and run like hell when she finds his dead body.

That's what I'll have to do. I'll even follow her every move once she's gone, maybe send a threatening letter to make sure she doesn't talk to the cops. I'll figure it out once I'm in there. I can't waste any more time thinking about this.

As silently as possible, I scan the keycard, and a small ding sounds off. With a hand on my nine, I gently push the door and let myself into what appears to be a large, dim, empty room. I close the door behind me, eyes scanning the expansive living room.

Not a sight of Carl or Izzy.

The floorboards creak beneath my feet as I take a step forward, and when I catch the sudden faint banging noise from my left, coming from behind a closed door down the hallway, I tighten my grasp on my weapon.

I listen for it again.

Nothing.

With my pulse beating in my ears, I remove my gun and slowly shuffle toward the hallway. My footsteps thud heavily as I inch closer until I'm before the white door that was left ajar.

Shoving it open a little at a time, I glimpse inside, hearing nothing, seeing nothing. But the room is huge and I can't see everything yet.

I proceed further, keeping my weapon cocked just in case he's hiding. That's what rats do, after all. But as soon as I glance to my right, my eyes expand.

"What the…?"

It takes me a second to process that Carl's tied up to a chair, a gag in his mouth, his head swung down like he's dead.

And before I can move toward him, something flies right into my face. I duck before it can hit me.

A knife drops right beside my leather dress shoe, nearly stabbing my big toe, the tip of the blade landing sharply in the floor.

Okay. Now I'm pissed.

"Whoever the fuck you are, you're damn lucky you didn't mess up the leather."

I glance throughout the room, staring at each closed door, not sure who is on the other side of it. Hopefully, Izzy left already and isn't dead somewhere in the suite.

"You either come out and tell me what you did with the redhead that was up here, or I find you and take your head as a souvenir."

A laugh echoes.

A woman's laugh.

"What the…"

No. Fucking. Way.

"No need to worry about me." Her voice is honey, edged sharper than the knife she just threw at me. "I can handle things pretty well on my own."

I would recognize that voice anywhere. I heard it enough today. Heard her laugh. Saw those eyes stealing glances.

Red.

How am I even more attracted to her right now?

"Here I was worried about you," I say smoothly. "But it seems as though I should've been more worried about Carl."

"Carl and I are long-lost friends," she purrs. "We were just having some adult fun when you rudely interrupted us."

I hear her from behind one of the doors, but I'm too far away to figure out which one. This room is too fucking big. She's like a ghost, one you hear but can't see. I'm getting closer, though.

"How about you go and save yourself the trouble?" she challenges.

My laughter pervades through the space, and I march a single step toward Carl, seated right beside the foot of the bed.

"I don't think I will. I kinda like trouble."

Six

GIO

In a flash, the middle door pops open, and there she is, strutting out, her eyes cutting into slits, gleaming like diamonds. I've never seen anything more beautiful in my entire life, especially this close. I march forward, unable to look anywhere but at her.

There's something about a strong, confident woman that gets me every time. But a strong, confident…killer? Well, that's a first, and I can't say I hate it.

"Who are you, and what the hell are you doing in here?" she questions, her eyes searing into me as though she wishes she could burn me alive.

My mouth twitches. "I could very well ask you the same thing, bambina."

A predatory curve of her lips has my cock throbbing.

"Don't worry about who I am," she tells me. "What you need

to worry about is getting the hell out of here before I carve up your pretty face."

"You think my face is pretty?" I chuckle.

"Not when you're talking." A single brow arches. "So why don't you be a good boy and shut the hell up?"

I grab my bowtie and loosen it. Goddamn, she's making it hard to breathe.

She lifts up a long, toned leg, her bare foot slipping onto the duvet as she hikes up her dress and removes a flip knife from the black leather holster wrapped around her inner thigh. Her dress hangs between her legs, denying me the view I'm craving.

I inhale a long, shallow breath, running a hand down my face.

"Christ," I mutter, almost to myself. "That's the hottest fucking thing I've ever seen in my life."

"Typical guy," she snickers. "Always salivating."

"I was giving you a compliment." I fold my arms across my chest, a satisfied look on my face.

She lifts a defiant chin. "Pretty sure I could live without it."

Oh, this woman… My hands are itching to throw her over my knee, hike up her dress, and leave my handprint on her curvy ass.

"Maybe I should teach you some manners, Izzy."

She laughs dryly, placing her foot back down and pointing the knife at me. "Izzy isn't even my real name."

And before I have a chance to ask her more, she throws that damn blade right at me, trying to kill me for the second time.

With a chuckle, I roll out of the way, rushing toward her just as she does the same, not an ounce of fear in her glare.

She throws a kick into my ribs, and with a grunt, I capture her soft ankle, spin her around, and wrap my forearm around her throat. My hand slips into my pocket and I retrieve the gun, digging the muzzle into her thigh.

"Well, Red, seems like you're in a bit of trouble now."

"Oh, that's so cute." She scores my firearm with her nails, almost fighting me off successfully.

"You keep trying to kill me…" I whisper right against her ear. "…while all I've been trying to do is keep you safe."

Her chest rises and falls steadily, the warmth of my breaths cruising down her slender throat. My large palm would fit perfectly wrapped around it.

"See, that was your first mistake," she retorts.

"And what was that?" I tighten my arm around her throat.

She groans low, her fingers digging into my arm. "Assuming every woman you meet actually wants to be saved."

"Everyone needs saving sometimes." My lips drop lower until my mouth traces the shell of her ear.

Her breath hitches. "Not me."

I beg to differ. But I won't argue. Not when all I can seem to think about right now is how we could stop fighting and do something else entirely. Preferably naked.

"Do you even play the piano?" I wonder gruffly, hissing as she inadvertently moves her hips, her ass rubbing on my straining hard-on.

The things I could do to her…

Her palm latches on to my wrist, trying to pry me off her, with the gun still pointing at her thigh. I chuckle at her attempt.

"Nope," she finally replies with wry laughter. "And I don't cook either."

Her bemused tone turns sinful, and it excites the hell out of me, which is a lot more than what women normally do for me. They're far too eager to drop to their knees and suck me off to interest me. Don't get me wrong, their mouths are pretty interesting, but that's all it ever is.

Her elbow connects violently with my ribs, and with a grunt, I inadvertently loosen my arm from around her.

She slips out, kicking my legs hard and dropping me right on my back, the gun slipping from my grasp.

That's what I get for being distracted.

Worth it, though, just for the view.

She stares down at me. A cold, calculating grin slithers to both corners of her mouth as she settles on top of me, lowering a blade against my Adam's apple.

I think I'm in love.

I grab a fistful of her hair and drag her face closer, until her lips brush against mine. "Do it, Red. Cut me."

"You think I won't?" She pushes the knife in deeper, and I know she nicked me.

"Good girl," I say through a tense grin, my skin throbbing where the blade pierced it, but I've never felt this alive before.

Her jaw strains at the praise, and it has me groaning, enjoying the quiet rage pulling at her features.

She could've easily done worse. But she didn't. I think I'm growing on her.

I take my time wrapping all that luscious red hair around my wrist, and her eyes grow heavy-lidded even as she fights me. Fights this obvious attraction coiling between us.

I've never fought a woman before. And I've sure as hell never wanted to fuck one while fighting her either.

"Come on now, Red," I whisper. "Do it. Kill me."

Her controlled, yet tight breaths rush out of her lungs. "Don't bait me."

She sinks that blade deeper, and I growl when it cuts me again. Her lips drop to mine until they stroke against me in a seductive, yet fatal way.

"You have no idea who I am," she challenges.

"But I want to." The confession slips easily. "You intrigue me."

She angles her chin, loosening herself around me just a fraction, but it's enough.

Instantly, I flip her onto the ground, pinning her beneath me. She gasps when my body molds into every one of her curves.

I settle between her thighs, and I know she can feel what she does to me.

"I can't figure out if you looked better on top or on the bottom."

"Asshole," she hisses, but I swear those hips move on purpose.

I stare into her eyes for long quiet seconds, and it's as though I'm staring into the eyes of my future.

It's crazy. It makes no sense. But it's what I seem to feel in this moment, and I'm not one to deny my own feelings.

"I don't even know why we're fighting. The last thing I want to do is fight you."

She scoffs. "Well, for starters, you interrupted me from completing my job." She glances away, frustration marking every one of her words. "And now that you can identify me…" She gives me a snarky glare. "I'm going to have to kill you. Which is quite a shame, since I did like looking at you."

I chuckle. "And I very much enjoy looking at you." My eyes drop to those full lips I want wrapped around my cock. "So, how about some kind of truce? Maybe we can even have a conversation like two civilized adults."

She narrows an unconvinced stare. She's quite the sexy thing, even when she's trying to plot my demise.

"You're here to kill Carl too, huh?" I ask. "What did he do, steal?"

"Yeah." She eyes me curiously. "He stole money from you too?"

"He did. A lot of it."

"So you weren't stalking me?"

"Well, I mean, I kinda was." My mouth curls. "I *did* want to make sure he didn't hurt you."

Something passes in her eyes just then. Something soft and vulnerable and utterly beautiful. And I swear I want to kiss her even more.

"Well…" She throws out nonchalantly, erasing a glimpse into the real her. "You can be sure he did no such thing. So how about you just go, and I'll clean up my own mess?"

"You're so cute."

Beneath her fluttering lashes, her eyes round. "Did you just call me cute?"

"And *so* fucking hot." The words slip on a shameless groan. "Is that better, Your Highness?"

"No." She tilts up her narrow jaw. "You're bleeding on me." She grimaces, passing a glance at my throat. "Might want to find your girlfriend to make your boo-boo feel better."

Shit. I stare down at her chest, drops of blood coating her dress, slightly camouflaged against the satin.

"How about you be my girlfriend and fix what you broke?"

She laughs. "Oh, goodness. Does your weak attempt at charm work on those poor women of the world?"

I shrug, sinking my fingers into her hair. "Usually."

"Well, it won't work on me."

"Pity." The back of my hand strokes down her cheek, my eyes locked with hers. "I'll have to try harder."

"You'll be trying for a very long time."

"I have all the time in the world."

Her features turn aroused, fighting the need skirting between us.

She rolls her eyes, denying that if I kissed her right now, she'd let me.

"How long are you going to suffocate me with your massive body weight?" she asks flatly, her gaze perched to mine once more.

"Until you learn how to behave like a lady." I stifle a laugh when her cheeks flush with indignation.

"You are just asking to die, aren't you?" Her breaths grow noisier.

"Bambina, I've got you trapped beneath me. What the hell can you do right now, except look good with those thighs spread wide, with me in between them?"

Her pupils dilate.

"I'm going to kill you slow," she warns, and it warms my cold, dead heart. "I'm going to let your blood drip from your throat as you realize you're about to die."

"Damn, baby. Keep whispering those sweet nothings to me. You're only making me harder." I thrust into her, and she squirms, her parted lips trembling, brows bowing.

"And all you're doing is deflating my lady boner."

"Liar. I bet you're soaking wet." My hand cruises up her hip, fitting it between our bodies. "Want me to slide a finger inside you and see for myself?"

"Please," she scoffs. "You'd be like all the rest of them, too worried about your own dick to care about whether a woman comes."

My low chuckling has her looking intently at me. "Someone hasn't been fucked right, huh? Is that why you're so angry, Red? How about I make it better?"

Her mouth forms a tight, thin line.

And I know I hit the bullseye. She's been sleeping with losers her whole life. But that's about to change if I have anything to say about it.

I lower my lips to her neck, my mouth coasting up to her ravaging pulse beneath. "I promise that when I fuck you—and I *will* fuck you—you'll lose count of how many times you come before I do."

She gasps.

"That's right. I very much care about your pleasure," I go on, peering back down at her. "I wouldn't come until you did. Over and over. On my fingers, my tongue, wrapped around my cock… until your body's trembling, begging me not to make you come again. But the son of a bitch that I am, I'd make you give me more. Until I've decided you've had enough."

Her breath hitches, chest trembling against mine, her fingernails biting into my shoulders while my straining bulge rolls between her thighs.

"So how about you let me finish him off and you get those sexy heels back on? And after that, I eat your pussy, then fuck you bent over that bed."

She lets a little moan slip while I grind my cock deeper into her core.

"Then…" I go on. "We can pretend we never saw each other. It's a win-win for the both of us."

Except there's no way in hell I'll ever forget about you. Wherever you go, I'll find you. That's a promise I intend to keep.

She clears her throat, flattening a hand against my chest and attempts to shove me off.

"Aww, that's adorable." She pouts, roughly trying to snap my hand away from her hair. "You think because you're the man, you get to kill him?"

Before I can even respond, she finds just enough space to hit my damn balls with her knee.

"Fucking hell," I grit, relaxing off her a fraction, giving her the chance to slide out and jump to her feet.

Without wasting a second, she grabs the blade from beside her and rushes toward Carl. The knife inches for his throat, her eyes fastened to mine while I slowly rise.

"He's mine, Red," I snap. "I'm the one who gets to kill him."

With every step, I cut the distance between us.

"Sorry, but he's mine. Finders, keepers and all." She shrugs casually.

"Doesn't seem fair." My hands ball into tight fists. "I couldn't seduce him like you could. I'm not his type." I smirk.

She flips a single hand in the air. "Being a woman has its advantages, I guess. But look at it this way. I kill him, and it solves your problems too."

"I've been hunting him for years." I edge closer. "He's mine. No matter how gorgeous you are."

"I've been hunting him for years too. You're not that special."

But you *are.*

"What's your real name?" I ask, needing it damn bad.

"Can't tell ya." Her tongue darts out, swiping across her mouth, and my cock jerks.

Jesus Christ, what is it with this woman?

"CIA?" I trek closer.

"I'm flattered," she replies teasingly, throwing a palm against the center of her chest. "But if I were, you'd already be dead, and your body would never be found."

"Noted." I chuckle. "You sure know how to flirt, my little bambina."

"If I were flirting with you, you'd know, but if you call me 'Red' or 'bambina' one more time, don't go blaming me when you get a hole in your head."

"I'd wear it like a badge of honor." I jerk up the gun still in my grasp and point it right at her pretty chest.

"You know you won't shoot me." She shakes her head with a scoff.

"Are you willing to take that chance?"

She flames me with an exasperated look. "This is getting quite boring." She clutches Carl's hair in her grasp, tilting his head back. "How about this? We compare how much he stole from the both of us, and whoever lost more gets to kill him."

My mouth thins into a flash of a smile. There's no way he stole more from her or whoever she works for.

"How do I know you'll be honest?"

"You don't." She narrows a snarky gaze, fitted with her amused expression.

"Fine." I exhale a short breath of laughter.

"How much did he steal from you?" she asks, the knife slowly beginning to dip into his throat.

"Ten mil."

Her self-satisfied voice echoes. "Aww. Well, at least you tried."

With a quick twist of her hand, she punctures the side of his throat. Blood oozes down onto his white dress shirt.

If I wasn't so pissed right now, I'd be even more impressed. She didn't even flinch.

"He took twelve million from me." She grins. "So looks like I won. Thanks for playing, though."

"Fuck, Red." I shake my head. "Really? I had a gun with a silencer right there." I jerk the gun in my grasp. "Would've been easier to use it. I would've given it to you if you asked nicely."

"Never said I was nice." She drags the blade out and starts for me, drops of crimson spilling across the ivory shaggy rug, as though she's doing it on purpose.

And she is.

"You like messes, don't you?" I ask, my heart racing the closer her body gets to mine.

"And let me guess?" She takes another step until she's right in front of me, gazing up. "You're afraid of a little mess."

With an arrogant look on her face, she lifts the knife and swipes it across my shoulder, the blood penetrating the cotton of my jacket.

"I'm not afraid of a damn thing."

I grab her jaw in a rough palm, my fingers digging into the hollows of her cheeks as I walk her to the bed and throw her on top of it. Her dress gathers at the knees, the knife still perched in her grip.

"Question is…" I run the muzzle of my nine up her thigh, and goosebumps prickle her arms. "Are *you* afraid of *me*?"

My body presses into her, and she lets out a little gasp, then immediately catches herself, her face hardening. Because for a woman like her, it may as well be a sign of weakness.

I brush my thumb across her cherry lips.

"I'm not afraid," she whispers, her breath hitching.

"Are you sure about that, bambina?" I ask huskily.

She swallows roughly, her gaze lowering to my lips, and hell, I wanna kiss her. Right here. Right now. With a dead man in the same room. I want to kiss the life into her frozen eyes and find out how good she sounds when she lets go. I bet she's soft everywhere. I bet she'd like it rough.

"What are you doing?" she murmurs, her warm exhales fanning across my lips.

My grasp around her jaw slides lower, until I have her delicate throat in the palm of my hand, my thumb deepening into her wild pulse.

She doesn't fight it. In fact, her body turns languid, allowing me the control.

"I have no idea…" I inhale her sensual perfume. "I can't seem to get you out of my mind."

Her exhales are sharp.

"You captivate me, and I'm not easily captivated."

I gaze back down at her, those eyes wild and begging me for something I shouldn't give her. It's like she's afraid to ask for it. Like it would make her weaker in my eyes. Or maybe her own. But that's the farthest thing from the truth.

"Is that another one of your compliments?" she asks in a sultry tone.

"It is, and you're gonna take it. You're gonna take anything I give you."

"Is that what you think? Or is that your ego talking?" Her eyes turn sensual, lips parted.

"No, sweetheart. That's your body talking." My hand tightens around her throat.

I know we should get out of here before someone catches us, but I can't focus on anything but her right now—this tough-as-hell, deadly, and equally as beautiful woman, who's staring up at me like she wants this just as badly as I do.

"Been wondering what your lips taste like from the moment I saw you."

"Oh yeah?" she breathes, lifting up her face, bringing her mouth so close to mine, it brushes against it. "And what do you think they taste like?"

"Like they're mine already."

"I don't belong to anyone," she whispers.

"Not yet." I stroke my lips against hers.

My cock grows heavier when her tongue swipes into my mouth. I groan, wanting to lift up that dress and feel her warm and wet.

"I saw you checking me out on that stage," she informs me.

"No, Red. I saw you long before, when you were with those two men you were talking to, pretending you were enjoying yourself. You like pretending, don't you?" I arch my hips between her thighs on instinct, my lips hovering, almost touching hers.

I crave this woman badly. It's like she's drugged me and made me fall prey to her spell.

"Pretending is a lot easier than reality." She utters the words on a whisper.

"And why's that?" I dare a tender look at her because somehow, I think she needs it.

I drop the gun on the bed for a moment, the back of my hand brushing down her cheek and her brows snap with a fleck of emotion. Something haunting courses through her eyes, something that resembles a raw kind of pain.

But just as quickly, it's gone, and that insolence is back on her features. "Because it's the only way to escape it."

I could easily fight him off of me. It wouldn't be too hard. But something inside me doesn't want to. Whoever this man is, he intrigues me just as much as I seem to intrigue him.

He shoves my dress up to my upper thigh with the muzzle of his gun, and I welcome it, the menacing way he's holding me captive beneath him, the shadows of darkness crossing his eyes, almost as black as death itself.

A pulsing need grows between my thighs, the emptiness inside letting itself be known the more I feel him on top of me.

Unintentionally, a moan slips from my lips, and he cinches his fingers tighter around my throat. I bet he can sense how much I like it when he's got his hands wrapped around my neck.

With a menacing expression, I grab the top of his hand and push his palm even deeper, wanting him to take all of my breaths.

Maybe it would hurt less. Maybe death is the only way to escape my past.

"I've never wanted to make a woman come this badly in my life," he vows, his voice straining, his rigid length driving into me.

Deeply. Forcefully.

My body grows achy, every molecule turned to a mess of lustful emotions. I've never been this turned on. Never wanted to sleep with a man with such fervor before.

Am I insane? Should I let him touch me? Have me?

But what if he's not some random rich guy with a dark side? What if he's part of the same world I'm in? Maybe he works for one of our enemies? There are so many factions in the underworld. He could be anyone.

Will we cross the same paths again? Can I sleep with him and then disappear? Because that's all this would be: a one-time thing. I don't do attachments.

After what happened, I don't get involved with men. Not on an intimate level. I fuck them once and hope for an orgasm that never comes.

He rocks his hips so expertly, I wonder if this guy is capable of giving me that one thing I've never experienced with a man. Sure, I've had plenty by myself. But my hands alone can't give me what I truly want: to be dominated.

Which, of course, I'd never actually admit.

His unrelenting gaze stays glued to mine while he thrusts, circling into me, pushing deeper against my clit.

My face flushes, my entire body warm and buzzing with desire. I can't control the rattling of my breathing, the beating of my erratic pulse.

What is this awful man doing to me?

The pads of his rough fingers climb up my inner thigh, waking my flesh with their intoxicating touch.

Slowly, he continues his journey higher, his eyes unnerving me as he stares into me like he wants to know what I like. What makes me feel…something. Anything.

And never until now have I felt it. This feeling of being free and alive, forgetting everything else but this intensity coursing through my limbs.

His digits ride up higher, feathering over the spot where my thigh meets my hip. I gasp when his thumb rubs my clit over my panties, and I find myself heaving, the knife slipping from my trembling hand. The one I forgot I was even holding. How have I not stabbed him with it by now?

"Say you want it," he gruffly demands. "Tell me you want my fingers inside this pretty little pussy."

I nod wordlessly, chest flailing, brows furrowing with every ragged breath.

"No, Red." He curls his fingers deeper into my throat. "Say please." He lowers his lips to mine, brushing them gently with an arrogant smirk.

If he thinks I'll ever beg him for anything, he doesn't know me.

His thumb pushes into me, the cotton of my panties along with his touch causing too much friction. My eyes roll back, temptation almost causing me to say those words he desperately wants to hear.

The worst thing is, the commanding way in which he speaks to me is only making me want him that much more. Desire unfurls in my gut, flaming out through my limbs.

When I can't manage to speak, the need scorching me into oblivion, he roughly pulls my panties to the side, his eyes still pinned to mine as he rubs his thumb around my pulsating clit.

Cursing out, I dig my long nails into the hardened muscles of his back.

"Don't stop," I gasp.

My toes curl as he holds me down by my throat like he owns me while finger-fucking me like he knows my body more than I do.

And right now, I swear he does.

The sounds I'm making would have me ashamed if I actually cared. But I don't. My body's climbing, soaring to the horizon. Two fingers slip inside me, his thumb playing me until my body trembles.

"Are you a screamer, Red?"

"No." I moan hungrily for release.

"Well, you're about to become one."

He pushes a third finger into my core, and when he curls them and drives them into my G-spot, I slam my eyes shut, wanting to fight this insanely addicting feeling.

But I can't give him what he wants. I can't scream. I won't.

"Open those eyes. I earned them," he grates.

And when I dare a look at him, his jaw tenses and the vein at his neck pops as though it wants to rip right out of his skin.

"That's it. Look at me. I want you to know who's about to make you scream."

A ripple of heat washes over me, the noises slipping from my mouth completely unhinged. He plays my body like it's his, like he owns the keys and notes.

Yet my mind is fighting it, even when my body wants everything he's doing. I want to forget it all and focus solely on how he's making me feel. Bathed in the hunger pulling us together, in this mere illusion created by our mutual animalistic need.

He pounds his fingers into me like he's lost all control, and every time he brings me close to the edge, he slows, driving me to madness.

I groan in frustration, needing to feel myself fall. But the bastard won't allow it.

"What do you need, Red? Come on, now. Use your words."

I grind my teeth. My body can't take a moment more of this sweet torture.

He strokes my clit between two fingers, and I'm so close…

"Please, please, let me come," I beg, hating myself, but not giving a fuck either.

"That's a good fucking girl," he growls, rubbing me in slow, tantalizing circles.

And the way he won't stop staring into my eyes has my heart racing and my pulse thrashing. Eye contact has never been my thing. It's too much. It's everything I've avoided. But he won't let me look away. It's like he's trying to untie the binds that keep me from falling.

The throbbing in my core grows until it becomes too much, until I need release so badly I'd beg over and over again.

He slows his tempo a fraction, an ominous warning in his eyes, and I'm about ready to tear his head off if he doesn't let me finish.

"Scream," he demands. "Show me what I do to you."

It's then his fingers piston inside me, until I do what I swore I wouldn't do. I scream. I scream so loud, the walls could shatter.

"Oh, God, yes! Don't stop!"

My hips buck, my hand clutching a fistful of his jet-black hair while I clasp my teeth as he wrings out every drop of pleasure my body is willing to give.

A roguish smirk lines the ends of his mouth, like he knew this was what he'd do to me.

My heart races as he says, "I can tell by your face, you've never come this hard before."

I want to deny it. But it never comes. So I say nothing instead.

"It's okay, Red. If you ask nicely again…" he whispers, lowering his mouth to mine, his soft, firm lips driving me wild. "I'll let you come like that as many times as you want."

Before I can admonish him for thinking he could *let me* do anything, he kisses me slow, his fingers still inside me, dipping in and out with an unhurried pace.

And he was right. I've never come this hard before. But I've never been kissed this way before either. Hard. Passionately. So earth-shattering that I never in my life could've imagined that this is what a kiss should feel like.

My God, have I been missing this all my life?

His tongue slips into my mouth, warm and wet, lips sucking and nipping and turning my world upside down in one single moment. This warmth coasting down my limbs, this out-of-body feeling as though I'm floating…it's something I've never even believed was possible.

And when my body climbs again, I don't even fight it. Because I know with him, there's no point in fighting anything at all.

GIO

After six mind-blowing orgasms, I let her rest, her breaths finally stabilizing while my body's still pressed up against her, refusing to let go.

Her flushed cheeks match the bright hue of her lips, and I very much wish I had kissed her the way I wanted to, tangled up in the bed, her body bare, my hands everywhere. But I could tell that what we've done so far alone was too much for her, and I wasn't about to go and push my luck.

I'll get her to open up once we get to know each other better, and we *will* be doing lots of that.

"Can you get off of me?" she huffs, her forehead crumpling as she attempts to push me off with her palms. She's quite unsuccessful, though.

I chuckle, and her eyes do that thing they do when she's planning my death.

My lips drop closer, and I kiss the tip of her nose, my heart beating faster the more she stares into my eyes. And I swear, hers grow tender.

The ice princess has a soft side.

I run a thumb across her mouth, and she doesn't even try to push me off.

My gaze takes in the contours of her face, the definition of beauty, sculpted to perfection, as though a sculptor spent years on her and her alone.

"What's your story, Red?" My voice grows low, like it's afraid she'll run if it gets any louder.

"Not everyone has a story."

"That's not true." I draw my thumb down her cheek, and her eyelids grow heavy. "Everyone has a story, and I'll find yours out soon enough."

A lazy smile grows over her mouth, and I swear it's a real one. "Good luck with that."

My other palm settles on her outer thigh, and she relaxes her body, like she enjoys my touch.

"Tell me your name, and I'll tell you mine."

"Nice try." She's pushing me off again with two hands against my shoulders. "Get off. I have to go."

Instead, I delve myself even deeper, plastering a huge cocky grin on my face, while she glares.

"Where?" I ask. "More men to torture?"

"About to torture *you* if you don't do what I say."

Just as she's about to answer, someone pounds at the door. "Sir, we need to get inside. Are you decent?"

"Fuck." I jump off, and she's frantically dashing for her shoes and slipping them on.

"I'm going through the adjacent door. That room is empty," she informs me, rushing toward it, hand on the knob. But suddenly she pauses, looking at me over her shoulder. "Come with me."

That damn near warms my heart.

"Why, Red? You worried about me?"

"No." She grimaces. "That would be horrifying."

I laugh faintly, unable to peel my eyes from hers.

Funny.

Beautiful.

Insanely skilled with a knife.

Suddenly, marriage doesn't sound quite so bad.

I probably won't live past forty with a woman like that, but at least we'd have a few short years of marital bliss. Wouldn't be boring, that's for sure.

"I'm just saying…" she goes on. "Why die if you can get away?"

"Don't worry, bambina. I'll be all right. Plus…" I stare back at Carl. "…someone left me a mess to clean." A smirk deepens over my face. "But as a thank-you, maybe give me your number. Hopefully next time, I can make you come without a dead body in the room."

Her face scrunches like she's considering it, and when another knock comes through, she says, "Ugh. Yeah, sure. Give me your phone."

Well, that was easier than I thought.

I remove my cell from my pocket and unlock it before handing it to her. She hurriedly types with both thumbs, then hands me back the phone.

Her fingers climb into her hair, and at first, I have no idea what she's doing…until she removes a pin and sticks it into the hole of the doorknob.

Not even five seconds later, the door opens.

If I wasn't already insanely attracted to her, this would have done it.

Over her shoulder, those bright ocean eyes take me in, a perfect blend of emerald and turquoise, a color as rare as the woman.

Her lingering gaze stays perched to mine for long seconds. My pulse drums. Why does it look like she's saying goodbye without actually saying it?

"I'll see you around." The corner of her mouth inclines. "Thanks for all those orgasms."

"Anytime, Red. But next time, I'll be using my mouth. Really wanna taste you and watch you fall apart on my tongue."

Her cheeks flush.

"Keep yourself alive until then," I tell her.

"Just come with me," she pleads, her brows knitting.

I grin, loving that she asked me twice. "I can handle this. You go."

"How will you get out of here?"

The entry door clicks.

"Go. Now," I whisper sharply.

That has her nodding, and with another long look, she's out of sight.

And I'm left wondering if I'll ever actually see her again.

Eight

GIO

I'm not one to play games. I tell a woman exactly what I want and what I don't. The women at the bars we run know exactly what they're getting with me: a one-night stand. Maybe two if the fuck was that good, but it usually isn't.

Yet, here I am the following day, sitting at my desk at work, unable to stop thinking about her. I stare at the number she added to my phone, naming herself *Call Me Red & Die*. I grin every time I see it.

I've contemplated calling her a few times today. She'll probably call me desperate and tell me how many times she envisioned murdering me since yesterday.

I chuckle to myself.

"Fuck it," I mutter, pressing on her number and letting it ring.

Once.

Twice.

Four fucking times.

I almost give up hope, and…

"Hello?" A voice vibrates through the line, but it's not who I was expecting.

My hand balls into a fist. Why the fuck is a guy answering her phone?

"Who the hell are you?" I bellow.

I don't even know her damn name. How am I supposed to ask for her?

He sighs like he's aggravated. "Not again."

"What the fuck did you say?"

"Look, did you get this number from this hot redheaded chick? Kinda tall, great body?"

How the *hell* does he know what her body looks like? My pulse slams in my ears.

"Who are you?" I ask instantly, my tone seeping with quiet rage, my temples throbbing.

"We hooked up ages ago. She didn't like it. And now, whenever she gets with some new guy, she gives him my number." His breath grows loud.

"How many men have called?" My thunderous tone drills through the speaker.

"Too many."

A muscle pops in my jaw.

"She's batshit crazy. Believe me, man, you're better off without her."

My knuckles turn white, straining around the edge of my black desk. *Fuck!* Blood rushes to my head. She played me like a fool and I fell into her trap.

"Do you know where she lives?" I ask the asshole.

"No clue. Don't even have her name. She's weird like that.

Even when we were fucking, she freaked out about taking off her clothes, so I didn't even get to see her fully naked. Damn shame." His voice trails, like he's using his own imagination.

I'm about to find him and put him to sleep.

"Did you *fucking* hurt her?" My chest rises and falls heavily, every inch of me drowning in red-hot fury.

Why would she do this to him if he hadn't tried hurting her?

"Of course not."

"I don't believe you." I crack a knuckle.

"Look, man, I've gotta go. Good luck finding the crazy bitch."

I draw in a deep breath, attempting to calm myself enough not to have this call tracked so I can kill him.

"Listen to me." My tone turns cold and ruthless. "If I so much as find out you did something she didn't like, I'll find out and I'll kill you. Do you understand me?"

His exhales intensify. "I don't know who you are, but I'll call the cops."

"Go ahead. I'll wait." I laugh humorlessly, taunting him. "But know this: that won't do a thing to stop me. And when I do come for you, you'll wish you'd taken your own life."

"O-okay, listen, I don't want trouble."

"Change your number, and don't talk about her again. Not a single word."

"Okay, yeah, I'll do that. I—I swear."

"I'll know if you lied."

Then, without hearing his pathetic reply, I end the call, squeezing the phone in my palm, realizing I don't know how to find her.

Little Red lied to me. She never intended to see me again. And once I find her, I'm gonna make her regret it.

ISEULT
FOUR DAYS LATER

"Are you trying to get yourself killed?" I yell out at Silas, one of my trainees.

He's only sixteen, and it's my job to grow him into a man who can handle any situation once he graduates. It's an honor to join Caellach, and not everyone is even allowed to try out. Your family has to be in deep with my father to get a chance.

We haven't had any girls join us, which is quite a shame. We need that. Girls turning into women who can handle themselves against the men of the world who try to suffocate them.

Of course, by joining Caellach, that also means they'll actually have to kill some people. But it's not so bad. Once you get the hang of it.

There is Kora, though. She's the only other female enforcer we have, and I guess she's also my friend. She basically forced herself into my life, and now I don't know what I'd do without her.

Before she joined, I was the only woman here. The guys tried to haze me, make me squirm. So I beat the shit out of them. They never did it again. If they can't handle me, they don't belong here.

"Sorry, ma'am," Silas breathlessly replies with sweat coating his forehead while his opponent, Oliver, is grinning, swiping blood from his brow.

Now, *he's* crazy. Seventeen. Joined us at sixteen. Ruthless as they come. He may be lacking a soul in there somewhere. But eh, I don't judge. It's better not to have one doing what we do. We all have our demons. His father and mine are good friends, so him joining us was a given as soon as he was born.

"Again!" I grab Silas by his t-shirt. "And this time, you better not get taken down."

He nods once, and the two guys start the self-defense routine again. We teach them everything here. Surveillance, weaponry, and survival tactics, just to name a few.

Kora laughs into my ear beside me, removing her boxing gloves.

"I think he pissed himself." She gestures with her chin at Silas.

"Well, he'd better get his pissing over with now unless he wants to fail out. And I swear, he's *this* close to getting kicked out."

None of the recruits want that. It would bring shame to their families.

"You're right. You have to be hard on them or they never learn." She pushes her blonde hair off her cheek, her hazel eyes concentrating on me, like she's trying to solve one of those crossword puzzles she loves doing. "You okay? You've been a little quiet the last few days."

Of course I'm fine. What is she talking about? It's not like I've been thinking about Orgasm Man for the past seventy-nine hours, three minutes, and—I glance down at my watch—fifteen seconds.

I wonder how pissed he was once he realized I gave him the wrong number. A laugh bubbles out of me.

Kora squints at me curiously. "Are you having a stroke?" She slaps the back of her hand against my forehead. "Fever?"

I scoff, shoving her hand away. "I'm fine. I was just…uh, thinking about something funny."

"Must've been something quite entertaining, since you literally never laugh."

"I laugh." I roll my eyes. "Sometimes."

"Uh-huh. Sure you do." She nods slowly, giving me a look that says she thinks an alien has taken over my body.

"Are you ready for tonight?" I quickly change the subject.

"Wow. Way to avoid talking about whatever it is you're hiding." She narrows a gaze.

And I don't plan on talking about him ever.

"Fine. Don't tell me." She shrugs, amusement laced in her tone. "Maybe I can get it out of you after a few drinks."

"We can't drink on the job."

"We can after." She winks. "You've gotta learn to have a little more fun."

If she only knew the kind of fun I had a few days ago. The kind I can't seem to get out of my mind, wishing I did actually give him my real number.

But of course I can't. That's dangerous. My identity must remain secret. Can't be messing around with a man like that—rich, connected. He'd figure out who I am, and I can't have that.

Kora's short ponytail flings in the air as she starts for the exit. She's got weapons training, and then tonight, we're off to New York City to clean up a mess. This time it'll be a lot less bloody.

The four-hour drive from Cherry Grove—our small town about a hundred miles from Boston—will be torture, but taking a plane is risky. I don't like being caught on camera or having too many eyes on me. I like keeping a low profile.

Our target tonight has a business meeting at a low-key bar, where we plan to take him out. He's supposed to be testifying against my father for assault, and he's the only proof the government has.

I do plan on going to my apartment in the city after that maybe for a night or two to decompress. It's my little vacation pad. Away from the chaos that is my family. Away from work. I can just sit in front of the TV, watch a bunch of shows I never have time for, and eat some good New York pizza. Already looking forward to a nice quiet night alone.

Or maybe you're just hoping you somehow run into that mystery man again and let him finish what he started.

Damn it. I hate it when my subconscious is right.

Either way, I'll be going. My father won't care as long as the job is done. He tries to give me space as much as possible. Guilt does have its advantages.

When I first told him I got a place of my own, far away from the family, he was not pleased. But I'm twenty-six. I need my own place. Not that I don't have one in Boston, but it's right next to him and my entire family. He's built houses here for my three brothers and me, while Eriu still lives with him.

The land my father purchased is acres upon acres of farmland. My father loves animals; taking care of them is in his blood. I'm not one to milk a cow. My sister, though? She loves it.

We're different, she and I. I'm loud, where she's quiet. I'm hard, where she's soft. She can talk anyone out of doing anything with her gentle way, while I'd beat them into submission. Two different people, but close as ever. I'd kill for her without any hesitation.

She only recently turned seventeen, and my father is going to want to marry her off. It's what's done within our families, but I plan to stop it at all costs. She doesn't want it, but she's too afraid to speak up. Not that our father would ever listen. But there's a better chance he'd listen to me.

Eriu has a right to meet someone and fall in love the normal way instead of having someone shoved down her throat on her eighteenth birthday.

The only reason my father didn't try that bullshit with me is because I was far too broken for him to force that on me.

I kinda just stayed broken, pretending I was fixed.

He knew that after what happened to me, I'd never marry anyone. I have no desire to fulfill some antiquated womanly duty. I'm better off on my own.

My father has no idea that sometimes when I think about what I've been through, panic grips its fist around my throat until I can't breathe. And he can't ever find out. If he thinks I'm weak, that I can't handle myself, he'll kick me out of the academy and not even blink. Enforcers can't be weak. They can't have baggage that could affect their mission or their life. And that's what I'd be. Baggage.

He'd apologize, sure. He'd tell me he's doing it for me. That he doesn't want to lose me like he lost Mom. But in the end, I'd lose the one thing I care for besides my family. I'd lose my job. And that means everything to me. It's the one thing that keeps me sane.

So every day, I fight to keep it together, not showing the world a glimpse into the woman I've been forced to become.

Nine

GIO

"**W**hat the hell do you mean, you can't find her? How can someone just disappear like that?" I holler at Grant over the phone.

It's been four days of her occupying my mind. Four days of fucking dreaming of her, God damn it, yet I can't find her. Can't make her pay for running off on me the way she did.

"I don't know what to tell you, but so far, she hasn't shown up on any of the cameras I've tapped into. If she had, I'd know about it."

"Do better!" I slam a fist on my desk at work, the glass of whiskey rattling beside me. "Did you try worldwide cameras?"

Grant chuckles. "How many countries are we talking?"

"All of them!"

He laughs harder. "You ever going to tell me what happened with the two of you?"

"No." I run a hand down my face, my voice lowering. "Just find her."

"I'll call you if I do." He pauses. "But I wouldn't hold my breath if I were you. She doesn't want to be found, Gio. You're going to have to get over her."

Never going to happen.

"I wasn't asking for your opinion, Grant. Just do your job." I hang up before he hears me break some shit.

I shove the chair back, rising to my feet, hands in my hair as I let out a frustrated groan. Not only can I not find Red, but the only lead on Bryce's killer was a dead end.

When I paid Donny a visit in prison, he swore it was him who killed Bryce. He even told me what went down and exactly how it went down. It matched up to the video I saw, which he doesn't know about. He's definitely covering for someone else.

I settle back on the leather chair and shut my eyes, and she comes into my mind.

Haunting me.

Red.

I can't eat. Can't sleep. It's become an unhealthy obsession looking for her the way I have. Whoever she is, she's making it her mission to stay undetected.

And finding her is going to be mine.

ISEUIT

I stay seated in the small, dimly lit bar with Kora on the stool beside me, chatting with the man we've been sent to extinguish, Lance, to her left. He never stood a chance when we walked in— short, tight black dresses, heels a good five inches long, our hair perfectly curled around our slender shoulders.

Once Kora and I sat down and ordered a drink, he and his business partner were keen on joining us. Men are so predictable. Dangle a carrot, and they come running like rabbits.

I will say, I'm kind of disappointed that Orgasm Man hasn't found me since I arrived in the city. I know it's delusional to think he could. It's like finding a needle in a haystack. Not as though he can see me through some magical crystal ball. But I had high hopes.

That number I gave him belongs to this asshole, Jack, who I once hooked up with. And ever since, it's been my mission to ruin his life. Whenever someone asks for my number, I'm always more than happy to give them his. Oh, and I also burned his Porsche and got him fired from his six-figure job at a bank. Wonder if he knew it was me who tipped off his boss about the past sexual harassment allegations he had against him.

He was one of those guys who didn't understand what the word no meant. Was rougher than he had to be. So I broke his hand in three places, and last I heard, it still doesn't work right. He's lucky I didn't kill him, because I wanted to. So badly. But I can't go around killing anyone without my father's approval. Sanctioned murders only. Not as though I can tell my father why I wanted the bastard dead. He wouldn't be too happy about my extracurricular activities. But I have two rules, and the first is never let a man get close, so sleeping with random guys when I get the itch is how I get by.

"So, what's your name?" Lance's business partner asks, pulling up his black-rimmed glasses on his wide nose.

He's my father's age. They both are. And definitely not my type. No itches are going to be scratched here tonight.

"Isabella." I grin. "And yours?"

"Benson." He lifts my hand to his mouth, staring into my eyes as though he can't wait to get me out of my clothes. "It's a pleasure to meet such a beautiful woman. What brings you here tonight?"

I twirl my hair around my finger, leaning my head into my shoulder. "My friend and I were just out having fun. How about you?"

"Business." His mouth slants up. "And hopefully some pleasure."

And there you have it, folks.

"That sounds like a fun time to me." I giggle.

"Lance and I have a hotel suite right above if you two want to come up and continue the party there."

I quickly glance at Kora, giving her a knowing look. "That would be perfect."

"Great. I—"

His phone suddenly vibrates across the bar, and his eyes immediately land on the caller ID once he picks it up. His face goes ashen, his demeanor shifting with displeasure.

"Would you ladies excuse us for a moment? We have an important call. Lance." He gestures with a tilt of his head, getting off his swivel stool, with Lance following behind.

"I'll be right back," Lance tells Kora. "Don't you go anywhere." He smiles on a chuckle.

"Wouldn't dream of it." She shoots him one of her sultry grins.

Then they're rushing out toward the exit, until they disappear out of sight.

"We can do it right now," I whisper to her.

"And miss all the excitement at their hotel room?" she mocks.

I reach into my handbag and remove a small tube of what appears to be mascara. Darting my eyes around the bustling place and not seeing anyone looking at us, I hand it to her.

She opens it discreetly and spills a few drops of undetectable, yet deadly liquid into Lance's drink. It's something new our chemist has concocted.

"I'm sorry about that, ladies," Lance says behind us, and my pulse quickens.

Kora slips the mascara tube into her bag.

"Shall we go?" Benson asks, extending his hand for mine.

"Can we finish our drinks first?" Kora flirts with a look on her face that has them sitting right back down.

"Of course, sweetheart," Lance says, placing his hand on the top of her thigh.

Instead of sipping on it, she downs the entire thing, and doesn't even flinch.

"Wow, you sure were thirsty." Lance ogles her with obvious desire.

"I was." She laughs flirtatiously, rolling her finger up and over his knee. "For you."

He clears his throat, a trembling hand picking up his own drink before he's gulping it down.

"You next," Benson tells me as he lifts his own beverage and cheers with me before he finishes his off. I swallow the remainder of my champagne, placing the glass down gently.

It'll take a good five minutes for Lance's heart to stop beating. Long enough for us to get to the elevators and for him to die before we even make it to their room.

Lance pays the tab, and together, we head out through the double glass doors. Benson wraps an arm around me while we wait for the elevator, and I instantly recoil.

Kora stifles a laugh, catching my expression.

"You truly are a beautiful woman," Benson whispers across my ear.

And before I can even thank him, Lance's hand flies to his chest, his eyes growing wide with terror.

"Oh my God! Are you okay?" Kora's voice trembles, and that has Benson turning toward his friend.

"Lance?" Benson's silver brows tighten.

But Lance doesn't say a word. Silently, he drops onto the floor. Dead within seconds. I don't even need to check his pulse.

Kora shrieks, ever the good actress, and soon enough, we're surrounded by a crowd, with Benson too busy worrying about his friend to watch us slip away.

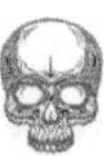

"So, that was kinda fun." Kora throws an arm around me, grinning as we stride down a busy city street, crowds of people walking by, taxis honking from every direction.

As many times as I come to the city, I never actually go catch the sights. Kind of wish I had a simpler life sometimes. One where I could go see a Broadway show or go all the way to the top of the Statue of Liberty. But I can't do any of those things. With the kind of work I do around the city—and everywhere else, for that matter—I have to minimize my exposure. The less I'm seen, the better. Sometimes it's unavoidable, but other times, I take careful steps to prevent being recorded, and the city is full of cameras.

"Oh my God. Look." Kora points to a Shake Shack. "Want to get some?"

"I'm kinda tired. I want to head to my apartment, and you have to drive back."

She knows me well enough to know I'd never invite her to stay over. I prefer to have my nightmares all by my lonesome. That way no one knows about them.

I can control the panic attacks, but I can't control what happens once I close my eyes. I know she'd never tell anyone, but I don't want her pity.

I feel like a total asshole for making her drive all the way back to Cherry Grove, but I know she'd never make me feel bad about it. Kora lives at the academy, in one of the spacious apartments built underground. It's like a damn city down there.

"Oh, come on! I want a shake damn bad," she begs, pulling my wrist toward the restaurant. "We may not get this opportunity again."

"Fine." I let go of her and cross my arms over my chest. "But hurry up. My feet are killing me, and I need sleep."

"You're getting one too." She hooks her arm through mine and practically drags me toward the entrance. "Gotta live a little, Iz."

If I didn't like her, I'd have killed her by now. She's all sunshine and rainbows, while I'm rainclouds and thunder.

But when she's working, when she's killing, there's nothing sweet about her. Kora is three years younger than me and joined Caellach when she was seventeen. Her father is my father's right hand, and he wanted her to be a weapon for our organization. He has no other kids and puts a lot of pressure on Kora. And of course Daddy Dearest couldn't refuse his friend. So here we are, two women in a sea of men who we have no problems putting in their place.

The guys at the academy are pretty respectful. Now. After they got their asses handed to them, which in turn earned us respect. Not that we needed it.

We step into the restaurant and order some Oreo shakes. Once they're ready and in our hands, we continue back out onto the street. I must admit the drink is pretty damn good.

"See? Wasn't this worth it?" She elbows me as we stroll back to her car, parked across from mine.

My mouth jerks as I continue enjoying the liquid dessert. But she catches my smile and smiles even wider.

"Okay, well, I guess this is goodbye," she says, giving me a tight hug once we're in front of her SUV. "We should come back to the city one night. Grab dinner at some fancy steakhouse, go dancing at a club."

I give her an *are you kidding me* look.

"What? We have to enjoy our life too, Iz. Life is so fragile, you know? Never know what the future holds." Her features tighten with melancholy.

She's right. We've all lost people. Family. Friends. Colleagues. Life is made up of tiny camera flashes, but we're too busy to ever look through the lens and grab hold of the present moments until it's too late.

Instantly, I see my mother's face, dark brown hair like my siblings, golden eyes. I miss her terribly. Even after all these years, there hasn't been a single moment that I've forgotten. The way she'd braid my hair, always so perfect. The way she'd wake us up with the corniest song.

Wakey, wakey, eggs and bakey, she'd say.

We'd groan and tell her to quit it, but right now, I'd beg for just one more song. Just one more morning. Just one more hug.

An ache pounds behind my eyes, and I fight it.

People leave. Sometimes they mean to. Sometimes they don't. But in the end, the reasons don't matter, because all you're left with is a gaping hole that hurts like hell and never quite heals.

It's easier not to get attached to anyone. Easier to be alone. To be responsible for just yourself. It's why I didn't want to befriend Kora when we first met. I didn't want someone else to worry about. But she's like family to me now. If something were to ever happen to her...

Forcing myself, I concentrate on her, dialing down the humming of my dreadful thoughts.

"The last time we went out to that dive bar…" I arch both brows. "…I had to carry you home. You probably don't even remember."

"I do." She flings a shoulder. "But that was six months ago. And, most importantly, we had a good time, didn't we?" Her bright pink lips wind up.

I can't help but return a tight sneer. "I guess."

"Oh, look, she smiles. If we can call it that…"

"Shut up." I swat her with the back of my hand. "You're sober, right?"

We never drink and drive, but we didn't want to mess up with Lance. He had to die before my father's court appearance.

"Yeah, I'm good. That champagne tasted like water."

"Okay. Go." I grab her shoulder and squeeze. "Make sure you text me as soon as you get back home, got it?"

"Yes, Mom." She salutes me.

"I mean it, Kora." My pulse hitches, those thoughts slamming into my head. But I shake it off. "Promise to text me."

She must note the harshness of my expression, because she stops smiling and places her palm against my forearm.

"Okay, Iz, I promise. Nothing's going to happen to me." She throws both arms around me and holds me tight. "I love you, stupid."

"Wow, you're a sweet friend." I hold her even tighter, closing my eyes as I do.

She sighs. "Okay, I'm going now. I'll see you tomorrow?"

"Yeah, probably."

"Call me when you get back," she tells me, and with a wave, she enters her car and starts it before heading out onto the road.

I watch her go, and then I'm crossing the street toward my own

SUV, getting inside and starting the car.

The drive to my place takes longer with the traffic, and once I arrive, I slip into a parking spot, conveniently across from my place.

"Good evening." The doorman lets me in as I thank him, and I head inside the twelve-story building that is my home away from home.

My heels clack along as I reach the elevator, pressing a button to call it down. The lobby is empty. No one here but a security guard.

The elevator dings, and I step inside, pressing twelve, when suddenly a hand shoots out, stopping the doors from closing.

"Caught it just in time," a man's husky voice announces.

And my heart ceases to beat.

Because I'd know that voice anywhere.

"Hello, Red." His lips curl on one end, dark eyes capturing mine. "It's been a while."

My head spins, and suddenly he's there, his body nearing mine, shooting me with a wicked glare.

Fuck.

He found me.

Ten

ISEULT

My heart hammers, words stuck in my throat as that handsome man I fought like hell to forget stares at me with madness clouding his large brown eyes.

It's as though he doesn't know whether he wants to wrap his fingers around my throat and drain the life out of me or throw me up against the wall and fuck the shit out of me.

"Nothing to say, Red?" He crosses the rest of the distance between us, taking predatory steps forward.

A finger reaches for a button, stopping the elevator from continuing its journey to my floor. It jerks to a halt while my palms hit the wall behind me to steady myself.

I keep gazing into those eyes, unable to stop myself. Drowning in want and untamable, unfurling desires. I never thought I'd see him again. Thought fantasies were all I'd get. All I should crave. But now, in this moment, I want more than just memories of what happened between us. I want it again. But this time, I want more.

Part of me doesn't know what to do with those foreign thoughts. I'm not used to them, yet here with him, I can't escape them either.

When I don't utter a single word, not sure why my mouth won't move, he presses his body right up against mine, like he doesn't need an invitation. Like he's a man who just takes what he wants, and I'm not about to say no.

His hooded eyes search mine, consuming every single inch of my face as though committing it to memory. He releases a burdened sigh, brows hunched, while his knuckles extend and gently stroke down my cheek.

The sound of my exhales echoes, and my chest turns heavy. And my heart? It beats and it beats. My God, it beats. Has it ever beaten this fast before?

As I continue to stare at this man, the shock that he's found me hasn't worn off. He not only found me, but he found my apartment, and that's really bad. How the hell will I get away from him now? He could follow me home to Cherry Grove. He could uncover everything. The rapid knock of my pulse grows louder in my ears.

"What are you doing here?" I angle my jaw and raise my voice above a whispered breath.

He flashes a mischievous smirk. And that mouth, what it does to me…

My stomach flips when he cups my cheek and holds me, unnerving me with untethered emotions. I've never been touched like that by a man before.

He smells good too, like a male woodsy concoction of heaven and hell, and he looks even better. Too good, in fact. Too tempting.

A deep navy suit fits his tall, well-built frame, a light gray dress shirt peeking from beneath with two buttons popped open. His thick black hair is brushed back, fuller at the top, buzzed at the sides. I have every wicked desire to run my hands through it—to tug and to pull, to feel the way I felt that one night we spent together.

"You lied, Red."

With a quick jerk of his large hand, he grabs the back of my neck and pulls me so close, my chest presses hard against him. His gaze hammers into mine with heated perusal, and I just about drown from overstimulation.

"Let me go," I demand, but it sounds more like I'm asking him to hold on tighter.

"No." He grinds his jaw, his deep inhales making his chest climb, his body pushing mine further into the wall until I'm almost one with it.

I stare at him with pounding heartbeats, unable to look away.

Why did he find me? What does he want? And why do I care enough to find out?

When a few strands of his hair fall wildly around his brow, I reach for them, pushing them off his face, my heart galloping the instant he shutters his eyes to a close, as though my touch alone can soothe him.

I immediately pull my fingers away, not liking this. Or loving it. I can't make sense of these conflicting, treacherous emotions.

His eyes instantly pop open, his gaze drowning over my face, his features tightening with unspeakable sentiments, like he feels whatever's happening between us.

But whatever this is, it can't happen. Not for me. Getting close to a man isn't part of my future. It never will be, no matter how badly I'm thinking about how good it might feel if I did. If I let it all go.

"Why'd you lie to me?" he asks, voice gravelly, a blend of all things savory and forbidden. "If you didn't want to give me your number, shoulda said so.”

"Was easier that way." I shrug, attempting to yank his thick wrist off of my nape, but he's like a damn brick.

He chuckles faintly, releasing his grasp, only for it to curl around the front of my throat. As he cinches his grip, his glare dares me to try and move him off of me.

"You need to understand something, Red." He drops his mouth close, his warm, intoxicating breaths dancing erratically across my trembling lips. "I'm not the kind of man who gives up easily. When I decide I want something, I go after it with full force." His mouth feathers against my lips. "And unfortunately for you, I've decided I want you."

He inhales slow, dragging air into his lungs as he draws back.

"Oh, that's quite the pity." I slip on a bemused smile. "See, this is why I gave you a fake number instead of telling you that I had no desire for you to call me. Didn't want you begging for it."

The vein at his neck pulses, eyes narrowing with a wicked stare. Then a chuckle rumbles out of him. Deep. Raspy. So carnal I want to bathe in the sound.

"Me? Beg?" He shakes his head real slow, flirtation curling around each one of his words. "No, baby. You're gonna be the one begging. I promise you that."

He arches his hips into me, my body imprisoned between his hard masculine form and the wall, feeling the effects I have on him.

He lowers his lips to mine once more, only a breath between us. "And once we're better acquainted, you'll tell me everything there is to know about you."

I'm the one laughing now. Really laughing. And when I'm through, all that's left on my face is a dark, cold expression.

"Funny. A few orgasms, and you think you're my god?"

"Not yet, I'm not. But I will be." His thumb strokes between my lips so achingly slow, my heart beats faster until it threatens to rip right out of my chest.

But he doesn't see it. He doesn't know what I feel. Or what I want. Or what I need. He'll never know.

"Good luck with that," I casually toss out.

"You know, Red, I've just about had it with your bullshit." His commanding hand crawls around to the back of my neck until he's got a fistful of my hair in his grasp. He yanks my head backward, his mouth coasting up my throat, hot breaths leaving a trail of utter destruction.

"Someone's going to catch us in here once security realizes the elevator stopped," I groan, unable to hold it back.

His mouth, his hands…it all feels too good.

"Let them." Teeth graze my jaw before his mouth lines up against mine. "No one can stop me right now. I've been looking all over for you." He wrenches himself away to stare at me with a possessed kind of hunger. "Do you know how insane it made me not to find you?"

"I can tell." A satisfied grin tethers to my face, and I nip the edge of my bottom lip.

He growls, his eyes zeroing on my mouth like he wants a bite too.

"How *did* you find me?" The words fall out breathlessly.

I need to know so I can fix what I did wrong.

"I know a guy." He flashes a devious smile. "He found you on a camera, and I followed you to the bar. Then I watched you in my car while you were having a ton of fun."

Fuck. This is exactly why I try to keep a low profile. And that damn camera inside the bar was supposed to be off. How the hell did he see me? Maybe he's bluffing.

He tugs my hair until it hurts, until it feels so good that the ache between my thighs roars to new heights.

His dirty, wicked grin widens. "I watched you kill a man."

Shit. He's definitely not bluffing.

"No idea what the hell you're talking about."

Hope he buys it, but his laughter says otherwise.

"I'm not here to arrest you, Red. In fact, we're the same, you and I." He drags in a long, sensuous inhale. "If anything, I'm impressed. And I'm not easily impressed."

I twist my face into a discontented expression. "Well, you have it wrong. I didn't kill anyone."

Kora did. I mean, I helped, of course.

"Yes, that's right." He nods thoughtfully. "You assisted. It was your blonde friend giving him that lethal dose."

My heart smashes against my ribs. If someone else sees that, Kora and I are fucked.

He seems really proud of himself. Fucker. I really can't decide if I wanna stab him in the throat with my heel or smash my lips to his.

"You can't tell anyone." My tone grows forceful.

My father would have my fucking head.

"And what will I get for keeping your secret?"

"You'll get to live." I narrow my gaze into slits. "Is that not good enough for you?"

Holding my stare, his eyes turn intense, his breathing heavy and tortured. "Oh, Red, every time you threaten my life, it only makes me want you more."

"You're insane," I huff out in utter exasperation, but also completely overtaken by maddening attraction, or maybe deep sexual chemistry.

But this feels like it's on a whole other level. Then again, I have nothing to compare it to.

"And you're beautiful," he replies softly, the back of his hand stroking the side of my face, like he can't stop touching me.

And my stomach flutters and soars—something I never dreamed it could do.

Every inch of me comes alive as though born from his touch alone. I instantly recoil, as though my mind's catching up, refusing to accept that my body could feel anything like this—an overpowering sense of loss of control.

"I don't want you to worry," he tells me. "I made sure to erase the footage I got permanently and had all the cameras showing you and your friend from around the city wiped clean."

I suck in a breath. "Why are you helping me?"

That mouth of his teases mine with a kiss he hasn't yet given. "Because, bambina, I'd like to consider us friends, and I help my friends."

"We're not friends," I declare, losing the untamable control of my own voice. "More like frenemies, maybe, and even *that's* pushing it."

He laughs, and it only continues to undo me. That gravelly rasp of his tone, it unfurls this deep-seated desire for things I never even considered before him: someone steady in my life.

It's stupid, I know. It sounded stupid as soon as the thought left me. But what if…

"Answer me one thing." He bores his piercing gaze into mine, and my pulse rises as though hostage to his command. "Have you thought about me once since the last time we saw each other?"

"I—"

"And try to be honest for once. I know how difficult that is for you." Amusement lines his expression.

"Fine." I roll my eyes. "Maybe once. Twice."

"Twice?" Both of his brows rise in a cocky way. "Wow. A lot more than I imagined."

I swat his chest, and he chuckles, catching my wrist and kissing the inside of it.

My heartbeats pummel, his eyes sinking into mine as his lips remain there, bound to my pulse.

I straighten my spine and clear my throat.

"I don't know what's going on in that big head of yours, but my thoughts of you literally lasted for seconds," I lie. "It was more like, 'Wow, those were some great orgasms. What's for dinner?'"

"Made that pussy come hard, and now you can't forget about me, is that right?" He smiles knowingly.

"That's not what happened." I huff, while pretending what he just said isn't in fact the whole damn truth. "I forgot about you. You were completely forgotten."

He shakes his head, unable to wipe that smug grin off his face. Then out of nowhere, his amusement dies, the smile fading away as though it never was, and in its place is a man sheathed with a raw kind of prowess.

My pulse hitches. With excitement.

His hand wraps around my throat like he owns me.

"Liar," he drawls, intensity brewing on his face, the hollows beneath his cheeks deepening.

Then, he smashes his lips to mine and kisses the holy hell out of me.

His palm tightens around my throat, his tongue invading the warmth of my mouth as he forces me to kiss him back, to undo the invisible chains that bind me, that he doesn't even know exist. The ones that keep me from the things that could've been mine if only my life wasn't so unspeakably changed.

His free hand roughs into my hair, tugging and pulling with

the roughened roll of his tongue around mine. He's groaning, desperate for more, while my hands act of their own volition, practically clawing at his shirt.

When I curl my arms around his shoulders and groan, his kiss gentles and deepens, an unhurried lull of passion seeping between us.

I want more of whatever this is. This everlasting high I've never known. I want his hands between my thighs, quenching this thirst I've never felt before. Want him to flip me around, bend me over, and fuck me until I see stars. A slip of a moan falls out of me, and a satisfactory growl rumbles out of him.

His teeth bite my lower lip, drawing it into that sinful mouth of his as he grunts deep in his chest. The kiss is unearthly, a shattering of my existence, a mere combustion of attraction and lust and desire.

I don't know what to do with it or how to stop it, and I desperately want to stop it. Or my brain does. But my body? It wants it all.

Breathlessly, he pulls away, his chest rising higher with each inhale, those eyes fastened with mine. "Fucking hell, Red. I knew you'd kiss me back like you meant it."

He groans low, the sound thundering as both hands sink into my hair, gripping roughly.

"I kiss everyone like that." I swallow thickly, trying to come down from the high.

"You don't even lie well," he retorts, eyes growing heavy-lidded.

I turn my head sideways, trying to fight a smile. Kinda, sorta succeeding.

"So adorable." His hand slinks out of my strands, an index finger tapping my nose.

I pitch him with a glare, and his smirk widens. I swear the man enjoys getting a rise out of me.

"You repulse me," I fire out.

His chuckle echoes as his hand glides down the side of my torso and climbs up my inner thigh.

"Are you sure about that?" That voice grows slicker, gravellier.

And fuck me, I get wetter the more he talks, the more he touches me this way.

"Yes…" I breathe, hating myself for sounding weak.

His darkened eyes trap me in his inescapable gaze, and with his hand clutching my hair, he flips me around and presses my front up against the elevator, pushing my cheek into the wall with his palm.

"I guess we're gonna find out how repulsive I really am." He yanks up my tiny dress, the cool air hitting my bare ass.

A finger runs between my cheeks, his thumb hooking into the thin strap of my white thong.

"I've been counting down the minutes till I have you under my grasp, and this right here…" He spanks my ass. "This is even better than I've imagined."

His words hunger for a taste of me, and I swear I'm about to give it to him. Roughly, he drags my panties down until they tighten around my upper thighs.

"Spread them," he demands, and like his little puppet, I obey.

My core throbs for his fingers, needing to feel myself come undone once again.

"Has anyone touched your pussy since I have?" he asks, as though daring me to tell him they have.

I shake my head.

"Brava ragazza…good girl," he grunts, relief swallowing his tone.

And I swear, if any other man ever called me a good girl, I'd deck him.

But coming from him, especially in two languages… I like it.

What the hell is happening?

Before I can think a second more about any of this, his heavy palm strikes me across my rear once more, my hair clutched in his fist as he snaps my neck backward.

"You're not going to run from me again, do you hear me?" His warm and heady breath wisps across the shell of my ear.

I don't disagree. I couldn't if I tried, not with the way I feel in this very moment.

But I will. I'll run, and this time he won't catch me. He can't. I won't let him get close. My secrets need to stay buried. My scars are not his to bear. I'm destined to be alone. It's the way it has to be.

"I haven't heard an answer, Red." He spanks me again, harder this time.

"I won't run," I breathlessly submit.

"That's my girl."

"I'm not your girl." My reply sounds like a lie even to myself.

"Not yet. But you will be. It's only a matter of time."

Then he thrusts his thick fingers inside me, filling me to capacity, giving me something no man has before: a sense of possession and yearning. An unexplainable feeling I've never felt.

Maybe it's the orgasms. They're loading my head with all kinds of stupid thoughts. Like maybe I can keep fucking the same guy and hold my secrets intact. Maybe he won't find out who I am or why I'm such a mess when no one's around. Or why I can't seem to get rid of the nightmares, no matter how long ago it happened.

But even as I try to rationalize it all, I know that's a fantasy. If I keep seeing him, he's bound to find out everything, and I'm not ready for that. I'll never be ready.

"Repulsive, huh? You get this wet for every man who repulses you?" He curls his fingers, stroking my G-spot with a gruff strain of his tone. He deepens his strokes, tugging my hair in his palm. "Your pussy is dripping, and I haven't even fucked you yet." He drives inside me, all the way deep.

"Oh, God, shut up," I gasp.

The more his punishing strokes assail me, the more he speaks those dirty words that apparently I'm very much into, the more turned on I get.

I let out a loud cry when he slides out and then back in with brutal force, like he wants to remind me I'm his to do with what he wants.

"Hush now." His lips fall close to my ear, velvety soft. "Wouldn't want an audience." He sucks my lobe into the heat of his mouth. "Unless that's your thing, bambina."

But I don't get to respond, because the man sends me headfirst into oblivion, so intensely I have no other option but to fall.

Hard and fast.

Completely unprepared.

With nothing to hold on to.

GIO

As soon as we're in her apartment, we're back at it, and she kisses me like her life depends on it. I don't think I've ever been kissed this way before.

Fuck, what is she doing to me?

She groans as she slides her tongue into my mouth, her hands slipping into the back of my dress pants, mine snaking into her hair.

I attempt to undo the zipper at her spine, to get that damn dress off, but she instantly jerks back, a sliver of panic in her rounded eyes.

"Don't."

Something dark and painful crosses her gaze as she swallows.

"I'm keeping the dress on," she warns while I stare, wondering why.

"Are you shy, Red?" My knuckles reach for her delicate face, running down her cheek. "Because if you must know, I find every inch of you to be perfect."

She sneers like she finds the thought hard to believe. "Just don't, okay? And stop asking questions. If you want to fuck me, then we do things my way."

"Okay, bambina." With both hands, I cup her face. "It's whatever you want."

Her eyes glisten, and her brows tug, unspoken raw emotions riding her face. And before I can ask her who put that pain in her heart, her lips are back on mine, stifling the questions as though she wants me to forget.

But I can't do that. I'm ravenous enough for her to put them aside. For now. But I will find out who hurt her, and I will make them pay.

"Bedroom. Where is it?" I growl, my teeth scoring up her throat.

Her lips pepper hungrily along my stubbled jaw as she points a thumb behind her. With my front to hers, I walk her backward, wrapping all that luscious hair around my wrist twice, mouth madly kissing hers, unsure if she's finally letting her guard down or playing me. I've come to realize that with her, one never knows the answer.

I have every desire to look through her apartment, to get to know this woman better. But right now, I'm consumed with thoughts of us tangled on her bed, her screaming for me while she gives me those eyes.

We step past the doorframe, and I throw her on top of the bed, her body falling over the soft white comforter, my frame molding over hers.

I settle my hips between her thighs, propping myself on an elbow while I stare down at her, wondering if it's true. If a person truly knows in their heart that someone was created just for them. Because I know in my damn soul that she was.

I don't know how.

I don't know if I've gone insane, but she's going to be mine.

I just need a way to make her believe it too.

"Would you stop looking at me like that and kiss me?" she clips, cheeks flushed, gaze dripped with agitation.

I've noticed she doesn't like it when I stare. Doesn't like to feel that connection I know she can't escape. It's like escaping your own destiny, and baby girl is trying hard to run from it. But this energy between us, there's no escaping it. It's palpable. Breathable. I know she knows it too.

I didn't expect you to come swinging into my life either, Red. But here we are, and there's nothing you can do to stop it.

My gaze roves down every curve of her face. "I enjoy looking at beautiful things." My fingers trace up her inner thigh. "And knowing…" I hook my index finger into the strap of her thong. "…you'll probably try disappearing on me again, it's making me desperate to remember every goddamn exquisite inch of you."

She gives me a little moan when I trace her wet slit, biting the edge of her bottom lip. I drop my face closer, inch by aching inch, my lips hovering, stroking hers in the softest way.

My pulse jerks. And I can't be sure whether it's from the passion swimming in the waves of her eyes, or simply because she makes me want to kiss her for the rest of my life. But either way, I know whatever I'm feeling, it's something I'll never feel again.

For anyone.

Scooping her up, I place her head on top of the pillows, wanting her comfortable.

She sighs, her eyes sinking into mine.

"You're so gorgeous, you know that?"

"I do now." Her voice grows faint, her lips flickering in what she'd consider a smile.

And when she does that, when she gives me one of those small smiles, her genuine ones, I'd do anything to make her keep smiling at me that way.

"Tell me your name," I ask, my lips brushing against hers, and her warm breathing fans across my mouth.

"Not gonna happen," she sighs, her fingers rolling up and down my back.

I drop my face lower, kissing her jaw, teeth grazing down her throat.

My hand returns between her silky thighs, and with a jerk of a finger, I push her panties all the way to the side, exposing her perfect little pussy. A single digit slides into her slit once more, feathering over her wet clit while I keep our eyes connected.

Her brows furrow, her back bowing while she gasps with uneven breaths. I tease and flick until she grows every bit turned on, making those sexy sounds, her body getting wetter and softer for me.

"I'm gonna spend my time tasting you," I promise, the words slipping past her ear. "And after that, you will tell me that name of yours."

"I'll never tell you," she pants.

"Oh, Red, you will." I chuckle, looking back at her. "You're gonna tell me everything."

I sink down her body, kissing along her throat and in between her breasts, leading a path downward until I'm right where I want to be.

Picking up the back of her knee, I spread her open, kissing the soft, velvety skin of her inner thigh, leading an upward trail.

Her hands ball around the comforter, her spine curved, her eyes shut tight.

Two fingers hook into each side of her panties, rolling them down her long legs until they catch in her high heels before hitting the floor.

She returns her attention to me when I palm her pussy, riding it slow while she writhes and moans.

"You look good on that bed, being obedient, letting me do whatever the hell I want."

Her eyes fill with quiet disdain while she grinds herself harder on me.

I knew exactly what I was doing. She likes it when I talk to her that way.

"I suggest you stop talking and get to eating me out," she demands, and my chest warms with a small laugh.

"I hope I get to satisfy Her Highness." I drag her dress toward her hips, her ass fully exposed.

"The dress stays just like that," she cautions, and I once again wonder why.

"You're one demanding hellcat," I whisper, my hands sliding under her ass, my mouth descending lower until I cup her pussy.

My tongue gives her a leisurely swipe from entrance to that throbbing clit.

"Oh my God…" Her eyes roll back, fingers splicing through my hair, yanking so hard she's about to rip off some strands.

My tongue snakes up and around that spot that has her thrashing wildly. I sink two fingers inside her, wanting my cock there, stretching her to fit me like a glove.

The erotic sounds escaping from her throat echo through the room while her hips roll like she's trying to both escape the way I'm making her feel and get more of it.

"Mmm," I groan when I feel her clutching my fingers like a

vise, her release getting closer.

"Don't stop," she quickly whispers.

I don't have any plans to. If watching her fall apart is the last thing I see before hell calls to me, then I'll gladly meet the devil with a smile on my face.

"Yes, yes, yes!" she cries when I thrust deeper, hitting her G-spot, sucking her clit into my mouth.

Her body shudders like she's about to let go, her whimpers of pleasure climbing higher. And with another swipe of my tongue, she screams out a curse.

"Oh, fuck!" Two fists pull on my hair as she comes all over my tongue, tasting like poison and honey twined into one.

Before she can realize what I'm doing, I gradually climb up her body while reaching into my pocket.

My body drops over hers, fitting just right, my cock rocking between her thighs as I lift her hand in the air. Silver cuffs dangle from my grasp, and within seconds, I have her wrist in one of them.

"Wha—what the fuck?" She looks up, trying to push me off just as I fasten the other end to one of the poles of her headboard.

She yanks her arm, eyes laced with rage, just as I start to rise off the bed. She stares up at her restrained hand before her gaze darts to mine, daggers shooting out of it.

"You have *two* seconds to let me go," she hisses, grinding her teeth.

I fold my arms across my chest, popping a brow. "Don't think I will."

The flush on her cheeks is all kinds of sexy, and so is that glare.

I stare with a satisfied expression. "You look too good lying there, all flushed and spread open like my personal offering."

She groans, balling her hands. "I'm going to kill you for this, whoever you are, whatever the fuck your name is. And nothing and no one will save you."

"I'd like to see you try, bambina." My eyes take a lazy stroll down her body, her pink pussy still completely bare and glistening. "Seems like whenever you pretend to hate me, we end up with you coming like my personal little whore."

"You bastard!" Her cheeks turn crimson and her eyes narrow. "This is *not* funny. You'd better let me go. Now!"

"Nah." A proud smile plays on my face. "I think instead, I'm going to teach you a lesson that lying to someone will get you into lots of trouble."

"What kind of trouble?" Her chest rattles with forceful breaths, her wrathful gaze hungry to make me her next kill.

"This kind." I settle on the edge of the bed, taking the right side, my hands cupping her hips, fingers delving deeper while she watches me, making no attempts to push me away.

She clasps the comforter with her free hand, her gaze hard, yet slinking with her unsurmountable desire.

When will she realize fighting me will get her nowhere? Though I do enjoy it when she fights.

Before she has a chance to protest, I flip her over, her hips on my lap, her ass mine for the taking. And what a beautiful ass it is.

"W-what the hell are you doing?" she stammers, peering over at me from behind her shoulder.

But the way her voice swells with an erotic current lets me know she has no qualms about what my palm plans to do to that ass.

I fist her hair, yanking her head back, keeping her head prisoner, while my heavy hand lands hard and loud against her round and curvy behind.

"Does that answer your question, Red?"

"You are *not* spanking me." Indignation settles on her features as she fights my hold, staring at me with a twist of her neck.

Yet…her hips grind against me like she's enjoying this a little too much.

So I do it again, spanking her ass harder with a grin on my motherfuckin' face. "Who's gonna stop me?"

"Shit," she cries when I let my palm slide under her, working her clit on it, forcing her to ride my hand as she groans.

She's fighting it, fighting the sensation drifting through her limbs.

She's slick and sensitive, throwing her head back, her low moan of satisfaction trembling throughout her body.

"Look at me." I slap her roughly. "Look at me, Red, or I stop and leave you here begging for it."

"Fuck you," she seethes.

My finger sinks inside her real slow, my eyes locked on hers as I curl it inside her, twisting and thrusting.

"Oh, shit," she whimpers with parted lips.

"You like that?"

She clenches her jaw.

"Stubborn girl." I add another finger. "I asked you a question."

I slam inside with a single thrust up to my last knuckle, pushing deeper with every stroke.

She tightens her thighs around me, not wanting to come. But her eyes roll and her features grow tense.

"Since you're really not enjoying yourself, bambina, maybe I should stop." I slip my fingers out of her and grab a handful of her ass, taking a little bite before I throw her back on the mattress.

As soon as I rise, she attempts to grab my forearm.

"Wait," she calls.

But I'm already walking away.

"Don't you *dare* leave me like this!" She flips to her front and roughly pulls down her dress, but that short thing barely covers her.

And I'm back to wondering why she didn't want to take it off for me in the first place.

"I'm not leaving." I stare at her pussy for a moment, flicking my eyes back to hers. "But I'm hoping in the meantime that the ache between those gorgeous thighs tortures you into obedience when I return."

"Where the hell are you going?" Her eyes narrow.

"Going to take a shower, then order some takeout. And if you're a good little girl, maybe I'll feed you." I give her a once-over, a smirk overtaking my face. "You look so good handcuffed to the bed."

She huffs with rage, her cheeks growing crimson as she stares at me like she's going to rip my head right off. It only eggs me on.

"Where are your clean towels?"

A vein practically explodes from her neck.

"Fine, don't tell me." I shrug. "I'll find them myself."

"Folded in the *fucking* bathroom," she hisses, ready to stake me. "Don't you dare go rummaging through my things."

"Why? Hiding a vibrator in your panty drawer?"

I start for the dresser, and she instantly sits up against the headboard, her shoulders rocking with such force, I wonder why there's no steam coming out of her head.

"Maybe I can use it on you when I'm nice and clean. Would you like that, bambina?"

She stares heatedly at me while I chuckle, heading for the top drawer, and as soon as I open it, my grin widens.

"Look what we have here…" My fingers skim across all those lace panties and bras neatly folded.

And just as predicted, there's a bright pink vibrator tucked in the corner, one end with a suction cup and a tongue-looking thing.

Wow.

"My, my. Little Red likes to play, huh? Well…" I grab the toy and stride back to her. "Lucky for you, I have all night to see how many times I can make you come with this thing." I lean into her ear. "Then if you're lucky, I'll let you come on my cock."

She stares at me with ire, scoffing as she glances at my dick. "Please. I bet you're five inches."

I extend a hand and grab her jaw, tilting up her face. "How about we double that number? Will that do, Your Highness?"

Her chest trembles as she pants like she's about to come. I watch her toes contort, her thighs tightening into themselves.

I drop her toy beside her and let my fingers skate down her torso, my eyes on hers as my fingers flick her clit.

She gasps right before I force three fingers inside her hard.

"Oh, God!" she screams, gaze perched to mine while I clutch her throat, thrusting so deeply and roughly that her walls clench, her sounds of pleasure loud and shameless.

She couldn't control this if she tried.

"Yeah, that's it. Spread those legs wider, let me finger-fuck that perfect pink pussy. And when I finally give you my name, that's all you'll be screaming for the rest of your life."

"I'll never say your name," she groans. "Unless it's to curse you to the pits of hell."

"Will you come with me, baby?" I decrease my tempo until I stop completely and slide out.

She grunts in frustration, fighting to get me back inside her.

"Greedy girl." I slap her wet cunt.

"Oh, f-f-fuck…" Her body heaves as she attempts to control her breathing.

Picking up the vibrator, I straighten to my full height and roll it up and down her thigh, purposely avoiding her core.

My smirk only pisses her off, blistering contempt snagging her features.

"Uncuff me and get the fuck out of here."

I place the toy on her nightstand. "I know you're used to telling people what to do, expecting them to listen."

I drop my face close to hers a second time, my lips fledging across her ear. Her breath hitches.

"But I'm not your boy-toy, Red. So I'm going to go take my hot shower, and when I'm done, I expect you to be on your best behavior."

I right myself, starting to undo the buttons of my suit jacket, shrugging it off before placing it on the edge of her bed. My fingers lower to my belt and I begin to remove it, the clinking reverberating through the room as she watches me, unable to take her eyes off my movements.

The shirt comes next, the pants and boxers following, until I'm completely bare. My cock is thick and heavy, and her eyes definitely don't miss that.

"Like what you see, bambina?"

"No," she snarls.

"I think you do." I fist myself, stroking nice and slow. "I think you like it a little too much."

"I bet you don't even last long." Her tongue swipes across her lips, her eyes bouncing between me and my dick.

"Oh, baby, you didn't just say that." In one quick step, I'm right beside her, my hand snapping around her nape, tugging her hair back and forcing her to look up. "Just for that, I'm gonna fuck you for hours until your body can't physically come anymore."

"That's not even possible," she challenges with a glint in her eyes.

"I'll make it possible."

Her exhales ravage faster, her chest climbing higher and higher, and goddamn, I have every urge to rip that dress to shreds and fuck every inch of her.

"Now…" I drop my hand to my side. "I'm going to go get clean, and I expect you to stay here and not cause trouble. Think you can manage that?"

"Go fuck yourself," she grates.

"I think I will, thinking about you." I take a lazy stroll down her figure. "At least in my fantasies, you're looking at me like you like me and not like I'm Satan."

She flips me off while I chuckle, turning to head out into the living room and finding the door to the bathroom. Stepping inside, I turn on the water, letting steam fill the room. The scorching drops run down my body when I walk in, washing away the invisible grime on me from someone I killed tonight.

Minutes later, the sound of a bang and then another loud crack swells through the room.

What the hell?

I quickly shut off the water and grab a towel from the stand beside me. Drying myself with one, I take another to wrap around my hips. I'm out in seconds, marching back to the bedroom, wanting to make sure she's okay.

But when I return, I don't see her at all, and that pole she was attached to? It's missing.

"Shit."

Before I can go searching, her roar registers behind me, and she's lunging forward with that missing pole. Anger seeps through her features as the metal reaches inches from my face.

I grab it and twist, but she jumps in the air and kicks me right on the side of my face.

"Holy hell, woman!"

I grow dizzy, and she takes that second and punches me hard in the jaw, pushing me onto the floor. With a grumble, she settles on top of me, the handcuffs still dangling from her wrist, the pole in her grasp edging toward my throat.

"I told you I'd kill you," she fires, an angry flush staining her cheeks.

But my blood only grows warm. The way I want her… It must be a sickness, her poison running free into my veins, because in this moment, staring up at her, all I want is to know her. Every bit of her. What makes her laugh. What makes her cry. What I can do to take away the hurt I can see so clearly in the veil of her gaze.

Gently, I reach up a hand, my knuckles caressing down her cheek. "It's okay, Red. Go ahead. If you're the last thing I get to see before I die, I'll die happy."

She gapes at me, then gets angry. The shift is instant.

"Fight me!"

"No." I gently shake my head.

She drives the pole deeper into the side of my neck until it hurts.

"You asshole." She grinds her teeth. "Fight me!"

My hand slides up the back of her head, the pads of my fingers burrowing deeper. "I don't want to hurt you, bambina."

"You won't." She snickers. "I've taken on worse than you."

"Maybe." My lips slowly bend up, raw emotions overtaking me as I hold her cheek in my palm. "But I don't want to be one of them."

Her unsteady breathing intensifies. "You're so infuriating."

Her brows knit together, her gaze washing over my face until it falls to my mouth.

"You have that effect on me too," I whisper, realizing my towel had fallen off, my cock hard beneath her and I know she feels it too.

"I hate you," she breathes, the pole falling from her grasp and landing with a loud clank against the wooden floor.

My fingers wind into her hair. "Then hate me, baby."

Her palms drop to the sides of my neck, her chest lowering to mine. "This doesn't mean anything."

Then she kisses me.

And I realize that all the other times I've been kissed before didn't mean a damn thing.

Twelve

ISEUT

Why couldn't I kill him?

I've never once hesitated ending someone's life. So why did I stop myself from ending his miserable life, and why the hell am I still on the floor, kissing him as though it's the only thing I ever want to do?

My hips rock against him, his erection pressing up deliciously into me, causing my body to ache with desperate madness.

His dick was definitely an eyesore. Who needs a dick that big? And why do I very much want to find out if he actually knows how to use it?

He flips me over, thrusting his hips in slow, tantalizing circles.

"Tell me to stop," he rasps, lips coasting up my throat, and I have magically lost my voice.

The only sounds I seem to manage are the little moans I've never given another man before. Because none of them have done to my body what he already has.

The men before were just a quick fuck. No foreplay. No nothing. I was bored every single time.

But this? It's like an escape. A feeling most akin to flying and never wanting to fall.

He groans when he doesn't hear my refusal, shoving the dress up my body until it hits my hips. He doesn't attempt to take it off. By now he knows I'd kill him if he tried.

His mouth lowers to mine, kissing me with such raw passion and savagery, I almost forget I'm supposed to hate him.

I've never been this reckless. Usually, I'll meet a man, then plan to meet him another day after running a background check. Then once we fuck, I never call him again.

But with this man, I don't even have a name. Yet I'm on the floor, letting him touch me like he paid for me.

I freeze, holding a breath in my chest when his mouth falls to my breast, kissing it through the thick material.

It's fine. He's not going to take off the dress.

My pulse quickens, and I close my eyes to steady my nerves.

I want to feel his bare skin on mine, his mouth everywhere, but I can't.

I concentrate on his fingers as they journey up my inner thigh, slipping into my warmth as he works my clit between two fingers. My body contorts on a gasp, the unquenched desire blazing through my body with such intensity that tingles spread across my limbs.

He rubs me faster, propping on an elbow as he watches me intensely, and my stomach roils, hating the way he's staring at me, but craving it all at once.

"I've been dreaming of touching you like this," he groans. "Gonna have this pussy wrapped around my cock, begging me to come."

"Fuck," I gasp when he curls his fingers and deepens his strokes.

My hand grasps a chunk of his hair while he continues his maddening tempo.

Men don't usually take such command of my body. I'm normally dictating their moves and rolling my eyes when they can't seem to listen. But this man doesn't need instructions. He's got my manual all figured out.

"Don't stop," I pant, tugging his hair harder, the release edging closer…until with a flick of his finger, I let out a scream. Loud and unashamed.

My teeth sink into his shoulder, and I swear I'm going to leave a mark. But he doesn't so much as flinch. Instead, he growls madly, as though enjoying it.

"That's it, bambina. Let me hear you. Let me hear what I do to you." He continues touching me, the waves of my release ebbing and flowing through me in rhythmic waves of unbending pleasure.

And before I realize what's happening, I'm lifted in the air and thrown on the bed, his body behind mine and my vibrator in his grip. He forces my legs apart, his hot breath against my ear.

"What are you…"

But the words instantly die in my throat, replaced by a cry when he cups my pussy with my toy and flips on the tongue. It flicks around my already sensitive clit, making my body shudder, my voice lost to the desperate cries.

"I—I can't," I gasp, unable to imagine having another orgasm.

He fists my hair, tilting my head to the side so I can look at him. "You're gonna come over and over until I tell you to stop. And right now, you don't have my permission."

He spins the toy over to the opposite side, and the vibrations from the wand make me scream and curse, my limbs shaking with unbearable intensity.

Then I'm flying again, soaring and begging for him not to stop.

And he doesn't. He increases the intensity, and before I know it, the need for release latches on to me until I cry for it desperately.

"You're gonna make me come so hard…"

He grunts, thrusting the vibrator inside me so deep, my fingers tremble and the sounds coming out of my mouth don't resemble me at all.

Before I know it, I'm falling once more, warmth sluicing up my body, tightening through my muscles, and never wanting this feeling to end.

He doesn't halt the sweet torture, lowering the setting to a dull hum over my aching clit, giving my body only a momentary stay until the tempo jumps between high and low, taking me to the edge once again, only to pull me back from it.

Everything inside me coils. My body trembles, the sounds I make too embarrassing to even think about, but it hits me again—the slam of my release—so hard I feel tears swell in the corner of my eyes.

In a flash, his hands are on my hips and he's flipping me on top of him until I'm straddling his muscular thighs.

He gazes up with those unspeakable emotions, and his palms hold my face within them, his thumbs tracing my jaw.

"Who hurt you, Red?" he asks with a whispered demand, staring at me with determination.

My heart tightens.

And I almost do. I almost tell him. Almost want to.

But I don't.

"No one," I lie, but my voice betrays me.

He gives me a sympathetic smile. "I'm gonna get you to trust me one day, and when that day comes, you will tell me. And if he's still alive, I'll make sure he dies slowly."

I inhale a rapid gasp, emotions clogging my throat.

My heart stills in my chest, unable to beat, to do much of anything.

And as I stare down at him, it's like he's begging me to climb up with him to the edge of the tallest mountain and not be afraid to fall.

But falling with the wrong person is the most terrifying of all.

My brows squeeze, and I harden my expression. "I don't need anyone fighting my battles, least of all a stranger I don't even know."

He concentrates his eyes on me, his palm on the back of my head, lowering my forehead until it's touching his. "You're so stubborn."

"That's what they tell me," I breathe.

"That's okay, baby. I like a challenge."

Then he's kissing me, ever so slowly, and I'm drunk on the high of these emotions he brings out.

And while every thought inside my head tells me to end this, my heart? It can't seem to. So instead of leaving, I cling to his shoulders and let him kiss me until he retrieves a condom from my nightstand. Until his body falls on top of mine. Until he rolls the latex over his thickness, pressing his cock against my bare core. Until I feel myself climbing again.

And with his mouth returning to mine, he slowly slips inside me, inch by tantalizing inch, refusing to look anywhere but into my eyes.

And I swear my heart… I never knew how good it could feel, to sleep with someone you have a connection with. It's madness and chaos and pure utter bliss.

I kiss him roughly, his tongue snaking with mine, his hands in my hair as he drives deeper with every stroke, as though he's trying to reach all the way inside and make me remember him forever.

And though I may remember him forever, I can't let him stay.

"Widen those thighs for me, Red," he groans.

When I do, he lifts up one of my legs and drapes it over his shoulder, rising on his knees, fucking me so hard my head hits the headboard.

My eyes close of their own volition, the intensity too much for me to bear.

"Look at me," his voice rumbles.

And I do. I can't seem to fight his forceful tone, not with what I'm feeling in every nerve ending.

His eyes fall to the place where our bodies meet and he mutters a curse, his gaze rising back to my eyes, and the faster he pounds into me, the more I beg.

And with his eyes latched on to mine, I fall, knowing it'll be the last time I do.

This will never happen again.

It can't.

He will never have me.

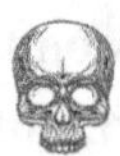

GIO

She's snuggled up against me, and I'm afraid to move even an inch, because if I do, she may realize I'm actually holding her. When a woman like this lets you hold her, you don't do a thing to ruin it. Because my Red, she could bolt at any moment.

I get that more than anyone. Relationships have never been something I wanted. I never did commitment. I had casual flings, and that was always the extent of it. I never had a reason to stay, to grab on to something. But with her, like this…I want to hold on. I want to latch on to something meaningful. Some*one* meaningful.

"How long have you lived here?" I ask.

"For a few years." Her fingers stroke my abdomen, and I close my eyes, reveling in the sensation of her hands on me.

"Where were you before?"

She chuckles. "I see what you're trying to do, and it won't work." She glances up, her eyes bright like two rare jewels. "You may have fucked me better than anyone has, but—"

"Whoa." I jerk back with a grin, and an uncomfortable expression settles on her features, as though she's just realized what she said. "Did you just admit I'm the best you ever had?"

"Uh, no." She grimaces, tightening her mouth to stop from grinning, a finger scratching her temple. "You must be hard of hearing."

"Mm-hmm." You couldn't erase that grin off my face if you tried. "The ice queen admitted I was the best fuck she ever had. I'm gonna get that tattooed on my chest."

"You're so annoying." She rolls her eyes.

With a laugh, I grab her jaw and drag her in for a long kiss, and the woman melts right into me, languidly rolling her tongue with mine, lazily groaning. When I draw away, she's utterly breathless and beautiful.

"Fine, Red. We can do this your way, but eventually you'll like me."

"I don't like anyone." She cocks a brow.

"You don't say?"

She plops her head back down onto my chest and sighs, almost under her breath. Without thinking, I lift up and kiss her on her forehead.

"What was that for?" she asks, peering up with softness bathing the tranquil ocean of her eyes.

"I have no idea." I brush the hair off her face with the pads of my fingers, and she lays a palm against my frantically beating heart.

"We should do dinner," I tell her.

"Was that you asking me out?" There's a smile etched in her voice, shining through her eyes.

"What if I am?"

"I'm not really a 'take me to dinner' kind of woman."

"Maybe you just haven't met someone worth asking you."

Her gaze widens before giving me a faraway look, staring to her right. "Doubt you're the one."

With two fingers, I tilt her chin and center her focus on me. "How would you know if you're always too busy pushing me away before I even get the privilege to know you?" I sweep her lower lip with my thumb, watching as her breaths grow ragged with every second. "So, dinner? Tomorrow?"

"I work tomorrow." I swear she wants to say yes, she just needs a reason.

"So take off."

She snickers. "It's not that kind of work."

"Who do you work for?"

She shakes her head, giving me a tiny smile. "You never give up, do you?"

"Finally, you're starting to realize that."

She props her chin on her palm and gives me a defeated look. "You're insane."

"All true." I wink. "I'll be picking you up at seven tomorrow, and I expect you to be fully dressed by then."

"Is that so?" She lays her cheek back down against my chest and sighs like she's content to be right here with me.

My chest swells with possessiveness for a woman whose name I don't yet know. As we lie there for silent minutes, my fingers massage her scalp while her breathing falls to a steady pattern.

"You have to go," she tells me as she yawns. "You can't sleep here."

"Why not?"

She peers up. "I don't let anyone sleep over. It's a rule."

"A rule, huh?" I continue to massage her. "What other rules do you have, Red?"

Why the hell does she seem so adamant about our sleepover? And how can I get her to change her mind?

"None of your business."

"Can I stay for a few more minutes?"

"Just a few more minutes. But then you really have to go." She groans, pressing her cheek back against my chest like she's made it her home.

My heart warms.

By the sound of it, she's about to pass out at any moment.

But I'm not about to tell her that.

Thirteen

GIO

She fell asleep about thirty minutes ago, and all I do is watch her. She's so at peace, I don't want to move and rouse her.

She said I couldn't sleep over, but she said nothing about what happens if she's the only one asleep. I could stay up all night if I get to have her like this.

My arm rests gently around her back, and I smile as I look at her. She's so perfect.

My phone vibrates beside me.

Fuck.

I can't let her wake up and throw me out. and I know she will. Grabbing it to shut it off, I see a text from Grant.

GRANT

Donny is still in solitary. He may be there for a while.

Fucking great. I need to talk to the asshole, and I can't do that when he's in a damn hole.

Red groans softly, her body giving a jolt, her shoulders rocking with heavy inhales. In an instant, I lower the phone back on the bed and grip her tighter.

"Stop," she whispers. "Don't. P-please."

Her voice is so low, I almost don't catch it.

"Shh," I say, realizing she must be having a bad dream.

"No, no. B-back away." Her voice grows frantic, her features pinched.

"Red? Wake up. You're having a nightmare."

But instead, she thrashes in my arms and I've never felt so goddamn helpless.

"Sweetheart, wake up." I shake her, but instead, her body shivers, rocking with tumultuous exhales.

"Please don't," she begs, and I instantly want to find whoever hurt her and rip out his fucking heart.

I gently shake her again. "Red, wake up *now*."

But she doesn't. Instead, she cries and tears swell in her lower lashes, tracing down her cheeks.

My heart instantly breaks.

"Help me," she sobs softly on a barely there whisper. "Someone, help me."

Fuck.

My pulse pounds in my throat.

"Red. Come on, baby." I gently nudge her jaw, cupping her cheek, not wanting to scare her.

And in a flash, her eyes pop open and she jumps to a seated position, her exhales roughly leaving her lungs.

Her eyes dart around the room and she blinks faster. "I…"

Her thumb swipes under her lower lashes. And when she sees

the moisture on the pad of her finger, anger takes over her face.

"You need to go. Now!" She roughly swipes the rest of her pain away from her eyes with the back of her hand.

I grab her wrist and drag her back to me. "I'm not going anywhere. Not when you're upset."

She swallows thickly and avoids my gaze.

"Who hurt you, Red? Just give me a name, and it'll be over. He's never going to hurt you again."

Her brows tighten, and when she stares back at me, it's through the eyes of a broken woman.

"It doesn't matter," she replies, her voice a bare whisper caught in the night. "It was a long time ago."

"It matters to *me*." I clasp her nape with a possessive grasp, dragging her forehead to meet mine. "Give me a name, bambina. That's all you have to do."

"I'm fine." She backs off, lifting up her chin, straightening her spine. "I can handle this on my own."

I hold her face in both hands. "I know you're strong. But sometimes you don't have to be. Let someone take the burden off your shoulders."

Her chin trembles, a momentary crack in her armor. "I can't." She drags my hands off her face, then starts to rise. "I'm going to take a shower."

"At this late hour?"

"I know. But it helps calm me."

"Okay. But I'm not going anywhere."

"I know."

A brief, dim smile lifts a corner of her mouth right before she disappears out of sight, leaving me wondering what I can do to help her.

ISEULT

My arms are wrapped around my raised knees, my back against the ice-cold shower wall. The water spills onto the floor like raindrops against the windowsill, concealing my quiet tears as I cry.

How could I have been so stupid? How could I have fallen asleep beside him, and why did I feel so comforted by his presence once I woke up? I hated that I wanted him to hold me as soon as I opened my eyes and saw him. But I wanted it so badly. And instead, I ran.

I cannot want such things. And not just because of whose daughter I am. That's not really the real reason, if I'm being honest.

It's because… It's because I'm afraid. There's risk in opening up yourself to someone, to your trauma and your deepest fears. Because if you do, if you show them what you hide underneath and they leave, that anguish… It's deeper than anything else.

And that guy out there? He wouldn't want me if he found out the extent of my pain.

No.

He'd be the one running.

I can't afford to let myself feel something for him—or any man—only to lose him in the end.

These nightmares and the panic attacks that I get come more often than I'd like, and I can't seem to stop them. I was seventeen when they began, and for nine years, I've endured them in silence. Hoping no one ever discovers that I'm not the perfectly strong Iseult Quinn that they seem to think I am.

Working is the one thing that helps to keep the demons at bay.

Killing. Fighting. It distracts me.

But this time, I wanted him to be the distraction. Which is foolish. No one can help me through this.

No. This is something I have to deal with on my own.

It's enough that he's sitting there thinking about how pathetic I am. Sad little woman who can't keep her emotions in check.

And now that he's seen me like that, it's even more important he doesn't find out who I am. He can't tell anyone. My father can't see me as a weakness. I can't lose Caellach.

Taking a deep breath, I get to my feet and finish my shower before drying off and slipping into my clothes.

With anxiety beating through my chest, I pull open the door and head back to the bedroom like nothing happened.

He's there, fully clothed now, sitting on the edge of the bed with his face in his palms.

"You okay?" He instantly jumps to his feet, concern flitted all over his face.

And I hate it: pity. God, I hate pity.

I don't want anyone to worry about me. It was enough that my father did for years after the incident, and it took a long time for me to convince him I was finally okay, even though I wasn't. I can't disappoint him now.

"It was just a damn dream." I wave off his concern, staring indifferently at him. "Don't make a federal case about it."

"Don't lie to me, Red." He comes closer, and I wait there, rooted in place like an idiot. His palm clasps my nape and pulls me in, his forehead meeting mine. "I know someone hurt you, baby, and I'm sorry we didn't know each other then, because I would've done anything to keep you safe."

My breaths catch in my lungs.

A raw ache hits the back of my eyes.

Don't you cry. Don't you dare do that.

I keep my head against his, not wanting to move. Not wanting him to see the tears coating my eyes.

You wouldn't have been able to help me anyway. My own family couldn't. He ruined me until I hated myself. And there's no coming back from that.

I clear my throat, blinking rapidly before I pull back.

Quickly turning from him, I pretend I need something from my nightstand. "I'm not some princess who needs saving."

Though I wish more than anything that someone had heard that girl screaming, begging for help, and come to her rescue. Maybe I would've turned out different.

"No, you're no princess," he says as strong hands clasp my shoulders, running down my arms until they wrap around my middle. His hot breath traces up my neck, goosebumps waking across my entire body. "You're a queen who doesn't realize that it's okay for someone else to hold her crown sometimes."

I bite down, emotions slamming into my throat.

I fight them. It's what I'm best at. But it's getting harder and harder the nicer he is to me. What the hell has become of me?

My cell suddenly rings on the nightstand, and I let out a silent sigh of relief. It's exactly what I need to get away from him—this man who, in a short time, has unrooted all the things I've kept neatly hidden away.

Hiding is easy. Being seen…that's what hurts the most.

Picking up the phone, I find that it's my father. I answer immediately.

"Yes?" I march a few steps away, still not facing the man at my back, yet feeling his eyes on me like I did that night at the charity event.

I feel his presence behind me right before I hear him walking close, the heat from his body gliding up my nape.

"I need you back." My father's voice is tense. "We have a job in a few hours, and it requires you."

"Of course. I'm on my way."

"Alright. Bye, darling."

"See you in a few."

I didn't want to say "Dad." Don't need this stranger to learn anything else about me.

"Are you leaving?" he whispers, his lips on the pulse thrashing in my throat.

"Yes. Work calls." My reply comes coolly as I swivel around and finally look at him.

He inhales with disappointment.

I don't want to leave either.

"You can crash here if you want," I tell him. "I'll be back tomorrow."

"Are you sure about that?" His deep baritone rushes over me, a feeling of warmth and desire and longing swaying through me all at once.

He clasps the back of my head and pulls my body flush against him. His gaze searches mine once. Twice. Then he kisses me. Slowly. Taking his time.

And I let him.

He drags himself back with a groan. "I want your number."

He pins me with a demanding gaze, and maybe that works on the rest of society, but not on me.

"I'm happy for you." The corner of my mouth tugs. "But you're not getting it."

"My God, woman." His heavy palm grasps my jaw and his lips hover there, breaths warm and inviting. Too inviting. "Do you have to be so damn difficult?"

My lashes lower, enjoying his rough hands on me.

"So, let me get this straight." I narrow a gaze. "You don't like messes or difficult things."

"I like you, though," he breathes, his lips brushing over mine, my arms twining around his neck. "So I'll wait for you right here until you return."

Strong knuckles trail down my cheek.

"Hurry back to me, would you?"

fourteen

GIO
FOUR DAYS LATER

She never showed.

I waited for her to return, remaining at her place until the following day, but she didn't come back.

She never came the day after, either.

Nor the next.

Nor the day after that.

I even sent people to watch her building twenty-four seven.

She ran again. Or worse…she's dead.

My Red could be gone.

A stabbing pain pierces my chest at the thought that someone hurt her.

Again.

And I wasn't there.

No.

I shake my head. She can't be gone.

She's still out there, hiding from me.

And I will stop at *nothing* to find her, even if it takes me a lifetime to do it.

Part Two

PRESENT DAY

Fifteen

GIO

"**A**nything new on Bryce since we last spoke?" I clench my jaw, hand wrapped around the glass of scotch in my hand.

"No, nothing," Grant replies from beside me, while my eyes jump to the two women who just walked into the small bar.

I'm instantly on my feet, rushing over, almost walking into someone else's table.

"Gio, where the hell are you going?" Grant's voice trails but all I see is her.

Red.

Even after all this time, I'm physically unable to rip her out of my mind, like she's permanently sewn herself into my flesh.

But as soon as I get right in front of the women, I realize that the redhead is not my Red at all.

"Um, excuse us?" Her head turns uncomfortably.

And with raised palms, I apologize and head back to Grant.

As soon as I sit back down, he grips my arm. "What the hell was that? What's gotten into you lately?"

"Nothing," I grumble.

Everything.

She's gone. I can't find her anywhere. I've tried hospitals. Morgues. Grant has done everything he could to find her too in this past year, but she either covered her tracks well or she's truly dead.

Throwing back the rest of my scotch, I slam the glass on the bar top.

"Fuck. It's her again, isn't it?" He shakes his head on a laugh, lifting a finger to the bartender, who pours him another scotch. "What the hell happened to the Gio who fucked around and had fun? Now you're miserable to be around."

"He met his wife and then he lost her," I mumble.

How could she do this? We had something. I felt it. I know she did too. And instead of facing it, she just left.

"You barely knew her." He shakes his head, not getting it.

Why would he? The only thing he ever cares about is money.

"And? I knew enough to know I wanted to know her."

"Do your brothers know how pathetic you've become?"

I shrug. "Michael's too busy trying to keep the Irish from killing Raph to worry about my problems."

"Well, if they knew, they'd tell you you're a jackass."

"What the fuck kind of friend are you?" I quickly order another drink and throw that one back too. Maybe if I'm hammered, I won't think about her.

Grant is right. I *have* become pathetic.

"I thought you were supposed to be good at finding people," I chastise. "How the hell can't you find one woman?"

He picks up his glass and empties it, dropping it back down on the bar top. "What can I tell you? She's good at disappearing. If you find her, I'd like an introduction."

My fist curls. He's not getting anywhere near her. Not with his reputation. Not that I think he'd try to screw her, but either way, I don't want any man near my Red.

"You should see your face right now." He chuckles. "I get it. You pissed on her and now she's yours. All I meant was that I'm impressed. I want to shake her hand on a job well done and maybe ask her to come work for me."

Now I'm the one who's laughing. "Believe me, you don't want her working for you."

I told him how we met. He knows everything.

"Why not? I could use her skills. Not many women out there doing that job these days."

"Because…that woman is her own boss. And she'd probably kill you." I give him a long look, and he returns a smug one. "Nah, she'd definitely kill you."

He snickers. "Well, I will say you need to give up the idea of finding her." A hand runs casually through his rich black hair. "You need to let her go."

"Never going to do that."

I won't stop until I get some damn closure. I'm not going to rest until I've found her, dead or alive.

And if she's alive, I'm going to make her pay for breaking my heart, the one I never knew could break until I lost her.

ISEULT

"Hey, Red."

I gasp internally, stopping mid-stride, my heart beating so fast

I almost grow dizzy.

But when I turn toward the voice, I realize it was Tiernan, one of the instructors at the academy.

With agitation seeping through my pores, I'm marching across the grass to where he's eating a sandwich. Kora walks close beside me.

The back of the training building, where Tiernan sits, has a high brick wall. That way the trainees and instructors can get fresh air, away from the prying eye of those who come to the estate to meet with my father. No one knows this place exists unless my father wants them to.

As soon as Tiernan sees my expression, he drops his sandwich and raises his palms in the air. "What did I do?"

I grab a fistful of his thick mahogany hair, his piercing hazel eyes assessing me like a wild animal let out of her cage. And I may as well be.

"You call me Red again and I'll take your balls."

Rian, his good friend and fellow enforcer, chuckles under his breath.

I turn to him sharply. "Something funny?"

"Not at all." He bottles a laugh, and it's a good thing, because I'm in a fucking mood.

Kora's chuckling her ass off. "Oh, boys…" She pats Tiernan on the shoulder. "Way to piss her off."

I drop my hands off Tiernan and start marching away. I hate that in one split second, he reminded me of the one man I have been fighting to forget.

"So…no Red, then?" he shouts with a laugh.

I swear I'm about to keep my promise and make him choke on his own tiny balls.

Kora jogs after me, her soft footfalls catching up until she's throwing her arm over my shoulder. "Um…what was that?"

"Nothing," I mutter.

"Seemed like quite a bit of something."

"Just quit it." I glare.

"Alright." She shrugs.

I can't tell her that the stupid nickname reminds me of *him*, the man she knows nothing about, and that no one else is allowed to call me Red.

It remains his.

Like it's sacred.

Oh my God. What's become of me? Sacred? Am I even hearing myself?

I need to get over him. He's gone. I moved on. He moved on. He was just a guy who gave me the best orgasms of my life. That's all he was.

So why haven't you stopped thinking about how concerned he was about you the night you had that nightmare?

Momentarily, I shut my eyes and force myself to stop this madness.

I haven't stepped foot into my New York City apartment since I left. I knew he'd keep looking. I stayed off cameras and wore disguises when I had jobs to complete in the city. I knew he wouldn't give up. He'd keep looking for me.

I tried to search for him online, but came up empty. I had barely anything to go on. What did I expect? I gave up months ago. It was better to forget him. Though forgetting him has been impossible.

"Want to grab dinner off-site later?" Kora asks.

"Can't tonight. Our father instructed all of us to be here for family dinner."

"Oooh. Sounds exciting. A Quinn family dinner."

"Yeah, real fucking exciting." I scoff. "Dinner with my

annoying brothers."

Fionn and Cillian are always trying to get under my skin. Kinda remind me of that someone who I'm not supposed to be thinking about.

"You mean your very hot brothers?" She shoots off a flirtatious grin.

"Really, Kora?" I stop and pivot toward her. "You're not fucking my brothers."

"Well, not all three of them. At the same time. Obviously." Her lips curl. "Unless they're into that…"

"Oh my God!" I cover my face with a palm. "I will never get that visual out of my head."

She purses her lips and laughs. "I said what I said, and I meant every word."

"That's gross." I shake my head violently starting down the road again. "They're my brothers, and you're not touching them."

"Okay…" She side-eyes me and pops a brow as though to say, *right, sure I'm not.*

She starts toward the main building of the academy and I follow. The red brick construction spreads across the lawn, like a looming haunting mansion.

My father's house is a short distance toward the left, which is where I'm headed. I promised my sister we'd grab lunch together.

"I swear, Kora," I add when she reaches the entrance. "If you bang any of my brothers, I'll kill you."

"No, you won't," she laughs.

No, I won't.

That bitch.

She strides up the three cobblestone steps, and disappears inside. The top level is dining and leisure, while the underground is reserved for sleeping quarters and additional training facilities.

We have a total of fifty recruits at the moment and about fifteen instructors.

I shake my head at the prospect of my best friend and any one of my brothers. No. Absolutely not. The visual alone is nauseating.

Minutes later, I'm entering my father's home, the grandeur of the foyer too gaudy for my taste. A large, sparkling chandelier hangs high above the cathedral ceiling, which is filled with painted angels floating in the blue sky, like one would find in a renaissance painting. My father had it commissioned and I will admit it is kind of creepy. I like things simple, and my dad isn't always a simple man.

"Eriu!" I call. "I'm home. Are you ready?"

I stalk off toward the spiral staircase only a few feet away.

Her footsteps register above me and then rush down before I see her, brown hair in a sloppy ponytail, her bright green eyes appearing panicked.

"What's wrong?" I ask once she's down, a black handbag slung over her shoulder. She closes the buttons on her black peacoat.

"Shh," she says, glancing up the stairs.

"What happened?" I place a palm on her shoulder.

Her face crumbles like she's about to burst into tears.

Instantly, my body reacts with a hammering pulse. "Someone hurt you?"

"No, it's not that," she whispers, swallowing nervously. "I overheard Dad talking to a man on the phone and…"

Tears well in her eyes.

"Whatever it is, you can tell me."

"He's going to marry me off, Iz," she cries, her words falling out faster. "I heard him talking to someone named Michael about it, and it's going to happen soon."

"What?" I grit my teeth.

Blood rushes into my head. Son of a bitch. He couldn't even wait a month? She just turned eighteen! She just started college. Her whole life is ahead of her. Rage boils over in my chest.

"Yeah," she goes on, unable to hold back her sadness. "He's in the Mafia." She sniffles, throwing her arms around me, sobbing quietly against my chest. "I don't want to marry anyone. I want to finish college. I want to become a vet. I want to live my own life." She clings to my shirt with a tight fist. "I don't want to be someone's wife, least of all someone from the Mafia."

I hold her tightly against me, my gaze climbing up the stairs, where my father's study is. He's going to be hearing from me very shortly.

"You don't have to do anything you don't want to do."

She laughs tearfully and weaves back. "You must be joking." She roughly swipes under her eyes with the back of her hand. "You know that's not true for girls in our position. You're lucky. You don't—"

Instantly, her face goes ashen and her eyes grow wide.

"Oh my God," she gasps, new tears misting her eyes. "I can't believe I just said that. I'm so, so sorry, Iz. Please forgive me!"

She curls her thin arms around me and squeezes.

I pat her back. "There's nothing to forgive. You were only eight when it happened. It's okay. It's in the past, anyway." I grab her hands and hold them in mine. "I love you. I'd do anything for you. You know that, right?"

She nods, looking sad.

I lean in and give her a quick kiss on her forehead. "I'll be right back. Give me five, okay?"

Her eyes grow as I start for the stairs. "Iz, no! Don't say anything. He's going to know I was listening."

"That's okay." I start climbing up. "You have a right to know what happens in your own life. And if this isn't what you want, then he's going to know about it."

She mutters something unintelligible while I rush the rest of the way and make a right toward his office.

I shove the door.

He looks up from a stack of papers on his oak desk. "Nice of you to knock, darling."

I march up until my palms hit the edge of the wood. "Are you seriously marrying her off to the damn Mafia?!"

"So, she heard, then?" He sighs.

"Yeah." I look him straight in the eyes. "She heard everything."

"Maybe you should teach her not to eavesdrop."

"Maybe you shouldn't marry your daughter to scum."

"They're not so bad, and it's what's in the best interest of this family. Or did you forget that our family…" Anger ravages his features. "…is what I've *always* been trying to protect."

"And forcing her into a marriage she doesn't want with a complete stranger is how you figure to do that?" My heartbeats rap against my ribs.

One of them killed my cousin. How could he think this is okay?

"Who cares that you'd be ruining her life?" My voice rises, and I don't care who on his cleaning staff overhears.

"Close the damn door before you wake the whole bloody city!"

I skewer him with an unflinching gaze for a few seconds before I stalk off and shut the door with my foot.

"Look, Iseult." He calls me by my full name, when no one ever does.

Though I do love it. My mother picked it. But when I started doing jobs, I began calling myself Izzy, so it stuck.

"This is what has to be done," he goes on. "After your cousin was killed by Michael's brother, we've been planning for war. But

Michael has offered a very favorable solution that your brothers and I are pleased with."

"My brothers?" I laugh coldly. "I'm sorry, are we still being sexist, Father? Because last time I checked, I've killed more men than any of them have, and I deserve a say here."

"That is valid." He nods curtly. "But either way, it's four against one."

I shake my head, disgust twining around my features. "And Eriu doesn't get a choice or even a vote?"

"No." His reply is cold. "She's merely a child who's having a tantrum. She does what I say, when I say it. That's all there is to it."

"You're ruining your own daughter's life." I grind my jaw, not knowing what to do or say to stop this from happening.

Maybe I can help her run. Make her disappear somewhere. She has a bodyguard on her, but we can fix that. One bullet here and there, and poof. Gone. Daddy wouldn't even know it was me.

I've gotta give it to her, though. She *did* piss off our father once by drugging Devlin, her last bodyguard. Of course then she got herself into a heap of trouble, and so did Devlin. But he did cover for her, and for that, I will always be grateful to him. But this new guy my father has on her? He means nothing to me. Killing him would be easy.

"Her life won't be ruined," he replies, dropping his attention to his papers. "Gio seems like a nice man, and he will take care of her."

"So love doesn't even matter to you, huh? Figures."

"What the bloody *hell* does that mean?!" He snaps his pale green gaze to me, his temper flaring around his enlarged pupils.

"You and Mom." My heart splits in half when I think about her, and I force down the ache lodged in my throat.

"I loved your mother." He grips the arm of the chair until his knuckle turns white.

"No, you didn't!" I bellow.

"You bite your fucking tongue!" He jumps to his feet and slams his fists across the desk, rattling the decanter of amber liquid set at the corner.

"You wouldn't be this angry if it wasn't true." I angle my chin.

He can't deny it. My mother told me everything. How she was forced to marry him when she was eighteen. How though he may have loved her in his own way, she never felt he truly loved her.

Years later, she discovered why. He was actually in love with another woman, who he wasn't allowed to marry. She found the letters he wrote to her, the ones he never sent, and it broke her heart. I would pity him if I wasn't so angry that he didn't love my mom the same way he did this mystery woman he called Fernanda.

Mom didn't want this for us—arranged marriages—and she told my father that right before she was murdered. Yet here he goes, spitting on her wishes.

"Leave. Now." His nostrils widen, thick gray brows shuddering. "Before I do something I regret."

His chest rises up and down, and there's invisible smoke coming out of his nose.

"She didn't want this," I remind him. "She may not be alive to vote, but she wouldn't want this for Eriu, and you know it."

"Eriu will marry Gio, and there's not a damn thing you can say or do to change that fact." He settles back in his seat, his breathing harsh and uneven. "Our bloodlines will live on, and that will avoid a war, hopefully for generations to come. Now go, and close the door behind you. I'm done with this conversation."

I hold his gaze for a moment before I spin on my heels and head out.

When Eriu sees me, hope fills her eyes. "Anything?"

I shake my head. "I'm sorry."

Her face falls. "It's okay. You tried." She blows out a defeated sigh. "I'm going to marry some crazy Italian who'll probably make me drop out of school and be his prisoner."

"We don't know that. Maybe he's not so bad."

But even as I say it to myself, I know it isn't true. The men of the Cosa Nostra know only one way to treat a woman, and it's not with respect.

Sixteen

ISEULT
ONE MONTH LATER

I almost forgot about my father's threat to marry Eriu. To the point, I stopped talking to her about it, hoping that maybe Gio, or whatever his name is, decided he didn't want a damn child bride.

I bet he's fifty and has been married twice. And probably offed both women for speaking out of turn.

But of course, I was wrong. Not about what this Gio looks like, but about my father forgetting about his awful plan.

Because this morning, he happily announced that we'd be welcoming Gio, Michael, and their father to his home so that Eriu and Gio could finally meet.

My sister hasn't stopped freaking out since.

Gio and his family are currently in Father's office, while Eriu stands shaking beside me in the den, doing everything in her power to put on a brave face, because our father won't tolerate anything different.

"I can't believe you assholes voted for this." I glare at each one of my brothers, shaking my head at them in disgust.

Tynan shrugs. "Wouldn't matter either way. He would've done whatever he wanted, even if all three of us voted against it."

"Well, you should've voted against it on principal."

Tynan doesn't say anything else, staring at me with indifference while seated on the sofa at one end, with Fionn in the middle and Cillian on the opposite side.

"It's going to be okay." Fionn rises and approaches Eriu, clasping her shoulder. "If he hurts you, he's got the three of us to answer to. You hear me?"

She nods, but doesn't appear relieved.

He wraps his arms around her. "I know this isn't what you wanted, but we would never let anything happen to you. I promise."

"Yeah, nice of you to help after she marries the asshole." I roll my eyes.

"Ignore her," Cillian says. "Our dear sister doesn't believe in love."

"Yeah," I snicker. "What's there to believe in? How many arranged marriages do you see turning into a blooming love affair?"

"See?" He grins, pointing at me. "Don't listen to her. It's going to be just fine. I've not heard anything that bad about him."

"That bad?" I march up, staring daggers at Cillian, his pale emerald-green eyes assessing me with humor. "What does that mean?"

"What he means is…" Fionn clears his throat, returning to sit beside Cillian, scratching the dark brown hair at his temple.

"Say it." I connect my eyes with his in a tight flare of my gaze.

"Well…Gio is, by all accounts, a bit of a playboy. Meaning, he gets around."

"So he's a hoe?" I throw my hands in the air. "Fucking great. Our sister is marrying a hoe. That's nice, guys, real nice."

"He's quite dashing, though." Fionn laughs.

I punch him hard on the shoulder, and when I pass a glance at my sister, she appears as though she's about to run out of the room.

"Jesus Almighty." Fionn rubs where my fist connected with him. "I forget how bloody strong you are."

"It's not funny," I tell them. "This is her life."

"I know it is, for fuck's sake…"

"So, uh…he isn't fifty?" I ask.

"No, not even close." Fionn fights another bout of laughter. "He's the youngest one, and you remember Raph, right?"

"How could I forget when he came storming in and started a damn fight with us?"

"Yeah. Well, he's the oldest, and Michael is the middle one. We've met in passing before."

Usually, the conversations my father has with the members of the Messina crime family have been over the phone, so I've never actually met the other brothers.

"Hush up. I hear them," Tynan announces.

I rush back to Eriu for moral support, and seconds later, my father walks in with a man around his age.

Eriu grabs my hand and squeezes, and I squeeze right back.

"Girls," my father says. "I want you to meet Giancarlo, Gio's father."

She smiles politely at the man, while I give him a curt nod.

Thank fuck that's not who she's supposed to marry, because if he were, I'd have to stake the bastard with my knife until there's nothing left of him to marry.

"It's a pleasure to meet you both." He walks to my sister, picking up her hand and kissing the top of it.

"It's wonderful to meet you, sir. I'm Eriu. Welcome to our home."

"What a polite young lady you are." He grins and assesses her like she's his bride instead of his son's.

My stomach churns, and in this moment, I instantly hate him.

"Gio is going to love you," he goes on, and I have every intention to find a fork and stab him in the eye with it for the way he's looking at my baby sister.

He moves on to me next, but all I do is glare, keeping my hands pinned to the small of my back.

"Yeah, welcome," I mutter.

I can see my father's disapproving eyes poking holes into me. Tough shit. This asshole sucks, and I'm not about to act all fake to please anyone.

"Well…" He lets out a wry chuckle. "Nice to meet you too."

His mouth forms a thin line, gray mustache jerking in irritation as he moves over to sit on the other empty sofa.

I don't fucking know why Eriu and I are standing here like a damn offering. But I don't feel like getting on my father's bad side at the moment by starting a full-blown civil war. When he pushes, I push that much harder. But I also know the concept of time and place.

I really don't want to be here to meet any of these assholes. I know I'm instantly going to hate this Gio.

Maybe I can plan his murder. That'll definitely get her off the hook.

Just then, multiple footsteps near, and when two men walk into the room…I gasp.

All air leaves my lungs.

Completely. Utterly. Gone.

No. No. No!

My head grows dizzy.

This isn't happening.

My pulse throbs wildly in my ears.

My heart quickens, faster and faster, because one of the men staring at me with equal amounts of shock is none other than Orgasm Man himself.

He stands motionless, eyes wide, while the other guy beside him peers over at him in question.

"Ahh, there you two are," my father says, but neither he nor I are paying attention.

His face goes practically white as he stares at me in disbelief, while his mouth moves slowly like he's talking under his breath.

Okay. Breathe.

This isn't so bad. Maybe he's Michael and the other dude with that vicious scar on his right cheek is the one marrying Eriu. Which also doesn't make me feel any better, because that man looks like he wouldn't know how to care for a puppy, let alone a wife.

"Let me introduce you to my two daughters," my father goes on.

But this man, this awfully stupidly handsome man won't stop gawking at me, flipping my whole heart in my chest.

I can't seem to stop staring at him either, an invisible chain forcing me to look at nowhere else but into those deep onyx eyes.

Nope. Not doing this. He means nothing. Absolutely nothing.

I should find a way to leave. Because it doesn't even matter if he's the one marrying Eriu or not. There's absolutely no chance in hell I'd ever get with him again.

Then why is your gut dry heaving at the thought of Eriu walking down the aisle to him?

I bite down in absolute frustration. Why did I have to meet him? I was doing just fine on my own. Never cared if a guy I hooked up with married someone else. Never felt a damn thing.

Not that I feel anything for him. I mean, except this insane desire to straddle him and kiss him again…and again…and again.

I instantly shudder at these horrifying feelings. What is happening to me, and how do I make it stop?

It's been a little over a year since we saw one another. Why does it feel like no time has passed, while at the same time, it feels like it's been years since I've seen him? Felt his arms around me. Felt…happy?

Oh, God. This is worse than I thought.

Imagine if he knew he had made me happy? He would probably get a tattoo saying that right on his chest. That smug, sexy bastard.

My father's eyes connect with him. "This is Iseult, my oldest."

It's then I know for certain. He's the one she's going to marry.

And I instantly want to die.

Oh my God.

What are the damn chances? Of all the people I had to fuck, it had to be my sister's future husband.

Of course.

My jaw grinds as I stare at the wall ahead, contemplating ways to murder the man. How the hell did he not tell me who he was? I mean, I didn't either, but still!

My father steps over to Eriu who glances at me right before my father introduces her. "And this? Is your bride, Eriu."

But Gio doesn't even look at her. From the corner of my eye, I can feel his smoldering dark eyes pinning me with a wild, hungry gaze.

His brother leans over to him, whispering something in his ear, and he says something back. They're too far to hear, but he nods at something, and I really wish I had vamp hearing. I can't seem to look straight at him, afraid if I do, I'm going to lose my mind and turn the damn room upside down.

"What are you boys talking about there?" my father asks. "Enlighten us. Please."

Gio takes a step forward, getting closer, and it's then I glance at him and instantly regret it. My pulse ramps up until I don't think it can go any faster while my arms break with a shiver because the desperate way his eyes cling to mine unearths me.

His brows tug and my heart does too.

We stare at one another for long, torturous seconds until I feel my soul ripping right out of my body.

I inhale a deep, quiet breath and force myself to look away. It suddenly hurts to be without those eyes staring back at me.

But I can't. I can't look at him anymore and feel all these things for someone I don't even know.

It's crazy and stupid. And now, it's also dangerous.

Because if he's to be my brother-in-law, I have to stay away from him. Nothing can happen between us anymore. If it does, my father will kill us both.

"May I go, please?" I peer at my father. "It doesn't seem like I'm needed here any longer."

"You may not." His voice is a sharp bite. "This is going to be your brother-in-law and our new family. Have some manners, darling. You will stay like everyone else."

"Yes, Father." I force a smile…but inside, I'm seething.

"It's so nice to meet you," Eriu says to Gio, her eyes darting to him, letting a small grin slip.

But Gio doesn't return it. He keeps glancing at me, unnerving me. How much more of this can I take?

My father doesn't notice the way Gio's eyes search my face.

The way he won't stop drowning me in these unexplained and unwelcomed emotions.

"Sit down, boys," he tells Gio and his brother, gesturing toward the loveseat. "I want you two to meet my sons, Tynan, Fionn, and Cillian, as well."

"Let the women sit instead," Gio says.

I fit him with a glare, blood rushing to my head, hating that he's here. I did so well hiding from him. Now he's going to be family, and there won't be any hiding.

"I prefer to stand," I say coldly while my sister moves around to settle on the other empty sofa.

"Gentlemen. You see that, Eriu? What a perfect husband for you," my father says, as though she's hit the lottery.

He's dangerous. He practically killed me. With orgasms.

And now he's going to do the same to her.

Nausea swirls in my gut.

I can't be here.

An ache hits the back of my nose; I wish I could bring my mother back to life. She was the only one I could talk to. I know that if she were alive, she'd be the one who I could open up to and tell her about Gio and me. With her, I could always be myself in ways I can't be with anyone else. I'm surrounded by fighters and killers. Being strong is how I've learned to fit in.

But Mom wasn't like us.

I miss her. The pain festers and gnaws like a wound that never quite healed.

Every time I remember how she died—burned alive by the Russians during the feud between them and my family, I begin to rage.

The bastard who did it is still out there, while she's not.

Not the time for these thoughts right now. I bury the anguish, not allowing even an ounce to seep through. Not when people are here to see me fall apart.

GIO

Fuck!

I can't believe she's standing right in front of me. How the hell is this even possible? How could she be Patrick's daughter?

I've imagined this moment so many times. That instant I found her again. Kissing her, holding her, spanking the shit out of her. But I never imagined this.

And now I have to marry her sister? There's no way that's going to happen.

As soon as I saw Red—*my* Red—I almost forgot why Michael and I were here. The world just shook under my feet, like an earthquake only she had the power to create.

I've finally found her.

After all this time, she's right here, staring at me like she wants to brand me with her knife.

My God, the way I missed her glare…and her smile. Will I ever see that again?

I watch as she starts for the exit once her father is distracted with Michael and his sons, her rich fiery waves flittering against the small of her back as she steps out the door.

She's not getting away from me that easy. Without drawing attention to myself, I begin to follow her.

"Where are you going?" Michael clasps a heavy palm across my shoulder from behind.

"Phone call."

He narrows his eyes and mouths, *be careful.*

I nod, and he lets me go.

He knows exactly where I'm going. When we walked in, I told him I couldn't marry Eriu because I had met Iseult before and wanted her instead. He told me he'd try to get me out of it, but for now, I had to keep quiet for the sake of peace.

Casually, I walk out into the foyer, seeing two of Patrick's armed guards—huge mofos, their expressions hard. They look like they'd be fun at parties.

"Did you see where Iseult went?" I ask them with a grin. "She forgot something."

Shit, I hope they don't tell Patrick I was looking for her. He'd wonder why the hell I was chasing after the wrong daughter, and we'd have a shit ton of problems we don't need right now.

"Outside," one barks.

I give them a tilt of my chin in thanks and get the fuck out the door.

As soon as I head down the steps, I stare out onto the acres of greenery, a few red bricked homes lined up on the right in the distance and a looming mansion set in the middle with another smaller one not too far from it.

"Where is she?" I mutter to myself, running across the grass.

She could be hiding anywhere. And if she left the estate, I swear I'm gonna take Michael's car and chase her down to the ends of the earth.

I keep running, hoping to see someone so I can ask them where Iseult had disappeared to. She's like damn Houdini.

Just as I pass the larger mansion, a blonde woman steps out, black leather jacket and tight jeans. The same one I saw with Red at the bar when they were drugging some idiot.

"Hey," I call to her. "Could you help me with something?"

She squints, assessing me up and down. "Who the hell are

you?"

"My apologies." I step up to her and extend a hand in greeting. "Gio. Here by Patrick's invitation."

"Well…" She grins. "In that case…" She shakes my hand. "What can I do for you?"

"I'm looking for Red—I mean Iseult. I have to talk to her."

Her eyes grow wide and she barely moves an inch. "Uh…what did you just call her?"

"Red. It's a long story." I chuckle. "I'd like to think she and I are friends. Even though she'd probably tell you different." A wide grin fastens to my lips.

"That does sound like her." She slants her head, her attention on me narrowed.

"So, do you know where she is? I really need to talk to her. It's urgent."

She folds her arms over her chest, those coppery eyes gleaming in challenge. "If Iseult doesn't want to be found, then I can't help you."

"Fucking hell. Come on. I promise I won't rat you out." I run a frustrated hand through my full hair.

Knowing Red, she could be halfway across the country by now.

"Who did you say you were again?" Her face grows wary, assessing me even more, her hazel eyes darkening.

"Gio. Italian."

"Shit," she whispers. "Are you the one who's supposed to marry Eriu, or are you the brother?"

"I'm definitely not my brother." I grin. "And I have no interest in Eriu." An exhale roughs through my lungs. "Look, if you're not going to help me, then I'll find her myself."

Muttering a curse, I give her my back and start down toward the grass. I won't leave this place until I have spoken to her. Because if she thinks I have forgotten her or what she did—or what we shared—she has another thing coming.

"Hold on," the blonde woman calls, rushing after me.

I stop and wait for her.

"How do you know Iseult? And don't lie to me." She props a hand on her hip. "I'm her best friend, and I'll kill you if you're here to hurt her."

There's indignation in those eyes. She'd do it.

"I'm not here to hurt anyone." I shuffle a step forward, shaking my head, not sure how much I should tell her. "We met about a year ago." I chuckle distantly at the memory. "Then she ran off on me. Twice, I might add." She listens intently as I go on. "So I've been looking for her for a year, hoping to talk to her, to explore the connection we had, but she was nowhere to be found. Until today. Until I saw her standing next to the one they say I'm supposed to marry."

"Oh…my…God…" she whispers, mouth parted, eyes caught in disbelief.

"What?" I ask, not sure which part surprised her the most.

"I'll tell you exactly where you can find her. Follow me."

Seventeen

ISEULT

I've returned back to my house and locked myself in my room in hopes that I don't have to see Orgasm Man for the rest of the day. Hopefully he doesn't return until the wedding.

Pacing, my cell in hand, I wrestle with what to do. Do I tell my father I know him and that we messed around?

No.

I let out a heavy sigh. That won't change anything. He'll just tell me that nothing can happen anymore and that Gio belongs to my sister now. I definitely can't tell Eriu. All that will do is make her feel bad. She's been through enough.

My God, I can't even think about her marrying that man without wanting to gouge out my eyes.

Am I jealous? Is this what jealousy feels like?

Lowering myself onto my bed, I drop my face into my palms

just as a soft knock interrupts me. I instantly know it's Kora from the sound of it.

"Yeah," I mumble. "Come in."

Gently, the knob turns, and she appears in the threshold.

"Why are you in here?" She walks in and shuts the door behind her. "Shouldn't you be with your family, meeting your sister's future hubby?" Her lips curl up as she stands before me.

"I don't feel like being there," I mutter, peering up at her through the slice of my fingers.

She settles beside me and throws an arm around my shoulders. "And why is that, *Red*?"

I pull my hands off my face and shoot her an irritated glare. "Not important, and don't call me that."

Sitting up straighter, I scold myself internally for being so damn pathetic. He was just a hookup. He's free to marry anyone he pleases.

Even my sister.

Totally fine. It'll be great. I can't wait until family dinners.

"Why are you here?"" I ask Kora. "I thought you were training."

"I was…" She shrugs. "But I finished early, and guess what happened when I was about to leave and grab some food?"

"What?"

There's a mischievous gleam in her eyes.

"Well, when I came outside, I saw this really hot guy running around like a crazy person, screaming for someone named Red."

A shudder runs down my spine.

"Yeah." Her gaze drills into me. "Can you believe it? I mean, who do I know that flipped her shit when someone else called her that?"

How could he be this stupid? He could've outed us to everyone! Now Kora clearly suspects. She's not an idiot.

"I seriously have no idea what you're talking about."

Maybe she'll buy it. I never told her about him. What was the point? I never intended to see him again. Until he decided to show up and marry my sister. Why does the universe hate me?

"Cut the shit, Iz," she huffs. "I know you've been extra cranky for a while now, and I couldn't understand why. Not until this Gio told me that you guys met a year ago, around the same time your mood got a lot bitchier." She laughs. "I can't believe you kept him from me this whole time."

"I'm always a bitch. Maybe you're just imagining things."

She raises a palm. "Stop lying to me. I'm supposed to be your friend, and friends are honest with each other." She shakes her head. "He called you Red. It's why you got pissed at Tiernan when he did the same, isn't it? It reminded you of Gio."

"Wow, you really are reading too much into this."

"Oh, Iz, you know I love you, but you need to stop sabotaging your own happiness. I know you didn't have it easy." She lowers her voice and grasps my hand in hers. "I know your mom's loss hit you hard and you try so much to keep people at a distance. But you can't spend your time living in the past. You have to surrender to the present and let it take you to a future you may not yet see. I promise…" She squeezes my fingers. "…there are people out there waiting to love you. All you have to do is let them."

"I'm not you, Kora." My mouth forms a thin line. "I'm fine alone. In fact, I prefer it."

Liar.

"Right." She begins to stand. "Whatever you say." Her eyes go to mine from behind her shoulder. "You're not unlovable, Iz."

A pang hits my chest.

"Yeah, I'll remember that." I snicker, hiding behind what I truly feel inside.

I hate it. I hate feeling and crying. My God, how much I cried when she died. I cried so much, I didn't know if I'd have tears left. But once I stopped crying, I took the reins over my emotions and I stuffed them deep. Crying gets you nowhere. Crying makes you weak and pitiful. And I wasn't either of those things.

But having Kora as your best friend makes it hard not to feel. That girl *is* fucking emotions. She's always saying crap to make me get this way—a sappy, stupid mess. But I can't live without the girl. I'm stuck with her.

What does she know, anyway? Who the hell would want to love me if they ever truly knew me. Truly saw me. I'm not her. I'm not Kora. I'm not perfect.

Opening the drawer to my nightstand, I pick up my cell and throw it inside, needing to do something to distract myself.

Just as she gets set to go, someone pushes the door open.

"I'm done waiting," says a voice I was getting used to avoiding.

But my heart races just the same, thumping wildly like it beats just for him.

"What the hell, Kora?!" I jump to my feet, fitting her with a horrified glare.

"You two need to talk. So talk." She gives me a stern look. "I'll be standing right in the foyer. So don't try running."

"Oh," Gio scoffs. "She's definitely good at that. Aren't you, Red?"

Reluctantly, I take in those deep, dark eyes staring feverishly at me, and I don't know if I'm angry that he's here or happy that he made the effort to find me.

"Okay, you two. Behave." Kora's face goes all serious, but cracks with a small smile. "Or don't."

Then she slithers out the door like the conniving snake that she is.

As soon as she's gone, I lock the door behind her. Just in case someone else manages to walk in.

If it wasn't for her bringing him here, he would never have found me. Our estate is so monstrous, you could hide underground for years and no one would be the wiser. In fact, one of my father's friends did exactly that when he was going to be arrested for embezzlement. He hid out here for five years until he was smuggled out of the country.

No one knows about Caellach. There are rumors, sure, but that's all it is. No one knows that it's actually all right here, right below their feet.

"Why the hell are you following me?"

I shove at his chest, and he growls low, eyes daring me to try that again.

"You need to leave. Now." I shove him again. "You're my sister's fiancé. You can't be here."

He doesn't move. Doesn't even budge. But the vein in his neck throbs.

"Touch me again, Red," he taunts with a glare. "See what happens."

I like the challenge in his gaze, so of course I shove again. Harder. Both palms against his hard, muscular chest.

And just as I do, he grunts, his hand snapping around my wrist, until he flips me around and wraps his arm around my stomach, pinning me to his front.

"Now…" His gravelly tone shoots down into my core. "This is a lot better."

I try to fight him off, but I'm only pretending. My body's fitted to his so tightly, I can feel his heavy bulge pressing into the small of my back.

"I'm very disappointed, Red," he drawls, warm against my ear.

"Or would you rather I call you Iseult?"

"Fuck you, Gio," I hiss. "You should've told me who you were. We could've stopped this before we slept together."

"You mean fucked?" He chuckles dryly. "Because that's what we did, Red. We fucked. Or do you need a reminder?"

He delves his hips into me, and I fight the desire to groan.

All those memories of us together come slamming back to the surface while I try to stuff them back inside. Yet the more he touches me, the more his breath cascades up my nape, the more I forget why it's wrong for him to be touching me this way. Or why it's wrong for me to like it.

"Why did you disappear?" he asks. "I waited for you at your place for days. I kept coming back, wishing you'd return. I even changed the locks, hoping it would make finding you easier. But you never came."

"You changed my goddamn lock?!"

"I sure as fuck did."

He's gloating. The insufferable man is gloating.

I release a heavy sigh. "None of this matters anymore, Gio. You're marrying my sister. Whatever we were or weren't makes no difference anymore."

"Is that what you think?" He cinches his grasp around my willing body. "That I'm the type of man to let go of something I want that easily?" His voice grows gravelly, his lips dropping to my neck, coasting down to my shoulder, kissing me through my sweater. "No, Red. Me and you, we're not done."

And in an instant, he spins me around and throws me up against the wall, his palms caging me in, his wicked mouth nearing mine, hovering there.

Oh my God. This is not happening.

My body shivers. My insatiable thirst for him nears the edge, my breathing coming in burning gasps.

His hot, unsteady exhales against my trembling lips taunt me with things I shouldn't want. But right now, it's hard not to wonder if Kora was right. If someone like me could be loved.

His palm sinks around my throat, fingers wrapped around it, thumb pushing into my jaw as he grinds his teeth.

"I've waited over a year to touch you again." His eyes search mine, gaze heated. And in it, I find intense emotions piercing right into my heart.

Before I can find it in me to fight him off, he slams his lips to mine and ends this unrelenting torture.

He steals my breath with a single, vicious kiss. The one I've wanted for too long.

With a moan, my hands climb into his hair, yanking and running my fingers through each strand I can grab on to, as though I can't get enough.

He sucks my tongue into his mouth, grunting deep in his chest when I yank his dress shirt out of his pants and run my nails up his solid bare back.

His skin feels so good, hard muscle beneath my fingertips.

The way he kisses me, nipping and tugging, it's like he's trying to punish me for what I did, and I deserve it.

I need his punishment.

I crave it.

His hands wind into my hair, pulling so roughly it burns, but I like it. I want more. I need him inside me again. I need him to make me feel the way he did the last time.

"I missed everything about you, Red," he groans as he wrenches away, his lips sucking along the curve of my jaw, teeth raking my skin.

"Oh, God," I gasp, unable to hide how good it feels to want a man this way.

"You're done running from me, you hear?" His chest rises and falls with heaviness as he draws back, his eyes pinning me in place.

When I don't answer, he tightens his grasp around my throat, so deep I fight for air. His free hand journeys down my sternum, lower until he brushes his fingers in between my thighs. And even through the jeans, I feel his touch, yearning for more of it.

"Say it," he demands, popping open the button of my pants and dragging the zipper down, the sound pervading the space around us. "Tell me you'll stop running."

I throw my head back when he slides his hand under my panties, almost where I desperately need him. He works my jeans lower, until they're stretching around my upper thighs.

This is wrong. He isn't mine. He's supposed to be hers. But I can't seem to make him stop. I don't want this to end.

A single finger dips lower until it skims my clit. And when I bite on my inner cheek to stop myself from screaming, he plunges two fingers inside me so forcefully, I can't help the sounds coming out of my lips.

"Yes…don't stop!" I groan.

A satisfied growl rumbles from his chest. "What a needy whore you are."

Thrust.

"So wet."

Thrust.

"So perfect."

Thrust.

"Oh, fuck…" I cry, his eyes delving into mine, unwilling to let go.

"I'm gonna have you coming on my cock over and over until you remember that you belong to me." Then he captures my mouth with a heady vengeance, swallowing my sounds of ecstasy, as though sealing his words with a blood oath.

But I don't belong to him. I never will, even if I wanted to.

He kisses me with a hunger permeating his marrow, his fingers sliding in and out with untethered depravity.

I grow languid, my body shuddering the more his thumb flicks over my clit. If it wasn't for him keeping me caged up against the wall, I'd collapse on the ground.

"Your pussy feels even better than I remember," he whispers against my lips, brushing them softly. "Or maybe I just missed you."

"I…I bet you've had plenty of pussy after mine."

He backs his face up, eyes narrowed, laced with a quiet rage that has suddenly grown as though out of nowhere. And then he's thrusting harder and deeper.

"Yes, yes, please don't stop…" My words are hoarse and achy and needy. And I'm not the least bit worried about any of it.

Tomorrow, though? Tomorrow I'll regret all of it. But it's not tomorrow. It's today. And right now, this is all I thirst for.

He chuckles. "Grew some manners since our time apart, haven't you, bambina?"

"Shut up and make me come," I grunt, gripping a fistful of his hair.

"That's the Red I remember." Then his fingers are curling inside me, stretching so good. But it's not enough. I need all of him. To make me feel the way only he can.

My lashes flutter shut and I drop my head against the wall, the fervor of my orgasm building.

"No," he snaps harshly. "Look at me. I want you to remember who's making you come, who you're begging to make you come."

Oh my God. Why the hell is that savage look in his eyes and

those domineering words making me want to drown myself in him?

"Iseult?" Eriu's voice suddenly slashes through the other side of the door, and it's like I've been doused in ice water.

My pulse pounds in my ears, blood rushing to my head.

"Get off," I whisper to Gio, shoving him, but his fingers remain inside me and a smirk curls over one end of his mouth.

I narrow my gaze, and when I do, he rubs his thumb around my clit and my eyes roll back.

"Iseult? Are you there?" Eriu turns the knob. "I really need to talk to you. Kora said you might be in the shower." She sniffles.

Shit.

Stop, I mouth to him, even when it's the last thing I want.

But my sister is right there. I can't make her think I'd hook up with her fiancé, even though that's exactly what I'm doing.

He drops his lips against my ear. "I don't think you want me to stop. You're so wet, you're dripping down my fingers."

He thrusts again, and I lose all ability to speak.

"Okay, I'll just wait for you." She huffs.

"Fucking hell," he mutters, slowly slipping out of me.

And when he does, I feel hollow, aching for him.

His fingers glisten with my arousal, and without his eyes leaving mine, he sucks them into his mouth until they're clean. "So delicious."

Why is that so damn hot?

The back of his hand strokes down my cheek, his gaze searching mine for things I can't give him. Because when I think about my sister out there, more guilt surfaces, and I realize what a horrible person I actually am.

"Look, Gio," I say breathlessly. "We can't do this again."

He cups my cheek, leaning into my chest.

"This was it. Do you hear me?" I whisper, my tone curling with annoyance.

He shouldn't still be this close to me. I shouldn't want him to be.

"You're going to be my sister's husband."

With intensity brewing in his gaze, he shakes his head. "No, Red. I'm gonna be *your* husband."

Something heavy slams into my gut, while my brain and heart wrap his words around them, turning them over and over.

I tilt up my chin. "That's never going to happen. I will never get married. Especially to you."

He doesn't realize how serious I am. He has no idea what I've been through. Everything changed for me when I was seventeen, and that included my future. I've accepted that. And I'm not going to let some guy make me believe otherwise.

"We'll see about that." His thumb runs across my lips, his eyes following its path, teeth clenching as they do.

He pushes himself off of me and struts toward the door leading into the bathroom. "Go tend to your sister. I'll see myself out once you're gone."

"Don't go looking through my panty drawer." I pop a brow while pulling up my pants and securing them.

"Why?" He runs a palm over my ivory dresser. "Afraid I'll find another toy I can fuck you with?"

My eyes turn to slits. "I absolutely despise you."

Humor lines his features. "But you kinda like me too."

Unfortunately.

GIO

Once she's gone, I look around her bedroom, everything neat and tidy and far too white to ever belong to someone as intense as Red.

Even knowing her name, I can't seem to call her anything but that. She's my Red. My goddess of fire and ice. And she's definitely got that *ice queen* thing happening, but fuck, does it make me hard.

That's okay, though. I'll take my time thawing her heart until it softens and lets me in.

I lower on her mattress, sitting on top of the white comforter perfectly tucked around the corners.

A photo frame rests in the middle of her ivory nightstand. Lifting it up, I see what looks to be a younger Red—early teens maybe—and a woman who looks more like Eriu.

Is that their mother? I know about her death. It was what continued the years-long war between the Irish and the Russians. I don't know what started it. No one truly does. But whatever it was, was bad enough for Sergey Marinov, the Russian Pakhan at the time, to kidnap Patrick's wife and burn her alive.

Patrick, in turn, killed one of Sergey's sons as revenge. And the war had continued…until his other sons called a truce. So many lives had been lost by that point.

But I have no doubt that Sergey was the one who started it all. He's always been insane. Unhinged and diabolical.

He's been gone for years now. He's probably in his late sixties. Rumor is he fled to Russia. That his sons banished him. Maybe he's dead by now.

I wonder how Red handled her mother's death. Must not have been easy. I'd imagine a girl and her mom to be close, and losing her when she was so young probably caused her a lot of grief. The need to hold her in my arms becomes ravaging.

I drop the photo back and open the single drawer, hoping to

discover something that lets me know her more. But when I see what's inside, a huge grin spreads over my mouth.

Definitely didn't expect that. But when a man gets a gift like this, he doesn't take it for granted.

I pick up her cell phone and press the side button, checking if it's locked. Sure enough, it is. But when your best friend owns the company that created her cell phone, unlocking it won't be that difficult.

Removing my own phone from my pocket, I call Grant. Only takes two rings for him to answer.

"Yes, Gio? What can I do for you today?"

"Shut up. I need you to unlock a phone."

"Excuse me? That would be a violation of privacy. Not to mention the amount of laws I'd be breaking." His tone is filled with mirth. He lives for this kind of shit.

"Yeah, yeah. I'm texting you the serial number. It's one of yours."

I lay her phone beside me, and quickly type it out and send it.

"Whose phone am I hacking?"

"Hers."

Seconds of silence fill the line.

"The woman you've been pining over?" His voice grows incredulous.

"One and the same."

"How did you manage that?" I hear him typing on his laptop.

"Long story. I'll fill you in later. Right now, I need into her phone because if she comes back and finds me, she's going to stab me to death."

He chuckles. "You'd probably deserve it."

"Yeah, I'd be careful if I were you," I tell him. "If she finds out you helped, you're probably next."

He lets out another laugh. "Okay, check her phone now. I deactivated the pin code. She'll have to put in a new one, so she'll know someone messed with it."

I grin. "Don't care if she does by that point. Thanks. Talk soon."

"Yeah." I end the call and place my phone on her bed.

Her cell back in my palm, I open her phone, finding a screensaver of her mom and her.

My chest instantly tightens, my finger running down her young face, feeling sorry for that girl, for the woman she is now.

Michael's name pops across my phone screen, telling me we're leaving in five. But I've already programmed my number into her cell. I text myself from her phone so that I have her number too.

I quickly shoot her off a message before leaving the phone exactly where I found it.

I'd pay a shit ton of money just to see the look on her face when she finds it.

Eighteen

ISEULT

"**M**aybe I could run away," Eriu cries as we walk side by side in the open fields behind the main Caellach building. "I can't marry him, Iz. I just can't."

She pants with gasping breaths, quickly swiping under her eyes.

"Hey, no…" I shake my head and throw my arm around her back, tucking her into me. "You're not running. We will figure this out. Together."

She backs off me and her brows bend. "There's no figuring this out. You know that. You tried, and he still went through with it." She shrugs, sniffling back. "I'm gonna end up marrying a complete stranger who won't even stay faithful to me." More tears track down her cheeks. "I'm going to be one of those women who lives in an unhappy marriage, knowing their husband doesn't truly love them."

"You don't know that." But as I say the words, it's like I'm chipping away at my own heart.

Her pain is mine. Yet it's different.

My sister's marrying the man who gave me the most earth-shattering kiss, a feeling that for women like me only comes once in a lifetime. But I can't be the cause of my sister's pain. Because if she were to find out that I was messing around with him without even telling her, it would hurt her. I have to stop putting myself in situations like that with Gio. That incident in my room will be the last of its kind.

"I don't want you to think that way." I bring my arm around her and we stroll together once again. "Maybe it just takes the right woman for a man like him to change."

"Do you actually believe that?" She sighs.

No.

"Yes."

"Well, I hope you're right, Iz."

"I guess if all else fails, I can kill him."

She stops dead in her tracks and widens her eyes at me.

"What?" My lips spread into a wide grin. "I was only joking."

She narrows a stare. "No, you weren't."

I shrug. "You said it, sis. Not me."

"I swear, if you weren't my sister, I'd be afraid of you."

I give her a wink and pop a brow. "I guess you're lucky you are. Now, come on. I'm taking you out for dessert."

"Ooh, can we go to that place that has those puff pastries served with ice cream?"

"Whatever my sister wants!"

She grins at me, smiling so brightly that for a moment, both of us forget our problems.

But sometimes even a moment is enough.

"You sure left mighty quick." My father glances up at me from his sofa after dinner, a mug filled with black coffee in his grasp. "Didn't care for the Italians?"

"Not particularly, especially the oldest one." I settle across from him.

It's been hours since Gio and his family left, and I'm glad to have gone out with my sister and kept her mind off of this damn marriage.

I was relieved to find out she had no interest in marrying Gio. She thought he was handsome, obviously, but she doesn't want this, which should make me feel a lot better about wanting to fuck his brains out.

But it doesn't.

"You mean their father?"

"Yeah," I snicker. "That one."

"Me neither." He drags in a long sip. "You should know something." His features grow tense. "This stays here."

"Of course. What is it?" I sit up straighter, adrenaline pumping through my veins.

"Their father is dirty."

My brows shoot up.

"Apparently, he killed Raph's wife and then tried covering it up."

"What?" I whisper with disbelief. "So he's the one who killed her?"

I remember how bad things were with the Italians after Bianca died. Raph blamed us, but no matter what my father said to convince him we were innocent, he went guns blazing and got my cousin killed.

See, me? I would've killed him by now. He may have been in mourning, and my father let him mourn in peace before he sought revenge, but I don't care. Raph should've had proof before he took my cousin's life.

"I've known that bastard Giancarlo for a long time," my father continues. "And he's always been a feckin' snake in the grass. But even this is too far."

"I agree. He has to go. Are they planning to kill him?"

"Aye." He nods. "Can't wait for that." He squeezes the mug tight, his knuckles going white. "That rat bastard. Wanna slice his goddamn throat." His eyes cast into the distance.

"I take it you don't like him, then?" My lips wind up.

"You're a funny one, eh?"

"I get it from you, I guess." A laugh rises out of me.

He nods thoughtfully, staring at me intently like he's trying to see through me instead.

"You doing okay? That stuff…" He clears his throat and shifts in his seat. "That stuff from before don't bother you anymore like it used to, right?"

Lie. Just lie.

Lying is safer. It keeps people from hurting. Nothing good ever comes from telling the truth. He doesn't need to know that not a single day has passed where I haven't thought about what happened to me.

"I'm fine, Dad. Promise." I even plaster on a nice big grin, like the cherry on top of a sundae.

"Good, then." He leans back. "Yer brothers left with the Italians, by the way, to help with the situation with Giancarlo. We might be heading to New York too, darling. Be prepared."

Shit. I'll have to see Gio again? This day is getting better by the second.

"Oh, yeah, no problem. I'll have my knives sharpened just in case."

He chuckles. "So, tell me, what did ya think of Gio?"

"Now you suddenly care about my opinion?" I fold one leg over the other and lean my back against the black leather sofa.

"My feckin' God…" He huffs, his eyes jerking up to the ceiling. "Are you ever not difficult?"

"Who else would keep you on your toes?"

I fight a smile, and he shakes his head, fighting his own.

"He's not who I'd want for my little sister," I tell him. "But nothing Eriu or I say will make much of a difference to you, so this conversation seems pointless."

"She doesn't like him?"

"No," I say sternly. "She wants to choose her own husband, you know? Since this isn't the eighteen hundreds?"

"Well, unfortunately for the both of you, this is who she must marry." He drags a sip of the steaming liquid into his mouth. "We've had enough war to last us a lifetime, Iseult. You of all people should know that."

My heart squeezes until I can't breathe.

As though I could forget.

"This is what must happen to ensure we can at least keep the peace with the Italians," he goes on, oblivious to my inner torture.

"Are the Russians giving us trouble again?" I ask, keeping the tone of my voice steady.

He shakes his head. "But you never know with them. His sons might decide to invalidate the treaty, and then we return to years of bloodshed. And I don't want any of my children to lose their lives. I've lost enough in my life." His gaze hits me intensely. "You understand, darling?"

I nod. "As long as I don't have to be forced to spend time with that irritating Gio.”

And his annoying laugh.

Or his breathtaking smile.

“He might grow on you.” My father brings the mug to his mouth.

“Doubtful,” I snicker.

“I do worry, though…” His eyes give a far-off look.

“About?”

“His reputation precedes him.”

My heartbeats tap against my ribs. “What kind of reputation?”

“He likes the ladies. A little too much, I might add.”

Oh, that's right. He's a hoe. How did I forget that little fact?

My stomach tosses as I picture him with others, doing to them what he's done to me. I fight like hell to keep my face from falling.

“Oh, yeah? You worried he'll cheat on her?”

“I am.” He rubs his gray stubbled jaw, a touch of black scattered within it. “I expect loyalty in a marriage, and I won't hesitate to put a bullet in him if he strays.”

Shit. If my father finds out about us, he will definitely kill us both. He doesn't tolerate disloyalty. From anyone. Even his own daughter.

“I think I'll invite him over for dinner soon, after all this business with Giancarlo is finished, so he and I can have a nice conversation about what I expect this marriage to look like.”

Awesome.

That talk with my father didn't make me feel any better. Gio has probably slept with most of New York City, while I hadn't been with a single soul since him.

I don't know why. Not like I haven't tried. But it just made me remember how bad sex was for me before he came along. The bastard has ruined me for the rest of my life. Because at this point, no one's going to come close.

Pressing my fingers into my eyes, I stop at the top of the stairs, finally back in my home again.

Walking into my bedroom, I shut the door, heading toward the nightstand, remembering that I had left my phone in the drawer.

I was so busy with my sister and then my father, it completely slipped my mind. I retrieve the cell, pushing the button to turn it on.

"What the…?" The password keypad has been deactivated.

My heartbeats quicken in my chest as I find a notification for a single text waiting for me. And I don't even need to read it to know that it's from *him*—my future bastard of a brother-in-law. He not only found my phone, but hacked it somehow.

I'm going to kill him.

Slowly.

I open the text and blink in disbelief at what he had the audacity to name himself.

FUTURE HUSBAND

> I'm glad we've reunited again, future wife. I'm going to enjoy getting to know every breathtaking inch of you all over again.

I quickly type out a reply.

ISEULT

> I don't even want to know how you got into my phone. But just know, you're officially number one on my hit list.

FUTURE HUSBAND

Hey, sweetheart. I miss you already.

ISEULT

Didn't you read what I wrote, you idiot?

A hot and awfully sexy idiot. But still an idiot.

FUTURE HUSBAND

Didn't I tell you already? Every time you threaten my life or insult me, all it does is make me want you more.

ISEULT

Unresolved trauma?

FUTURE HUSBAND

The only trauma I have is from when you disappeared on me. But don't you worry, Red. I promise to thoroughly punish you for it.

ISEULT

You're not going anywhere near me. Not only are you MARRYING MY SISTER, but I hear you're a bit of a man-whore. And by a bit, I mean I heard you fucked your way through all fifty states.

Seconds trickle by while I wait for a response. Then minutes vanish into thin air without a single reply from him.

I stare at the phone, turning it on and off, wondering why he hasn't written back. My pulse races faster and faster. Does he not want to talk to me anymore? Did I push him far enough?

With a frustrated exhale, I drop the cell on my bed and fall backward against the mattress. It's what I wanted anyway. I can't be involved with him. It'll ruin everything.

Ding.

I gasp, jumping to a seated position and immediately picking up the phone. His name's displayed with an unopened text. I click to read it.

FUTURE HUSBAND

> Neither one of those things are true. I will never marry your sister, and I haven't touched a single woman since I touched you.

A shiver races up my spine.

I can't breathe. He's stolen all the air from my lungs.

And I'm not even sure whether to laugh or cry or do both at once.

Surely he's lying. There's no way in hell that is true. A man isn't going to give up sex for over a year.

My fingers hover as I attempt to type out a response. But I don't know what to say.

I want to tell him not to lie to me. That it doesn't matter how many women he's been with since we were together, but I can't seem to say any of that.

Because if I'm being truly honest with myself, it does matter.

It matters a lot.

I stare at the phone. At his name. *Future Husband*. And my stomach tightens.

Because for one quick moment, I wonder what it'd feel like to have one.

GIO

As soon as we flew back to New York yesterday after leaving Patrick's, we were thrust into a war. With my father, of all people.

My brothers were keeping me in the dark about the things he was up to, like how he planned to have my oldest brother, Raph, killed so he could hide the affair he was having with Raph's wife.

I instantly wanted to kill him. I was mad as hell at them for keeping me in the dark. Still am. But I'll get over it. I understood why they did it. They were worried I'd lose it and mess up the plan they've been working on to get rid of our father.

And they're right. I would've murdered him.

Sitting in Michael's den with Patrick's sons, I pour myself a drink.

It's been interesting to have them here while they assist us with our father.

Tynan clearly still hates our guts after the whole thing with his cousin. I hear they were close. His cousin left a son behind, who is now an orphan after his mother died. Tynan adopted the child. I feel really sorry for that poor kid to end up with the likes of this grumpy fuck.

"You want another drink?" I ask Fionn, who's emptied his third glass of bourbon.

"Aye, would love some more." He rises, marching over to the bar, while his two brothers are seated on the sofa, still drinking their second.

The house is dark and silent, except for us. My niece, Sophia, is sleeping soundly upstairs, while neither Michael nor Raph wanted to join us for a late drink. Michael isn't one to socialize and Raph's too concerned with finding Nicolette, his dead wife's sister, to care.

"So, what time is Iseult coming in tomorrow?" I ask them.

"Not sure." Fionn laughs. "She didn't give us a memo."

"We can tell her you asked about her, though." Cillian chuckles. "She'd *love* to know you're so concerned about her whereabouts."

"Yeah," Fionn adds. "She'll probably stab you for it."

Wouldn't mind if she did.

If I were smart, I'd probably be more discreet about my line of questioning. But I was never very smart.

I've been unable to think about anything but her in the last twenty-four hours, especially when Cillian let it slip yesterday that something did in fact happen to her. I had my suspicion after she had that nightmare with me. But that confirmed it. When Fionn joked about her having a mean streak, Cillian had said, *Leave her be. She hasn't had it easy.*

Why the fuck would he say that if that's not what it meant? And why would Tynan immediately shut his brother up when he said it?

"What did I tell you about messing with our sister?" Tynan's voice grows irate with his brothers once again. "Leave Iseult alone, or she'll claw both your eyes out."

I stare at Tynan, and something passes between us I can't name.

And it makes me want to know what happened to her that much more.

Nineteen

ISEULT

Yesterday, my father and I arrived at Michael's, and I did everything I possibly could to avoid Gio.

That was harder earlier today, though, when we all went to interrogate Giancarlo together. By interrogate, I mean torture him until he told us where he's keeping Nicolette. But he told us more than any of us bargained for.

Thanks to Giancarlo, I finally learned the truth of who owned my father's heart all those years. Instead of giving his whole heart to my mother, half of it belonged to Gio's mother, Fernanda.

Yep, *that* Fernanda.

Of all people in this fucking world. She's the one he loved.

No. *Loves*, apparently! He's *still* in love with her!

My stomach churns as I wander into the foyer, back at Michael's home.

I can't handle this.

My mother deserved better.

We both know Fernanda was always too good for you, he told Giancarlo. *But circumstances and bloodlines prevented me from being her husband the way I was always meant to be.*

"Fuck!" I groan, aimlessly roaming around this damn house, climbing up the spiral stairs where I don't have to hear my father talking to Fernanda. Probably planning their damn future together, now that nothing is stopping them.

I pace into a large, dim hallway, wishing I had driven my own car from Cherry Grove so I could get out of here. But my father said it would make sense to take his car and come to New York together.

How could he do this to Mom and to her memory?

She deserved more than to be married to a man who didn't love her like his whole world revolved around her. She deserved more than to be scorched alive, to die in such excruciating pain.

A raw ache pounds behind my eyes, and I feel them coming. The tears. The endless river of grief. It comes whenever I think about her. Whenever I recall the vivid details of her death. And seeing your own mother die like that is something you never forget.

Silently crying, I lower onto the floor with my back against the wall and bury my face in my lap.

Suddenly, a door squeaks from my right. Michael's six-year-old daughter, Sophia, widens her big brown eyes at me, rays of bright sunlight flitting behind her, with her long, chestnut-colored hair glistening from around her shoulders. I met her already when I first arrived, but I never actually said a word to the girl.

"Are you okay?" she asks, squinting, her voice syrupy-sweet.

That has me plastering a wide grin and wiping under my eyes, hoping she didn't catch those damn tears of mine.

She continues to assess me with a speculative expression, and it's a bit unnerving. I need to get the hell out of here.

"Yeah, just fine. Sorry," I mutter, quickly rising to my feet. "I didn't mean to be up here."

"That's okay." She smiles widely, bright pink lipstick on her mouth. "You're our guest." Her brows knit from the doorway. "You were crying?"

"I was not." I clear my throat, brushing my hair off my cheek.

She throws a hand on her hip and stares knowingly at me. "I know what I saw, and you had tears on your cheek. Why would you have tears on your cheek if you weren't crying?"

Where the hell did I just end up?

"You're six. What do you know?"

We're arguing with kids now, Iseult? Really?

"You don't have to be embarrassed." Her words are laced with kindness, and I swear my body breaks with hives.

"Okay, kid." I draw my features into an uncomfortable grimace. "Gonna go now. Nice chatting with ya." I turn, giving her my back.

"You know…" she goes on, halting me in place. "It's okay to cry. Mabel tells me that all the time."

I exhale sharply, staring up at the ceiling because now I really wanna know who the hell this Mabel is so I can tell her how wrong she is.

"And who is Mabel?" I whirl back around, finding her just where I left her.

"She's the nice lady who cleans our house and also babysits me sometimes. She's also my friend and very smart." Her little mouth pinches with a smile, cheeks just as rosy.

Was I ever this happy? Because this child, she's happy. If I was like her once upon a time, I don't remember. Sometimes I wish I could recall all the days I spent with my mom from when I was little. I'd hold on to all those beautiful memories.

"Sophia?" a woman's alarmed voice rings from behind the little girl.

Sophia turns, just as a strikingly attractive woman appears. Her long black hair is pinned up in a messy bun, her dark brown eyes bouncing from me, then to the child.

"I go to the bathroom for five minutes and you're already making new friends?" She smiles politely at me, and I force one back. "Daddy said to stay inside, didn't he?"

"Yes…" Sophia curves her neck up to look at the woman. "But I heard someone in the hallway and saw Iseult crying."

"I was *so* not crying!" I twist my face with a scowl.

"Elsie and I were just having a dance party. Wanna join us?" Sophia's face lights up at me, ignoring what I had just said.

So this is Michael's wife. I haven't had the chance to meet her since she arrived yesterday.

"A dance party? Me?" I shake my head, tight-lipped. "No. Not my thing. But thank you for the offer."

But she ignores me. Again. Instead, she dashes toward me, her fluffy pink dress fluttering as she grabs my hand and pulls.

"Come on, just one dance," she pleads. "You'll see how fun it is, then you can leave."

Her eyes twinkle, and she drops her head to her shoulder with a pout.

Oh my God. Does that actually work on people? I roll my eyes to myself.

But instead of staying firmly in place, I find my feet moving until I'm in her bedroom, my ears bleeding from girly pop music bathing in the distance. I much prefer eighties rock. Hell, I'll take anything but this. *Anything*.

Sophia continues to drag me further into her room. A large canopy bed with a light pink comforter to my left, shelves with books and stuffed animals set neatly against one wall.

What the hell just happened and how did I end up here?

"How did she just do that?" I lean in and whisper to Elsie, who laughs softly just as Sophia drops my hand, wanders toward a cell phone, and changes songs.

"Magic," she whispers.

It has to be, because there's absolutely no way in hell I'd ever willingly agree to a dance party.

When I glance back at Elsie, she sighs as her tender eyes go to the girl who's already twirling.

She loves her. It's not her biological daughter, but to her, it clearly makes no difference at all.

That familiar gnawing hits my gut, and I instantly want to bolt. Seeing them together reminds me of all the years I missed out on with my own mother.

Maybe it's better that she's gone. She's not here to see what kind of disappointment I've become. She'd barely recognize me.

"Dance with me!" Sophia says.

"Ugh."

Elsie laughs at my dissatisfaction. "She's not going to leave you alone until you agree to do whatever she says."

"Great," I mutter.

"Come on." Elsie grabs my hand. "Let's get crazy and forget our problems for a little while."

I look to her, holding her stare. Does that even work?

The little girl squeals with excitement as we approach.

Once a new song starts, I kneel and grip Sophia's shoulders. "Okay, kid, before we do this, you have to promise me something."

"What?" Her eyes grow like I'm about to ask her to keep the biggest secret of her little life.

"You have to promise to never tell your uncle Gio I did this."

She giggles. "Why?" She lifts a shoulder and gives me a knowing look. "Do you have a crush on him?"

My mouth parts and I quickly right myself, scratching at my temple. "I absolutely do *not* have a crush on him." My eyes dart to Elsie who looks at me with amusement. "Would you two stop staring at me like that?"

"You're blushing." Elsie purses her lips to hide her smile.

"What?" I pat my cheeks with the backs of my fingers. "I don't blush."

Sophia giggles again. "Does Uncle Gio kiss you on the lips with tongue like Daddy kisses Elsie?"

"Nope! We are *not* doing this, kid." I huff out. "You know what? Forget I said anything." I fall back a step. "Tell him whatever you want, because your uncle and I are just friends. Actually…" I pause. "We're not even friends. He's so…"

I grit my teeth in frustration, throwing my hands in the air while Elsie's gaze grows a fraction, probably thinking I'm insane. And clearly I am.

"You don't like Uncle Gio?" Sophia gasps. "But he's the best. He tells funny jokes, he takes me to the park, and he can eat more pizza than even Daddy." She places both palms on her hips and inclines her chin like she's about to fight me for insulting her dear uncle.

I seriously just entered the scariest room in this house.

"He sounds great." I grin wide, hoping she leaves me alone and ceases this form of questioning. "But he's supposed to marry my sister, so I kinda can't be kissing him."

Even though I want to all the fucking time, and it's a major problem.

"But he doesn't want to marry her," Elsie challenges.

I level my attention on her as she goes on.

"Last I heard…" She pinches her lips. "He's got a thing for someone else."

Shit. She knows. Gio must've told Michael, who told her.

"Well, it doesn't matter what he wants," I retort. "This arrangement can't be broken."

"Why not?" she questions.

I laugh nervously, groaning under my breath. "Can we dance now?"

I grin at the girl, whose gaze zigzags between Elsie and me.

"I thought you don't like to dance?" Sophia counters.

My God, this child.

"I changed my mind, 'kay?" I grab her hand just as an upbeat song plays.

That's when Elsie joins us, increasing the volume until the sound pervades the space around us, until the questions have been forgotten. All three of us throw our hands in the air, jumping around, swaying side to side, our laughter filling the room.

And I get it now, what Elsie said. Because for a few minutes, I forget why today was such an awful day, and I have the most fun I've had in a while.

GIO

Never in a million years did I think my mother and Patrick fucking Quinn were in love when they were young.

Surprise, surprise.

It's sure as hell been a day for that. Apparently, my mother had to leave Patrick because of an arranged marriage to my father. But she never forgot him.

Raph is too messed up about our father kidnapping Nicolette, his sister-in-law and the woman he's in love with, to worry about this right now. All he wants is to get her back.

Yes. My family is the definition of dysfunctional.

I step into Michael's foyer, hoping to find Iseult, to see how she's handling the news about our parents. And just as I'm about to go searching for her, I find my Red climbing down the stairs.

I instantly freeze.

She does too, staring at me from the top.

But when I scan her face, I split into a fit of laughter. And the more I look at her, the louder I laugh.

"Don't you dare say a word." She points an accusatory finger at me, climbing down.

"So, I see you had a playdate with my niece, huh?"

She brushes past me, heading for the door, but I catch up to her, her bright pink lips set to a tight line, her eyelids with way too much green and purple eyeshadow on them.

My little niece loves to do everyone's makeup, and clearly Iseult couldn't resist her charm either.

"You look quite stunning, bambina."

When her palm lands on the doorknob, I catch her wrist and pull her flush against me, then press her back against the door, forcing my body into hers.

Her inhales are loud as I drop my lips against her ear. "I especially love your cheeks. I think they're even pinker than your pussy."

She shoves at me, her mouth falling open. "You're an ass."

Her eyes instantly turn to slits. Right on cue.

"I think it's adorable that you're warming up to my niece, seeing as you'll be her aunt eventually."

Her expression is seeping with silent rage. "I don't know what you think is going to happen in this imaginary future you have built up, but I will never marry you."

My mouth twines up. "I'm going to enjoy proving you wrong, Red." I lower my palm to her hip, curling my fingers around it. "I love how much you keep fighting our destiny. But marrying you is exactly what I'll do."

It's what we need to end the war between our families. A marriage. And who better with than Patrick's other daughter? The one I actually like.

But convincing this feisty little fox of that will be a lot more difficult.

"Get off!" she whisper-shouts, pushing my arm off her, looking behind me as though to make sure no one's coming.

My fingers reach for her face, gently swiping her hair behind her ear. Her chest rises and falls to a steady rhythm, her eyelashes flickering.

She feels this too.

How can she not?

My mouth drops to hers, lips softly brushing. "Why do you fight this?"

I skim my lips with hers, and she groans quietly into my mouth, the sound setting me off. I grab a fistful of her hair, about to kiss her—fuck the consequences.

"Iseult, darling?"

She gasps into my mouth and practically shoves me across the room at the sound of her father's voice.

Her eyes bulge at me accusingly as she quickly swipes at her mouth as though there's evidence of me there.

With hands in my pants pockets, I stare smugly at her.

Yeah, she definitely wants to kill me right now.

"I'm here," she tells Patrick.

Seconds later, he appears.

"Hello, Gio." He nods toward me, and I return it before he's peering at her. "What happened to your face?" His chuckling grows.

"Don't ask," she mutters.

"Okay, then… Well, we didn't have time to talk about everything you heard…"

And I know he means him and my mother.

"Yeah, it's fine." But the tightness of her voice says otherwise.

"You don't appear fine, darling. Spare me a few moments, would ya?"

"No can do, Dad. Gio is going to drive me to my apartment right now, and seeing as he has a *very* busy schedule ahead, we can't be wasting his precious time. Isn't that right?" She hits me with a look that says if I don't back her up, she's going to stake me with an ice pick.

"Yeah, I have quite a lot to do with finding Nicolette, so we really must be going."

"Fine," Patrick huffs. "I expect to have a word tomorrow. Alright?"

He gives her a stern look, one she matches, the intensity brooding in her gaze.

"Yeah. Great." She turns on her heels and opens the door, practically running out of here, with me following closely behind.

"So I'm driving you where, now?" I pause beside my black Rolls-Royce.

"You heard me." She juts out her chin. "And I want the new keys to my apartment. And if you have your own copy, I suggest you burn it."

Her eyes narrow, the greenish-blue tint even brighter now that the sun has clung to them.

I intend to do no such thing.

I chuckle. "So demanding."

The woman is a force to be reckoned with, especially when she's pissed.

"I will give you the keys on one condition."

"And what's that?"

"I spend the night."

She's the one laughing now, throwing her head back. "That's cute." Her features lose all sense of hilarity. "But you're not sleeping over."

"Okay." I back off the car. "Then you can sleep at Michael's. There's plenty of room. Better yet, come over to my house. We'll be all alone, and you can scream as loud as you want to when I'm inside you."

Her nostrils widen, and if she didn't have all that makeup on, I bet she'd be blushing.

"No way in hell would I ever stay at your place."

"Then I guess you only have one choice." I push a button on my car keys, and the single beep opens the doors.

With a frustrated groan, she pops open the passenger side, practically ripping the door off its hinges and settles on the seat.

This is going to be quite the enjoyable ride.

Twenty

ISEULT

We arrive back at my place, and having him here is already making me uneasy. I can just imagine when I'm in bed trying to sleep, worried he'll hear me have a nightmare.

It was enough that he had seen me at my worst the last time. What if it happens again? I can't have that. But I also don't have a choice…unless I do kill him, in which case my father will kill me. So don't think that's much of a plan.

"You're sleeping on the couch," I inform him briskly.

He makes himself at home on my ivory suede sofa, his arms extended out, a smirk settling on his mouth as he gazes up at me.

"My, you're some host," he teases with a lopsided grin that has me feeling all kinds of ways. None of them acceptable.

I pop a brow. "I'm not hosting you. You literally invited yourself."

"I may have." His eyes scan the room, leisurely taking a swipe of my one-bedroom apartment.

There's nothing particularly exciting here. Just a flat-screen TV on the wall with a bare round glass coffee table and a shaggy gray rug beneath it.

"I like your place." His attention returns to me. "I didn't have much time to tell you the last time, being that you were practically devouring me with that sexy mouth of yours."

My eyes narrow. But I can't deny it. I was.

"I'm going to my room now."

I don't care if it's still early. I need to put distance between us, or else very bad things are bound to happen and someone is going to end up getting hurt. And the last thing I'd want to do is hurt my sister or make my father angry with me. I can't lose my family over a man.

"Blankets and pillows are in the closet." I point to a white door to my left. "Don't bother me for the rest of the night."

I try to walk away, but just as I turn, his fingers wrap around my wrist, roughly pulling me on top of him. His eyes bore into mine, his hands cupping my hips as he easily lifts me a fraction and forces my thighs on both sides of his.

"Now…that's much better," he husks all deep and gravelly, a sinful concoction of all things I shouldn't crave. "I was starting to feel the distance between us." His lips brush mine. "And I hated it."

"What are you doing?" My voice grows raspy, belonging to anyone else but me.

There's no way I sound this needy. This wanton. This free.

"I've missed you, Red." His fingers curl around the small of my back, tracing up my spine until he weaves them into my hair, palm locked around the back of my head.

"Well, I'm sorry." My lips twitch. "Wish there was a pill you could take for that."

"And not feel what I feel for you whenever you walk into a room?" He lifts a hand and strokes his knuckles down my cheek. "That would be a sin, bambina."

"Gio…" I breathe, not sure what I'm asking for.

"Yes?" He kisses the corner of my mouth, warm breaths scattering across my lips.

"We can't do this. Someone will find out." But instead of trying to get off, I find myself grinding my hips, his rigid cock pressing right where I need him.

"Let them find out. Let them try to tear me away from you."

"You don't know what you're saying."

He groans, arching himself into me.

"This will start another war between the families. None of us want that."

He drags himself away and looks at me, his gaze swimming with unparallel emotion. "You're worth fighting for."

My pulse picks up speed.

But I'm not, I want to tell him. *I'm not worth much of anything.*

"We can talk to him," he goes on. "Make him understand."

I let out a bitter laugh. "Even if this was something I wanted, it wouldn't matter. When my father makes up his mind, that's it."

"Why couldn't it be you? Why was it your sister?"

I let out a sharp exhale, feeling the weight of his eyes settling on mine. "I never wanted marriage. He knew that. He let me off the hook."

"Your father doesn't seem like the type of man to do that."

My gut tightens.

"What happened to you?" he whispers.

The air traps in my lungs, his gaze unrelenting.

"Stop," I tell him, my palm inadvertently cupping his face. "Don't ask questions you'll never get the answers to."

"I'm not the enemy." He pins his forehead to mine. "I want to help. Let me help you."

Twined in his words is honesty—heavy, blistering honesty—but it doesn't matter.

"I'm beyond help, Gio," I admit the words I've often been afraid to say out loud.

But with him, right now in this moment, it feels as though I can say them.

"I refuse to believe that, baby." A wrinkle deepens between his brows.

He actually believes that.

My heart stutters.

It feels almost like I'm stranded on the edge of a cliff, attempting not to free-fall right into his arms.

"Just don't," I say. "I don't want to talk about it anymore."

He clutches the underside of my jaw, his gaze intense, bleeding with his emotions. "You're so beautiful, Iseult. I hate knowing someone hurt you."

A poignant smile slips from my mouth. "I'm still here, though. I fought. I survived."

"Yes, you are." His voice cracks a little, and my heart clenches.

With his palm against the back of my head, he pulls me against him, gripping me in his arms, pressing me into his body. My cheek hits his shoulder, his pulse maddening beneath my ear, and I don't know if it's from being close to me or what he assumes happened to me or both.

He softly brushes his hand up and down my back, and I let him because no one has ever held me or touched me this way. I never even realized how much I needed it until now. I nestle my arms around his neck and hold on tight, not wanting to overanalyze what any of this means.

His arms squeeze, and he kisses the top of my head, unleashing feelings in me too heavy to put into words.

He's my sister's fiancé. Yet he's holding me like he's mine.

"Why were you so upset today when the truth came out about your father and my mother?" he asks, his baritone smooth and deadly, enough to send me straight to hell.

"Because no matter how many years have passed since my mother's death, I love her. And my allegiance is to her."

"Was he not good to her?" He keeps stroking me still, and I could grab hold of this moment for as long as I live.

"He was. My father never did a thing to my mom, but he was never truly in love with her. Not completely." I sigh. "She knew. Then I knew, and I'm kind of angry about it."

"You? Angry?" He chuckles gruffly.

"Shut up, you idiot." I laugh, and my God, if Kora saw me now, she'd think I've had a stroke for sure.

"I like it when you call me an idiot." The cadence of his voice sparks a match in my heart.

"Really?" The smile on my face grows, and I couldn't fight it if I tried. "Do you hate yourself that much?"

"It's just, when you say it..." He sighs. "It sounds like something more."

Because it is.

I've never been good with affection and words. It makes me feel naked, too exposed for someone else to pick apart my wounds. It's easier to hide behind insults. Easier to pretend I don't need anyone.

From within my pocket, my cell vibrates, and I slink down a hand to drag it out, straightening my back so I can see who's calling.

Kora's name appears. But when I try to get off so I can speak to her, he holds me hostage with both arms wrapped around me.

"Answer it," he demands, an obvious challenge in both his words and his eyes.

And instead of fighting him, I press the call button.

"Hey, Kora."

"Hey. How's it going over there?" She's loud enough for him to hear.

"It's going. How's everything back home? How's Eriu?"

Gio's eyes drink me in, large hands splayed across my hips. His thick bulge thrusts into me deliciously, and my body scurries with a warm current he put there.

"She's fine. I'm keeping her company."

I clear my voice, paying attention to the conversation.

"I was just calling to find out if you went shopping for your birthday party yet?"

"Your birthday's coming up?" Gio instantly asks, sitting straighter, fingers dipping into my flesh.

My eyes widen with disapproval.

Shut up, I mouth. I can't have anyone knowing we're spending time together.

But he only grins like the smug bastard he is.

"Wait. Who are you with?" Kora asks before a gasp splits through the line. "Oh my God. Is that him? Are you with him? Did I just interrupt a bone session?"

Great. Now she knows.

"No one is boning anyone."

"Hi, blonde friend," he says, dropping his mouth into the phone.

"You're totally fucking him."

"I'm not," I argue with her.

He opens his mouth to say something to her with a grin on his face, but I swat him hard across the chest to keep him quiet.

Laughter rumbles out of him.

"Going to hang up now," I warn her.

"Wait! I wanted to know if you want to go shopping for some new outfits for your party. We need new dresses."

"What party?" Gio asks, curiosity bathing his eyes.

He's definitely not invited to that. It was Kora's doing. I didn't even want a party. I'm turning twenty-seven. Who cares? But she insisted, because she's Kora. And of course, she invited everyone at the academy. My siblings too. I hate parties, and I especially hate being the center of attention.

"There is no party," I quickly tell him.

"Liar!" Kora yells out. "It's in five days at Iz's place. You should come."

"I'll be there," he tells her confidently, his eyes locked with mine like he dares me to argue with him.

Fuck.

The last person I need there is him. I can't let anyone find out about us, and if he's that close, someone may see something and catch on. I can barely fight this attraction as it is.

"You may not be able to," I tell him. "With looking for Nicolette and all."

"I'll find a way." There's determination wedged between his words, and I know for certain he's going to be there.

"I swear, Kora…" I grit. "If I didn't actually like you, I'd move you to the top of my kill list."

"Who's number one there now?" she asks.

"Gio." I look him dead in the face.

Her laugh fills my ear. "Sounds to me like your kill list is more like people you don't actually want to kill."

"Wanna test that theory?" I quip back.

"Nope. I'm good. 'Kay, gotta go. Love you. Nice talking to you, Gio. See you soon."

The call ends, and I swear I'd throttle that girl if she were here. She knows I can't be with him, even if I wanted to.

Which I don't.

"I'm going to go to bed now," I tell him, starting to get off, and this time he lets me.

"You always go to bed this early?" His mouth twitches, arms folded across his well-toned chest.

My eyes rove down his body, and he doesn't miss it.

"Want me to take off my shirt so you can get a better look, bambina?"

"Not particularly."

His lips wind up at the corner.

That cocky bastard.

"How about we order takeout?" he offers. "Maybe eat at the table together like civilized people. Then I'll let you go to bed."

"*Let* me?" I scoff.

"That's right." His expression matches my intensity. "Now, how about you be a good little girl and sit down at the table so I can properly feed you."

My stomach rumbles like the treacherous thing that it is, and the demanding tone in his voice has me wanting to deck him and kiss him at the same time. It's really confusing.

His chuckle is gruff as he climbs to his feet. "Come on, let's order something."

He grabs my hand, and as he does, it tingles.

What the hell is happening to me? And why do I like it?

Hours later, and I'm finally in bed, while he's out there on the sofa watching TV. I actually had a nice time with him.

We ate together in the kitchen, then watched a documentary about a serial killer and found time to actually talk.

I told him how close I am to my sister. That I'd do anything for her, kinda like he would for his brothers. It's important to have a strong family bond. It's why I can't fuck it up. I can't have my family turn away from me for betraying Gio and Eriu's future marriage.

I settle on my pillow, throwing the comforter over myself, when my cell dings with a text and Elsie's name appears. We kind of bonded while dancing to those corny pop songs and getting our makeup done by the tiny tyrant.

Elsie asked if we could exchange numbers, and my first instinct was to say yes. I like her. What can I say?

ELSIE

Are you okay? I heard your dad wanting to talk to you. But you ran off with he who shall not be mentioned before I could ask.

ISEULT

Yeah, and he's here in my damn apartment annoying the fuck out of me as always.

ELSIE

Just promise me when you two get married that I can at least be one of your bridesmaids.

ISEULT

If I ever agree to marry that idiot, promise to get my head examined.

ELSIE

Just give him a chance. I mean…I did. The first time I met him, he drew his gun on me.

ISEULT

Lucky he didn't do it in front of me, because he'd be dead right now.

ELSIE

Aww, she really likes me.

ISEULT

Eww. Please don't get all girly on me.

ELSIE

I'm going to hug you so hard the next time we see each other.

ISEULT

Please don't.

I can just hear her laughing.

ELSIE

No promises. But look, Gio and you? I have faith. You have to believe it too.

I want to tell her she's wrong, that there's absolutely no future for Gio and me, but I know all she'd do is try to convince me that there is. So instead, I say something else.

ISEULT

I'll let you believe that for the both of us. I've gotta get some sleep. Talk later.

ELSIE

Night. But this conversation isn't over.

ISEULT

Oh, believe me, I know.

A heavy breath leaves my lungs as I lay the phone down beside me. Staring at the ceiling, I wonder what my mom would think about what I've been doing with him.

Would she understand? Would she try to talk to my father and explain why Eriu shouldn't marry him? Would my father even care?

Of course he wouldn't. All he wants is to protect us from a war. Nothing else matters to him.

I force my eyes closed, my mother's beautiful face appearing before my eyes, and slowly I drift off to sleep, seeing her there too.

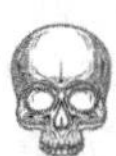

AGE 14

I face the full-length mirror in my bedroom, assessing myself just as someone lightly knocks on my door.

"Come in," I say, knowing it's Mom from the sound.

I stay where I am, running my fingers through my ginger curls, releasing a huff.

"Hi, darling. You alright there?" She smiles when I turn to her, already dressed to drive up to see my aunt who's about to pop out my new baby cousin.

"What are you doing in front of the mirror?" she asks, her thick brows knitting as she settles on one end of my bed.

I lean against the wall, looking at her, wondering why I don't look like her. Mom is gorgeous. Her hair is this perfect rich brown color that falls just past her shoulders and just shines all the time, while her eyes are a golden blend of honey and warmth. As though she's the sun, heating everyone around her.

"I'm just..." I flip my hands in the air, shaking my head, my exhale sharp. "Why am I the only one in the family with red hair?" I lift my eyes to the ceiling before facing her again. "I look like I'm adopted." I shuffle closer to her.

"Adopted?" She chuckles.

"Yeah. I mean, look at me, Mom. Are you sure I even came out of you? Because I wouldn't be mad if I didn't. Definitely couldn't have had a better mom than you, anyway." I blow out a breath just as she gives me a sympathetic smile.

"Come here, child." She extends both arms.

And with a twist of my mouth, I do. I sit right beside her.

Her eyes glisten as she settles her gaze on me, her arm wrapping around my shoulders simultaneously. "First of all, if you were adopted, I'd never hide it from you, sweetheart. But you very much are my biological daughter. I mean, I can show you the stretch marks you gave me." Her lips purse in a comical way, and I can't help but smile.

"Then how come I don't look like you guys? You all have brown hair. Even my eyes are a weird blue green, while you have your hazel and Eriu and the boys all have Dad's light green eyes."

"What is this about, Iseult? Did something happen at school

today?"

"*No.*"

Yes. It's Samantha Britson's fault.

In English class, we were reading about this character who was on a quest to find her birth family. Samantha the Serpent sits right behind me, and the whole time she kept whispering that maybe I should go find my real family too, saying I was adopted. And after school, she and her little friends decided to tell me how hot my brothers are and that I look like the ugly stepsister. What a great start to the school year.

But the problem is, I've had those thoughts a bunch of times already. And when I heard that bitch say it out loud, I just thought, what if it's true?

Mom drags in a long breath, her eyes locked to mine in deep concentration. Her arms unwind from me and she's patting my knee.

"Did I ever show you a picture of your great-grandma, Maeve?"

"No…" I yank my head back curiously.

"Well, that's completely my fault. I forgot I had them until now." She quickly gets to her feet. "Give me a minute to run to my bedroom and grab some photos. I think you're gonna wanna see them."

Her mouth widens in a huge grin, her perfect white teeth sparkling just as she rushes out the door.

I've never seen photos of Mom's extended family. I knew my grandma and grandpa—and of course, my aunt. But that was it.

Minutes later, she returns, clutching a black leather binder.

"Okay, let's see where that photo of her is." She sits in the same spot as before and opens it, revealing a photo album.

She skips a few pages before she stops at one. "So, this was your great-grandma, Maeve, when she was just about a few years older than you."

She points to a small black-and-white photo on my side. My eyes widen.

"Anything look familiar?"

With my mouth parted, I glance up at Mom for a second before I'm staring at...me.

"Oh my God," I whisper. "It's like looking at myself in the mirror if I were in black and white."

"Yep. You're her clone, and just as beautiful. You have her red hair and her beautiful eyes." She runs a hand down my curls. "Not only was she beautiful like you, but she had a warrior's heart, and you are every bit her granddaughter."

"I'm not a warrior."

"Oh, yes, you are." Mom clasps my cheek. "You just don't know it yet." She sighs, her affectionate expression concentrating on me. "I love you so much, do you know that? I'd do anything for you."

"I love you too, Mom."

Gently, she leans in and kisses my forehead. "You take care of your sister while I'm gone, okay?"

I return a nod.

"I have to leave in a few minutes before it gets too dark."

I hate that she has to go. It's hours of driving, and it's already after five in the evening.

She places the album on my bed and gets up. "You keep that. I want you to have it."

With my heart beaming, I lift it up and place it against my chest. "Thank you, Mom."

"Of course, baby."

"Call me as soon as you get to the hospital, okay?" I tell her.

"Of course I will, sweetheart."

But she never does. She never calls me. That was the last time

I saw her.

"Iseult," someone calls, the weight of it laced with a tremor. "Wake up."

Arms pull at me, rousing me from the clutches of a nightmare I can't seem to escape.

"She's burning…help," I cry, gasping for air, my lungs suffocating on the smoke.

My mother screams as her body turns to something completely unrecognizable, the bright orange flames dancing around her body while he laughs, a cunning kind of laugh. The kind you hear like a shadow following you wherever you go.

He's always there, like a phantom of my worst nightmare. Except he's very much alive, and I know he's hoping to find me and finish what he started.

"Fuck, baby, please wake up," Gio's voice calls from a faraway distance, like he's attempting to drag me back into the light, as though his heavy hand is yanking me out of the dirt one inch at a time.

I instantly shoot upright, my body trembling, my breaths firing out in gasps.

"It's alright," he says so calmly, it reminds me of a lullaby. "I've got you, Red. No one's going to hurt you anymore."

My body feels as though it weighs a million pounds, my chest heaving and heaving. Oh, God, it hurts. Everything hurts.

His arms wrap around me, my face falling over his shoulder, my eyes staring blankly into nothing at all.

It's as though I'm still back there, inhaling the smoke. Still trapped with her, like we were there at the same time. But in my nightmare, I'm actually with her, tied up, unable to get to her, watching helplessly as she melts into the fire.

Until her screams are replaced with silence.

Until she's gone.

My heart races at an abnormal pace, nausea swirling in my gut. I can't ever forget what he did to her. What he did to me. Not any of it. To this day, I'm still afraid of fire, like my mind retreats back to that young girl who was alone with a monster with no one to help her.

They tell you time's supposed to heal even the deepest wounds. But I wear mine. They never go far. They pick and gnaw until they're fresh as the day I got them.

"Talk to me, bambina. Tell me what I can do." His palm grips my cheek so tight, it's like he's afraid I'll disappear again.

But there's nothing he can do to erase what's been done. All talking about it will do is make me remember everything all over again.

Being vulnerable equals weakness. And I'm not some broken little bird whose wings need mending. I stopped being that bird a long time ago. And I grew into a woman who doesn't have room for self-pity.

I back off of him, clearing my throat while he searches my gaze.

"Don't," I say, getting to my feet. "Don't ask."

His jaw clenches just once before he's getting up too. "Go get your shoes on."

I incline my head, confusion seared in my expression.

"We're going on a date." A deep smirk lines the edges of his mouth, and something in it feels familiar and homey, like that favorite spot in your house where you can cozy up and forget your problems.

"A date at one a.m.?" I narrow a stare.

"Just trust me."

"I don't."

My heart races when we lock eyes.

I do.

GIO

"What is this place?" she asks as we enter a bar and coffee shop in one, her hand tucked in mine as though it belongs there.

I wonder when she'll finally realize she's actually holding my hand and snap it away.

"You'll see," I tell her, leading her to the back where the real fun happens, where she can let loose and hopefully forget whatever she refuses to talk about.

Her black hoodie is wrapped around her face, her chin lowered like she's afraid to run into someone she knows.

"Don't worry, Red. There are no cameras here, so you can stop hiding."

She side-eyes me. "How do you know?"

"Because the owner is a good friend, and he never turns them on. They're all for show."

We reach the far end of the room, a black curtain parting off the other area. I fling it open, and we move into the game room with a bowling alley on one side, arcade games on the other.

She looks around, then tracks her eyes to mine.

"Do you even know how to bowl?" Her face brightens with a teasing expression.

"Well enough to beat you." A smile tips up my mouth. "I'm pretty damn competitive too."

Grant, Bryce, and I would come here to get drinks with Xander, who owns the place. Sometimes, when we were the right amount of hammered, we'd play. I still can't believe Bryce is really gone.

She narrows a playful stare, flipping her hoodie down, exposing all that gorgeous hair I want wrapped around my hands.

"Good luck with that," she taunts, her eyes lighting up.

My heart swells seeing the genuine happiness tangled in her features. On instinct, I curl one arm around her back, the other one sinking into her hair, bringing her flush up against me.

With a groan, I lean in slowly, my lips brushing her mouth.

Her hot and heavy breaths, the way her hands are moving up my back, the way she looks at me… It makes me want to kiss her today, tomorrow, and all the days in between.

Before I can stop myself, I do just that, and she doesn't dare push me away. A hungered growl escapes from my lungs as my lips take hers like I own her. Like she's letting me.

With a moan, her nails pierce into my back, climbing up my spine. And when she slants her face to kiss me deeper, I suck on her tongue, fisting her hair, pulling it hard until those little noises she makes vibrate between us.

She kisses me with a maddening fury, while my teeth tug on her lower lip, pulling it roughly.

The need to bury myself inside her grows. And so does the

desire to remind her that she isn't alone. That I know what that feels like, and neither one of us has to feel that way again. But I can't say that to her. She's not ready to hear it.

Breathless, she pulls away, her chest rising higher with each inhale.

"I like it when you kiss me, Red."

The back of my hand wanders down her cheek and her lips tremble, her long golden lashes fluttering right before her features shift into something less intense.

Her hand clasps my wrist.

"Don't get that excited," she retorts playfully. "It doesn't mean anything."

My heart races. "You say that, yet somehow, it always does."

ISEULT

I don't remember the last time I had this much fun.

I, of course, kicked his ass in bowling. But unfortunately, he's kicking mine at this damn shooting game.

I'm in his lap while I fire at some zombies, hoping to catch up to his score. I'm never going to, though, and I'm okay with that. Because tonight actually felt normal. Like I'm one of those people who can do things like this. Play video games with a guy.

"I can't believe someone so good at doing this for a living…" he breathes into the crook of my ear. "…sucks so bad at this game."

I scoff with mock horror and elbow him in the chest.

"Ow!" He chuckles behind me, and his gravelly tone has my heart wanting things it shouldn't.

I know nothing can come of this, yet I can't seem to move off his lap.

One strong arm fastens around my front, and I want it there. It feels too good to be in his arms. So good, in fact, that I'm afraid of what it could mean. I never needed a man to make me feel safe or cared for. But in his arms, I want both.

Stupid. The whole thing is stupid.

Yet I settle deeper against him and fight a smile.

"You want me to get you more salsa?" he asks, while I attempt to finish off as many of these damn zombies as I can.

This bastard is gonna gloat.

"No, I'm officially stuffed. We ate too much."

I think he bought everything off their menu. Burgers, tacos, mozzarella sticks, wings. He made sure I had everything. And most importantly, he made sure I forgot why he brought me here in the first place. Admittedly, this was exactly what I needed.

And even worse, having him this close to me is making me question all the reasons why I can't tell my father that I may have accidentally started liking my soon-to-be brother-in-law.

"Last one. Make it pretty," he drawls, his lips pressing into the ravaging pulse trapped beneath my throat. "Though I'll still win by a hundred points."

"Shut up," I breathe as a fevered rush of goosebumps runs down both of my arms right before I aim the gun at the head of my last kill and pull the trigger.

Dropping the plastic weapon into the slot, I quickly get off of him.

I'm being reckless. What if someone who knows my family sees me here? What if they mention my being with a man and my father puts two and two together? I can't let him catch me like this, sneaking around. He'd never understand.

Gio shakes his head, his eyes growing heavy-lidded. "You're doing that thing again."

He slowly rises, while I'm standing there as though waiting for him to touch me. My heartbeats thump against my ribs as his gaze drinks me in slow, his hand reaching for me, fingertips gently gliding across mine.

"Doing what?" I whisper, unable to fight this pull between us, this aching to know what it feels like…to be wanted. To be loved. To love someone in return without the fear of losing them.

"Running." The corner of his mouth winds up a fragment.

"It's what I'm good at." My breath stalls from the intensity brewing in his stare, as though he's taking me apart only to put me back together better than he found me.

"How about, for once, you stay?" He cups my cheek, his thumb softly brushing over my bottom lip.

"I don't know how to…" My voice trails.

"How about I show you?"

And this time when he kisses me, it's slow and filled with passion, holding too much meaning. Giving me all the things I didn't even know I wanted in the first place.

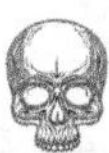

THREE DAYS LATER

After that night, I avoided him as much as possible, which wasn't difficult, considering I returned back to Cherry Grove.

Thankfully, Gio and his family have been busy with Nicolette's return. They finally found her a couple of days ago, and I'm glad they have. I know that fear too well. Not knowing if you'll see your loved ones again, not knowing if you'll live or die.

I texted him to let him know I was happy she was back and he was too. He called and texted me a few times in return, but I never answered. The time apart made me realize there was no point in continuing this, because there's no future for us in this world.

A text from Elsie comes through while I fling the clothing racks, pretending to look for a dress for my birthday party, which I still don't want to attend.

ELSIE

I'm really sorry that I won't be there for your party tomorrow. If my parents weren't coming by, you know I would be.

ISEULT

Please don't even worry. Because I'm not. I wish Kora hadn't planned this stupid party in the first place.

ELSIE

It's your birthday! Just have fun! You have to treat every year as a gift. Don't ever forget that.

"Iz?" Eriu calls, holding up a light pink skater dress. "What do you think of this one?"

ISEULT

I'll try. Gotta go. Being forced to buy a dress for the party.

ELSIE

That sounds terrible.

I know she's teasing me, but this *is* terrible. I hate shopping. I much prefer to order things online.

"So? Do you like it or not?" Eriu goes on.

I blink a few times, trying to focus on her. "Oh yeah, I like that."

She appears unsure, twisting her mouth as she reverts to scanning other dresses.

"Look at this," Kora calls from the other side of the boutique we're in.

I march over to her as she holds out a tight cobalt-blue dress that will probably hit her knees.

"Pretty," I mutter.

"Good." She shoves it into my chest. "It's for you."

"What?"

"Yep." She pops a brow. "You're literally walking around watching us shop. So I picked your dress for you. You're welcome." She nonchalantly turns around and continues to look at more clothes.

With a shake of my head, I start toward the cashier, intending to pay for the dress and be done, when Eriu walks up to me, handing me a rust-colored dress instead.

"Have you heard anything about when the wedding is supposed to be?" she whispers, glancing at the cashier, who doesn't hear us as she takes our items.

"That'll be four thousand and fifty dollars," the woman informs us, her brown eyes peering at me through a pair of red-rimmed glasses.

I hand her my card.

"No," I tell my sister. "Have you asked?"

She shakes her head. "I'm afraid to remind him. Maybe he hasn't gotten around to getting it planned yet."

"Thank you," the cashier says as she hands me the bags and card.

We settle on the white upholstered bench, waiting for Kora to finish.

"Look, Eriu…" I face her, placing the bags on the other side of me. "You have to talk to him. You have to tell him you don't want this."

"But he won't listen to me." Her eyes glisten with anguish, as though the color within them is draining with each passing moment.

"Maybe. But you have to let your voice be heard, or else you'll disappear behind everyone else's desires for you. This is your life. Speak up." I clutch her forearm, meeting her helpless stare with my hard one. "Even if he doesn't hear you, at least you know you tried."

She sighs, and it doesn't appear as though I've convinced her.

"Can I tell you something?" she says really low, her eyes glancing around the store like she's afraid someone will overhear.

I squint, leaning closer. "What is it?"

"Devlin is out." Her cheeks flush.

I look intently at her, not sure what that flush on her face indicates. "What? How?"

"His lawyer got him off somehow."

"Oh…" I guess I haven't been paying close enough attention.

"Yeah. I'm so glad he's free." Her eyes turn doleful. "He shouldn't have been there in the first place."

"I know that." I nod, remembering why he went to prison in the first place.

But there was no choice. The detective on the case was hungry to pin this on someone, and there was outside pressure, especially from the prosecution side. So Devlin sacrificed himself.

She sighs dejectedly. "I hate that he did that. We shouldn't have let him."

I grab her hand and squeeze.

"It's done," I whisper-shout. "We can't go back, so I don't want to hear you talk about it anymore. And he's out now. So it's over."

Her gaze lowers. "I don't think it will ever be over."

I release a weighty sigh. And then it hits me.

"Wait a minute…" I arch a questioning brow. "How do you know he got out when *I* didn't even know? I'm pretty sure you didn't ask our father about Devlin, so…"

Her eyes pop.

"You're blushing again."

"What? No, I'm not." She clears her throat.

"Of course not." I press my lips to stop from grinning. "So, are you going to tell me how the hell you found out that he was out?"

"Promise not to tell Dad?" She grimaces. "Devlin is already ashamed of what happened, and I don't want Dad to hate him even more."

"I would never tell him."

She nods, looking nervous. "I've been writing to him while he was in jail."

"You what?" My jaw goes slack.

Well, that's one thing I didn't see coming. I kinda suspected she had a childhood crush on her bodyguard, but I didn't realize they remained in touch.

"Yeah." She huffs out a breath. "I felt so bad while he was in there. I just—I don't know."

"Missed him?" I offer.

"No… Yes." She grimaces. "I don't know."

"You like him."

She shrugs. "Doesn't matter. He's not the one our dad wants me to marry."

No, he's not. And he never will be. Marrying him won't stop the war between the Mob and the Mafia. Marriages in our circles usually involve a purpose…other than love.

"I'll have to accept my fate," she says glumly. "I'm marrying Gio."

The words are like gasoline, burning me where I sit, scorching my body to ash.

"Do you like him?" She's the one asking this time.

"Who?" My heart races even as I try to listen to what she's saying.

My sister is going to marry him.

"Gio." She eyes me curiously, her head slightly tilting.

Right. Him.

My pulse thumps in my ears. How the hell am I supposed to answer that? *Yes, I like him. He's really good with his tongue. He's also kinda sweet, which I will never admit out loud.*

"He's okay, I guess." I scratch my temple.

Her body sags with a sigh. "I don't want a husband I don't love, let alone someone who'll cheat on me."

My heart races. Because he's already cheating on her…and it's with me.

Twenty-Two

GIO

I walk into Red's place about thirty minutes late, parking my car beside a bunch of others. The only reason I even knew what time this party was going to take place is because Fionn told me. He knew I was invited and offered the information easily.

When I arrive, her house is packed with people, drinks in hand, the place dimmed, music blasting. This doesn't seem like Red at all. Holding a small box in one hand, I shove past a group of guys, wanting to find her so that I can hand her the gift I bought her. I even wrapped the damn thing.

But as I move past more bodies, my eyes greeting the curves of her figure, hugged beneath a deep blue dress, blood rushes to my head. Hard and fast like I've been struck in the back of the head with a baseball bat.

My feet are moving quickly, my pulse filling my ears.

I squeeze the box in my fist, not caring if I'm destroying it. Because seeing her with another man is destroying me.

His arm is wrapped around the small of her back, and neither of them see me. Not yet. But they will, and whoever he is, he's about to have his hand permanently detached from his wrist.

"Get the fuck off of her," I snap through gritted teeth and that has them both turning, and when I see the man beside her, rage fills my veins.

The weapon at my waist burns with the need to wrap my palm around it and put a bullet into Adriano Scutari, the son of the boss of the Grazia family.

Iseult doesn't glance away from me, her features indifferent, as though she's doing nothing wrong standing beside a man who isn't me, letting his fingers stay settled on her hip.

"Gio." Adriano nods, while my glare shoots between the two of them. "What seems to be the problem?"

He pulls her in closer, and my chest rises with one quick inhale. And before he can blink, my hand whips out the gun and I'm pointing it at him.

But just as quickly, he snatches his from his waistband and points it at me.

I don't know who's catching wind of this besides Kora, who's near Iseult, and a few guys on my right who are talking in hushed tones, but we're about to have a party of our own if this asshole doesn't stop touching her.

"The problem is you have your hands on her," I tell him, fury and readiness slamming into my chest. "You need to leave. Now."

"And why is that?" His tone is taunting, dark eyes narrowing. "I was invited."

Iseult places her palms on each of our weapons. "Drop your fucking guns before I take out mine and shoot you both dead."

I fix her with a piercing gaze, and she doesn't even attempt to look away.

Adriano chuckles, shaking his head as she widens an angry stare at me. But he starts to lower his weapon, and I quickly follow.

I have nothing against him or the Grazias. But right now, I'd kill my own flesh and blood for touching what's mine.

If I kill him, I will start a whole new war. But I wouldn't be the only man on this planet who's gotten his hands bloody over a woman. And she's not just a woman. She's my Red.

"We need to talk. Now," she seethes, grabbing my forearm and dragging me away toward the kitchen on the opposite side of the floor.

She shoots me a venomous look filled with unmitigated fury. "What the fuck was that?"

She shoves at my chest, while I remain still, taking slow deep breaths.

"Were you trying to let everyone in there know we're fucking?" she whisper-shouts.

She throws another palm at the center of my chest, while anger spirals from the pit of my stomach. And when she attempts that again, I grab her wrist, spin her body around against the counter, and press myself up into her.

With a curled fist at one side, the other hand reaches for her throat, wrapping my fingers around her delicate flesh. She swallows hard, the vibrations rolling down my hand.

"We haven't fucked in a year, Red," I remind her.

My lips drop close, stroking her soft trembling mouth.

"Believe me, I remember exactly how long it's been. And don't you fucking dare..." I nip her bottom lip with my teeth. "... diminish us to just fucking. I've fucked plenty of women before. None of them meant a damn, because none of them were you."

"Gio…" she breathes.

Grabbing a fistful of her hair, I say, "Don't you fucking *Gio* me, baby." I kiss her once, hard and fast, groaning when I pull away. "Go out there and be a good girl and get rid of him."

"That'd be rude," she whimpers when my fingers cinch tighter around her throat, her eyes turning heated and aroused.

"Get rid of him, or I will walk back out there and kill him in front of all your guests. What would Daddy say then?"

My eyes fall to her mouth, while hers fall to mine. Desire unfurls between us as it always does when we're this close to one another, consequences be damned.

"You're insane," she whispers, her breath hitching.

"You have no idea how right you are. And you, my little bambina? You will pay for this. How much, depends on how quickly you make him leave."

"He's my date, Gio." She grabs my wrist to try to yank me off, but with those words, I squeeze my grasp around her throat even tighter so she feels how badly those words just hurt.

"Date, huh?" I laugh coldly before my face twists into something dark.

I force her body to bend backward until she's pinned to the counter and mine's looming over hers.

"Let me clarify something, baby, because I don't think we've established the rules." I brush her mouth with my thumb while her eyes narrow into slits. "The only man you'll ever date is me. The only man who'll ever get to kiss you, and fuck you, and love you, is *me*." I fall in close to her ear. "Do we understand each other? Because if we don't, I'll drag you back into that room, bend you over that couch, and fuck the shit out of your pretty pink pussy while they watch you take it. Because we both know how good you can take it."

She groans.

I grind my throbbing cock into her. "Is that what you need? For everyone to know that you're my whore? My everything?"

"You need to let me go," she utters breathlessly, her eyes boring into mine. "We have to stop. Your marriage to Eriu isn't just going to disappear. I won't hurt my sister, no matter how good this feels…"

The last few words strangle in her throat the harder I grind into her.

"My feelings for you won't disappear either. So why don't you go and tell that asshole there was a misunderstanding. That he's no longer invited."

I back off while she fixes the hem of her dress and shakes her head in frustration.

"You can't do this again," she says in a whisper. "Not when there are people all around us."

I gnaw my jaw.

"I will not tell you again, Red. Get. Rid. Of. Him." Every word is a growl.

Her chest lurches with quick inhales, my eyes scanning her breasts, practically spilling out of the V-cut. When she doesn't say anything, I go on.

"And if I find out you let him touch you or kiss you…" I curl and uncurl a fist. "He's as good as dead, and you? Oh, Red, you'll be in so much fucking trouble. The kind that even your feisty temper won't save you from."

"He didn't…" Her words trail.

"Lucky him. You just saved his life."

"Is everything okay?" Eriu's voice causes us both to sharply turn toward her.

"Of course." Iseult plasters on a fake smile and rushes toward her sister. "Let's go dance."

"Uh, you hate to dance." Eriu peers questioningly at her.

"I don't right now," she mutters.

"Red," I warn, and she glances behind her shoulder right at me and nods.

"Let me do one thing before we dance though," she tells Eriu, dragging her away, leaving me there with my demons.

ISEULT

The party has long wound down, and my sister and Kora are cleaning up before heading to their respective homes.

Kora enjoyed the show Gio put on, saying he must really care about me to risk his life like that. Because if my father had found out about us, he'd definitely not react kindly. He may not have been at the party, but he's got spies everywhere, and it could very well be any of the instructors who were at the party.

I admit cozying up to Adriano wasn't the most brilliant plan I've ever had. But once I saw Gio park his car, I started talking to Adriano, thinking if I could get Gio to think I wasn't interested, maybe he'd back away.

But, of course, it's Gio, and I should've known better.

Mafia men are really not my type. Except one, apparently.

And though Adriano is a handsome man—six-three with a chiseled jaw that definitely has women drooling, especially when paired with his black hair and dove-gray eyes—I have zero interest. It's why he was the perfect date of sorts. Because no matter how badly I try, the only man I'm interested in is the one I shouldn't have.

"So, why was Gio so mad at you?" Eriu asks, picking up the

empty charcuterie board and bringing it to the sink.

"Yeah, Iz, why was he so mad?" Kora tightens her lips beside me as we follow my sister, throwing some empty beer bottles into the garbage.

Shut up, I mouth, giving her a deathly glare.

She stifles a laugh.

"I don't know," I tell Eriu as she glances over her shoulder, scrubbing the board before drying it.

"I thought maybe you were fighting about me," she sighs. "I didn't even get a chance to speak to him."

"Did you want to speak to him?" My heart races, wanting more than anything for her to say no.

"Well…" She shrugs. "If he's going to be my husband, I think I'm supposed to at some point, right?" She laughs nervously, leaning back against the counter.

"Right." My smile is tense; I'm not sure what else I can say. "Well, thanks for a great party, but I'm tired." I force a yawn, making a big show about it.

"Oh, right, of course." Eriu starts moving out of the kitchen, grabbing her handbag from the table.

Kora rolls her eyes and throws an arm around my sister. "Come on, let's leave the old lady to her sleep."

"I'm not old." We march toward my door, and Eriu opens it.

"At twenty-seven, you may as well be ancient," Kora teases, her eyes narrowing as she examines my scalp. "Is that a gray hair?" She pulls on a single strand.

I scoff, slapping her hand away as both she and my sister laugh hysterically at my very unamused expression.

They both start to head out, and I shove Kora out the door. "Goodbye, and don't come back."

"Have fun with Mr. Tongue," she quips back, a glint in her eyes as she whirls back around.

"Who's Mr. Tongue?" My sister's eyes bounce between us.

"Oh…" A mischievous grin slinks to Kora's treacherous face. "That's your sister's vibrator."

Eriu's gaze pops wide. "Wha—"

I shut the door in their faces, locking it before I lean against it, hearing Kora's laughter falling further away.

Once I don't hear them any longer, I start thinking about him all over again, wondering if he got home safe.

He was so angry when he left, I was worried about him driving all the way back to New York. I wanted to text, but I didn't want to distract him while he was behind the wheel.

He should be back by now, though. I take out my phone and find his name… Well, not his name exactly.

ISEULT

Are you home?

Gripping the cell in my palm, I stare at the screen, hoping he returns my text, or I won't be able to sleep. If I caused him to have an accident, I'll never forgive myself. Minutes fall into the distance and he still hasn't replied.

ISEULT

I don't care if you're still pissed. Just tell me you're okay.

FUTURE HUSBAND

Pissed? Oh, Red, pissed is a fucking understatement.

Instant relief washes over me.

He's okay.

ISEULT

Well, I'm glad you're not dead. So... goodnight.

I gawk at the phone like a damn teenager, hoping he says something back. Which of course is crazy, since I'm trying *not* to have him want me. Damn well that's going, considering how badly I wish he were here.

He's probably shirtless, lying in his bed, hating me. I wish I was in his arms right now. I kinda like it there.

With a rough exhale, I start for the stairs, needing out of this dress and shoes. Maybe I will use Mr. Tongue tonight while thinking of him. I love Mr. Tongue so much, I have two of him.

Reaching the top of the stairs, I shuffle toward my bedroom, the upstairs immersed in darkness. I get to the second door on my right, turn the knob, and strut inside.

Switching on the light, I suddenly gasp, my pulse slamming into my ears.

Fingers clutch my chest, my heartbeats hammering against them as I come face-to-face with the one person I didn't expect staring back at me.

Twenty-Three

GIO

The shock on her face was worth waiting for. When everyone thought I had left the party, I instead went up to her bedroom, trying to calm the fuck down before I killed that son of a bitch Adriano downstairs.

When I saw him leave out the window, that's when I finally relaxed enough not to go back down there.

But I remained in her room for hours, waiting for that damn party to end so I could finally get her alone. So I can remind her who she belongs to, whether she realizes it or not.

"What the hell are you doing here?" She stomps closer while I sit there on the edge of her bed, taking in the woman that I know in my heart is destined to be mine.

And though I've never been a patient man, I vow to wait for her for as long as it takes her to get that damn stick out of her ass and realize what we could be together.

I inhale a single sharp breath, climbing to my feet. And without my eyes leaving hers, I grab her jaw and yank her mouth close to mine.

The quick jerk of her inhale has her eyes glistening with something other than fear, something that smells and tastes like desire. It's unmistakable.

I drop closer, my lips stroking hers.

"I've been waiting all this time to give you your birthday present," I say, wanting to kiss her.

"The best gift you can give me is you going home," she whispers, but nothing in her voice or the way her hands cling to my shoulders lets me know she means a word.

"Stop denying what you feel for me," I tell her, pushing her body backward until it hits the door with a soft thud.

She gasps as she does, while my other palm slides up her arm until my fingers wind though her soft strands.

"You need to understand something, Red. I'm not the kind of man who'd allow another man to touch what belongs to him."

When she opens her mouth to speak, I place a finger against her full lips.

"Shh…" A smirk tips up my mouth as the words die in her throat. "This will serve as your one and only warning. Pull that shit again…" Roughly, I yank her head back by her hair. "And I will show you what I'll do to anyone who so much as looks at you. Do I make myself clear?"

The challenge in her eyes is mingled with her apparent yearning. She grits her teeth, her eyes narrowed.

"I asked you a question, bambina. And you will answer it."

Her lashes flutter, and her mouth quivers. What is it about her that makes me want to fight every war, to lay my life on the line just for a chance to have her? I may not know her well. I may not know her past, nor her demons. But I know one thing well, and that is that she's mine. Irrevocably mine. And soon enough, the whole world will know it too.

"Is it true?" Her voice grows raspy. Lustful and dangerous. And altogether inviting.

"What's that?" I ask, unable to stop looking into those eyes, her steadfast gaze slowly undoing me bit by bit.

"Did you really not sleep with anyone since me?"

A small smile fastens to my mouth, and I draw my knuckles up and down her cheek. "I haven't kissed a single soul, not so much as a touch since I've touched you, Red."

She drags in a slow, shaky breath.

"Why?" The word falls out so softly that I wonder if it came from her at all.

"I told you, they weren't you." I cradle her cheeks in both palms and lower my mouth to the corner of hers, leaving a kiss there. "No one will be. Not ever." I return my gaze to hers. "Since that very moment you tried to kill me, I saw something in you. I still see it, baby."

I let my forehead meet hers, wanting to get lost in her.

In us.

Her arms entwine around my back, holding me tightly against her.

"Gio…" she murmurs like she wants to believe in what I'm saying, wants to believe in this feeling, this moment. "We can't…"

She tears herself away, and her brows furrow.

"We can," I remind her. "You can be the one I marry if you tell him you want to. I think you can tolerate me long enough to fall in love with me."

An easy smile inches up my mouth, but hers never comes.

"Falling in love with you would be the easiest thing in the

world," she confesses, jumpstarting my heart.

It meant everything to me to hear her say that. She isn't the kind of woman to say things like that so easily.

As she goes on, she sighs brokenly. "It's falling in love with *me* that'd be the hardest part."

I let out a chuckle, cupping her face tightly, blood rushing into my veins from the extent of my affection. "How could anyone not fall in love with you? Sei la donna più bella che abbia mai varcato questa terra."

"What does that even mean?" she whispers.

"That you're the most beautiful woman that ever walked this earth."

She scoffs. "You deserve someone normal and kind like Eriu. She would be a good wife for you."

But the way her face falls…she doesn't mean it.

"I don't want a good wife, Red. I want *you* as my wife." My palm snaps around her nape, and in my eyes, I hope she sees the truth of my words.

"Well, I'm sorry, but that isn't possible."

I let out a frustrated groan. "Che cazzo, donna. Sei una spina nel fianco!"

"What d—"

"Wanna know what that means?" My nostrils flare. "It means you're a pain in my fucking ass." I shake my head as I stare up at the ceiling for a second until my eyes are back on hers. "I can't wait until we're married so I can remind you how crazy you made me before we got there."

She snickers. "When are you going to get it?"

She tries pushing me away, but I stay where I am, tugging her closer around the back of her neck.

"Get what?"

"That we'll never be together. It just won't happen. This was fun, I won't deny that, but it's over now. I can see you're a good guy and you'll treat my sister well, and I'm happy with that."

"Fuck!" I growl in absolute frustration, throwing my hands in the air as I fall back a step. "Are you ever going to get tired of lying to yourself? Of denying the truth?"

"This *is* the truth, Gio. You may not like it, but it is."

A cold, brutal chuckle wisps out of my throat. "Just answer me one thing, Red."

"And what's that?" She folds her arms around her chest and glares.

It's like a protective shield she wears, a mask of sorts, to keep people away. But I see right through it.

"Why the hell are you really pushing me away?"

"Are you kidding?" Her tone is laced with annoyance. "Because you're supposed to marry my sister! Because we have to keep the peace between our families, and this is how we can do that."

"No." I erase the steps between us, our bodies mere centimeters apart. "That's not the real reason."

"Well, I'm telling you it is." She remains against the door, her eyes tracking me as I take another step toward her.

"A woman like you does not just back down that easily, especially when you know your own sister doesn't even want to marry me."

"How the hell do you know that?" She grimaces.

"Because I heard you two talking in the kitchen during your party."

"You were spying on me?" Her eyes widen.

"Not exactly." I shake my head. "You two are loud, and I just so happened to be standing very close."

She pinches the bridge of her nose and stares at me with a

glower.

"So why are you really pushing me away, Red?" I grip her chin in my palm. "You make me want to be a better man, Iseult. You make me want things." My voice falls. "So why? Why won't you give us a chance?"

"Because," she whispers, her eyes falling to a close. "I just can't."

"You can't what?"

Her lashes flutter until she looks at me again. "I can't fall in love with you!"

"Why not?" I graze her lips with my thumb, my heart damn near breaking.

"Because…" Her whole body sags and she lets out a defeated sigh. "Love is fragile. It makes you weak. And I'm done being weak."

I search her eyes, wanting to erase every instance of pain written within them.

"You're afraid of getting hurt, aren't you?" I ask, pausing between the next set of words.

I know they may hurt her, but sometimes the only way to heal is to push on the wound deep enough until it gives you all its pain. Until you can let it heal for good.

"Is this about your mother?" I ask. "Are you afraid of losing the ones you love?"

Her nostrils widen, her eyes full of wrath. "Don't you *fucking* talk about my mother!"

"Why not? You still miss her, don't you?"

"Fuck you!" She shoves past me, but as she does, I grab her wrist and bring her flush against me.

"I'm sorry, Red." I cup her jaw and kiss her softly. "I don't want to hurt you, but I know what happened to her, and I'm sorry.

I'm sorry that she left you and that it still hurts."

"Get out!" she grits, her voice almost to the point of shattering. "Get the fuck out and don't ever come back!"

Tears shimmer in her eyes, but she won't let them fall, holding them hostage like the calming sea before the storm.

"One day you'll realize she'd want you to let go and be happy, piccolina."

"You have no idea what she would've wanted!"

I heave a ragged sigh and let my hand fall away from her, knowing I have said enough for one day. "You should rest."

My hand hits the doorknob, seconds trickling as I stay there with my back to her, not wanting to go.

"Wait!" she calls, and my pulse punches in my throat.

Ask me to stay.

"Call me when you get home," she says instead.

I turn toward her, her features clouded in despair.

"You worried about me, Red?" A tiny smirk lines my lips. "I love it when you worry about me."

"I'm serious." Her voice grows alarmed, and she appears before me in a few quick steps and grabs my hand. "Don't forget. Promise me."

Something dark crosses her face, like a ghostly shadow.

"I promise." I squeeze her fingers like an oath. "As soon as I step inside that door."

She nods and lifts up her chin.

"Goodnight, beautiful."

She swallows hard. I can see her throat vibrate.

"Oh, and before I go, don't forget to open the gift I left you." With my head, I gesture toward the box I placed on her bed.

"Thanks."

"You don't even know what it is."

She shrugs a single shoulder. "Doesn't matter."

Fuck.

And she thinks it wouldn't be the easiest thing to fall in love with her.

As soon as I leave her, I already miss her. It's a strange feeling, to miss a woman, yet here I am missing her anyway.

I head toward the large parking lot on Patrick's estate, a short distance from her house. But when I approach my car, I register footsteps behind me. Hope erupts in the marrow of my bones, wanting it to be her.

My pulse quickens.

But when I turn around, I find Tynan there instead.

Under the streetlamp, his stare is hard and unrelenting.

"What are you doing here?" I ask, my tone matching his hardened expression.

"I should be asking you that." His eyes burn with ill-consumed indignation. "What the hell were you still doing at my sister's?"

I really don't like how the son of a bitch is looking at me, and I'm seriously close to shoving my nine into his face.

"I was at the party," I reply cooly, pivoting to open my car door to get the fuck out of here.

"Party's been over for hours, and everyone thought you left."

"Seems like I didn't." I grate my jaw, keeping my back to him.

"What the hell are you doing with Iseult? Is this a fucking game to you? I saw you at the party. Everyone did."

I turn around sharply and walk into his space. "Does it look like I'm playing games? Do you think Michael asked when he arranged a marriage between Eriu and me?" My face tightens with a glare. "It's not my or Iseult's fault we met first. She's the only fucking Quinn I actually like."

"Does my father know that?" His voice grows with irritation, and I no longer care who knows I have feelings for her.

"No. If it were up to me, he would, but she doesn't want to tell him. And I have to somehow convince her to."

"If you care about her, you'll let whatever this is go and forget her. Because if my father finds out, you're as good as dead."

"I can't do that." A cold smile slips over my face. "She's impossible to forget."

"Even if my father allowed it…" he goes on. "She doesn't want to get married. So you'd be wasting everyone's time."

I inhale a strained breath. I don't need him telling me what Iseult wants.

"Before I met her, I didn't want to get married either. Things change."

"She doesn't." He eyes me with an edge. "She does better alone."

"No one wants to be alone, even when they tell you they do."

His jaw tics. "I've known my sister far longer than you have, and her stance on marriage will not change." He runs a hand down his face like he's recalling something. "She's a little bit broken."

With the remote I retrieve from my pocket, I click the door to my car open.

"Well, it's a good thing I find broken things beautiful."

Then I get in, turn the Bugatti to drive, and get the hell out of there, hoping Tynan doesn't fuck things up and tell his father what's been going on.

ISEULT

As soon as he walked away, I wanted to run after him and tell him to stay. Would he have? Would he still want me if he saw all the things I try desperately to hide?

There's no way he would. No one would want someone like me.

I stare down at the small square box, the black and gold wrapping paper neatly tucked around the edges. It's a little heavy, and I start to wonder what he could've gotten me. Not that I need anything, but it's nice that he thought of me.

Ripping the paper off, I toss it into the garbage in the corner of my room and gently open the black box.

And when I see what's inside, I start to laugh.

Of course he got me a gun, because he knows just what I would've wanted.

This one, though? It looks custom made. It's got a bright red grip with a shiny black barrel. I can't wait to test it out. Maybe on him.

A smile freezes over my face as I pick it up, and it feels nice to smile this way. To be happy. As I aim the muzzle at my wall, my thumb rests on the trigger before I place it on the nightstand.

Taking out my cell from my pocket, I dial his number. It rings once, and I hope he doesn't answer it so I can leave a voicemail. Hearing his voice makes my heart beat faster, and I don't think he realizes just how much it does.

But two more rings, and his voice comes through the line.

"You must've opened your present," he rasps, and the sound wakes up every inch of my body, like I've been dead for years until he came along.

"I did…and I think this is my favorite gift."

"Ever or just this year?" he teases.

"Ever…" I run a fingertip over the black metal, admiring the craftsmanship. "Other than this one gift I got when I was younger."

As soon as the words leave me, I instantly regret it. I didn't mean to say that out loud. Didn't mean to remember.

Emotions clog the back of my nose.

"And who was it from?" he wonders while I slowly settle on the bed, quiet for a moment, afraid to speak about her.

Talking about her out loud makes her loss hurt more than it already does.

It's then I see her, her full smile, the twinkle in her warm eyes as she walked out of my room for the last time.

My pulse beats unevenly.

My chest stiffens.

My lungs burn with every inhale.

I fight the tremor rolling through my muscles, that grip of panic clutching my throat. My head spins, but I fight it, jumping to my feet.

But as soon as I do, my left arm tingles and the left side of my chest grows heavy, like someone is weighing it down with cement.

"I can't breathe," I whisper, gasping for every ounce of air. "I can't breathe."

If I didn't know better, I'd think I were dying of a heart attack, but this isn't the first time.

My breaths come in gasps and I drop to the floor, the phone landing beside my thigh, while my hands claw my chest. My heartbeats fire out of me so quickly, I'm afraid that I'm really going to die this time.

"Red?" he calls with alarm. "What's the matter, baby?"

I can barely hear him, the sound falling into an echo.

"Iseult, answer me," he demands.

But I can't get out of this, not once it's embedded so deep into my subconscious.

My hands tremble. Or I think they do. Or maybe I'm dizzy.

Oh, fuck. I can't let this happen again.

I have to stop thinking about her. About what he did to her. What he did to all of us.

But I can't. The more I tell myself to stop, the more I see it play out in my head. The flesh at my back throbs, like the pain is all too real. Like it's happening all over again.

It's okay. I'm okay. This is not real.

If only I'd begged her not to go, maybe she'd still be here.

"Hold on, Red," Gio calls. "I'm coming back."

The roaring of the engine sounds off in the distance while I recall the gift my mother gave me a few months before she was killed.

It was a simple silver heart-shaped locket, and inside there was an engraved photo of our entire family.

I still wear it every single day as a reminder of what was taken from me.

Twenty-Four

ISEULT
AGE 14

*S*he didn't call. She didn't text. It's been hours since she should've arrived at my aunt's, but I haven't heard from her. No one has.

My father's downstairs freaking out, talking to some police officers he's friends with. Many people have gone out searching for Mom, but all I can do is keep calling her.

Over and over and over.

But all her phone does is ring.

Aunt Shannon confirmed Mom never got to the hospital. She had the baby already. And I know Mom would never have missed that. Not for anything.

Something definitely happened to her. I know it in my gut.

My hand trembles around the cell phone in my palm as I pace around my room, completely terrified.

I can't even imagine something bad happening to her. My brain won't accept it.

No. Mom would want me to be positive. She would want me to believe she's okay, so I will. I'll pray and beg whoever is listening for my mom to be okay.

My father's voice rises, and my heart explodes like a bomb when a heavy shattering of something like glass startles me.

I scamper toward my bedroom door and open it gently, wanting to know what happened. Maybe they found her. Maybe he was relieved and broke something on accident.

I drift down the stairs, my tight breaths rising out of me so quickly, I'm afraid my father will hear them.

He ordered me to go upstairs while he talked to everyone. But my brothers are there, right alongside him. If they're allowed to be there, I should be too. Fionn isn't even that much older than me. He's eighteen, which in boy years is like eight.

As I slowly climb down, my father's voice booms.

"Play it!" he demands harshly. "Play the fucking video!"

"It's not a good idea," one of the detectives says.

"Don't feckin' tell me what's good for me. Play it. Now!" He bangs a fist on the counter.

I tiptoe toward the edge of the wall, peeking out from my right into the kitchen, where my father and brothers have their back to me and two detectives I recognize from earlier face my way.

"Pat, you don't want to see this. Trust me, you don't want to," Fred, the taller gray-haired detective, tells him.

His brown eyes grow sympathetic, and I don't understand why. Nothing is making sense right now. What does my father want them to play?

"She was my fucking wife! You play it, or I swear I will rip out your bloody throat!"

W-w-was?

Like…like she no longer exists.

No.

He misspoke.

She's fine. Mom is fine.

My chest heaves and nausea curls in my gut.

He didn't mean that. Tears burn my eyes.

"Maybe tell the boys to go, then. No child should see their mother this way, no matter how old they are."

Instantly, my father snatches the collar of Fred's dress shirt. "My boys are no boys. They're men. Play the damn thing."

"Just do it." *Roy, the other detective, presses his fingers into his eyes.*

"Jesus Christ, Pat," *Fred mutters, picking up a laptop I hadn't seen from behind him, and looks toward my direction.*

I quickly snap my head back, breathing faster and faster, hoping he didn't catch me.

Seconds later, I hear her.

"No! Please!" *Mom screams, fear wedged between each word, yet I cannot see her from where I hide.*

"Kak zhal', chto ya dolzhen ubit' takuyu krasivuyu zhenshchinu," *a man I've never heard before says in what sounds Russian.*

My insides churn.

"Please," *she begs with a wilting sob.* "Please, I'll do anything. Just name your price. My husband will pay whatever you want. Just call him."

"Your husband…" *he replies in a thick Russian accent.* "…is the reason you're here."

"What?" *Mom pants.*

"Nu da, moya dorogaya. He didn't give me something I wanted, *so I take something that belongs to him. I say that's fair, yes?"*

"Oh m-my God, I beg you, please. No! I have children. Don't do this…" Her words end in another earth-shattering wail.

My gasping breaths turn faster, matching the panic fastened in her tone.

I want to come out. I want to see what's happening, but I can't seem to move. My legs are as heavy as lead, bolted in place.

But as soon as her blood-curdling scream hits my ears, I emerge from hiding, slowly trotting out, and what I see has me stumbling backward in sheer horror, tears throbbing behind my eyes.

I run as though that will somehow save her from the flames leaping around her body.

"Mom!" I shout with a heavy cry. "Mom!"

"Iseult! Go upstairs now!" my father shouts as he pushes to stand.

All eyes are now on me, the laptop turned away in a flash.

I whimper, almost collapsing, unable to stop hearing her voice. Seeing my poor beautiful mother burning alive, the fiery orange flames dancing to a frantic rhythm.

"Help her!" I roar tearfully at my father, tears streaking down my cheeks. "Help her! Do something!"

His fists tighten until his knuckles go white. And I realize he's hurting too.

Tynan rushes over to me and puts his arms around me, holding my crumbling body against him.

"I've got you," he tells me as I grip his shirt and cry.

My mother is dead. No one can save her.

How do I tell Eriu? How do I tell a five-year-old girl her mother will never come back? And it's then I realize she'll probably never remember her when she's older. Never recall how much she loved us. But I promise to myself right here and now to always remind her every moment of every day how special our mother was. How loving and kind and beautiful she was.

Even as I think these thoughts, I can't process the fact that she's dead. It's not possible.

She was just here!

But now she's gone.

Someone took her from us. I'm never going to see her again. I'm never going to talk to her. Feel her arms around me.

And I cry even harder, wailing against my brother, wanting to die too.

"Who—who hurt her?" I ask Tynan, choking on a sob. "Who d-d-did that?"

My words collapse out of me with shattering torment.

"You don't have to worry about that." Tynan kisses the top of my head, ever the big brother at nine years older.

But not even he can keep me safe from the sheer agony.

"Take her upstairs!" Dad bellows. "She can't be here."

"She can't be gone," I snivel. "She can't leave us."

Tynan shushes me as he takes me up while I'm huddled to his side.

"I know," he says as we walk into my bedroom.

"Who was that man? Tell me!" I plead. "What if he comes for us too?"

My body jerks with my shallow breaths as I clutch his shirt in both palms, staring up wildly at him.

"He won't, I promise. No one will hurt you or Eriu."

My, how wrong he was.

GIO

Now back at the Quinns' estate, I realize I hadn't even thought about how I'd get through the damn security gate. What reason would I give for my return? I wait a few feet away while the armed guards stare at me.

Gonna have to figure it out, or I'll shoot my way through just to see if she's okay. But six against one seems like a sure way to get myself killed before I'd even get a chance to see her for myself.

So I do something I may regret. I get out my phone and dial Tynan's number. He's the only one here who knows there's something between her and me, and maybe if he understands how frantic she sounded on the phone, how terrified she seemed, he'll let me go see her.

He groans as he answers. "What?"

"I need you to call the security booth and let them know I'm allowed in."

He mutters a curse. "You're back again? You're like a damn leech we can't get rid of. What the hell are you doing back?"

"In any other instance, I'd tell you to fuck off, but she needs me right now."

"Who?"

"Re—Iseult."

"My sister doesn't need anyone. Why are you really coming back? And don't fucking lie, or I'll order one of the snipers to shoot you before you even reach the gate."

I chuckle, shaking my head. Fucking crazy Quinns.

"I was on the phone with her, talking about the gun I got her for her birthday, and she was about to tell me her favorite gift. But instead, she went silent, and then I heard a bang and her crying."

"Fuck," he mutters. "Hold on."

The sound of him fumbling with something takes over for a few seconds.

"Okay, they know you're allowed to pass."

"So, you know why she was upset?"

"I do."

My pulse pounds. "Are you going to tell me?"

"No. Not my story to tell."

"Fucking hell."

"She's my sister. I'm not about to violate her trust." He pauses. "I just didn't realize she was still having—" He cuts himself off.

"Having what, man? Just tell me so I can help her."

"You can't help her. She has to help herself," he says. "But I'll let you in anyway so you can be there for her just in case. Because Lord knows if I tried, she'd chew my bloody head off."

I let out a small laugh, but worry etches into my bones.

"Okay, I'm here," I tell him, popping my head out from the window for the guys at the booth. "Giovanni Marino."

One of them nods, and the iron gate parts for me.

"Let me know how she is. And don't tell her I asked," Tynan says.

"Will do. I've gotta go." I drop the call and place the phone in my pocket.

Rushing out of the car, I jump up the four stone steps and knock loudly on her door.

"Red, open up." I place my ear against it, not hearing a sound.

Fuck. What if she's hurt?

"Red, I need you to open the door."

Waiting an additional thirty seconds, I try again, afraid if I knock any louder, someone will notice and find me here. When I start banging again, the lock on the door clicks and the door starts to part.

And when I take in her bloodshot eyes, her wet cheeks, my heart shatters.

She forces a trembling smile. "I'm fine."

Yeah, she's fine, alright. She looks like a damn ghost.

"You're not fine."

Walking in, I lock up before I'm taking a few steps closer until I'm right in front of her. My palm latches around the side of her throat, my gaze cutting into hers.

"I promise I'm okay now. You didn't need to come." She blinks back the quiet moisture building in her tattered stare.

"I didn't *need* to," I tell her, stroking her cheek with the back of my hand. "But I wanted to, Red. There's a difference."

Fresh tears coat her lower lashes.

"There's nothing you can do," she whispers, staring right at me, pain seeping through. "And it's over now. I'm fine."

"You keep saying you're fine, baby, but nothing about you looks fine right now."

"Are you saying I look like shit?" A small laugh trickles from her lips.

My thumb brushes over her jaw. "Like a damn tornado."

She scoffs playfully, but her pain is still there, blinding me, and I want more than anything to make it all disappear.

"How about I run you a bath?" I cradle her cheek in my palm, her skin warm and soft.

Her eyes shutter and she sighs, burrowing into my touch. But seconds later, she exhales roughly and her demeanor shifts.

"Look, Gio—"

She attempts to remove my hand off of her, clutching my wrist, but I squeeze my fingers around her.

"Here we go," I say through a strained breath, searching the eyes of the woman I've come to care deeply for.

"Here we go, what?"

"Here comes the part where you push me away." I snicker. "I was ready for it."

She rolls her eyes and fights another smile.

"All I want to do is run you a bath. That's all." I drop my lips to her cheek and kiss her. "So shut up and let me take care of you, bambina."

Goosebumps thread over her arms when I draw back, my eyes locked with hers.

She sucks in a long inhale. "You don't get it." She shakes her head. "I've never depended on a man for anything before."

"I don't need you to depend on me, Red. I want you to want to." An arm loops around the small of her back, and I mold her to me. "I know you're strong enough to do it all." I cup her face with my free hand. "But let me hold your crown just once so you can breathe without suffocating from the weight of it."

She stares with awe, her brows knitting as I continue.

"I just want you to trust me a little bit. Trust that I'd never do a thing to hurt you. Trust that you're not alone anymore. I will fight by your side. I will kill by your side, and I'll do it with a damn smile on my face." My lips jerk while her nostrils flare, fighting the emotions filling her features.

When she doesn't say anything, I go on.

"So how about I go start on that bath and let you know when it's ready?"

"How do you even know how I like my bath, let alone if I even do?" She swipes under her nose with the back of her finger.

"If I remember correctly, water calms you." I slant my mouth across her forehead, breathing her in just once as I kiss her before I pull back. "And as far as how you like it, probably as hot as hell."

She laughs. "Yes, you'd be right." Her brow arches. "And maybe add some bubbles. They're on the corner of my tub."

She pinches her lips while I chuckle at the thought of her liking a bubble bath.

"Don't judge." She swats my shoulder as I angle back, heading for her master bath.

"Coming right up, Your Highness. Try not to run."

And as I walk away, I hear her say, "Couldn't if I tried."

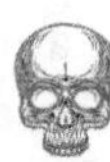

I run my hand through the water, making sure it's warm enough for her. Picking up the bottle of bubble bath from the jacuzzi tub in her spacious bathroom, I pour a few drops and let the suds fill up the tub. Seconds pass, and I close off the faucet when the water is almost to the top.

"You can come in now," I call, and her footsteps trudge closer.

She slinks inside, her eyes on me, a smile tipping up her mouth.

"Thank you," she says, leaning a hip against the doorframe, and somehow, coming from her, it means more than it maybe should.

Her eyes are still bloodshot, and I'd do anything to erase the reasons why.

"I'll be right outside." I approach her, taking her hand in mine and bringing her palm to my lips.

When she nods and doesn't say anything, I let go of her and give her privacy. As I start back toward the den, I hear her soft voice.

"Gio?"

I turn back. "Yes, bambina?"

There are a few inches between us, and all I want is to kill all the distance, take off her clothes, and bury myself inside her like

I'm worthy enough to be there.

"If I were the marrying type, you're the kind of man I'd marry."

Before I can process what she just said, she rushes into the bathroom and shuts the door behind her.

Think my Red just admitted she wants to be my wife.

Twenty-Five

ISEULT

Once upon a time, the thought of any man doing anything nice for me would have made me want to jump off a cliff to my own death. But not now. Not with him.

It's nice to have someone care enough to run me a bath. To turn back around and check on me. Not many would. I matter to him, and up until this point, I hadn't grasped that fact.

I'm glad that my sister will have a man who has a heart big enough to care. Because in the end, no matter how I may feel about him, nothing has changed. I'm still me—a damn mess—and he's nothing more than a fling.

With a defeated sigh, I start removing my clothes, taking off my t-shirt, then my leggings.

When I start to dip one foot into the inviting water, the door opens, and my heart jumps out of my throat.

"What the hell are you doing?!" I let out a scream.

Flipping around, I cover my breasts with my palms.

But it's too late.

He inhales sharply, his eyes enflamed as a hand balls at his side.

He saw.

He saw it all.

And I just want to crawl into a hole and die.

GIO

"Who did that to you?" My voice roughs out of my lungs, blood-curdling rage filling my veins.

"Get out!" she hollers.

But I merely shut the door and lean against it, trying to control the anger brewing within me before I tear this place apart.

Someone hurt my Red, and they hurt her bad. Whoever did it better hope he's dead because if not, I'm coming for him. And there's not an inch on his body that I won't mar.

She glares with a tight gaze, and with a shake of her head and a muttered curse, she fits down into the water, her body now covered by the suds.

But all I can see are those scars.

Thick, angry scars across her back.

"You're not going to leave, are you?" She runs a hand down her face, her hair floating around her in flaming waves.

"Not until you tell me who did that to you so I can find him and kill him." My nostrils expand and my pulse races savagely.

"It doesn't matter." She gives me a pointed stare.

Doesn't matter? Does she think so little of me? I'd never ignore what I saw. I'd never forget that someone hurt her.

"Why?" I ask, gritting my teeth. "Is he dead?"

She drops deeper into the water, until her neck is covered, her eyes bouncing to the ceiling, her gaze lost, like she's back there with her ghosts.

"No," she replies quietly.

"What?" Heat rushes into my body.

One word. One fucking word, and I've never hated it so much.

She turns her hardened expression toward mine. "It doesn't matter anymore, Gio. I was seventeen when it happened. And no one has seen him since."

Seventeen? Fuck!

I grind my molars, taking heavy steps toward her. Emotions battle inside me. Too many at once. I want to kill something. Want to hold her and kiss her and care for her. My God, what she's been through.

My Red…

I settle on the edge of the tub, my hand gripping the porcelain until all the blood leaves my knuckles. "Tell me who it was, baby, please, because I'm about to go crazy."

Her lashes flutter to a close before she's looking at me again. "Promise not to do anything stupid?"

"Define stupid."

A mirthless chuckle escapes her as she shakes her head. Her mouth parts, and my heartbeats ravage in my chest, waiting for a name, needing it like my next breath.

"It was Sergey," she admits. "The same man who killed my mother."

"Son of a bitch." The words fall out on a growl as I do what I can not to lose it in front of her.

But inside me, there's already blood on my hands. I'm coming for him and his sons. All four of them.

"Gio," she scolds as she takes me in through a narrowed gaze.

"Whatever you're thinking right now, don't."

She gives my hand a little squeeze, drops of water penetrating the cotton of my dress pants.

"It's over now," she goes on. "I want it to stay that way."

"Tell me what happened." There's a buzzing noise in my head, too much noise. I don't know if I can handle hearing what he did, but I need to know.

"After my mother was killed, I'm sure you know my father murdered one of Sergey's sons, but what no one knew was that he waited three years to take me." She takes a deep breath, like the rest is becoming difficult to say. "After I got free, the other Marinov brothers signed a treaty with my family to end the war. They knew their father was insane. Everyone knew." Tears line her eyes. "He started the war over turf. He killed my mother over money, Gio. Over fucking money! She was worth more than that."

I cup her face, my need to undo her pain, to right her wrongs is too great to put into words.

"Come here," I whisper, opening up my arms.

The savage need to hold her, to comfort her, to give her the safety she never had back then, becomes intense to the point of breaking me.

Slowly, she rises out of the water, like a goddess from the heavens climbing out of the ruins to claim me.

With a wave of another bout of anguish, she settles her naked form on my lap, drenching my clothes from her wet skin. And with my arms enclosing around her, she quietly shatters.

Iseult isn't the type of woman to cry, I know that much, and the fact that she allowed herself to do that in front of me makes me feel like the most powerful bastard that ever walked this earth.

She's utterly beautiful—and not just her body, but her mind and her heart, and her absolute resilience.

I'm in awe of her.

Yet, as she rocks with soft cries, it physically breaks me to hear it, more than any gunshot or any physical pain I've endured. Because this right here, her pain, that's the worst kind of torment of all.

"How long did he take you for?" My fingers glide up and down her arm.

"A week," she confesses with a whisper.

Fucking Christ.

A slice of pain lodges in the back of my throat. "Who got you out?"

She pitches back to look at me. "*I* did."

Twenty-Six

ISEULT
AGE 17

"**P**lease," I cry, choking on my sobs. "Please stop!"

"Zatknis', malen'kaya suka!" Sergey bellows, his foot pressed into my nape, the blowtorch feathering over my back as it burns through my flesh. "I'm not done yet. Must be patient."

The heel of his shoe delves even harder, but I don't feel it because the torment he rains across my skin is far worse.

No matter how many times he tells me to shut up, I can't. The pain is unimaginable and indescribable.

All I want is to be free.

But it's been days, and no one has come for me. I'm all alone here with a monster. And not the kind they tell you about when you're a kid. The real kind. The human kind. He's the only monster I've ever met, and I'll never be rid of him, whether I survive this *or not.*

With my eyes slammed closed, the raw screaming escaping my lungs, I imagine my mother the day she died.

Is that how she felt as he burned her alive? At least I could still breathe. She couldn't. I could still survive. If only someone finds me before I'm dead too.

"You know…" he chimes through my brutal snivels. "If your father was an honorable man, we could've avoided this, but…"

The torch swallows me up again, and I shatter, barely hearing his words.

Burning…

Skin charring.

"He was never a good man, your father," Sergey goes on while I'm barely able to listen. "So you can blame him for this."

"F-f-f-fuck y-you," I grate through a snarl, my neck turned to him, staring up into his dirt-filled eyes.

He laughs cruelly, his shoulders rocking. "My God, you're a tough one, aren't you?"

Hatred blooms inside me as he shuts off the torch and shakes his head, as though mocking me.

"All the things I have done to you and you're still talking back to me, huh?"

For one fleeting moment, I think that maybe he'll finally leave me alone for the day. Maybe he'll let me lie here and rot.

But instead, he kneels, torch in hand, his putrid breath invading my nostrils, like the decaying of flesh. Or maybe all I smell is me.

With his teeth gritted, he grabs a fistful of my hair and twists my head back until my neck spasms.

"You better watch your mouth when you talk to me, you got it, suka?" And as he straightens himself, his foot connects hard with my ribs.

"*Ahhh!*" *I scream, new tears rolling over my old ones, crusted to my face.*

I remain here on the floor of the warehouse crying, wishing I could just die.

My back pulses, the burns on my front almost numb, but I still feel the throbbing pain from when he burned me days ago.

I can't take another moment of this. Where is my father?! Why hasn't he found me! I know he'd never give up hope. But I'm close to giving it up.

It's been seven days of this. Seven days of torture. Seven days of hell.

I close my eyes, my body cold, trembling, my shirt burned into my skin, and it's then I see her: my mother, her beautiful smile, her hair gleaming in the sun.

"Get up, Iseult. Don't you dare give up."

Her voice. Her face. It's as though it's right here. Right in front of me.

"I can't, Mom. I can't anymore," I speak under my breath.

"Did you say something, sweetheart?" he taunts, his leery grin churning my stomach.

My mother's voice is still there as I stare into the devil's face.

"You have a warrior's heart. A warrior keeps fighting, Iseult. Keep fighting, darling. Don't let him take your light."

When he comes nearer once more, a wicked sneer beneath a set of pale yellow teeth, something blooms in my gut. Something wild and free, a whisper of the girl I was before he snatched me and made me his victim.

But I've never been good at being a victim.

When he kneels this time, I don't think. I just react.

With a grunt, my body flips to my side, my foot connecting hard with his balls.

"Suka!" he growls as he stumbles backward, collapsing to the ground, the torch clinking beside him.

I gasp, not wasting this opportunity. Rushing to my feet, I run for the torch, my entire body surviving on the sheer will to make it out alive.

He groans, holding his crotch, sagging in a fetal position as I jump over him and turn on the torch, and that's when his eyes grow.

"What are you do—"

I stomp on his balls harder, hoping I busted both his tiny nuts, and when he screams, a grim smile tugs at one end of my mouth.

The torch flips to life in my hand, and I stare at the brilliant blue light. So beautiful, yet so deadly. And I swear that when I survive this, I will be like this flame.

"I'm gonna kill you!" he shouts, but makes no move to get up.

And slowly, torturously, I lower the flame until it meets his eye, until his screams scratch up the walls, until there's nothing there but blood.

His hand grabs for my ankle as he shrieks. I fall to the floor, the torch collapsing on the ground, almost connecting with my thigh.

My pulse thrashes as the silent fear returns, as he glares at me with one good eye. But before he can, I grab the torch once more and let the flames eat away his thigh. He screams in agony as I leave the torch behind, away from his grasp, staring at the man who tortured me for seven days.

He starts to rise, and fear and anger creep up my spine. And as much as I want to kill him, I know that I must get out of here before I end up dead myself.

Jumping up, I rush out of the room, down the metal steps, and out into the assailing light. Two cars honk as I blink against the rays of the sun, getting my eyes to adjust.

My heartbeats are a deafening sound in my ears, the enveloping fear eating me alive as I will my legs to run, needing to find a phone.

"Hey!" Someone rolls down the window of their black SUV.

A woman. Mom's age, maybe older.

"Are you okay, honey? Do you need an ambulance?"

"I...I need to call my dad."

"Do you want me to drive you to a hospital?"

Her eyes are kind. Soft brown, golden flecks within them. Like my mother's. Tears fill my eyes, and I smile, knowing that somehow my mother sent this woman to me.

"I need a ride home. Please."

"I...uh..."

"Please! Someone is after me."

"O-okay. Get in."

I rush around to the passenger side, and when I pass her windshield, I can see the moment she takes in my full condition, and her own eyes water.

Stuffing down my emotions, ignoring the roaring of my stinging pain, I open the passenger door and get inside.

"Please just drive," I beg her just as Sergey rushes out the door, looking every which way for me.

I lower myself down and she looks at me, perplexed, before she glances to her left and sees him.

"Just go!" I whisper-shout. "Before he kills us both."

When the light turns green, she keeps the car at normal speed and gets us away.

My breath rushes out of me, and when we're finally gone, all my emotions pound at me, and I burst into silent tears.

She lets me cry, not saying a word. But a second later, she's handing me a phone.

"Call your dad, honey. I'm sure he's anxious to know you're okay." Her voice trembles.

I nod, taking it, and as soon as I dial his number…

"Hello? Who's this?"

His gruff, tortured voice only makes me wail.

"Iseult?" He breaks into a cry. "Darling? Is that you? Oh my God. She's on the phone!"

Voices. So many voices. Tynan. My other brothers.

"Where are you? Tell me where you are so we can get you."

"I r-ran. A lady picked me up and is giving me a ride. I…" I sniffle. "I need a shirt."

Silence. The silence grows until it's all I hear.

"Okay," I hear Tynan next, as though my father can no longer handle it. "We'll bring it. Tell her to drop you off at the restaurant on Sixth."

"Yeah. Okay."

"Iseult, I'm so sorry. I'm so fucking sorry."

"It's not your fault, Tynan."

"It is. It was up to me to protect you, and I failed. Fuck!"

Something smashes in the distance.

"I've gotta go. I'll see you in about forty-five," I tell him.

"Okay. I love you."

"Ditto."

GIO

As she recalled the time she was taken, all I could do was stare at her in disbelief.

"You were just a kid." My words are filled with awe. "Fuck, Red." I clasp the back of her head. "My little fighter even back then, huh?"

She shrugs. "My mother once told me I had a warrior's heart. I guess it kinda stuck with me."

Her lips jerk, and she smiles softly now. It's good to see her smile that way, even while reliving all that trauma.

"He didn't take me far," she goes on. "Some abandoned warehouse about thirty miles from home. I was glad he didn't take me to Russia. If he had, I know I'd have ended up dead."

"Did your father go back there? The place he held you?"

"Yeah." She nods. "It was empty. He searched everywhere. My brothers too. They didn't stop for years. I don't think they ever did. They just don't talk to me about it anymore. Tynan took it the hardest out of the three of them. He felt like he failed me."

She lays her cheek against my beating heart, my utterly broken beating heart.

"And no matter how many times I reassured him it wasn't his fault, he wouldn't stop hating himself for it."

"Shit. Speaking of, I was supposed to text him to let him know you're okay."

"What?" She jerks back and her eyes enlarge, but she makes no attempt to escape my arms. "What did you tell him?" Her voice turns feverish. "What does he know, Gio?"

"Hey." I brush a hand down her hair. "I just told him you might be upset and to let me pass the gate."

"Is that it?"

"Mm, well…" I grimace.

"Oh, no…I don't like that face you're making. What did you do?" She punches me in the shoulder.

"Fuck, woman, you gotta hit me that hard?"

She glares like she's got my death certificate already written. "You know…I have a new gun I've been dying to test out."

I chuckle. "As long as you let me hold you for a bit more before you kill me."

"Gio…" Her eyes expand. "Tell me."

"Okay, okay. Geez." I clear my throat. "After he caught me leaving your place earlier, I told him I liked you."

"You said *WHAT*?!"

I don't think I've quite seen her face this red before.

"He won't say anything. So stop worrying."

She sighs heavily and drops her forehead against my shoulder. "My life has imploded ever since you walked into it."

"Well, my life has only gotten better since the moment you stabbed your way into it."

"I didn't stab you." She gazes at me once again. "Not really." Her mouth jerks. "I should've, though."

"You should've…" I whisper, my voice cracking, the back of my hand stroking softly down her cheek.

Her brows draw together while my unwavering gaze holds hers, not wanting to look at anything else for as long as I live. Breathless seconds pass between us. And I feel it in every beat of my heart.

And in this moment, I know we both know that something has shifted between us, something new born from this vulnerability she allowed me a glimpse into. She handed me a gift in the form of trust—with her story and her scars. And I'd never take that for granted.

I love how strong Iseult is, but there's something beautiful about her when she's at her weakest.

I start to rise, and she clutches her arms around me, holding me to her with a wounded gaze. And I feel it—that sinking feeling in my gut, that squeezing inside my chest like she's there reminding me who my heart belongs to.

"I'm just going to undress so I can join you," I say, getting to my feet.

I start with the buttons of my shirt, slowly undoing each one.

Her eyes close and her face slightly crumbles as she dips into the water. "Look, you don't have to stay. Not after what you saw."

She tries to sound strong, but I can read between the lines. She's afraid I'm going to reject her.

"I wouldn't blame you for it," she goes on, staring into the wall ahead. "I know they're hideous. I know what I look like. I can barely look at myself. Why would you want to?"

I toss off my shirt and remove my cell from my pants pocket, placing it on one of the towel shelves, before I find myself hurrying toward her. When I slide a foot inside the tub with my pants still on, she gapes at my chest.

"Gio…? What is that on your shoulder?" Her eyes rove down my body, her wild expression taking in the tattoo I completely forgot about in this moment.

"Oh, that?" I flex my bicep as I smirk. "Let me get in and I'll explain."

She makes room for me and I settle into a seated position in the warm water. "Come here, baby." I drag her closer with an arm curled to her back. "I need to hold you. I couldn't stand another second of you thinking that I wouldn't want you."

My hands reach for her hips, lifting her up gently and placing her on my lap facing me.

Her fingertips trace the vivid red and black tattoo.

"When did you get this?" she whispers in awe.

"After the first night we were together." I grin. "I needed a keepsake."

I recall how hard she bit me, leaving a mark.

"So you decided to get the bite mark I gave you permanently tattooed on your skin with my name right under it?"

"That's right. You have a problem with that, bambina?"

I expect her to make fun of me. To laugh at how ridiculous I am. But the last thing I expect…is for her to burst into tears.

"Shit, baby," I weave my arms around her as she sobs against the tattoo. "I'm sorry you think it's so ugly that you're crying about it. I can have it removed."

She laughs tearfully.

"Shut up," she mutters. "I love it."

"Aww, you mean you're capable of loving something?"

She weaves her head back just as she punches me in the ribs.

I groan on a chuckle.

"Just because my utter disdain for you has lowered to minor hatred doesn't mean I won't kill you."

I hold her naked body tighter against me. "You wouldn't be my Red if you didn't threaten me at least once a day."

My lips slant up and I inhale deeply, feeling fulfilled and at peace just merely being with her. Like this right here is enough for me. Enough to make me happy.

"You're beautiful, Iseult. Nothing has changed for me. I need you to know that. If anything, I only want you more."

She sniffles. "Well, clearly you were kicked on your head a good few times."

"No." I hold her cheek in my palm. "I just know a good thing when I see it."

She blinks back the moisture welling anew in her eyes.

"Why do you have to be so nice to me, you idiot?" She presses two fingers into her eyes with a tattered laugh.

"Just so I can hear you call me that."

And when she inhales sharply, emotions threaded in her gaze, I grasp the side of her neck and watch her eyes light up right before I kiss her.

With a grunt, I slide my tongue past her lips, her moans tangled with the rumbling sounds of satisfaction coming from deep in my chest.

My perfect woman thinking she's anything but that in my eyes is a damn sin.

I fist her hair, tugging her head back, sucking on her jaw, her tongue. My other hand drifts down her spine until I can feel the grooves of those scars, until she flinches away.

"Hey," I tell her, my palms returning to cup her face. "Stand up."

"What?" The momentary fear seeping in her gaze has my heart lurching.

"I said stand up, baby. I don't like repeating myself."

She mutters a curse before she slowly climbs up in the water. Bare and beautiful. Water drips down around the slope of her full breasts, those hard pink nipples calling for my mouth. She can barely look at me as my gaze traces lower and I take in that first scar around her lower abdomen. A long groove extends around her belly button, like he was drawing on her with fire, like he was toying with her as she screamed.

My heart can barely take it.

Fuck.

I didn't see those.

I can make out her heavy breath while my pulse races to an unnatural speed, unable to contain my level of fury.

Say something, or she's gonna think this changes something for you.

Both my palms clasp her hips and I bring her close to my mouth. As I look up at her, my lips drop to what she believes are her imperfections, and I kiss them.

"You."

Kiss.

"Are."

Kiss.

"Beautiful."

I spin her around, my mouth coasting up every scar across her lower back, all six of them, not missing an inch of her gorgeous skin.

I kiss her a final time before lifting to my feet. Grabbing her jaw, I stare intensely at her, drowning in the weight of my feelings, then smash her lips to mine. Our kiss is maddening, my groans desperate, like a man who needs her to survive.

And I do. I need her.

"You take my breath away, Iseult." My forehead meets hers. "I see you, baby—the person you are underneath—and I'm not the least bit afraid at the thought of falling in love with you."

She gasps, disbelief clouding her expression.

"It doesn't turn you off to look at me?" Her voice cracks and sways with emotion.

With the tips of my fingers, I trace her scars with my rough fingertips while I deepen my gaze with hers.

"My beautiful girl. There's nothing about you that could ever turn me off. You are art. It's a privilege to look at you."

"I think you're a liar," she whispers.

"Then I'll spend my whole life proving you wrong."

Her chin trembles as she shakes her head. "Oh, fuck, I'm gonna regret this."

And she's the one kissing me now. Through her agony, through her tears, she kisses me like she never wants to let go.

And I hope like hell she won't have to.

Twenty-Seven

ISEULT

After the bath, we showered together, his big strong hands in my hair, washing me with care. He didn't attempt to touch me, which I was grateful for. It was not what I needed. And without even asking, he just knew exactly what to give me.

He took me to bed and held me all night, and for once in a very long time, I woke up well rested, without the nightmares claiming me.

With my head propped on my hand, I watch him just starting to wake. He's a breathtaking man. All of him is, which is a shame, because I have no idea what to do with us. No idea how to tell my father that I'm starting to develop real feelings for a man I have no right to.

He groans, his eyes not even open yet, but his mouth forms a huge smile. It's as though waking up beside me makes him happy.

"Good morning…" His palm cups my ass and squeezes my abdomen up against his erection.

"Good morning to you too." I arch into him, and his husky laughter has me aching between my thighs, needing him there.

"I'd say I was sorry…" He scoops me up and, in one quick move, places me on top of him. "But I'm not. You make me hard as a rock."

His sinful smirk forges a fire deep in my belly, desire unfurling in my bones. I widen my legs to feel him rub against my center, so thick and firm.

I let out a raspy moan that has him growling.

He fists my hair and drags my jaw to his mouth. "I'm gonna feed you, then fuck that greedy little pussy."

"Oh, God…" The words fall in a whisper as he circles his hips into me, giving me exactly what I need. Just a little more, and I could come.

"You miss my cock inside you as much as I've missed feeling you stretch around me?"

"Gio…" I hiss. "Don't talk dirty to me unless you're gonna do something about it."

He slaps my ass hard with a chuckle.

"Come on, baby…" He kisses and sucks at my neck while I moan in sheer ecstasy. "Get up."

His hips stop moving, and I groan, grabbing his face and giving him a quick kiss. "You're so mean."

"I know." He winks. "But I did tell you I'd pay you back for Adriano, and I'm not done yet."

"So you still haven't forgiven me for that?" I tease, nipping against the stubble lining his well-defined jaw.

"Every time I see you with him, his hands on you, I want to find him and kill him. Does that answer your question?"

"Please don't do that."

With a huge grin, I lay my head against his racing heart and sigh.

Seconds stretch between us before I say, "I'll have you know I don't cook. At. All."

His fingertips stroke up and down my back. "Don't worry, I do."

"Really, now?" I prop my chin on the top of my hands as I peer at him.

What doesn't he do?

"That's right, my future wife." His burly chest rises with each of his breaths. "And I do it well, too."

"Must win you lots of Brownie points with those ladies."

"Wouldn't know." He grabs my jaw and kisses me hard. "Never cooked for them."

"Oh, let me guess." My lips curve. "I'm special."

"No," he scoffs. "I'm just hungry."

I swat him, narrowing a humored gaze that has him chuckling.

And I'm laughing too, wondering why it took me this long to laugh again.

"Sit, woman." He pulls out a chair for me and points a finger at it.

"Demanding even in my own home?" I settle into the seat.

He spins me around in the swivel chair, his body towering. "When I marry you…" He grabs my throat possessively and bends to me. "I'll move you into my home and command you there too. I think you love it when I do."

"I do not."

He brushes his lips to mine.

I so do.

It's my new secret obsession to be spoken to this way by Giovanni Marino.

He rights himself and heads for my fridge, opening it as though he didn't just make me want him to fuck me on my kitchen table.

He peers inside, rummaging. "How do you survive with nothing in this damn thing?"

"There's usually food at my father's, or I grab stuff I can toss in the microwave."

He shakes his head, grabbing some milk and eggs. "That's not happening anymore."

"What does that mean?"

"It means you have me to take care of your needs, like making sure my woman is well fed."

"Your woman?" I pop a brow, biting on the inside of my bottom lip to stop myself from smiling.

"That's right." He fits me with a serious stare. "And *try* to give me lip about it."

I bring my fingers to my mouth and pretend to zip them.

"Good girl. Now, where's your flour and sugar?"

I point to a cabinet on the corner. Reaching over, he grabs two containers, after which I tell him where the pan is.

Silently, he starts throwing ingredients into my standup mixer and starts it. "Have you ever used this thing?"

I pinch my lips. "Not even once."

He shuffles over to me. Lifting my hand, he kisses my knuckles. "It's a good thing you have me now. I'm gonna unvirginize the shit out of your mixer."

"Why the hell did that just sound so hot?"

He laughs, big and beautiful, and I'd do just about anything to watch him laugh like that for the rest of my life.

GIO

"Open your mouth," I tell her, standing by her side as I cut into a piece of the pancake I've just finished making.

There's something about feeding a woman, and throw in the fact that it's something I made with my hands… I don't know, it makes me want to go all caveman on her.

She squints like I've grown another head. "I'm fully capable of feeding myself."

She tries to take the fork away, but I yank it back.

"If you don't hush up, I'll force you to sit on my lap while I feed you."

She laughs like I'm crazy, not realizing how serious I am.

"You asked for it." I drop the fork and easily lift her off the chair, one arm under her knees and the other around her back.

"Hey!" she squeals while I sit down, placing her on top of me, my forearm enclosed around her front, keeping her caged.

"Now, this is much better. Wouldn't you say?"

"You're so frustrating," she groans, but doesn't fight me any longer. Instead, she sags against me.

"Me?" I jerk back. "I'm frustrating?" With a fist, I yank her head back by her hair. "Have you had a good look in the mirror lately, baby?"

She rolls her eyes while my gaze drops to her lips, wanting—no, *needing*—to taste them. I growl under my breath, lifting the fork back up and picking up the abandoned piece of pancake.

She opens her mouth, and my teeth grind as she locks her lips around the metal and sensually sucks while her eyes stay glued to mine throughout. Even her damn chewing has me throbbing.

The fork slinks out, and I cut into another piece.

"I like it when you're obedient."

She hits me with a wrathful gaze I saw coming miles away. "I'm anything but obedient."

"Well, seeing as you're sitting pretty on my lap eating what I made you, I'd say you're being pretty damn docile."

"It's been a while since I've threatened to kill you." She narrows her eyes, grabbing a chunk of my hair.

"Damn, bambina. I love it when you talk dirty to me."

That sultry look in her eyes is telling me she's hungry for something other than my blood. The need to throw her on the counter and spread her thighs for a taste has my cock jerking beneath her.

My fingers sink into her hair, and I groan as my mouth lines with hers, wanting to own this woman, body and soul. And as I'm about to skip right to dessert, my damn phone rings in my pocket.

"You should answer that," she tells me huskily, her mouth hungrily sucking along the curve of my jaw.

"I'd much rather do this…" I curl her hair around my fist and snap her head back, lips teasing and sucking along the slope of her throat.

But whoever it is keeps calling and calling.

"Fuck." I release a frustrated groan as I give her an apologetic look before my hand is sinking into my pocket, fishing out the phone.

Grant's name appears on the caller ID.

"Yeah?" I answer, my eyes still glued to hers, hoping he has a damn good reason for interrupting what was about to be one hard fuck.

"I have a lead on Bryce, and it's time-sensitive."

I instantly sit straighter, and she must notice my change in mood, because she does too.

"What is it?" I ask him.

"There's a homeless man one of my guys found. He wants to talk. Says he saw what happened to Bryce. Claims he squats in that empty house right next door to the alley and was looking out the window at the time."

"You fucking serious?" I start to get up, kissing Red on the temple. "You think he's telling the truth?"

"Maybe. That abandoned building is prone to squatters, and he mentioned two women and a man arguing."

"Are you saying he saw two women that night with Bryce, not one?"

"Yeah."

That really solidifies the fact that Donny wasn't directly involved. He was definitely covering up for someone.

The bastard recently got out on a technicality, and though Grant and I have tried locating him, we couldn't. It's as though he's vanished.

"When are we going to talk to him?" I ask Grant.

"I'm not. You are. I'm about to walk into a meeting I can't get out of. My guys are with him now, feeding him at a restaurant in the city, waiting for you."

"Shoot me the address. I'm in Cherry Grove, so it will take me a while."

"That's fine. I'll get him a hotel room. Make him king for a day, and hopefully he remembers even more."

"I hope this is it," I say, my pulse ramming in my ears. "I hope we finally find out what happened."

"Keep me informed as soon as you can."

"I will." I hang up and place the phone back in my pocket. "I'm sorry, Red, but I have to go."

I start for the door.

"What happened?" she asks, concern zipping through her features.

I battle with whether I should tell her, but there's no reason I can't. I whirl back around as she edges up to me.

"I had a friend who was killed about a year ago. We haven't been able to find out what happened. But there's someone who may have seen something from that day, so I have to go and speak to him."

"Let me come with you. Maybe I can help." She appears genuine, like she actually wants to.

"You don't have to do that."

"I know." Her entire face turns dark and distant. "But I know how it feels to lose someone you care about. And it's obvious that whoever he was, you cared a great deal about him."

Twenty-Eight

GIO

Hours later, and we're stepping foot inside one of the top hotels in the city. A glimmering chandelier sparkles above us, the shiny black marble flooring dazzling as Red's heels clack beside me.

Her tight jeans leave very little to the imagination, and her long-sleeved silky crimson blouse looks both professional and sexy as hell.

Every man turns to look at her, and I have every desire to gouge out their eyes for what their minds are surely doing to her body. Instinctively, I bring my arm around her, gritting my jaw at a man to her left who just looked at her ass.

"Did you have to wear jeans this tight?" I mutter close to her ear as we make it to the elevators.

"Oh, I'm sorry. I didn't realize I needed your permission on what I'm allowed to wear."

"You sure as fuck do when every man has his eyes on your gorgeous ass," I whisper. "I think you forgot who this ass…" I grab a handful. "…belongs to."

"My, my, Gio…" She marches into the elevator after a group of people shuffle out. "Are you jealous?" She pushes on the twelfth floor.

My pulse hammers as I catch that teasing sparkle in her eyes. And as soon as the elevators close, I'm on her in a flash, pushing her up against the wall, my fingers curling around her throat, the other palm cupping her pussy.

She grins, her eyes heavy-lidded. "If I didn't like being pinned to the wall by you so much, I'd have my knife at your throat already."

I chuckle, my lips hovering above hers. "Promises, promises."

My fingers climb to her waist and pop open the button of her jeans, my hand snaking inside, where she's warm and already slick.

"Fuck," she whispers on a groan. "What are you doing?"

"Reminding you who owns you."

I rough two digits past her panties, flicking her wet and warm clit.

"Oh my God," she rasps, her nails raking my back as the elevator dings past each floor.

I sink my fingers inside her, my lips dropping to her ear, sucking her lobe into my mouth.

"You can wear whatever you want, bambina, but it makes me murderous when another man looks at you like he wants to fuck you."

"No one has fucked me since you," she whimpers when I rub her with my thumb while sinking deeper into her cunt.

"I knew you were a good wife. I can't wait to be inside you again." My teeth graze her jaw, her pulse hammering beneath my fingertips.

"Stop calling me that," she challenges even as her eyes roll back.

"You're right. We haven't even gone on a honeymoon yet." My mouth trails down to her shoulder as I yank the blouse down to taste her skin. "I hear the Maldives are romantic."

"Oh my God. Stop talking," she cries on a breathy moan when I stroke her faster. "More… Please."

The elevator dings one final time before the doors open.

She gasps, trying to stop me from touching her, but I keep her where she is, looking over my shoulder at a pair of elderly women in pearls and black knee-length peacoats.

"This one is occupied," I growl.

Their eyes grow wide while I reach over and close the doors, then stop the elevator midflight. It jolts while her chest climbs with heavy inhales.

I tighten the clutch on her throat, stroking my lips with hers. "Please what, Red? Her Highness is going to have to beg for it."

"Bastard," she groans, attempting to ride my hand.

I slip my fingers out of her and pinch her clit, making her moan so damn loud, I'm sure those old ladies hear her.

"Please what?" I do it again, stroking her harder, and her mouth parts into a perfect O, a cry strangled in her throat.

"Please…fuck…" She throws her head back hard against the wall. "Please let me come!"

Two fingers ram inside her, my thumb back to swirling her clit. "Oh God, Gio!"

"That's right, you keep saying my name like that," I growl.

Her walls quiver around me while I bring her to the edge and take her off of it, over and over until her hands tremble, until the words coming out of her make no sense at all.

"Yes, yes…that's it," she cries, closing her eyes.

"Look at me," I demand. "I want you to know who's touching you. Who's making you feel this good."

She obeys, staring into my eyes as I increase my tempo, working harder, faster, until—

"Yes, Gio!" she screams out, and a smirk curves over my mouth knowing I just made my little Red scream my name twice.

Slowly, she climbs down from the high and lets out a woosh of an exhale while she buttons her jeans back up. "I don't know what that was, but you have my absolute permission to do that again."

I chuckle, unlocking the elevator and hitting our floor again. "Pretty sure I never asked for your permission in the first place."

"Asshole," she mutters, but there's a grin on her face that I put there.

The doors open, and I grab her hand in mine, strutting out together toward the room where Grant's men are holding our witness. I knock once, and a guy dressed in a short-sleeved black tee and black pants opens the door.

"He's inside." He motions with his head, extending the door all the way to allow us access.

I let Red move in first, following right behind her, seeing another two men with their arms crossed. An older one, maybe in his sixties, sits at a glass table, eating a bowl of ice cream as though he's never had any.

I greet the other men with a tilt of my chin, and it's a good thing neither makes any attempt to check out my Red, or it'd be a pain to explain to Grant why I killed his guys.

"I hear you've seen something," I tell the old man, dragging a chair for Red, which she takes, while I sink into my own beside her.

"Like I told your friend…" He wipes his mouth on the sleeve of a clean gray sweater, staining it brown. "I don't know how much help I'll be. It *has* been a long time."

There's a glint in his dark eyes, the wrinkles around them deepening. I bet he wants more money for talking. Grant was already paying him a fair sum.

"You know…" Iseult says, leaning toward him from across and picking up a fork from beside his bowl. She runs it across the table, slowly reaching the top of his hand. "There are always ways to convince someone to talk."

A callous expression crosses her face, and that has his eyes growing large. He drops his spoon, backing up into the chair, fear clouding his wild gaze.

"I don't want no trouble, ma'am. I was just trying to be a good Samaritan, offering to help when I saw those men questioning one of my friends about a murder. I was there. I saw things. Just don't know if it's what you folks be needing."

His thick gray brows bunch into one another as he shakes from fear.

"Now, honey, is that how we treat friends?" I say, taking the fork from her.

She pivots toward me. "I suppose you have a better idea?" She tilts a single brow.

"In fact, I do."

The corner of her mouth tips up just a little, and I suspect she doesn't mind playing a little good cop, bad cop.

Removing my wallet from my pocket, I open it up and take out a wad of cash, full of hundred-dollar bills. I place them before the man, who keeps staring at the money with an unblinking look, his mouth practically salivating.

"What's your name?" I ask him while he's unable to peel his eyes off the cash.

"Uh…I…Walter." He finally glances up.

"Well, Walter, being that you're such a good Samaritan, helping me find my friend's murderer, I say you deserve some more cash."

"Yeah, I, um…think that's fair." His hand trembles toward the money, but before he can touch it, I drop my palm over it and shove it back to my side.

"First, you're going to have to tell us in detail what you saw and heard."

"Yeah, 'course." He clears his throat. "So, as I said, it was late, and I was peeking out the window next to that club the young kids like to go to. I kinda like to see what's going on, so when I heard people arguing, I peeked out from the window and saw a man—maybe like your height, pretty big dude—dragging a girl."

My pulse turns erratic; I can practically taste it. "Go on."

"It was dark, so I couldn't make out faces, but the girl was either dead or drugged or something?"

Red shifts uncomfortably. "Where was this?"

"You know that place called The Bang Room? Right next to it."

"The Bang Room?" Her voice drops, the color draining from her face, but she quickly recovers, straightening her spine.

"What is it?" I ask, leaning in. "Do you know something?"

"Me?" Her face upturns with irritation. "How would I know something?"

"Never mind," I say, unable to take my eyes off how uneasy she suddenly becomes.

"What else?" I ask Walter, who scratches his shaggy white beard.

"So, while he was dragging the girl, another one came screaming. She kept telling him to let the girl go, that she was going to call her father and that he didn't want that. The man laughed and said he worked for some powerful people and that no one could save her friend. He told her to run before he took her too, but she wouldn't leave. She was a tough one."

"Fucking Christ," I mutter, not understanding any of this.

What the hell was Bryce doing? And what people could he have been working for? We would've known. There's no way he was keeping secrets from Grant and me. None of this is making sense.

"What else?" I ask. "Better be more if you want that money. And don't lie to me. I want the truth."

"No, sir." He shakes his head. "I don't lie." He nervously glances back at Red, who steels her gaze. "Um…s-so the man dropped the girl on the ground and went right at the other girl, like he was going to hit her. She told him to back away, that she was gonna shoot him if he didn't let them both go." He pinches his lips. "I have a daughter who's probably in college right now, and it made me think of her, ya know?"

He blinks back his emotions.

"Anyway, he laughed and said she probably didn't even have a gun. But then she reached into her purse and was pointing one at him. I saw it clear as day. The guy seemed afraid, holding out his hands and moving back. Told her to put it down before she got hurt." He pauses in between uneven inhales. "She told him to leave, but instead the idiot darted right at her, and when he did, she shot him. Just one bullet, and he was on the ground."

I curl a fist against the table, my pulse banging in my ears. How can I believe Bryce was trying to kidnap a woman, but how can I deny that he was doing something shady?

"After he was shot, the woman put her gun back and ran toward her friend," he goes on. "Dragged her against a brick wall by a large trash can. She sat there with her for a while until other people showed up."

"What people?" I growl.

He takes a long pause, his gaze bouncing between Iseult and me. "Maybe fifteen minutes later, a man showed up. A scary man. The girl called him Devlin, I think."

Red sucks in an audible breath, circling her index finger on the table. She's either nervous or upset. I can't tell yet.

"You definitely heard that name? Are you sure it wasn't Donny?"

"Absolutely. Because I remember thinking I never met a Devlin before."

"What did he look like?" I ask.

"His hair was kinda long for a guy, and his voice was cold when he told the girls to come with him, and he was tall like the dead guy was."

Donny had long hair too. Definitely not a fucking coincidence.

"Did the women go with him?"

"Yeah. He took the girls with him. That's all I know."

I hand him the cash.

"May I go now?" he asks.

I look up to the men behind him and gesture with my head to take him out of here.

"Let's go," one tells him.

He quickly takes another two spoonfuls of his ice cream, finishing it all, before he gets up and scurries out of the hotel room.

Once he's gone, I look over at Red, but her eyes are cast in the distance, as though she's not even here anymore.

And I wonder why.

ISEULT

This is bad. So fucking bad.

"God damn it!" I slam a fist onto the wheel of my car, speeding back home.

As soon as I found out who Gio's friend was, my body grew ice cold. I wanted to run. But I couldn't. I had to sit there and pretend I wasn't dying inside. Dying because the man I've been sleeping with is friends with the enemy.

I know exactly the kind of man Bryce was and what he wanted to do that night.

And now Gio will find out everything. It's only a matter of time. He heard Devlin's name. He's going to piece it all together, and I can't let that happen. He can't find out.

When Gio was talking to Grant and mentioned a Bryce, I didn't think it was *that* Bryce. But once I heard Walter describe what he saw and the name of the club, I knew. I tried to deny it at first, but I knew as soon as I heard that bastard's name.

What are the chances?

Does Gio know what Bryce was into? Is he involved too? If he is, I can't let Eriu marry him.

And you can't let yourself continue to fall for him either.

Did I read him wrong? Did I develop feelings for a man who would do the kinds of things Bryce did?

No, I refuse to believe that. He can't be. But then again, he *is* in the Mafia, and I know the kinds of things the Cosa Nostra have their hands in.

Finally getting home, I pull into my driveway, just sitting there—confused, pissed. How will I ever face Gio again and pretend everything is okay? I don't do fake with the people in my life. If I'm angry, you sure as hell will know about it.

But this is different.

This isn't just about me.

This is about all of us.

Twenty-Nine

GIO

With my face in my palms, I replay yesterday over and over, seeing Red's reaction to what we were being told about Bryce.

I didn't want to see it then.

I didn't want to believe that she could possibly be involved.

But what if she is?

I caught tension in her body and the way her entire face turned hard the more that man told us. But how the hell would she know Bryce? Were they involved somehow?

Fuck!

I can't ask her either. She'll deny it. I know her well enough to know that.

I have to figure out a way to find out who was with Bryce that night. If only I could find Donny and beat it out of him.

"Who's the lucky girl?" my mother asks as I wait for Michael in his den.

He's on a business call, and after that, he needs me and Raph to discuss expansion of our properties overseas.

But I need our meeting to end quickly, because I have plans today and they involve Konstantin Marinov. I'll be paying the oldest Marinov a visit. And he will tell me where his father is, even if I have to bleed it out of him.

Faintly, I look up at Ma. "What are you talking about?"

"Well, you look like you haven't slept for a week, and your whole face looks tense." There's a knowing glint in her gaze as she takes a seat beside me, gently laying her palm on my shoulder. "And there's only one thing that'd make a man look that way." Her mouth quirks up. "A woman."

I give her a long look.

"So, what's her name, Gio?"

I scrub a hand down my face. "Ma, you're with Patrick now. We can't be discussing this."

She scoffs. "I don't care who I'm with. You're still my son, and your happiness matters to me a great deal. So, if there's someone other than Eriu, then I want to know about it."

"What difference would it make anyway? She doesn't even want to try."

"And who is *she*?"

My jaw grows tight, looking at her while I consider telling her what's been going on. Maybe she can talk to Patrick for us and make this shit with Eriu go away.

Fuck no. That's a bad idea.

If Iseult finds out Mom talked to him, I'm going to lose Red for good. She has to be the one to tell him, and it has to be before he publicly announces my wedding to her sister. And since I won't actually be at my own wedding, Patrick will be pissed either way.

May as well piss him off sooner than later.

"You can't tell Patrick any of this, Ma." I look her square in the eyes. "I mean that. If you can't keep secrets from him, I understand. But then I can't tell you."

"He doesn't have to know if it doesn't directly involve him," she counters. "So tell me, because now I'm starting to worry."

"I have feelings for Iseult."

Her brows shoot up. "Well, that's a plot twist I did *not* see coming."

I chuckle dryly at her amused expression, groaning as I cover my face with a hand. "It's not funny, Ma."

"Well…it's a little funny."

I shake my head as I level a gaze at her. "I don't know what to do, and now I think she may be involved in something else that may mess things up even more for us."

"Listen," she says. "Do you have that feeling in your heart that's telling you she's worth it? Worth pissing off Patrick? Worth angering the world just so you two can be together?"

I nod.

"Then there's your answer." She smiles. "Go ahead and burn the world to the ground, my boy, because sometimes that's the only way to fight for what you want."

"Are you advocating that I piss off your boyfriend?"

She grimaces. "Eh, why does that word sound so vile at my age?"

My shoulders rock with laughter. "What the hell do you want me to call him? Your baby daddy?"

"That's even worse." She whacks me on the back of my head, but she's grinning.

"I'm sorry, Ma. I'm just kidding."

"I know, sweetheart." She sighs. "I want you boys to have

better than I did. I was never in love with your father, and both you and Eriu deserve better than that. So if you want me to talk to Patrick, I will. Though that man…" She shakes her head and widens her eyes. "Stubborn then, and even more stubborn now."

"No, don't say anything. Iseult needs to be the one to tell him."

"You're right. But you'd better convince her to do it soon before he finds out on his own."

That's what I'm afraid of.

A little while later, once Mom's busy in Michael's kitchen, Sophia's staring inquisitively at me. Her big brown eyes twinkle as she twirls a makeup brush in her hand, me her latest victim. This kid loves makeup. I think she gets a new set every few months from someone in the family. There hasn't been a person in this household whose makeup she hasn't done once in their life.

"I think I need more color on my cheeks," I tell her while she narrows her very serious expression, like she's examining a science project.

"I think you're right, Uncle Gio." She nods real slow. "You're too pale. And maybe more lipstick too. Red looks good on you."

She sure as fuck does…

She giggles when I wag my brows, her large Bambi eyes shimmering while she dips her fluffy brush in her pink powder.

She returns to dabbing my cheeks with precision. I'd be surprised if twenty years from now she wasn't some famous makeup artist.

"She likes you," she throws out nonchalantly, and I instantly sit straighter.

"Who?"

"Iseult." She lays the brush down on the coffee table and picks up the eyeshadow, rubbing some purple on my eyelid.

"And how do you know?"

"Well…" Another dab. "When she danced with me and Elsie a few days ago, she was acting like she doesn't have a crush on you, but I could see she was just shy, kind of like when I get shy when Connor says hi to me in class."

More eyeshadow hits my other eye, but I have completely tuned out that she's making me look like a clown.

"She danced with you?"

"Yep!" A big toothy grin appears. "She didn't want to at first, but then I made her, and we all had *so* much fun."

"You did?"

"We did." She nods, her forehead scrunched as those thick brows rise to her hairline. "She's pretty, Uncle Gio." Her lips twine up. "You should marry her."

"Don't tell anyone," I whisper, leaning in closer, and she concentrates all her attention on me. "But that's what I'm trying to do."

"Really?" She grows all giddy.

"Yeah." I give her a secret wink.

If the woman doesn't kill me first, that is.

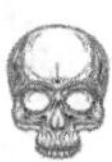

"If you think I'd allow you to go and confront the Russians, you're out of your goddamn mind!" Michael's fist slams on his desk. "You don't think we've had enough fighting with our father and the Irish? And now, when things are actually good, you want to bring the fucking Russians to our doorstep?"

Yeah, I mean, I figured he wouldn't be *too* thrilled to learn what I was planning to do. I didn't exactly mean to tell my brothers, but sometimes I get too worked up and can't keep my mouth shut.

But when Michael questioned why I was in such a hurry to end our meeting, I blurted it out like an idiot.

Which led to me telling Raph and Michael that Sergey had hurt Iseult and that I needed to find him to make him pay. I didn't give them details—that's not their business—but it was enough for them to know he harmed her.

In our world, if someone hurts the ones we care about, especially our women, then there's no conversation unless it's done with weapons or our fists.

And Red is every bit mine.

"Listen to me, Michael." I get to my feet and drop my palms across the edge of his cherrywood desk. "If you think I'd sit idly by after finding out someone hurt her and is still alive to tell about it, then you don't know me."

"That's the problem," he snickers. "I know you too well. You'd have shown up unannounced and gotten your head blown off. And if I send the men with you, Konstantin will take it as a show of force, and then we will have to go to war."

"So what do you fucking suggest I do?" I glare with indignation.

"I'll go with him," Raph offers.

I turn to my left to find his stare filled with understanding.

"Call Konstantin," he tells Michael. "Tell him we'll be arriving today to have a sit-down."

"And if he turns it down?" I challenge.

"He won't." Michael blows out a breath. "He knows keeping things peaceful between us is wise. He isn't his father. He's much smarter than that. But going there is still dangerous. And the way you planned to show up…" He shakes his head. "I swear, if you weren't my brother, I'd have killed you by now for your recklessness."

I admit my plan wasn't very thought out. I was going to drive up to his complex and shoot my way through if he refused to see me.

I chuckle. "It's a good thing we're family, then." I step back and head for the leather sofa, settling into it. "Call the son of a bitch. The drive to Jersey is probably going to be a pain, so I want to head out there ASAP."

He removes his cell from his pocket and looks pointedly at me. "You know you'll probably get us into war with the Irish and the Russians, right?"

"I'll find a way," I tell him. "Patrick will let me marry Iseult instead."

"Or he'll kill you." Raph shrugs, chuckling.

"He might." I smirk. "Would be worth it, though." I extend both arms across the back of the sofa. "At least Iseult will finally realize I'd rather die than marry anyone else."

"Jesus fucking Christ," Michael grumbles, staring at the ceiling and shaking his head before he stares my way again. "If Konstantin tells you he doesn't know where his father is, you leave it at that. Do you understand me?"

I mutter a response, which almost sounds like, "Okay."

He grits his teeth.

"You have my permission to shoot him in the leg if he acts out of hand," he tells Raph.

With one look at me, Raph laughs. "Don't worry, I'll make sure he behaves himself."

Michael glares at me, because he knows me well enough to know I won't.

Thirty

GIO

We drive up a private double road, both sides lined up by tall trees, obscuring the view beyond them. Konstantin lives on acres of empty land, the entire complex like a fortress.

Can't say I've ever had the displeasure of meeting Konstantin in his home. It's usually at one of their strip clubs or one of their underground mixed martial arts fights, both of which help launder their money.

But the Bratva also have their hands in narcotics, and that has made them filthy rich. They have a solid system. They supply arms and ammunition to drug traffickers in places like Colombia, who then give them cocaine to sell across many parts of Europe.

The Russians are fucking ruthless. It's kinda why I've always liked them, yet hated them at the same time.

Raph turns on a curved road that leads to a tall iron fence, with two men on each side, their rifles across their black hoodies.

"What is your business here?" one asks in a thick Russian accent.

"Giovanni and Raphael Marino," my brother offers. "Konstantin is expecting us."

The other takes out a phone and presses a few keys, his almost black eyes narrowed as he puts the phone to his ear.

"Oni zdes." He pauses, staring at us with a cold demeanor. "Khorosho."

Seconds later, the gate slowly parts on a squeak, and then we're driving through it, past another long road that ends with a monstrosity for a house, spread across acres of green.

Tall white columns sculpted into angels wait for us on each end of the entrance door. Another armed soldier is there too, but there are definitely more around; we just can't see them.

Raph parks his car next to the three sports coupes, and we get out. As we shuffle toward the cobblestone steps, Raph clasps my shoulder, halting me.

"Let me do the talking," he says.

And with one look into my unwavering expression, he shakes his head. Because of course that isn't going to happen.

She's mine. They hurt her. So I'm the one who'll talk. And being the Pakhan now, Konstantin is the one I have to speak to.

The double brown doors open and two men appear, dressed similarly to the ones at the gate. They approach us and start patting us down. When one tries to take the gun at my waist, I push him off.

"The guns stay."

"If you keep guns, you can go." He glares while I clench my teeth.

"Fucking bastards," I grit, letting him take all three weapons, while the other asshole takes my brother's.

"Let's go," they tell us.

We follow them into the foyer with its white marble flooring. My eyes land on the spiral staircases while a gaudy crystal chandelier hangs above a cathedral ceiling.

"This way."

The men lead us left to a large sitting room with a fireplace at the far end wall and two ivory sofas with a gold glass table in the center of it. Konstantin is already there, sitting back, a glass of clear liquid in his right hand.

"Gentlemen, welcome to my home." He places his drink down on an end table. "Have a seat. May I offer you some beverages? Tea? Coffee? Vodka or cognac perhaps?"

"None for me," Raph says, taking a seat opposite him. "Thanks."

"And for you, Giovanni?" His mouth twists into a smile, while his dark dirt-colored eyes glare, and I instantly want to kill him.

"I'll take a whiskey neat."

He turns toward one of the men and lifts a single thick brow. "Bring us the Macallan 1926."

The guy goes off behind Konstantin and opens the cabinet behind the bar. He brings over the most expensive fucking whiskey bottle ever sold. Almost two million. And I know he's doing this on purpose.

His eyes go to mine as he's handed the opened bottle, two glasses placed before him.

"Since we are friends, I'd like to offer you my finest bottle. I won it at an auction, and what better way to open it than with friends?"

He leans forward, pouring some for me and for himself, then picks up my glass and extends his hand toward me.

I take it from him, needing to get this bullshit over with so we can talk. But before I can bring the liquor to my mouth, he reaches his glass for mine.

"Boodym zdarovy," he says, lightly clanking my glass to his, then drains his drink.

I tip the liquid down my throat and, fuck, does it taste like the best whiskey I've ever had in my life.

"Good, yes?" He slams it on the table and leans back. "So, what can I do for you, gentlemen? Your brother said it was important."

"I need to know where your father is." I cock my head, my tone seething.

"A man who doesn't bullshit. I like you." Konstantin's mouth tips up at one corner. "But I'm afraid I don't know where my father is."

"Cut the shit. I know you know where that piece of shit is."

His eyes narrow and a hand balls at his side before the smile returns to his face, a cunning smile.

"I welcome you into my home, give you my finest bottle, and you disrespect me by speaking to me like that?" His nostrils flare. "I may like your brother, Michael, and I respect him and our mutually beneficial friendship, but don't for one second think you can speak to me like that in my own house."

"Your father…" I inhale a shallow breath, feeling Raph's eyes burning a hole into my temple, but I don't give a fuck. "Your father hurt someone I care about. You may know her name. Iseult, Patrick Quinn's daughter."

"Ahhh…" He inclines his chin and nods slowly. "It is most unfortunate what happened to her."

"You mean what your father did to her and her mother."

"Yes." He pauses, leaning back into the leather sofa with outstretched arms. "And I will tell you right now I did not approve of what he did. That was squarely on his shoulders."

"And that somehow absolves you?"

"Perhaps not." He flips a hand in the air. "But I do not know where he is. Last we heard, he ran to Russia after what happened with the girl. That was, what? Almost eleven years ago?" He considers cooly. "He's probably dead."

"Well, I'd like a confirmation."

"Would you like me to take you to Russia on one of my jets?" His shoulders rock with a laugh.

"We have our own jets," I counter, grinding my molars.

Fucking wish I could kill him.

"Yes. Maybe." He smirks. "But yours won't get you into the country. Mine will."

"Just tell me where in Russia he was last seen."

"You'll never find him, my friend, because even I cannot. And believe me, we have looked. If I had found him, he'd already be dead." A line creases between his brows. "What he did to that girl is—"

"What he did to *my* woman," I clarify, dropping my elbows onto my knees and leaning in.

Raph places a palm on my back to steady the rage that zaps through me like lava, splintering through my bones.

"I can see you're upset, and in your predicament, I would be as well," he goes on. "But I can assure you, if he's alive, he's somewhere no one can find." He shrugs. "Probably in some small village, hiding out like a rat. Just imagine he's dead. It's what I do."

"Unlike you, I can't do that," I strain through a tense jaw. "If there's a chance he's still out there breathing the same air she does, then I *will* kill him."

"On kak sobaka," one of the men behind him laughs. "Ruff, ruff."

I jump to my feet, my nostrils flaring, marching around the sofa toward the prick. "What did he just say?"

Raph follows suit.

"Relax," he whispers in my ear.

"Now, now." Konstantin lifts a hand, while my eyes zero in on the asshole who definitely just insulted me. "Our friend is just very loyal to those he loves," he tells his men, tilting his head backward with a stern look that gets the guy to instantly stop grinning. "Sit, please." He gestures to me with a quick jerk of his fingers. "I can see this is a very difficult subject for you. You care deeply for this woman, and I sympathize. I do. But I cannot help you, I'm afraid. Though I wish I could."

Fuck! How the hell will I find Sergey without this bastard's help?

"I understand why you want to locate him, but he isn't someone you'll find. It's as simple as that. When he wants to lie low, he knows how to." His expression sobers as he sighs heavily. "My father still has many loyal connections back in Russia who'd do anything for him."

He rises to his feet and starts toward the exit, indicating we're not welcome anymore.

"Even the police there haven't been able to find him for me. Believe me, I want his blood just as badly as you do."

We shuffle out toward the foyer after him.

"He has burned too many bridges for the family," he goes on. "And my brothers and I have no loyalty to extend to him anymore."

One of Konstantin's men opens the front door.

"It was a pleasure to see you both. Please come back anytime."

Then he closes the door in our faces.

Asshole.

Thirty-One

ISEULT

It's been days since I've seen him. Days since we spoke. He's texted, though, acting like his usual self, which I hope means he doesn't suspect that I know something about Bryce.

I've wanted to ask him if he knew what kind of man he was friends with, to tell him I was involved. Because if he were to find out I knew things and kept it from him on purpose, there's a good chance he'd stop talking to me.

And in the end, that's what I want, isn't it? To come to terms with the fact that I can't have him. No matter how badly I want to.

I came close to telling my father, but I chickened out.

I've never been afraid of a single thing as much as I'm afraid of losing my family and my work. My father will never forgive me for this. He won't accept that I've been having an affair with Gio. It's what he'd call it. In his eyes, an engagement would be just as bad as a marriage.

I'll lose everything.

But can I live with losing Gio? Could I walk through a life where he isn't mine?

Tomorrow, I'll have to come face-to-face with him at a dinner hosted by Michael and Elsie. All of us have been invited. So I'll have to sit there and act as though staring into his eyes doesn't unravel me. Doesn't make me feel like I'm wanted and free for the first time.

He's seen my body. Seen the scars that I've loathed since they've been imprinted on my skin. I've spent years hiding them, hating myself. But he touched and he kissed every single one and he told me I was beautiful. And that meant more than he'll ever realize.

There was this one time some asshole I was hooking up with yanked the zipper of my dress down before I could stop him…and he gasped. Asked what happened, then pretended he had a meeting to go to and I never saw him again.

He didn't mean a damn thing to me, but the rejection… It hurt, more than I care to admit. I felt ugly. I *was* ugly. No matter how pretty my face was, my body was marred.

And when Gio walked into that bathroom and saw me, that fear, that rejection—it came back. I thought he'd run. I thought he'd be like that other man.

But…he was Gio.

He didn't run.

He didn't turn away.

He stayed.

And he held me while I did something I never do: cry.

Staring at the cell in my hand, I find another text from him, and it immediately puts a smile on my face.

FUTURE HUSBAND

Don't wear panties tomorrow.

ISEULT

I'll make sure to wear two.

FUTURE HUSBAND

Try it, bambina. I'll rip them off of you and stuff them in your pretty mouth so no one hears you scream my name while I'm fucking you.

My toes curl at those dirty words, my body warming and tingling for more.

ISEULT

You wouldn't dare with my family there.

FUTURE HUSBAND

Of course I would. And if I were you, I'd wear a dress.

ISEULT

I'll wear the tightest jeans.

FUTURE HUSBAND

You're only making it harder on yourself, baby. Because I will make you come with everyone seated at the table, you next to me, my fingers stroking your clit while they're all oblivious, not knowing what a dirty whore you are for me.

Fuck. My cheeks flush, the hunger for him unsated.

Why the hell is he so far away? I'd have driven to his place right now and let him do whatever he wanted to me. And I definitely wouldn't be wearing panties.

ISEULT

You better not do that. We'll get caught, and then I'll kill you.

FUTURE HUSBAND

Think you can keep quiet the whole time I finger-fuck you? I can't wait to watch you try.

ISEULT

I'm going now.

To take a cold shower.

FUTURE HUSBAND

Can't wait until you're mine, Iseult Marino. Damn, does that sound good together.

ISEULT

Who said I'd ever take your name?

FUTURE HUSBAND

You will take my name. You'll take everything I own. My body. My possessions. My heart. They're all going to be yours. It's only a matter of time.

ISEULT

In your dreams, Gio.

FUTURE HUSBAND

In my dreams, you're already mine.

Stepping through Michael's door, we immediately hear voices and Sophia's giggles rising from the near distance.

Fernanda's heels click closer until she's walking into the foyer with a huge grin, her hair perfectly framed around her face.

"I'm so glad you could all make it," she says as she embraces my father.

I don't think I'll ever get used to him hugging another woman the way he's hugging her.

"Hello, darling," he tells her, and her face beams.

And though I'm still angry that my mother was never the object of all his love, I can't hate this woman. She's not a bad person. In fact, every time I've been around her, she's been nothing but kind. And the worst thing is, I think my mom would've liked her.

She quickly separates from him and strides over to Eriu. It's the first time they've met, and Eriu does know the status of our father's and her relationship.

"It's such a pleasure to meet you." She gives Eriu a gentle hug, and my sister smiles at her as they part.

"You too, Mrs. Marino."

"Oh, please call me Fernanda, will you?"

"I can do that." My sister removes her black peacoat.

And that's when Gio strides into the foyer, both hands in the pockets of his black trousers. A baby-blue dress shirt with a single button popped open is perfectly sculpted around his muscular frame, his biceps jutting out.

My God, I want my hands on them. What have I become?

His eyes rove down my body, as though already ripping off the black dress that hits right above my knees.

A slow crawl of his mouth has the breaths in my lungs gasping for air, my stomach rolling with the kind of need that would have me begging for relief if we were alone.

"Look who's here," Mom tells him, staring at me, then my sister.

My brows furrow as I glare at Gio with a tight expression. Does she know? Did the idiot tell another person we're…fooling around?

I don't even know what we are.

A fling? A disaster?

Or is he right? Could there really be a future for us?

"Hello." His eyes are on mine, and I couldn't look away even if I had a knife to my throat.

This is why being around him is dangerous. I can't handle my emotions when he's this close. And right now, with those eyes gazing at me like I'm the only one in the room, all I want to do is take his hand and let him kiss me right in front of everyone. To tell them we're together. But not everyone gets what they want. Least of all me.

Slowly, he steps toward me, fingers gently brushing across my back, and I don't even flinch. His arms circle around me as though in a normal greeting while soft lips discreetly graze my cheek.

"You're fucking beautiful," he rasps under his breath, and desire stirs in my gut, my arms breaking with a shiver.

He pulls back, walking over to my sister as though he didn't just make me die a little inside. He gives her a quick hug, then shakes my father's hand and greets my brothers with a quick jerk of his head.

I don't miss the clenching of Tynan's jaw as something passes between them.

"Let's head into the dining room," Fernanda adds. "Everyone else is already there."

My father drapes an arm around her shoulders, tugging her closer as they lead the way. I allow everyone else to go before me. Everyone except Gio, who nonchalantly locks the door and sidles up beside me.

"You shouldn't be here," I whisper, avoiding eye contact as we march right past the large kitchen.

He ignores me, his hand snaking out for my ass, squeezing it before crawling it up my hip.

"Good fucking girl," he breathes. "No panties."

Before I can say something snarky, we're in a dining room with a black table that can seat sixteen.

"Fionn!" Sophia yelps, jumping from her seat and running up to him.

My brother immediately picks her up in his arms and spins her.

"Hey, little miss. How are you doin'?"

"I'm good." She tilts her head and grins. "Do you want to sit next to me?"

"I thought you'd never ask." Fionn laughs, placing her back on her feet.

She grabs his hand and leads the way. Michael chuckles, kissing the top of Elsie's head before they climb to their feet and Elsie wanders over to me.

"I love that dress," she murmurs. "And I think someone else does too."

She gives me a knowing look, glancing to her left. And when I follow her line of vision, I find Gio there, staring at me.

I grab her wrist and pull her nearer. "You're a bad influence."

"I like you two together," she tells me. "And I don't think it's right that you can't be with whoever you want."

"It's not how it works in our families," I stress under my breath.

"Well, maybe it's time you changed that."

She squeezes my fingers and walks over to my brothers, while I'm left not knowing how to respond to that.

Everyone takes their seat, Eriu settling into one beside Gio. And when I try to get away, he discreetly grabs my wrist and tightens his grasp, as though daring me to sit anywhere but beside him.

He extends the chair for me. And with a frustrated scowl, I lower into it, right next to the man who makes every cell in my body tingle with pure unease.

Everyone begins to eat, my father thanking Elsie for the beautiful meal she has prepared.

"So, Eriu," Fernanda asks, passing my father a platter of clams. "What are you going to college for?"

"I want to be a vet," she says with a shy smile, taking a sip of her water while I bring my glass of red wine to my lips.

"Wow, that is wonderful."

Gio's hand clasps around my upper thigh, while he eats with his other. I glance at him from the corner of my eye, but he definitely doesn't appear like a man who's currently dragging up my dress, thick, masculine fingers sliding up my inner thigh.

He pops a piece of sausage into his mouth.

"And you, Iseult?" Fernanda turns her attention to me. "What do you do?"

I shift uncomfortably just as he runs a single finger between my slit.

Oh. Fuck.

"U-um…" I stammer, my hand trembling around my wineglass when he brushes his thumb over my clit.

My brother Cillian chuckles, and Fernanda gives him a curious look.

"Did I somehow put a foot in my mouth?" Her cheeks redden, and my father drops his face to her ear and whispers.

Her eyes grow as they hold mine for a moment, her mouth parting as what I assume is the shock of my real contribution to the world finally sinks in.

"Well…" She fixes the collar of her maroon blouse. "I definitely didn't expect that. But good for you." She pauses, her eyes flicking to Gio. "I can see why, umm…"

"Why what, sweetheart?" my father asks while Gio gently strokes me between my legs, like he's warming me up.

"Uh…" Fernanda's face tenses and she forces a laugh. "Why she's got such a strong personality."

Yeah, this is going quite well.

"She sure has that." My father reaches for the pasta and adds a hefty amount to his plate.

The conversation flows, and I try to force the penne a la vodka down my throat, but Gio's fingers languidly slink inside me while another rolls around my clit.

The air stills in my lungs, my fingers squeezing against his powerful forearm.

This is how I die, isn't it? This is how it all ends. At his mercy, succumbing to an orgasmic obliteration.

I bite down on my inner cheek to stop myself from moaning or jumping off the seat. He continues to torture me, rubbing me in slow, agonizing circles. And though I try to force my thighs closed, he's too strong, pushing himself further inside me, two fingers sinking inch by breathtaking inch until his last knuckle.

"So, Gio," my father says. "I did want to discuss my expectation of your marriage to my daughter."

He hits Gio with a hardened stare while I clear my throat, cupping my mouth to stop from screaming in undulated pleasure.

The bastard lets a little smirk slip while he curves those devilish fingers inside me, rubbing me with renewed fervor.

"Of course. What would you like to discuss?"

Gio thrusts deeper and harder, not allowing me a second to compose myself. I grasp the edge of the table and squeeze until my palm aches.

My body heats up, sparks igniting in my core, shooting out to my toes.

I'm so close…

Oh my God…

This can't be happening in front of everyone.

My shaky fist slams against the table, so loudly that my glass of wine almost tips over.

All eyes go to me, and I breathe out, "Sorry," sounding like I'm going to be sick.

If I could just grab the nearest knife and stab him with it, that'd be fan-fucking-tastic.

It's a good thing Sophia is the one seated beside me, because I think anyone else would've noticed. And I'm really thankful for the long tablecloth hiding the dirty things his hand is doing.

My clit pulses, my core growing slicker the more he touches me.

Fuck. I can't seem to breathe.

"As I was saying…" my father continues. "I have heard the rumors about you." He gives Gio a knowing glare that I'm barely paying attention to. "I expect you to be faithful to my daughter. Will that be a problem?"

"Not at all."

Gio pumps his fingers all the way inside, then back out, driving me to near desperation. I writhe and wiggle, while he works me to delirium.

I gasp back a sharp inhale, fighting the quivers overtaking my entire body.

"I plan to take my vows *very* seriously," he promises, and from the corner of my eye, I find his lips shudder.

"Well, that is good to hear. I hope that is a promise."

"It is. I always keep my promises."

Thrust.

"I can't wait to marry your daughter."

He rubs my clit faster, and my heart rate spikes to a violent pace.

"I'm glad to hear it." My father picks up his scotch and takes a sip.

The chatter picks up, Elsie talking to Nicolette, my brothers speaking to Michael, while the man beside me brings me to the edge, then back from it, torturing me to never-ending heights, like he's daring me to scream out his name in front of everyone.

The faster he moves, the more my eyes start to roll. I drop an elbow to the table, squeezing my eyes with two fingers, almost there. Almost—

"Oh my God!" I gasp as the most intense orgasm bursts through me, wave after wave of pleasure.

Everyone instantly stops talking.

Their eyes on me.

Shit.

My stomach dips, my nipples straining against my tight dress.

"Are you okay, darling?" Fernanda asks. "Is the food not agreeing with you?"

"N-no." I drag Gio's hand out from between my thighs. "It's f—"

"I, for one, think the sausage is amazing," Gio offers, popping the fingers that were just inside me into his mouth and gives me a salacious smirk. "Don't you think, Iseult?"

"Yucky, Uncle Gio." Sophia giggles. "Don't suck your fingers."

"I'm sorry, but I just couldn't help myself." His eyes sear into mine. "I'm a man who enjoys delicious things."

My walls clench.

I hate him.

My cheeks heat up while I pour myself some water, swallowing every last drop.

I can't believe I just came in front of my entire family.

"Well, boys, Fernanda and I are getting married next week," my father suddenly announces after dessert.

They're what?!

My pulse slams like a pummeling fist across my throat. He can't remarry. He can't just erase my mother like that.

I mutter a curse under my breath, while Gio's eyes go to me from across the den.

"What? Are you serious?" Michael asks, looking as dumbfounded as everyone else.

I mean, they only *just* started up again. What's the hurry? Then again, I guess when you're older, the clock runs differently.

"I love your mother," he tells Michael. "Always will."

He stares at her like he's the moon revolving around her sun, and all I want is to be gone from here so I don't have to see any of this. I should've skipped out after dinner like I had intended, but my father wouldn't allow me to leave and go to my apartment.

"I lost her once," he tells us all, his eyes warm. "And I'll never do that again. So if you have a problem with that, Michael, then we will have another reason for war."

I know I should be happy for him. But I'm not.

"I don't—" Michael tries to say.

"Pat, No." Fernanda frowns, shaking her head. "No one will be fighting. You got it, boys?" She tosses both Patrick and Michael a stern look. "I'm a grown woman, and this is my choice."

"Can you two let me finish?" Michael goes on. "I have no problems with you two getting married. In fact, if you two do get married, then would it be necessary for Gio and Eriu to do the same?"

My eyes widen.

Maybe my father will listen to Michael. Maybe there's a chance Eriu won't have to go through with this. I squeeze her hand beside me on the sofa, and she returns it.

It's then that I cast Gio a look. I don't even know what it says, but his mouth curls just slightly, and I wonder if I could ever truly marry him.

It's what my father wants: a marriage alliance. And I am his daughter too. But an alliance means kids, a family. Am I even built for that? I'm not my mother. I'm not kind. Or affectionate. I don't have what it takes to be a mother. Eriu does. Eriu is every bit our mom.

My father chuckles coldly. "Clever. But…our deal stands, Michael. I don't want to speak of such topics when I have just announced my upcoming nuptials. But…" He inhales sharply. "My nephew is still dead. And this is part of the price your family must pay to secure our future bloodline. It's not negotiable."

Anger curls in my gut, and I rise to my feet, excusing myself to the ladies' room. My feet are moving faster, my lungs releasing a heavy breath while I rush down a long corridor leading God knows where.

But I don't care. I just need to be far away from everyone, and far away from *him*. I find the nearest wall and throw my head back, shutting my eyes, not knowing what I want.

Except I do. And it scares me. Irrevocably terrifies me to want him the way I do.

Iseult Marino.

It did sound good. Too good.

The way he holds me. The way he kisses me. Touches me. It's not just physical. It's deeper. And that's the worst thing of all.

"What are you doing here?" The possessive rumble of his voice has my chest heaving, wanting his hand around my throat, his mouth on my lips.

"Leave," I whisper.

But he only moves closer, and my heart? It beats, over and over like the pounding of hail against the windowsill.

"I asked you a question, Red." Only a few feet remain between us.

"And I chose not to answer." I take in his rugged masculinity, a few strands of his hair falling across his forehead in the most alluring way.

Those eyes…they drink me in, like I'm the taste of whiskey he so desperately craves.

"Does it make you crazy to imagine me fucking your sister? Being inside her?" He's in front of me now, gripping my jaw while his teeth grit. "Because it makes me homicidal to imagine you with someone else."

He drops his mouth nearer, lips stroking mine with a low growl. He looks both ways as he opens the door behind me, and with a quick pull, he drags us inside.

With both palms around my hips, he throws me up against a pool table, his eyes aligned with mine, his brows snapping tightly. "We can tell him tonight. We can tell your father we want to be together."

"Are you insane?" A nasty laugh rolls out of me. "First of all, I never said I wanted to be with you. This is just sex!"

Lies. Awful lies. Because I want him. I want him so badly. And I hate that I do.

He groans with a deepening of his voice. "You fucking liar. I don't know why you're denying this, but I won't let you."

"Oh, yeah? And what are you going to do about it?"

With a low, raspy chuckle, his hand wraps around my throat, fingers biting deeper. He pushes my body across the pool table, forcing his chest into mine. His hard muscles pin against my body, until he's molded across every inch of my heady flesh.

My pulsing need for him spirals until I grow dizzy with lust.

"He will disown me." My voice falls. "I can't tell him."

"We can try." He pins his forehead to mine. "I want you, Red. I'm not willing to let you go."

The deep baritone of his voice swells through the room and into my heart. No one has ever wanted to fight for me before.

"You don't understand," I try to explain for what feels like the hundredth time. "My father doesn't tolerate disrespect, and doing what we've been doing, it's disrespect to the family. He'll throw me out of the academy and out of this family." I release a ragged sigh. "I'll have nothing, Gio."

He stares at me with understanding, pitching back a drop. I force my eyes shut, knowing there's no way to get out of the hole we made. I have to find a way to end it, as much as it kills me. Between my father and the thing with Bryce, it's for the best. We were always meant to be temporary.

"Go!" I shove at his chest. "Leave me alone. You don't mean a goddamn thing to me, do you understand?"

But he doesn't move. He doesn't so much as breathe. He stands there like a statue, his eyes fastened to mine, tearing me from the only things I once thought I needed: my job, my family. But now? I need him too.

He shakes his head, his chest rising and falling with taunting breaths.

"Be with her!" I push him off once more. "Be with my sister. It's what you have to do."

"I'd rather die." His fingers snap tighter around my throat, refusing to let go.

"Now you're being dramatic." My words fill with emotion. I despise it, yet I can't help it.

"Wanna see dramatic?" His lips stroke the corner of my mouth.

And before I can do a thing about it, he kisses me, soft, yet with a passion rivaling madness. Like a beautiful melody that beats and forces you to listen.

And with every brush of his lips, it's as though he's saying, *I want you, and this is how much.*

His fingers twine into my hair, mine scratching up his back, wanting to feel his warm skin against my flesh.

"You're mine, Iseult," he reminds me, his lips glistening as he returns to ravaging my mouth.

He sucks my tongue, rolling his hips into me while this insatiable need curls inside my core.

But a sudden, loud knock has us both jumping upright, our eyes scanning the outside of the glass door.

"I'm leaving." I quickly fix the hem of my dress and rush for the door, not sure where else I have left to go.

Thirty-Two

GIO
ONE WEEK LATER

Can't believe Ma's officially married. But I'm happy for her. She always deserved more than my father ever gave her.

She planned the wedding to Patrick quickly, but my mother is the queen of party planning, so none of us were surprised when she told us when it would be.

I think she wanted to start a life with Patrick as soon as possible, something she never got the chance to do when she was younger. And now that our father is dead, she can have the kind of life she always wanted.

From across the dance floor, I watch Red with Sophia, twirling while holding hands under the tent on Michael's estate. She's laughing with my six-year-old niece like she's already part of our family. And if I have anything to say about it, she will be soon. I just need to convince her to talk to her father before I do it myself.

She's managed to evade me since the incident at Michael's a week ago, ignoring my texts and my calls. Ignoring everything we shared.

Typical Red. Always running.

I would've driven up to Cherry Grove, thrown her up against the wall, and reminded her just how well running from me really works, but Michael had sent me overseas to secure some properties for our hotel expansion. It's been plane after plane until I returned yesterday just in time for Mom's wedding.

"You going to keep staring at Iseult, or are you going to ask her to dance?" Hudson Mackay, our lawyer, asks, smirking at me as he approaches from my left.

Hudson is the one everyone calls when they have a problem. Everyone as in Mob or Mafia. He's the one that can get you off for just about anything. He was Patrick's lawyer even before he was ours. That's how we met him.

"Shut up," I mutter, returning my attention to the woman who won't even look at me.

He snickers, staring straight ahead at his wife, who's off speaking with Elsie, both of them with a glass of champagne, black gowns hitting the floor.

"You look at her like I look at my Hadleigh."

I have no desire to deny how I feel about her. I want the whole fucking world to know.

I eye him with a tight glare. "Pretty sure you weren't being forced to marry her sister."

He chuckles. "Hadleigh doesn't have a sister."

His eyes bounce over to me for a second, a grin deepening on his face before he watches his wife fling a hand through her shoulder-length chestnut hair.

"Look, man." His light blue eyes assess me. "I've known that family a long time. Sure, Patrick is a hard-ass, and sure, he'll be pissed once he finds out you've got a thing for his other daughter." He laughs. "But after that initial shock and probably a punch to your nose—and maybe a bullet or two—he'll come around."

"Funny, asshole." I release a breath. "That's not how she sees it, though. She's afraid to tell him."

"She just needs time." He slaps me across my shoulder blade. "Patrick told me the marriage was for an alliance, right?"

I nod tightly, glancing at him from the corner of my eye, my gaze still fixed on my Red.

"An alliance is an alliance." He shrugs. "And for you, Iseult makes way more sense." He nods with a curl of his mouth. "But…" he warns, his expression stoic. "It's better you tell him soon before things happen between you two. Because he won't forgive that."

Yeah, a little too late for that…

"Noted," I say under my breath, watching her twirl Sophia around, and just as she does, her eyes go to mine.

And that feeling—that unexplainable feeling in the pit of my stomach—it hits me like a tornado. And I know, right here in this moment, with all these people around us, that no matter what happens and no matter how many women I meet, it will always come back to her.

Seconds feel like minutes the more she stares, the more her gaze tethers to mine from across that room, holding me there like she's already mine and I'm already hers.

But just as quickly as it came, she twists her face away and reminds me that she'll always be running.

"Jesus," Hudson mutters. "What the hell was that?"

He runs a hand through his dirty-blond hair.

I ignore him, watching her as she continues to dance, that long green dress hugging her curves, accentuating every inch that I've tasted. That I've imprinted into the marrow of my bones.

"Thanks for the chat," I tell Hudson. "But I need to get out of here before I do something stupid."

"Don't do that." He scoffs. "I may be good at my job, but I'm not *that* good."

"You'd have to." I start to head out of the tent, walking backward with a grin. "If not, then I'd have to kill you, and I don't want to kill you."

"Yeah." He chuckles. "I kind of don't want you to kill me either. I'd never want to leave Hadleigh alone." He sighs longingly, staring at her.

Just before I turn to walk out, I say, "Hey, that Donny guy. Did you ever talk to his lawyer about who hired him?"

Hudson had been keeping tabs on the case for me.

"Yeah. He said his fees were paid anonymously."

I nod. Of course they were. Whoever Donny is covering for must've been in a grateful mood.

"Look…" Hudson approaches. "You may never find out who killed Bryce, and you're going to have to accept that."

I chuckle dryly. "Come on, Hudson. You've been my family's lawyer for a while now, and you know I never let anything go."

"That's what I'm afraid of." He shakes his head and blows out a breath. "Whatever he was doing in that alley, it wasn't good. You must suspect that."

Hudson knows all about getting his hands dirty. He's been dirty for so long, he doesn't even know what it means to be clean.

"Maybe," I admit. "But I won't know for sure until I find out the truth, whatever it is." I march up, crowding his space, my jaw set tight. "If he was up to something, I want to know about it. Do you hear me?" I lock eyes with him. "So if there's something you find out, you'd better share it with me first."

That was my friend. He was practically family, and I *will* get answers, no matter what they are.

Just as I'm about to get the hell out of here, the music ceases and Patrick appears on the stage next to the band, tapping the microphone.

"Is this thing on?" he jokes, and the crowd erupts in laughter.

He holds Ma's hand, her face gleaming beneath the purple and blue LED lighting, her smile big as she peers up at him.

"My bride and I just wanted to tell you all how grateful we are that you could join us."

Whistles and cheers fill the space before he continues.

"I never thought this day would come for Fernanda and me. But here we are, finally married, and I can't wait to spend whatever days I have left with you, my darling wife." He brings their joined hands up and kisses the top of hers, staring straight at her.

From the corner of my eye, I watch Iseult, her eyes glancing down to her feet, her face riding with intense emotions. She's not happy. I get that. If I felt like my father was replacing my mother, I'd feel the same way.

"But our marriage isn't the only marriage that will be happening between our families," Patrick goes on.

Mom's brows furrow, and her smile begins to fall. And for a quick second, her eyes go to mine before they land back on him.

Fuck. He's about to make this public.

"My beautiful daughter Eriu and Giovanni Marino will be tying the knot in three months from now!" he announces.

"Like hell we are!" I yell, but no one hears me over the roaring of the celebratory cheers.

Mom's eyes grow with shock. She had no idea he was going to do this either. She gently grabs his forearm and presses her mouth to his ear, faking a smile while saying something that has his face growing taut.

They continue to speak, both of them looking anything but pleased.

The bastard ambushed me. He fucking knew he was going to do this.

Iseult kneels to say something to Sophia, then rushes out of the tent.

I start to go after her, but a soft hand lands on my forearm. I turn to find Eriu there, not an ounce of joy on her face either.

This is more like a fucking funeral.

"Did you know?" she asks, glancing down at her feet before she looks at me again.

"That your father was gonna pull that shit? Not at all." I glance behind me, wanting to know where Iseult ran off to.

Her shoulders drop with a weighty exhale. "Me neither." Her pale green eyes concentrate on me for a moment. "You don't really want to marry me, right?"

"I…uh…" I scratch my temple, unsure what the hell to say without sounding like an asshole.

"It's okay. I get it." Her pause stretches as she stares at me. "You like my sister."

"What?" My heart pounds.

She laughs. "I won't tell my father. Don't worry. But he'd be stupid not to see it, because I do."

I stand there awkwardly, hoping this conversation ends before my mother's wedding breaks out into a full-blown war. The more people know, the more likely he finds out before we can tell him.

And time is running out.

"I love my sister," she goes on. "She's always looking out for everyone but herself. But she deserves to be happy too."

I nod, hoping to go after her stubborn ass right now and convince her of that.

"Go find her." She smiles softly. "I'll cover if anyone asks about you guys."

"Thanks. I'm sorry it won't work out for us." I smirk.

Her eyes gleam as she shrugs. "Don't worry. You're not my type anyway."

Chuckling, I rush out of there, hoping my future wife hasn't gotten far.

ISEULT

Three months.

My damn father has been orchestrating a wedding with God knows whose help and decided to stab me in the heart at his own wedding.

Of course, he had no idea he was doing that to me, but he did. It's like my heart has been permanently sliced open.

This is what getting close to someone gets me. Feelings. Fucking feelings. I hate them more now than I ever did before.

How could I have allowed this to happen? And what can I do to stop it?

I don't have many options. I never did. It's either I fess up to my father and face the consequences or risk seeing the only man I've ever cared about marry someone else. And not just anyone else, but my own fucking sister. Their marriage will always be in my face. I'll never be able to escape it.

"Fuck!" I shout, hiding near Michael's golf course, far away from the outdoor wedding.

Sitting on a bench, watching the water fountain illuminated

with bright blue lights, I think about when I met him. Back then, I thought he'd be a fun little hookup. Pretty sure I didn't see any of this coming.

Maybe if I had a penny, I could drop it in and make a wish.

"Wish for what?" I say to myself. "A happily fucking ever after?" I snicker.

"Talking to yourself?" Hadleigh's voice looms.

I gasp at the sudden realization that I'm no longer alone.

She struts down the grass from my right, her gown trailing behind her as she comes to stand before me.

"I'm having a day." I hunch over, face in my palms. "Let me live."

She lowers to the empty space beside me and shoves her shoulder into me playfully. "Wanna talk about it?"

"Not particularly," I grumble.

I've liked Hadleigh since the moment we met back when she was just dating Hudson. She's one of those genuinely nice people. So nice that she has no idea that most of the people her husband represents, the people he's been friends with—like us—have blood on their hands. She thinks we're just rich folks with too much money and too much time.

In her mind, the Mob and the Mafia are just fables, nonexistent in the perfect world Hudson made her believe they're living in. She has no idea what I do or whose daughter I am. To her, I'm Iseult, trust-fund kid of one of the richest families in Massachusetts. I sometimes wonder what she'd do if she were to find out that Hudson has lied to her about the kind of life he leads.

Would she still love him? Would she leave? They're so nauseatingly in love that it'd be awful to imagine if they weren't.

From the moment he met her, she's been all he talks about. I don't know what he'd do if he ever lost her.

"Does it have anything to do with your sister marrying that dashing man?"

I keep looking at the water, hoping she stops this line of questioning before I confess all my sins.

"No." I glare at her without blinking.

"Really?" Her voice rings with amusement. "Then why do you sound like someone died? Would think you'd be happier."

"I am happy. See?" I grin all facetiously, and she bursts with laughter, her hazel eyes gleaming.

"Geez. If that's your happy face, Iz, kinda would be afraid to see what you look like when you're angry."

Definitely don't want to see that.

"I just think my father's rushing it, and on top of that, Eriu doesn't really want this," I explain.

"Yes." She nods. "Hudson did mention the marriage is for business purposes, which to me sounds quite archaic."

"Have you met my father?" I pop a brow.

She laughs again. "I can't imagine being in love with Hudson and then being forced to marry someone else. I'd probably pack my bags and run."

Then you don't know my father. There's no running from him.

"I'm not in love with Gio."

"Have you told your face that?" She curves a brow.

"Shut up, Hadleigh." I swat her arm with the back of my hand. "Who asked you, anyway?"

"I wish there was something I could do." She lays a hand on top of my knee. "I'm sorry, Iz."

"It's whatever. We can't all be perfect like you and Hudson."

She releases a burdened sigh. "Believe me, we're not."

I sit up straighter, concern filling my gaze. "Is everything okay?"

"Yeah." She waves off my concern. "Nothing we can't handle."

"You can talk to me if you ever need something," I say. "I hope you know that."

"That means a lot. Thanks, Iz."

I nod. "I'm glad Hudson met you. He was quite pathetic before you came along."

"I find that hard to believe." Her full mouth bends up, her eyes full of adoration.

But she has no idea who Hudson was when my father found him. She has no idea the kinds of things he's done. And she will never know.

"I should probably get back," I say, quickly rising to my feet before she starts prodding even more.

This woman is too easy to talk to. If you're not careful, you'll find yourself spilling all your secrets before you realize what you're doing. She should've been a therapist, but I guess a teacher is not that far off.

She follows me up, and together, we start back to hell. And by that, I mean the tent. I just want to be away from everyone.

"What were you doing here anyway?" I ask her as we stroll, bathed in peaceful darkness.

"I saw you leave the party and wanted to check on you. It looked like you were upset."

"Oh."

That's all I can manage. What else can I say?

Just as we return, I find Gio pacing right at the entrance of the tent. As soon as he sees me, he looks up.

"Where the hell did you go? I looked all over for you."

Hadleigh looks curiously between us. "Well…I shall leave you two alone."

She pinches her lips and scurries inside.

"Are you crazy?" I whisper-shout.

His eyes are cold and hard. The muscle in his wide neck tremors before he blows a breath and grabs my wrist.

"We need to talk," he says through clenched teeth.

He forces me away, taking me to the back by the thick shrubs lined neatly in the grass. When we're alone, he throws my body up against his, his arm snaking around my lower back, dragging me so close, his hot breath slinks across my lips.

"I'm done pretending." His eyes bore into mine, and even in the moonlight, I can see them talking to me, begging me for something I've always been afraid to give: my heart.

"I want you more than I need my last breath."

"That sounds ridiculous, because then you'd be dead," I whisper, even as my throat clogs with emotion.

"Fuck, you're such a pain in the ass, Red." His responding laugh is thick and heavy with emotion. His knuckles softly brush down my cheek. "But you're *my* pain in the ass."

My heart flips in my chest.

How can this hurt so much?

"We'll give your father and my mother a few days, but after that, we're telling him."

"That's easy for you to say. You have nothing to lose," I say bitterly, burrowing into his firm palm, wanting nothing more than to be touched the way he's touching me.

"That's not true." He grips my jaw with his free hand. "I lose *you*. And I can't live in a world where you're not mine, Iseult Marino."

Tingles and warmth breathe life into my body, like every cell only knows him.

"You don't understand, do you?" he asks.

"Understand what?"

"That I've been a man with a body, but no heart, until you, and that's because you *are* that heart, Red. Are you truly willing to rip it right out of me again?"

"Will it hurt?" I twist my lips and fight my insurmountable emotions.

"So damn badly," he whispers, lowering his mouth to mine until it lingers there, the erotic current between us zapping through my body.

"Then yes…" I kiss him once. "I'll take my time carving it out of you."

With a growl, he fists my hair, teeth grazing my jaw as he yanks my head back. "You damn insufferable woman."

Then he smashes his mouth to mine, kissing me raw, with unrestrained savagery while he practically rips my dress, yanking it up until his fingers find me bare and wet.

"Fuck," he grunts as he winds back. "You had no panties on for me all night?"

"Who said it was for you?" I challenge. "Maybe it was for one of the other handsome men at the wedding."

He rocks with a cold laugh, fingers languidly playing with my clit until his eyes narrow. "I don't find that funny, baby."

He thrusts his fingers inside me until I gasp with a throaty moan.

"There is no other man for you, Red. You're mine."

Then he proves it. Over and over again, until he practically has to hold me up as we make it back to the party, pretending he didn't do what he just did.

thirty-three

ISEULT

"Have you found anything new about your friend?" I ask once we're back at the wedding, sitting alongside one another.

Our table is empty. The rest of the guests are on the dance floor, my sister having fun with Sophia. Because who doesn't have fun with that kid?

Spending time with her earlier almost made me feel like I was capable of the whole mom thing, but of course that's a load of bull. Being a mother is a lot more than twirling around with your daughter.

"No," Gio says, his face turning intense. "I haven't been able to find Devlin, and I need to talk to him to see what he knows."

I almost feel bad that I can't tell him what happened. He should know. He has a right to. But it's bigger than he realizes.

I've thought a lot about his connection to Bryce, and there's no way he was involved in whatever Bryce was doing. It just doesn't fit. But at the end of the day, if he were to learn what happened that night, things between our families could change. And instead of finding peace, the truth could throw us into a full-blown war.

"I'm sorry," I tell him, placing my hand over the top of his.

His brows knit, and his gaze leaps between my eyes and our bound hands. "You feeling okay, Red?" A wide smirk takes over his face. "For a second there I actually thought you were trying to console me."

"What?" I yank my arm back. "Not in your dreams."

I bite the edge of my lower lip to stop from smiling, watching his bemused face from the corner of one eye. He throws an arm around me and pulls me against his side.

"You're already such a good wife," he whispers and kisses the top of my head.

"I'm not your wife," I breathe, trying to remove myself from his heavenly grasp before someone sees us.

"Not yet." He holds me closer. His voice turns all raspy. "But I really like how that sounds, you being my wife."

"I wouldn't be good as anyone's wife. Or a mother," I admit, staying locked against him, loving the way it feels to be held by him.

"Look at you, already planning our children." His eyes gleam teasingly. "I definitely wouldn't mind practicing for that. How many should we have?"

"Shut up, Gio." I throw a punch into his ribs, and he lets me go with a bemused groan. "I don't want kids. I'd be a terrible mother."

"No, you wouldn't be." He stares at me raptly. He sounds so sure of himself, as though he knows it to be true. "You care. You'd do anything for the ones you love. We both know that, bambina. And at the end of the day, that's all there is to being a parent. I can see that with Michael." He picks up his glass of whiskey and takes a long swig. "And if that angry fuck can be a good dad, you'll be fine."

I can't help but laugh. And my mind…it does this thing whenever I'm near Gio. It starts wondering, creating a future I'm not ready to come face-to-face with.

"Excuse me?" A young waiter approaches me.

"Yes?" I stare inquisitively at his hand, an envelope in his grasp.

"You're Miss Iseult, yes?" he asks nervously, his cheeks almost bright red, his curly brown hair falling over his ears.

"I am." I dart a curious gaze at Gio, who returns it.

He extends his hand. "I was told to give this to you."

"Uh…thanks?" I take it from him while he scurries away.

"Who would send you something at Michael's house?" Gio questions while I start to open the envelope.

"I have no idea…" This strange, unsettling feeling drops into my gut.

I tear open the flap, unfolding the paper within.

With a sudden gasp, I read the words to myself. Over and over. Hoping this isn't real. It can't be.

"Red?" I hear Gio call, but I don't see anything but those words on that paper.

I jump to my feet, rushing after the waiter, grabbing his arm when I get near.

"Who gave this to you?" I spit out.

He turns to me. "Ma'am?"

"The envelope! Who gave it to you!" With both hands, the paper crumbled in my fist, I clutch the collar of his tux.

"It—it was a woman. She didn't give me a name."

"A woman?" My heart pounds. "Are you sure? What woman? Is she here?"

The words fly out of me in a hurry, and my pulse thumps in my ears.

"Red? What's going on?" Behind me, Gio's voice carries with concern, a hand brushing up between my shoulder blades. At all other times, it would comfort me, but not now.

"I think she left, ma'am," the waiter continues. "She had on a short black dress and had black hair. I've never seen her before."

Nothing is making sense. Fuck!

Nausea swirls in my stomach, my head growing dizzy. I clench a fist to steady the build of panic thrumming through me.

"What did this woman say?"

His eyes grow, fear slinking through them. I can tell he's not involved. It's the only reason I haven't beaten him for information.

"She just said it was very important that you get this and looked very serious." His breaths turn heavier the longer he stares at my enraged expression. "She pointed you out to me, and when I looked around the room, taking my eyes off of her for a second, she was gone. Did I do something w-wrong?"

My fingers press in between my brows.

"Just go. Get out of here. But if you see her, let me know immediately. But don't say a word to her. Got it?" I glare.

"Yeah…uh…I'm sorry." He's practically trembling, his throat bobbing as he swallows thickly.

Once he starts toward the bar, I plop down onto the seat.

Gio pulls his chair right up against mine. "What's going on, baby? Talk to me. Let me help."

"I don't need help. I've got this."

With my palms digging into my eyes, those words on the note appear vividly in my mind, as though conjured up by him.

Privet, moya dorogoya. Ya skuchal po tebe. Ne mogu dozhdat'sya, kogda my snova budem vmeste.

Yeah, I've missed you too, asshole. Can't wait until we're together again either, so I can take both your eyes.

Sergey has returned for me, and this time it looks like he's not alone.

Now I have to figure out who's helping him so I can kill them both.

I left the wedding a little bit ago, unable to think with all that noise. Nor with Gio there, trying to get me to tell him what was on that paper.

But I know what would happen if I did. He'd want to save me. He'd go hunting for Sergey and probably get his ass killed over me.

I can't let that happen. This is my fight. My kill. And I *will* kill that bastard once and for all. I owe it to myself, and most of all, I owe it to my mother.

Placing my cell on speaker, I call a number I have never needed to call. My phone rings and rings, while my fingers curl around the steering wheel, heading to my apartment. An SUV to my left honks wildly at me when I almost sideswipe it, but I curve around it and speed ahead.

I knew Sergey would return. I knew he wasn't dead. Men like him are vermin. They always find a way to survive.

But he doesn't know me anymore. He only knew the seventeen-year-old girl I was. He has no idea the kind of woman I became thanks to him. He can't do a thing to hurt me now. He already did that. I wear the scars as proof.

Visions of what Sergey did to me fill my head. The way he'd

burn me while I cried. While I begged.

The way he laughed. My God, I still can't get his laughter out of my head, no matter how many years have been wedged between us.

"Hello?" Konstantin finally answers, his voice a smooth baritone. Calm and collected, like always. But underneath, he's just a savage in a suit.

"Where is he?" I shout.

"I'm sorry, but who's this?" he asks casually.

"You son of a bitch. You know exactly who this is."

"Such a dirty mouth on you." He chuckles. "Not much has changed, I see, Iseult. What might I do for you on this fine evening?"

"Tell me where he is, Konstantin, or I will drive all the way to your house and burn it while you're sleeping."

"You know I don't take threats very well, right?" His tone turns callous. "So why don't you tell me what has you this upset, and maybe I can help."

"Your father. Where the fuck is he?" I grit, my pulse filling my ears.

"Oh, not this again." He sighs like he's bored, and I wish I could see him right now just so I could put a bullet between his eyes. It'd be worth dying for. "Like I told your boyfriend, my father is in—"

"I'm sorry?" I interrupt, my mood growing frustrated. "I don't have a boyfriend, so what the hell are you talking about?"

He laughs again, like I'm a fool. "Giovanni came to see me."

"What?"

"Oh, yes. A little over a week ago, in fact." He pauses. "He was very upset to learn what my father had done to you, and like you, he wanted to find him. But I did explain that my father isn't here. He's in Russia or dead."

"No, Konstantin. He isn't," I clip out, my vision growing cloudy from the hatred I feel for this entire family.

There's growing silence between us.

"Did you hear me, asshole?" I ask, contempt weaving through my words.

"What did you mean by that?" he questions tonelessly. "Do you know something about my father that I do not?"

"Your father sent me a note while I was at Michael's. And in it, he said he couldn't wait to see me again. It was signed by him."

His breaths grow monstrous. "Do you have the note?"

"I do."

"Send me a picture. I will confirm his handwriting."

I quickly pull over on the side of the road, grab the paper from the passenger seat, and snap a photo before sending it to him.

"Blyad," he mutters a Russian curse.

After I got away from Sergey, one of the things I did was learn Russian. I wanted to be ready in case he ever came back, and knowing his language was one way.

"So it's definitely him, then?"

"I'm afraid so."

Good. I want his blood.

"The waiter who gave me the note said a woman with black hair had given it to him to pass to me," I go on. "Do you know who could be working for him?"

"Black hair, you said?"

"Yes. Do you know her or not?"

He pauses for long, torturous seconds. "I do not know who it could be. My father has no alliances in America. I made sure of it. So whoever she is, once I find her, she's good as gone."

Like I said, a savage in a suit. If anything stands in their way, the Russians extinguish it.

"Did you happen to get a photo of her?" he asks.

"The waiter claimed she left as soon as she gave it to him. There were a couple hundred people at the house. It will take forever to comb through security footage."

"Then I suggest you ask your boyfriend for his help."

"He's not my boyfriend."

"Are you sure he knows that?" He chuckles. "A man who storms into my home the way he did definitely doesn't do it for just anyone."

"Lovely chatting with you, Konstantin. Let's never do this again."

He laughs as I end the call, and then I'm dialing someone else's number.

Michael answers on the third ring, music from the wedding playing in the distance.

"Iseult? Where are you calling me from?" His voice booms louder than the melody. "Aren't you at the wedding?"

"Uh, no. I actually had to skip out, but listen. I had a favor to ask, and please don't tell my father."

"Go on."

"Can you ask the videographer to email me the raw footage from the wedding? I want to make something for my father and your mom. Like a wedding gift, you know?"

A long stretch of time passes, and my pulse thumps in my ears. *Come on. Don't say no.*

"Text me your e-mail," he says, and I breathe a silent sigh of relief. "Is that all?"

"Yep. Thanks. Tell Elsie I said bye." Quickly, I end the call before he gets suspicious.

Then I turn my car back around.

Seems like I won't be going home quite yet.

Thirty-Four

GIO

The wedding began to wind down not too long after she ran off, so I went home. I kept calling until she finally texted back telling me she was fine and that she needed to deal with something on her own.

Of course she did.

Having her accept my help is like asking for the impossible. But whatever was on that note scared her at first before it made her angry. I wondered if it could be Sergey. If he'd returned and decide to taunt her. It would be like him.

If it is…fuck, the things I'll do to him. She wouldn't be able to stop me, either. I know she can handle things alone, but she shouldn't have to. I'm here now.

As I'm about to go take a shower, my phone vibrates. And when I look on the screen, hoping it's her, I'm fucking disappointed.

"Yeah?" I growl at my security detail stationed around my

large property.

"Sir, there's one pissed-off woman demanding to be let in," one of my armed guards informs me.

"You tell him to open that fucking door right now!"

Aww, my wife came to see me.

I grin instantly.

Of course, I completely ignore the fact that she sounds like she wants to rip my head off. But I don't care as long as she's here. Where I can touch her. See for myself that she's okay. She actually used the address I gave her. I wanted her to know where I lived just in case.

"Let her in," I tell him.

"Yes, sir." He disconnects the call while I head for the front door.

As soon as I open it, her emerald eyes turn to slits, and before I know what the hell is going on, her hand slices in the air and lands hard across my cheek.

"Damn, baby." I rub at the sting. "You missed me that badly, huh?"

She kicks the door closed behind her, her features flared with her fury. "You idiot! Were you trying to get yourself killed?"

She pushes at my chest with both palms while confusion settles around my head.

"What are you talking about?" I keep a few inches between us, because I can tell that if I touch her right now, she's going to go off like firecrackers on the Fourth of July.

And the only time I want her going off like that is when I'm inside her. Then again, her being angry at me usually does lead to...

Her high heels snap across my porcelain floor as she proceeds inside, flinging her arm in the air. "What the hell were you thinking, going to the Russians?! Do you realize Konstantin wouldn't hesitate to kill you?!"

She stares at me, her eyes gleaming with ferocity. And through the crack of her anger, her shoulders sag and she exhales heavily.

Oh, damn. My baby was worried about me. I feel like a kid on Christmas morning.

My mouth jerks as I shrug. "Well, since you don't want me, why would it matter to you if I got myself killed?" I take one step forward.

She shakes her head and lets out a grunt, balling her hands at her sides. "You're such a reckless idiot." She stares deep into my eyes, her chest rising and falling with intensity.

"How about you come a little closer and tell me more about what an idiot I am?" I march another step.

Her jaw strains. "I'm serious, Gio. He could've killed you." Her brows snap as her voice falls.

My heart flips in my chest. "So you do actually like me, then?"

A slow-growing smile falls on my face.

She throws her head back and releases a rough exhale. "Oh, shut up, will you?"

And it's then she erases the rest of the void between us and rushes into my arms. Her gaze fits me tight as though, for once, she wants to stay.

"I like you enough not to want you dead. So don't die, okay?"

I brush my knuckles down the side of her velvety cheek, and she closes her eyes and sighs.

"Is that all this is?" I whisper. "You liking me just enough?" My mouth leans into the corner of hers, leaving a barely there kiss behind. "Hmm?"

My fingers snake into her strands, and I yank her head back with force.

"Gio…" she groans, making my heartbeats leap and my cock harden.

"Say it, bambina. Tell me I matter to you. Tell me that you see no one else but me in your future…" My lips hang above hers, only a breath between them. "If you do, I promise that the next time I decide to do something stupid, I'll ask your permission first."

"No, you won't," she breathes, all throaty and hoarse.

"No, I won't," I chuckle. "Especially not when it comes to your safety."

"I don't need you to protect me…" Her hands sink into my hair.

I nip her bottom lip, fisting her hair in a rough palm, searching the depths of her eyes as though searching for her soul.

"I know you don't, but I want you to want me to, Red. I want to be the one you think about, the one you call when you have something to say. The one who has your back while you have mine." I let my thumb brush against her jaw. "Don't you get it by now? I want *everything* with you."

She roughs an inhale, her eyes glazing over, expressing things she's afraid to say out loud. "What if we never get everything? What then?"

"How would you know if we don't try?"

I stare at her, wanting to kiss her, to strip off all the layers that keep her from giving me everything—body, heart, and all those insecurities. I'd take care of the first two while extinguishing the third. But every time we're one step forward, she takes two steps back.

"What are you afraid of?" I ask. "That this might actually work out? That I fall in love with you and that you, by some goddamn miracle, fall in love with me too?"

She flattens a palm against the center of my chest.

"I never wanted this," she whispers.

"Never wanted what?"

Her lashes flutter to a close for a single fleeting moment before they open and she releases a heavy sigh. "I never wanted to feel safe in anyone's arms before, but I feel safe in yours."

My pulse pounds louder. Those words…they've jumpstarted my heart. I make her feel safe. This brave, strong, incredibly beautiful woman feels safe with me.

My hand comes to fit around the side of her throat. "You're always safe with me, bambina."

She lets out a bitter laugh, her pulse thrashing against my touch. "You have no idea who you're getting yourself involved with."

"I think I've known since the moment you threw that knife at me and tried ending my life."

My chest swells when she gives me a tearful smile.

"I'm a mess, Gio." She shakes her head and scoffs, vulnerability etched on her face, so much of it that I just want to cradle her.

"It's a good thing I like to clean," I challenge.

"I'm also not a morning person," she informs me with a tilt of her chin, as though she wants to find something that will make me turn around and run.

I kiss the tip of her nose. "Then we sleep in."

"I'm stubborn."

"You don't say?" I chuckle.

She swats my shoulder with the back of her hand, her grin unraveling the fused parts of my heart that have been waiting for her to unlock them.

Her brows slant into a frown. "I cry sometimes."

I clasp my hands around both sides of her face and look straight into her soulful eyes. "Then I'll be there to let you."

"Gio…" she whispers, and my heartbeats grow unsteady from the sound of her broken voice.

"You don't get it, do you?" I grasp her jaw and kiss her. "I don't want to run from this, baby. Not when there are a million reasons to stay. And unfortunately for you, you're every single one of those reasons."

Her bottom lip quivers, and she slams her eyes shut, squeezing them as I go on.

"I'm never going to tire of you, Iseult. So you can say whatever you want, but nothing will ever push me away."

"You don't know that." She looks back at me, tears battling to drip down her cheeks, but it's as though she fights them with everything she has.

"Don't ever tell me what I know."

Her breaths ghost across my lips, warm and enticing.

"You were destined to be mine, Iseult Marino. So, go ahead…" I grab a handful of her hair with my other. "Run. I dare you. But know that in the end, I'll always find you, and my arms will always be waiting to bring you home."

A frown lines between her brows. "Why the hell do you want me?"

"Because you're it for me, dummy." The corner of my mouth winds up.

"Wow." Her tear-stricken laugh is damn adorable. "That was so romantic."

"What can I say?" I curl an arm around the small of her back and tug her to me. "You bring it out in me."

"What else do I do?"

I drop both hands off of her, taking a few steps back, hoping I'm not about to single-handedly ruin this moment. "You make me happy. And I didn't know what that meant until I met you."

Slowly, I drop to one knee.

"W-what are you doing?" she whispers incredulously, her eyes growing round. "Get up. Please get up."

But I don't. Instead, I reach into my pocket and remove the ring I bought her last week.

"I've never been a perfect man," I say. "And hell, you're probably the least perfect woman I've ever met."

She scoffs. And laughs. And cries, the tears freely rolling down her cheeks.

"But the thing is, Red, I don't need you to be perfect. I just need you to be mine. And I knew for quite a while that I was going to make you my wife. Now, I'm actually doing it."

"Gio…we can't," she pants, her hand slowly lifting to cover her gaping mouth when I open the box.

"We can." I hold her gaze. "If your father wants an alliance, then we'll give him one. And we're going to make it one fucking hell of an alliance, because I plan to knock you up as many times as possible."

She swipes under her eyes. "You're insane."

"Insane is right, because sometimes what I feel for you feels like I've lost my mind."

My heartbeats throb, waiting, hoping… I don't know what I'll do if she says no.

Actually I do. I'm gonna shove that ring down her finger and cement her to my bed, because this woman isn't getting away from me.

"You really do have a way with words." She releases another laugh, and my God, I could listen to her laughter for the rest of my life.

"I'm falling in love with you, Iseult Marino."

She gasps softly. "You can't love me."

"Well, I do, my little bambina, and you're just gonna have to live with that."

Her teeth tug her bottom lip, her watery gaze full of confusion and disbelief.

"So what do you say? Want to be perfectly imperfect together, or are you going to keep me guessing until I've died from old age?"

With a rough exhale, she glances up to the ceiling before her attention returns to me. "Fine, you idiot. I'll marry you."

Then, with a huge grin, she extends her hand toward me. And fuck, do I rush to take the damn ring out and stick it right on her finger just in case she changes her mind.

She stares at the four-carat solitaire with a rose gold band. It reminded me of her: beautiful, strong, shines brightly all on her own.

"It's…wow," she whispers, unable to peel her eyes off her finger.

I rise to my feet. "You know this actually means you're going to have to marry me, right?"

"Unfortunately." She grins.

"Then why the hell are you smiling?" My palm rounds her jaw, tugging her mouth for a quick kiss, growling when she makes a moaning sound.

"Just shut up," she whispers, then smashes her lips to mine.

She groans as I take over, ravaging her mouth while her feminine sounds of pleasure come in waves. Her hands are on my back, nails clawing as I grunt deep in my chest.

I want to fuck her like a damn animal. Just throw her on the floor, ass up, pounding into her while pressing her cheek to the ground with my palm.

Without my mouth leaving hers, I curl my arms under her thighs and lift her up in the air, her body sculpting perfectly to mine. Her arms loop around my neck as I lead her up my spiral staircase. Pushing open the bedroom door with my foot, I lower onto the bed, still kissing her, my body dropping over hers.

Her fingers are everywhere as she groans, the sounds vibrating between us while she grinds her hips around my throbbing cock.

With a shove across my chest, she forces herself on top of me, sitting there and staring down at me like she's a goddess on top of her throne.

Her eyes take in the ring on her hand, a smile twitching on her face. "I'm gonna tell him tomorrow when I get back. I'm gonna tell my father about us."

I rise on my elbows and fasten her hair around my wrist, dragging her down against my mouth. "You don't know how happy I am to hear that."

My teeth graze her jaw, my cock thick and ready for her.

"I think I can tell." She moans, rocking herself against me.

"That's it, baby. Let me hear you."

Her hands go to my hair, gripping hard as she gyrates into me, making my cock ache to be inside her. She's still wearing that dress from the wedding, and I glide my fingers up the top of her thighs, slowly drawing up the gown. And it's then I remember…

She's not wearing any panties.

Instantly, I flip her under me, pushing my weight into her body, yanking up the dress until she's exposed. My length is pulsing, wanting desperately to feel her bare.

"Stay right there, and don't you move," I warn while I rise off the bed, watching her chest flail with barraging intensity.

My hands go to my tie, undoing it while I stand between her feet, hanging off the bed, her body ragged and turned on as she watches me.

"Sit up," I demand when the tie is free.

"Why?" There's a glint of challenge in her gaze.

"I won't ask again, bambina. Sit up."

Her inhales and exhales grow shallow as she does what I asked, squirming on the bed, all aroused. I lean over and wrap my tie around her eyes.

"What are you doing?" she asks on a whisper, but in her voice, there's more excitement than fear.

"It's been too long since I've been inside you, Red." The back of my hand strokes the curve of her jaw, and every hair on her arms rises to attention. "Too many nights spent thinking about you. Too many nights remembering how good it felt when I was inside your wet and warm cunt."

She shifts uncomfortably, her cheeks flushed.

"I've missed you, baby, and I'm done waiting. I need to feel you clenching around my cock. I need to feel you come."

With a palm, I push her back down on the bed.

"Lift up your dress and spread those thighs wide."

Her throat bobs as those fingertips roll over her pebbled nipples, poking from within her dress.

"Come on now, bambina. Show me that pretty pussy before I rip that damn dress off of you."

She groans, squeezing her tits together before she traces her fingertips down her body, reaching the mid-thigh as she gathers the material in both hands and lifts it up.

An approving growl rumbles out of my throat when she spreads those legs open and shows me that glistening pussy I'm about to make a meal out of.

"So beautiful…"

My hand draws closer, knuckles brushing up inside of her thigh. And with a quick jerk of my palm, I give her pussy a hard slap.

She cries out when I hit her clit, so I do it again, pressing on her sensitive flesh with my thumb.

"You like that, don't you, my dirty girl?"

She moans a heady reply, and I give her another hard blow, grinding my palm against her achy flesh. Her hands fist the sheets as she rolls her ass deeper into the mattress. I haven't been inside her in over a year, not since I used those cuffs on her in her apartment and she escaped them.

I haven't even so much as looked at anyone else since her. Because there is no one else who could hold a candle to this woman.

I love that she can't see me, won't see the things I'm gonna do to her, the things I'm gonna make her feel.

My fingers roll up her knees before I start undoing the buttons of my shirt, tugging each sleeve while I watch her squirm. I toss the cotton on the ground, and my hands go to my belt next.

Her curves contort languidly when the sound of clacking resonates through the room. Folding the belt in half, I run the cold metal buckle in between her breasts.

"Gio…oh God, what are you doing to me?" she pants, writhing beneath me.

With both hands, I palm her breasts, squeezing them. Before she realizes what I'm doing, I grab hold of the V of her dress and roughly split the material in half, exposing her full breasts, cupping them, kneading them in my palms as I groan at the utter perfection.

"You're a damn dream," I say while I loop my belt into double handcuffs.

Her gasping breaths come in waves as I run the belt over one stiff nipple, drawing the leather down her body until I slide it between her wet slit.

"Oh, fuck," she mutters with a whimper when the rough edge of the belt flicks over her clit, until she's arching her back as though she needs more. "I'm so close!" she cries, begging for release that

I'm not ready to deliver.

"Not yet," I warn, withdrawing my touch, reaching toward the nightstand to pick up something special I purchased just for her.

She curses in frustration, her hips jutting out for more.

I slip my palms under her hips and flip her onto her stomach, harshly tugging the rest of the dress down until it falls past her curves, pooling around my feet.

It's a good thing I have clothes for her in my closet, the ones I had my assistant from work purchase. I was hoping there'd be reasons for Red to wear them.

Her face turns as though to look at me even though she can't see a thing. And slowly, I let my fingertips trace down every scar, every instance of pain she was made to feel.

She flinches, her breaths jagged and uneven. I hate that she's still uncomfortable for me to see her scars. I hate it so much it fucking hurts.

"You're mine, Red. Every breathtaking inch of you is mine." I drop a knee beside her and replace my fingers with my mouth, kissing up her spine.

"I'm not breathtaking," she breathes.

Knowing she thinks of herself that way makes me want to find Sergey and torture him for years until I give him the mercy of death.

Gently, I swipe the hair away from her shoulder and lower my lips to her ear.

"That's where you're wrong, bambina." My whispered words are rough and thick with meaning. "But that's okay. Don't believe me. We have years for me to convince you."

I fit a hand between our bodies and stroke her between those thighs. Her pleasure-filled sounds make my cock jerk.

"I'm gonna remind you how beautiful I think you are." My

warm breath laces up the nape of her neck. "Do you trust me?"

"Yes." She nods.

My eyes fall to a sharp close, and I inhale a long breath, a smirk curling over my mouth. Because this is the first time she admitted out loud that she trusts me. And to her, that means something.

"You're safe with me. Remember that." Then I take both of her wrists and loop them into the belt cuffs I created, tugging one end until they're snug around her.

"You better not leave me like last time," she teases with a slow wind of her mouth.

"Not a fucking chance." I rise momentarily, just enough to flip her back around and settle myself on the bed, placing her on top of my chest. "Sit on my face, Red."

"What?" Her mouth trembles.

"Come on now, baby. Don't pretend to be shy. Scoot up and sit on my face. Give me that pussy."

Her nipples harden, and I pinch them between two fingers, eliciting a groan from her pretty lips. She trembles on top of me, her breath quivering as she starts to shimmy higher up my chest, until she's got herself settled on my chin.

I chuckle. "I said my face, and I meant it."

Gripping her hips, I lift her up in the air and lower her right over my mouth until all I can breathe and taste is her and her alone.

ISEULT

His tongue rolls in tantalizing circles over my clit, his breaths hot and ravaged around my most sensitive flesh.

He follows a slow, torturous path until he rims my opening, growling when my nails claw his upper thigh, fingers feathering over the crown of his heavy cock.

I can't touch him how I want, nor see him, and that only makes me more desperate and needy.

I feel myself wet and wanton, thrashing around his tongue like I want him to stop, yet I don't at the same time. The sensation coils in my gut, skirting through my limbs. Every time he brings me to orgasm, it feels like it's better than the last time.

He thrusts his tongue inside me with ruthless force, like he's feasting on the essence of me, the taste and the thrill of knowing he can make me this way—his whore, his everything.

"Oh, fuck!" I grind myself on his mouth, no longer shy or caring how insanely intimate this is, not the way I felt the moment he told me what his intentions were.

I've never actually had a man eat me out this way. But my God, Gio doesn't even care. He growls as he flicks and fucks and makes me become a woman I've never even dreamed I could be.

His palms round over my ass, grabbing each cheek before he gives it a hard slap. That only makes me warm and depraved, needing to reach that precipice only he can take me to.

He growls, long and deep, saturating me with his brand of seduction, the vibrations piercing through my limbs. I can feel it around my clit, and it makes the hunger, the burn swimming through my veins, flame out brighter.

"Yes, just like that. Don't stop!" I beg.

I'm almost there. Just a little more.

He spreads my ass cheeks until it hurts, then tugs my clit between his lips while his tongue draws wildly around it, nibbling and flicking until the sensations grow insurmountable. He gives me more, grunting with a fury, and the need to shatter comes until I fall. Hard and fast. My head dizzy, my heart racing, my eyes rolling.

But he doesn't stop. He keeps going while I fight it, this feeling too overpowering.

"I can't, Gio. N-not another one," I stammer with a shaky breath.

But instead of granting me reprieve, he slaps my ass and goes harder, flattening his tongue and forcing me to ride it.

"Oh, God!" I scream as a powerful sensation snaps around my body and I'm climbing again.

Before I can even comprehend what's happening, he pushes me back a little, and instead of his mouth, the most intense vibrations hit my core.

"Fuck!" I scream. "Wha-what's that?"

I go breathless, crazed to the marrow of my bones, needing that release with barbarity.

"It's my present for you. Knew how much you enjoyed your toys."

He switches the settings to a faster pace and I can't even formulate a response while my body convulses. He thrusts his fingers inside me, and I fall across the top of his body, open and bare for his eyes to take in everything. And knowing that he's looking at my most intimate place while he's doing this to me is only making me more aroused.

He curls his fingers, the vibrator pulsing with rapid beats until the need overtakes me.

My body arches as I scream. "Oh my God, I can't stop coming!"

"Yeah, that's it, baby. Take it like my little whore, and scream like one too."

Before I can come down from the most powerful orgasm I've ever had in my life, I'm lifted in the air, his big, strong hands around my waist, my body thrown facedown on the mattress.

My wrists strain from the belt tugging around, but I like the burn. I like everything he's doing to me. I crave the desperate way he wants me. The way he takes me like I'm his to control, to own.

"On your knees, Red." His demanding tone has my core pulsing, desperate to be filled. He slaps me hard across my behind. "Ass up."

I yelp, rising, my wrists on the small of my back.

"You're so fucking beautiful tied up, at my mercy, your pretty pussy dripping onto the bed."

I exude no shame at the knowledge of what my body does for him.

Lowering my chest flat against the mattress, I arch my hips higher.

"Good fucking girl," he growls, working a palm over my achy core while I hiss, the intensity almost unbearable.

"Fuck me," I gasp as he works two fingers on each side of my clit, making me delirious once again. "Please, Gio. Give it to me hard."

"I love hearing you beg for it. I'm gonna fill you up with my cock. Don't you worry, baby."

He doesn't stop touching me, making my knees weak, unable to keep myself upright. But I do. I stay just like that. Open and pleading and needing all of him.

I feel the instant the crown of his hard-on enters me, and I cry out his name, needing all of it.

He stays just like that, just the tip inside me. He fists my hair roughly, tugging my head back as far as it'll go.

"You wanna get fucked? Is that it, bambina?"

"Yes…please." My panting ravages through my lungs.

I whimper when he inches just a little more, my body stretching for him.

He leans closer to my ear, his hot breath fanning across my

pulse.

"Okay, baby," he rasps with a groan. "I think it's time you met the devil."

And with a single vicious thrust, he impales me until I scream. But he doesn't ease or allow me a second to take in his power. Instead, he plows into me like a savage, clutching my hair tighter until my scalp throbs, the sounds of our bodies adding to the erotic current in the air.

He takes me for hours, I'm sure of it. Until my body grows weak, until every muscle burns and aches, yet my veins fill with the desire to take everything he's giving.

Like a man who won't let anything stop him from taking what he wants, and what he wants…is me.

Thirty-Five

GIO

Sunlight splinters in through the slice of my curtains as the most breathtaking woman wakes up across my chest, her head tucked between my shoulder and my neck, her body clearly satiated from last night. She's sighing, unable to erase the satisfied smile on her lips as I stroke the back of her head.

"How'd you sleep?" My voice is gruff.

Both of us are naked, skin to skin, and it's the closest I've felt to anyone in my entire life.

"Your bed is comfortable enough." A teasing smile lines her mouth.

"You mean *our* bed." I tilt her face up with one finger under her chin. "It's going to be yours when you marry me."

She raises her head and props it on her chin. "You know, with all those rumors about you, it's hard to believe you're the same man."

"That's because I'm not the same," I easily admit. "I've been a different man since the moment you pierced those sharp claws into my back and refused to let go."

The back of her fingers trace over the stubble of my jaw. "You make it kinda hard to let you go, Giovanni."

I jerk my head. "Wait a minute."

I quickly flip her onto her back, and she squeals when I start to tickle her ribs.

"Did you just admit you like me?"

She laughs, trying to push me off. "Never said that!"

Her laughter grows, making my heart beat right out of my chest. I shake my head.

"You ever going to just say it?" I still, my heart beating ferociously the more I stare into the serenity of her gaze.

"Say what?"

"How I really make you feel?"

All amusement slowly dissipates from her face.

With a sigh, she clasps my cheek. "Fine. But I will only say this once and probably never again."

My pulse slams into my ears.

"Do go on, Your Highness." I grin.

"Oh, God…" She shuts her eyes for a moment. "I can't believe I'm doing this, but here goes." She clears her throat and stares back at me. "Ever since my mother died, and then after what Sergey did to me, I hated getting close to people. I had my family, Kora, and that had always been enough. But now…"

Silence stretches, and my God, my heart is gonna cut in two if she doesn't say more.

"But now, the very thought of never being close to you again kills me. Imagining you in bed with someone else, loving someone…it physically hurts, Gio." Her voice lowers as she picks up my hand and places it in the middle of her chest. "It hurts right here, and I don't know what to do with that."

I stare, the magnitude of what she just said overwhelming me.

"Are you going to say something?" she asks. "Or are you going to just stare at me and make me feel like an asshole for confessing all of that? Because I'll have you know I've never said that to any man before."

With a groan, I grab her jaw and kiss her hard before I stare back at her.

"You don't know what that meant to me, bambina." I drop my forehead to hers. "Your heart is safe with me," I whisper across her lips. "Is mine safe with you?"

She lets out a sigh, but she doesn't say a word, and that fucking terrifies me.

I palm her forehead, circling my hips between her soft thighs. My shaft is rock hard, wanting to be welcomed home, needing that connection between us.

She flattens her hands around my back, nails piercing into my muscle. And without taking my eyes off hers, I thrust inside her with one quick move, going slower than last night, driving inside her until I'm all the way in.

I stay that way, still, wrapped in her warmth and heat as I gaze down into her eyes, gently stroking the back of my hand across the pale softness of her cheek. "You feel too good, bambina."

"Faster," she begs, curving her hips upward.

My palm clasps around her throat, her pulse beating frantically against my fingertips.

"Spread those thighs wider," I demand, and she instantly complies, letting me deeper inside her.

I drop my mouth to hers, kissing her slow, the passion and raw need seeping from my lips. And the way she makes me feel, no one ever has and no one ever will. It's something different, something earth-shattering and something completely ours.

My hand reaches down, stroking her clit between our sweat-ridden bodies.

She groans, her walls gripping me tight, her body ready to let go. And I don't stop. I take everything, her sounds of pleasure around my tongue, her insatiable body mine to please.

And with her eyes on mine, I watch as she falls apart, wave after wave, all mine for the taking.

I follow her there too, spilling inside her, wanting this feeling to last for eternity.

ISEULT

I've never felt more alive than I do whenever I'm in his arms—a man who has seen me at my worst.

Yet he's still here, wanting me. Looking at me like I'm his entire universe.

The ring glistens on my finger, and I can't believe I said yes. It was reckless and stupid, but it felt right. Mom would be happy. She'd like him. I'm sure of it. I bet he'd make her laugh.

His words ring in my head. *I'm falling in love with you*, he said. And though I felt that all-consuming feeling to say it back, I just couldn't.

Because what the hell do I know about love?

His large, powerful hand is fastened around my back while I'm cradled against his beating heart, feeling the magnitude of my emotions reflected in his wild heartbeats.

"What are you thinking about?" he asks, tilting back to look at me.

Can a man be both beautiful and fierce all at once? Like a giant mountain that terrifies you, yet makes you awestruck.

"Just thinking how unfortunate it is that I'll have to be stuck with you for the rest of my life," I quip.

"My God, woman," he chuckles. "Can't even be nice to me after I just made love to you?"

My heart skips a beat.

Made love.

Not fucked.

He made love to me.

That's what he said.

Emotions I can't name drift through my body like I'm drowning in a flood I can't breathe through, see through—like it's too much, yet not enough.

He made love to me.

Yet if I'm being honest, I already knew it. Felt it when he was inside me, taking bits of my soul.

A lazy smirk greets his sinful mouth. "No one has ever made love to you before, have they?"

I shake my head, unable to pacify my shallow breaths.

"It's a good thing you'll be stuck with me for the rest of your life, then," he adds, his gaze filled with intensity. "Because even though I enjoy fucking you like I hate you, I much prefer making love to you like I don't."

And before I can even wrap my head around what he just said, he palms my cheek and presses me onto his chest, leaving a kiss on the top of my head.

With my feelings overtaking me completely, I curl my fingers around him, hoping my father accepts that I may be falling in love for the very first time.

"Ugh," I groan as my phone rings, loud and annoying.

I don't want to get up. I'm content with staying in his bed forever, not wanting to move to see who's calling. He tightens his arm around me.

The cell stops, but seconds later, the irritating sound continues.

"I have to get that…" I stretch my arm and feel for the phone on top of his nightstand.

As soon as it is in my hand, I maneuver out of Gio's grasp and see that it's my father calling. My pulse pounds, as though he can somehow find out where I am. It's still very early in the morning, and he doesn't normally call about work-related things until at least after lunch.

Worry echoes through my mind as I answer.

"Hello?" I yawn. "Is everything okay?"

"No," he fires. "Where are you?"

My heartbeats thrash. He sounds enraged.

"What's wrong?" I ask, immediately jumping to my feet while Gio sits up against the pillows, rubbing his face, the muscles in his triceps straining.

"I asked you a question. Where are you?" His tone is a sharp bite, sending a chill down my arms.

"At my apartment in the city. It was easier to go there after the wedding than drive back home. Tell me what's going on."

"I need you home immediately."

"This can't wait until tomorrow?" I ask, gauging the seriousness of the matter.

"It cannot. I'll be waiting." Then the line goes dead.

I stare at the cell in my hand, unable to make sense of why he sounded that way.

"What's going on?" Gio moves to sit beside me. "What did he say?"

I shrug, my heart hammering. "That he needs to see me immediately." I glance at him, before peering back down at my phone. "I have to go home."

"Text me as soon as you get there," I tell her.

"That's usually my line."

He clasps a palm around my jaw. "Well, now it's mine."

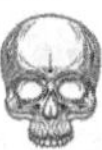

"Sit. Now." My father's glare hardens as I pull a chair and take a seat across his desk.

As soon as I walked into his house, I felt this instant dread hit my gut. The home was silent, except for the foot soldiers who instructed me that my father was already waiting for me.

He rocks back and forth on the swivel chair and eyes me with something heavy and unspoken.

My fingers brush over my bare ring finger, grateful I remembered to take off my engagement ring before I walked inside. It's currently in my glove compartment, and I'm paranoid I'm going to lose it.

"So, are you going to tell me what's going on?"

He pulls himself toward the desk, elbows hitting the wood with a thump.

"How long?" he asks through gritted teeth.

"What?" My expression twists, my eyes leveled to his.

"Don't play me for a fool, darling."

I scoff. "I'm too tired for guessing games, Dad." My arms cross over my chest. "Just tell me what I did to piss you off this time."

He balls a hand until his knuckles pale. "How long have you been screwing around with Gio?"

All air leaves my lungs.

How the hell did he find out?

"You're just going to sit there and deny it?"

A cold, brutal chill rushes up my back.

I tilt up my face and shrug, so tired of hiding. I don't want to hide anymore.

"You know what? I'm not. Gio and I are together." I throw one leg over the other while his eyes turn to slits.

"How dare you? He's your sister's fiancé! How could you bring such shame upon our family?" Rage and disappointment battle for space on his features.

I hate seeing him look at me with shame. "How did you find out?"

"I didn't, but I suspected." He shakes his head. "And you just confirmed it."

It doesn't matter at this point, does it? I was going to tell him about Gio and me today anyway. Maybe I can make him understand that this isn't just a hookup.

"I didn't mean to disappoint you. I met him before you made plans for Eriu. This wasn't random. I really think I l—"

"Silence." His nostrils widen as he hunches over the desk. "Do you know what you've done to your sister?!"

"Patrick, stop!" Fernanda walks in, tightening a long, white robe around herself, her brown hair up in a low bun.

Her kind eyes greet me before her attention reverts back to my father. And though I hate seeing her here, in my mother's home, I get it now—the hurt from not being with the one you love. They once cared about each other, yet couldn't be together, torn apart by her family. And instead, she was forced to marry Gio's horrible father. It wasn't fair what happened to them when they were young.

"I love you, Fernanda, with all my heart," my father tells her, taking her hand in his. "But this is between me and my daughter."

"But they love each other, Patrick," she stresses, begging him for his understanding. "Can't you see that?" Compassion fills her gaze as she darts her attention toward me. "Let them be together, sweetheart. It's the right thing."

"No…" He roughs an inhale. "What would've been the right thing was for them to come to me and talk to me instead of sneaking around, bringing shame and embarrassment to the family." He bounces his attention to me. "People saw you at the wedding. I saw you. There's no excuse!"

"It wasn't intentional. I didn't even mean for it to get this far. It just happened." I try to make him understand, but he can't see past his anger.

"While your sister was engaged to him? Is that what you're trying to excuse?! What you did was a sin! A *vile* sin that I cannot forgive." He takes a long pause, running a hand down his face. And when he stares back at me, there's pain in his eyes. "Your selfishness has caused your sister to run off."

"What?" I slowly rise, my heart pounding, my knees going weak.

That can't be right. She never wanted to marry Gio. Even if she were to have found out about us, she wouldn't run away because of it.

"That's right." My father's chest flails roughly as he pulls open a drawer and removes a piece of folded-up white paper. "I found her note this morning. She left." His tone grows exasperated by the second. "She must've found out about you two before I did, and she left."

Oh, God. I've got to find her, especially with Sergey looking for me. What if he takes her as revenge for what I did to him?

My throat closes in, thoughts of what Sergey could be doing to her making me insane. She has to be okay. I have to find her. If I had anything to do with her leaving, I have to apologize.

I rush over and grab the paper from his hand. Opening it up, I read the note.

Dear Dad,

I'm sorry, but I needed to go. I can't marry Gio. I'll call you when I'm ready to talk.

Rage simmers in my gut, because the more I read the words, the more I realize this isn't all on me. He has no right to make me feel guilty while he pretends he's innocent.

"Nothing in here says she ran because of me!" I crumble the paper in my fist, narrowing a glare. "How the hell do you know this isn't *your* fault?"

My sneer causes him to grind his jaw, but I don't care. I continue, boiling over.

"She never wanted to marry Gio! If anything, you have yourself to blame, always trying to do things we don't want for some guise of family allegiance." I laugh bitterly. "You just do things to please *you*, the almighty. So you can sit there and blame me all you want, Daddy." I fling a palm in the air. "But she left because of *you*."

I point an accusatory finger at him, and his cheeks turn a deep shade of crimson.

"You have some feckin' nerve to talk to me like that." He jumps to his feet, fists on the desk. "No daughter of mine would go screwing her own sister's intended. Get out. I don't want to see you."

"Fine." I shrug. "I'll go."

My laughter is cold, but inside every inch of me hurts. I could tell him about my true feelings for Gio. I could try to make him see what he's starting to mean to me. But right now, my father won't care. Eriu is gone, and that's all he sees.

"Don't expect to see me again."

"Oh, that's fine, darling." He snarls. "Neither this family nor Caellach need you anymore."

I flinch.

Fucking dagger to my heart.

"Patrick!" Fernanda's tone is horrified. "Don't say that. They didn't do anything wrong."

"Of course they did, my love." His voice grows softer for her. "The only reason your son will get to keep his life is because I love you, but their actions are reprehensible."

The back of my nose burns, but I keep my face together, breaking a little fragment at a time. Everything I was afraid of is coming to fruition, and even if I get to keep Gio, how can I live without everything else that matters?

"Patrick, don't you do this!" Fernanda urges, her voice anguished as she darts her gaze between us. "He's my son, and she's your daughter. This isn't right."

"None of this is right. But they did this. And she has to pay the price for her actions."

"Not like this…" she cries.

"It's okay, Fernanda," I tell her. "Now you know who my father truly is."

Then I turn on my heels and storm out the door, not sure if I'll ever be welcomed back.

Thirty-Six

ISEULT

My head grows dizzy as I walk out of the house. My heart physically aches.

He's just mad, I attempt convincing myself. *Once Eriu is back, he'll get over it.*

But I don't know if that's true. My father is even more stubborn than I am, and cheating is one thing he doesn't easily forgive.

I try my sister's cell as I head to Kora's, wanting to say goodbye to her before I head back out to New York. When she doesn't answer, I quickly leave her a voicemail, telling her to call me as soon as possible.

Where the hell would she even go? She has some friends in college, but no one she would trust like that. I don't even have their phone numbers.

As I get closer to the Caellach building, I spot Tynan walking toward my father's house. As soon as he sees me, he lifts a chin in greeting.

I march up to him, needing to know if he had anything to do with why my father found out. Maybe my father lied and someone said something.

"Hey," he says, attempting to trail past me.

But I stop him with a glare. "Did you say something to our father about Gio and me?" My chest rises with quick, jerky breaths. "I know you know. Don't deny it."

"You should know me well by now. I'd never do that." A concerned crease forms between his brows. "What happened?"

I back off a step, pressing my fingers into my temples.

"God, I hate this!" I grab my head from both sides and squeeze.

I can't lose everything. I just can't. My family, my work, it's everything to me. But Gio has become important to me too, and I can't deny that.

Anguish plunders into the very depth of my heart. The raw pain claws in the cavity of my chest at the realization that my father may not forgive me when everything is said and done.

"Hey." Tynan places a gentle palm on my arm. "What did he say?"

"He confronted me about my relationship with Gio." I sigh. "And when I didn't deny it, he told me he suspected it. That it's unforgivable. I don't know…" I throw my hands in the air. "I thought maybe someone said something."

I close my eyes, a tingle forming in my left arm, and I know a panic attack is going to come if I don't relax. But attempting to calm myself when an attack is brewing is like trying to stop myself from spinning when thrown into a tornado.

Tynan's arms come around me, holding me like he used to when I was younger. "You're okay. I've got you."

After I got attacked, he was there for me during my episodes.

He centered me. He calmed me. He reassured me. I don't know how I'd have survived the aftereffects without him.

Though he can be a real son of a bitch sometimes, he's also the best person I know.

"He said I'm out." My throat goes dry, a burning sensation pinching the back of my throat. "The academy. The family. I'm out, Tynan." I force a broken smile, my vision cloudy.

"That's fucking bull!" He pivots his head back and grabs my shoulders, looking intently at me. "We're not going to let that stand, you hear me?"

I nod, even though I know no matter what he says to our father, it may not work. But looking at my brother, looking at the certainty ingrained in his gaze, I grasp on to hope.

"I'll talk to Fionn and Cillian," he declares. "We will knock some sense into the old man. And if you think any of us give a shit what he says, then you don't know me."

He drops his hands to his sides, and his eyes flash with thunderous darkness.

"He can kick you out from his life if that's what he wants, but he will never kick you out from mine." And my brother, who barely smiles, lets a small one slip. "You've always been a pain in the ass. Always had to cover your messes, but you know I'll always have your back."

Don't you dare cry.

"Thank you." I blink back my emotions. "Ditto."

He nods. "But I think until we figure this out, you have to stay away from Gio."

"Okay."

I realize it may be over for good. My father will never let us be together. And if I marry him anyway? Then what? Never be invited to family dinners or birthdays? Have my brothers and sister come around on their own without our father? No, I can't live a life like that.

But the thought of never being with Gio, never knowing if we could build a life together, tears me up inside.

The ring he gave me, the way it looked on my hand…I want that. I want to be his wife. I want the safety of his arms. The way he laughs with me. The way he makes me feel—both within my body and my heart.

But is it worth it to give up everything else to have him?

I clear my throat, fighting all thoughts of him, remembering that Sergey is out there and I have to focus on finding him. I'm on my own with that. I don't want to involve anyone else. He's mine to kill. But knowing Sergey, he's going to hide in a hole until he decides to come after me. It's what I fear: a surprise attack.

"He told me Eriu left," I add. "He said it's my fault because she found out. But it can't be true, right? She didn't want to marry him."

"Fuck, that's probably why he called me. I was out. Just got in." He pinches the bridge of his nose. "We'll find her. I'll get her phone tracked."

"Okay. It's still on. I called it just now."

"I'll get the crew on it immediately, unless he has already."

My eyes flutter closed, emotionally exhausted from it all.

"Where you off to now?"

"Going to see Kora before heading to my apartment."

"Alright. I'll call you once we've found Eriu. She couldn't have gone far." He shakes his head. "I don't know what she was thinking."

"She was probably thinking she didn't want to marry someone she didn't love."

"Love." He snickers. "What the hell does love have to do with marriage?"

"Wow," I scoff. "I finally found someone who hates marriage more than I do."

"Come on now, Iseult. You don't hate marriage. You just don't want to trust anyone, which is fine. I get that. But for me? Marriage sounds as good as getting thrown into a volcano."

I laugh at his grimace.

"You laugh, but I'm not joking. I'd probably prefer the volcano."

I shake my head, laughing still, knowing my brother isn't kidding at all.

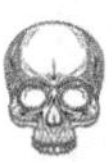

"I'm gonna miss you." Kora lets out an aggravated sigh, holding me in her arms.

"You know I'm not actually going to a different country, right? I'm only like four hours away."

She backs off, her expression crestfallen. "New York City may as well be a whole other country." Her brows climb to her hairline. "I really can't believe he's throwing a fit about this. It's not like you were really having an affair." She rolls her eyes. "He forced that damn engagement. This is so stupid."

"I know, but it's how it is in our world."

"Well, the world sucks." She plops down on the bed, her underground apartment spacious enough with a modest bedroom and a similar-sized kitchen and living room. "No one is going to force me to marry anyone. This isn't the sixteen hundreds."

"Believe me, I know."

"You can just stay here with me." She frowns. "I won't tell."

"Thanks." I laugh dolefully. "You're a good friend. But I have to go."

I start for the door, and she rises to walk me out.

"He's an ass." She hugs me tight one last time.

Yeah, he is.

Just as we part, I say, "If you hear anything about Eriu, let me know, okay?"

"Of course!" She shakes her head. "Your poor sister. God knows where she is. I hope no one hurt her. She's not like us, you know?"

Her worry is reflected in my rapid heartbeats.

That's exactly what I'm afraid of.

GIO

She's been gone for a while now, and other than a text to let me know she got home to her father's, I haven't heard a word. I'm hoping she's telling Patrick about us. I want everyone to know we're engaged. I don't want us to hide like what we feel for one another is wrong. Because none of it feels wrong.

My cell starts to vibrate, and I instantly reach for it on the coffee table, hoping it's her. But I see that it's my mother instead.

"Hey, Ma."

"Gio? Have you heard from Iseult today?"

I sit up straighter, registering the alarm in her tone.

"What's wrong? Something happen?"

She exhales roughly. "Patrick somehow found out about you two, and he was really angry."

"Fuck," I mutter under my breath. "I was afraid of that."

"Yeah, sweetheart… He threw her out." She tsks. "Poor girl. She looked so upset. And I'm furious with him!" She curses him in Italian. "He's been asking for my understanding and forgiveness. But I will not let him have an ounce of it until he blesses your union."

I'm already on my feet, grabbing the car keys, rushing out the door. "Do you know where she went?"

"No, I don't… And there's one more thing."

Blood rushes to my ears as I open the driver's side door and start the car, putting her on speaker. "What is it?"

"Eriu ran away. No one knows where. Patrick is going crazy with worry. He's got everyone looking. I fear she got herself into trouble. And I know Iseult loves her sister, and with everything Patrick said to her, I'm afraid she's blaming herself."

"That asshole!" I pause. "Sorry, Ma."

"Don't be sorry. He *is* an asshole. I love him like no one's business, but my God, I want to bang his head with my frying pan."

I chuckle as my car roars to life, gunning it down the road, getting onto the main street, heading toward her apartment. I hope she's there. We have to talk before she shuts me out again.

"I'm going to find her," I tell my mother.

"Let me know when you talk to her, okay?"

"I will. Thanks, Ma."

"Always." A heavy exhale wooshes out of her. "I want my boys to be happy."

"She makes me happy."

"Then that's all I need to know."

"There's something else you may want to know," I throw out.

I'm not sure if I should tell her, but fuck, I want to tell someone. "What's that?"

"Can you keep what I'm about to tell you between us?"

"Of course."

Seconds drift. My heart pounds. "I asked her to marry me yesterday."

"Oh my God!" she screams, then whispers, "Oh my God."

"Yeah," I chuckle. "But I'm afraid Patrick's actions may have just cost me my wife."

She scoffs. "That man is going to come around if my frying pan has anything to say about it."

Even through my worry, I laugh harder.

"You just find her," she tells me. "And convince her that you're meant to be together."

"You've met her, right?" I let out a snicker. "Because that woman is stubborn, Ma."

"All the good ones are." She sighs. "All the good ones are."

Thirty-Seven

ISEULT

It's not like my sister to make me worry. She wouldn't just not answer her phone. She'd find a way to call me.

I've managed to track the numbers to everyone she knows. I've called her high school friends and college friends. But no one has seen or heard from her since she left. And the last ping on her cell Tynan said they had was at a gas station about ten miles from home. Then the phone was turned off and they have been unable to gather info.

My father has everyone on payroll—the dirty cops, the equally dirty politicians. And they're all on the hunt for her. I feel useless, sitting here staring at my phone, now back in my apartment. I hate this. I hate not knowing if I'm the reason she ran. If I hurt her without realizing it.

Picking up the cell, I call the one other person who may know where she is: Devlin.

The phone rings a few times before his deep, broody voice comes on. "Yeah?"

"Hey, Devlin. It's Iseult."

"I know."

I don't wait for him to say anything else. He's always been a man of few words.

"Have you heard from Eriu at all in the last couple of days?"

He pauses, and I can hear his heavy, taunting breaths.

"What happened to her?"

He's always been protective of my little sister, maybe even more than a bodyguard should be. I sort of see that clearer now, more than I ever did then. Seems like my sister isn't the only one with feelings involved.

"She ran off. Didn't tell anyone. Left a note on her bed that she'll call when she can, but she would never not call me back. I was hoping she was coming to see you."

"If she was, she didn't tell me. Why would she run?"

"My father arranged a marriage for her to the guy I've been involved with, and—"

"What?" His temper flares. "She's getting married?" His sharp inhale shoots through the line. "To who?"

"Mafia. But she doesn't want to. I'm hoping that's why she ran, and not because she found out I was involved with him."

"Bloody hell," he spits out in a thick Irish accent.

He doesn't say anything for what feels like a minute.

"She knows where I live, but she hasn't come."

I register the noise of something shattering. Like he just broke it.

"Okay, thanks. If you hear from her, call me."

"Aye. You too."

The line goes dead, and I throw the phone on the couch and

pace.

With Sergey out there, my worry for Eriu grows. I hope she's safe, wherever she is. I just need her to fucking call me.

My cell beeps, and I jump at it again, seeing an email from the videographer at my father's wedding. I've been waiting for that, hoping to find out who's working for Sergey and make sure she pays. I read the note from the photographer.

> Please find the link to the drive containing the video file you asked for. Thank you.
> -David.

I quickly hop on my laptop, download the video, and press play. Cillian and Fionn give their toasts, and then more guests do the same.

I start to fast-forward, my eyes scanning for a woman with black hair and a black dress. I sit there for over an hour, fast-forwarding to the time when the waiter handed me the note.

Once I find that exact moment, I see her. The woman walks up to the waiter, her back to me, her hair up in a bun. She's only with him for a few seconds before she hands him the envelope, then she struts out of view.

"Damn it!"

I slam a palm on my desk, continuing to watch until it's over, and I'm not any closer to finding her or Sergey.

"Open the door, Red!" a voice booms.

I startle, lifting my head up from my desk, realizing I'd fallen asleep. With a groan, I rub my face with a hand.

"Come on. I heard what happened," Gio's voice carries. "We

need to talk."

A heavy bang echoes.

Gio.

A twinge tightens in my chest.

And it's then I realize I'm going to have to break his heart, in turn breaking mine. But I can't seem to gather the courage to do it. To move from this spot, open the door, and end it.

Because I don't want to. I don't want to go back to the days before—before he was mine and I was his.

Shutting my eyes, I sit frozen as he continues to call for me, asking me to talk.

With deep breaths, I attempt to muster the courage to appear as though breaking things off isn't going to destroy me. But I know it will, whether I show it or not.

How can I let him go? How can I leave the comfort of his arms? The one place I felt more at home than I've ever felt anywhere else.

The stabbing pain in the center of my chest comes swiftly, and my palm fastens around the anguish, fruitlessly attempting to contain it.

And it's right here, in this moment, that I realize that I'm falling for him too. Why else would the very thought of never seeing him or talking to him hurt this badly?

"I saw your car!" he booms. "I know you're inside. So either you open this goddamn door, or I'm breaking it."

He's bluffing.

Two seconds later, the loudest slam I've ever heard sounds off, and my eyes pop wide.

Okay. Soooo, he wasn't bluffing.

With a deep inhale, I start for the door. "Alright, I'm coming!"

"That's right, you are."

I can just *see* the intensity on his features, and I can't help but smile.

I've never had anyone fight for me like this before.

As soon as I open the door, he's there, an arm raised against the doorframe, hair disheveled, strands falling over a thick brow. But my God, he's still so insanely sexy. I want to run my fingers through his hair, to grab him, pull him close, and tell him how badly I've missed him.

He's in a black button-down, two buttons popped open at the chest, changed from when I saw him earlier.

His eyes narrow.

His nostrils flare.

And the way he's looking at me… It's like he's a hungry predator waiting for me to run just so he can catch me.

His jaw clenches, and my heartbeats quake. I lick my lips, watching him, watching as his mountainous bicep jerks when I take him in.

My body roars to life, owned by him. Completely and utterly owned by this man that I want more than anything. But we can't get everything we want in life. Sometimes, we have to let things go.

Before I can find the right words to send him away, his hand reaches for me, fingers curling around my jaw, his thumb deepening into my pulse. And with a growl, he wraps his other arm around my back, throws me up against the wall on the outside of my apartment, and smashes his lips to mine.

He groans when my tongue dances with his, my tempo just as ravenous, just as depraved. My hands are everywhere—clawing his back, grabbing chunks of his hair. His hand slinks downward, clutching my throat as he kisses me like he's punishing me for everything I've ever done to hurt him.

Every hard inch of his body is so tightly molded to mine that it'd take an earthquake to separate us.

He draws back, his gaze daring me to say a word that would contradict what he feels for me. And the more he looks at me that way, the more every piece of me dies.

I don't want to let you go. But what choice do I have?

My brows snap and he closes his eyes before he lowers his forehead to mine. "Whatever you're thinking, don't."

"Let's go inside where we can talk."

"We can talk out here," he challenges, pitching me with an irate gaze.

"I can't say everything I want to out here…"

"That's the damn problem," he snaps.

And with a harsh pull of his inhale, he takes my hand, drags me inside, and shuts the door behind us.

"Talk." He leans against the door, arms folded against his well-defined chest, muscles clinging to his shirt. "And I swear, it better not be you ending this."

"You don't get it, Gio." A defeated sigh escapes me. "Eriu is gone. She ran, and my father is blaming me." I tilt my head up to the ceiling and stare momentarily before I find the right words, then I return my attention to him. "We were temporary. You had to know that. We were getting ahead of ourselves." A cold laugh breaks from my treacherous lips. "My father will never allow us to be together, even if I wanted that. And I don't."

The words hurt coming out of my lips, but I had to say them.

I reach into my pocket and retrieve the ring he gave me, extending it toward him.

He drops his arms.

An icy glare shadows across his eyes.

His chest climbs with ravaging breaths.

He takes a menacing step forward, then another, while I stay rooted, waiting to see what he'll do.

With a final stride, he grabs a fistful of my hair and bores his gaze to mine. "Do you think I'd let you go that easily, bambina?"

He lowers his mouth to mine, his lips hovering, breath against breath, chest against chest. My heart rate kicks up, air never reaching my lungs.

"Do you think I go around buying rings for every woman I fuck? Because I don't," he whispers gruffly, brushing his mouth with mine. "It means something to me, Red. *You* mean something to me. Clearly, I don't mean shit to you."

He continues to trap me in his inescapable hold, not allowing me space to move, yanking out my ability to speak. His free arm snakes around me, his palm latching on to my ass.

"Let me make something clear to you." His eyes catch with a fierce kind of possession. "This bullshit with you trying to push me away isn't going to work anymore. You're mine," he declares like an omen, winding my hair around his wrist like a chain. "Do you hear me, baby? You. Are. Mine. And I fucking dare you to open your mouth and tell me otherwise."

I run over the different things in my head, figuring out what to say to make him believe it when I myself don't. I could continue making the lies come out of my mouth, but I don't even want to anymore. I hold on to my engagement ring tightly, not wanting to give it back.

"Come on, Red," he says. "Go ahead, tell me how you can't marry me. How you made a mistake when you said you would." His features turn with his subdued anger. "Better yet…" He reaches into his waistband and retrieves a nine-mil. "Here, go ahead." He shoves the gun into my hand. "Kill me. Because if you're planning on giving me that ring back, you already have."

I choke on a laugh. Or a cry. My God, I don't even know, because this man… I just don't want to live without him.

"Always so dramatic." A tiny blink of a smile falls over my face, tears casting over my lashes.

He takes a single long breath and drops his mouth to my forehead, and every time he kisses me that way, I give him another little piece of my soul.

"Ho più bisogno di te che del mio prossimo respiro," he says, staring back at me.

I have no idea what it means, but looking into his softened expression, I know it means something beautiful.

"I think I need to teach you Italian," he whispers with a smirk. "Just so you know what I say when I make love to you."

Thump.

There goes whatever's left of my heart.

"I'd love that, Gio." I palm his face and kiss his mouth, just for a moment.

"I need you more than my next breath is what I said, bambina. And it's true. I need you and I want you. So don't go."

My chest throbs. "I wish things were easy, but they're far more difficult now than they were before."

My fear kept me from talking to my father, but in the end, I ruined things anyway.

"Look, baby, I know you're scared," he retorts. "But we can get through this together. This is hard for me too. I never saw what a healthy relationship was like. My parents…well, you know." He snickers. "But I want to be different, Red. I want that with you."

"Why? Why me? Why the hell would you want me? I'm messed up, Gio. I'm not the kind of woman men fall in love with."

"Too late for that. Already in love with you."

I pant breathlessly as he leans in and kisses me slow, so achingly slow I melt, tingles spreading throughout my body.

"I was dead set on never getting married," he goes on. "But when I met you, I just knew you were gonna be my wife, and I instantly wanted that more than anything."

He traces my cheek with the back of his hand, and I'm running out of excuses why this can't work. Why I shouldn't tell my father to go fuck himself, because Gio is my future.

"Could you stop being sweet?" I tease. "It's making it real hard to come up with ways to insult you."

"Come on, sweetheart. I have faith in you." He kisses me quickly, groaning, like he can't keep his mouth off of me.

"You're such an irritating idiot." I roll my eyes, warmth flitting through my heart.

"See? I told you." Then he grins, kissing my forehead, my cheeks, the corner of my mouth.

"Put that ring back on your damn finger." He yanks it from my grasp and practically rams it down my hand.

I laugh.

"You think this is funny?" His eyes grow dark. "Just try to take it off again, and I'll throw you over my knee, yank down your panties, and give you one hell of a spanking you'll never forget."

"Promise?" My mouth tilts up and I pretend to take off the ring.

"You want a spanking, baby girl?" He clutches my hips. "All you had to do was ask."

Then he's lifting me in the air, throwing me over his shoulder, and keeping his promise.

For hours.

Thirty-Eight

GIO

My throbbing cock rocks into her from behind just as my phone rings.

"Fuck whoever that is," I grunt in frustration. "I'm too busy reuniting with my fiancée."

She moans while I trail kisses down her neck, nipping her shoulder.

But the ringing doesn't end. Someone calling two, three…five times.

"Just gonna see who it is."

I told Grant about Eriu, and I'm hoping it's him calling with a lead.

Retrieving the cell from the nightstand, I find his name on the screen.

"Hey," I groan, thrusting deep inside her while she grips the sheets, twisting her neck to find me staring right into her heady eyes. "You better have a good reason for calling."

She smiles, and my pulse goes faster.

"Where are you?" he asks.

I instantly recognize the serious nature of his tone. I ease off of her and sit up, and she follows suit, concern tethered to her expression.

"I'm with Iseult. Why? Did you find something?"

"Shit…" he mutters. "I did, but it's not about her sister. Gio…I need you to check your email. Right now. It's about Bryce, and you're not going to like it."

"What are you talking about?"

Whatever he's about to tell me, it doesn't sound good.

"Just look at the damn email."

He hangs up, and I enter my account and find his name at the top of today's emails.

"What's going on?" Iseult asks, my gaze shifting between her and the phone.

"Grant called. He found new information on Bryce and emailed me something to look at."

"Oh? Do you know what it is?" She slides closer, peering at my phone.

"I'm about to find out."

Her foot bounces as she clears her throat.

Why the hell is she so damn nervous?

Opening the email, I find a single attachment.

And something inside me says not to open it, that whatever is in there is going to break me.

I give her a lingering look, and she returns it, her brows knitted with emotion, as though she doesn't want me to open it either.

Before I can change my mind, I click on it, waiting for it to load.

And when it finally does, I can barely breathe, staring at the face of my fiancée, a gun in her hand while my best friend is dead behind her.

Her eyes close, and she inhales long and deep.

"Fucking look at me." I grab her jaw and turn her face to mine. "Tell me I'm not seeing what I'm seeing. Tell me I'm wrong and that you not only killed my best friend, but lied about it too."

"I didn't lie." Her face turns cold. "You never asked if I did it." She pushes off my hand and gets to her feet.

Anger coils around my heart as I glare. I try to control the stabbing of my pulse in my ears but it's no fucking use.

She killed Bryce.

The evidence is staring right at me.

But why? Why the hell did she do it?

Following her up, I plow toward her until I force that body up against the wall, my hand trapping her throat.

"Get your fucking hands off me," she snaps, fighting to get my arm off her.

But I tighten my grasp instead. "Start talking, baby. Because you're not getting out of here until I know everything that happened that night."

She laughs. Icy, taunting laughter. "You want to know what kind of sick, perverted asshole you were friends with, then I'll tell you."

Oh, hell…

I don't know if I'm ready for this.

I knew it had to be something bad, but when it's someone in your inner circle, you don't want to believe they can do the unforgivable. And I just know what she's about to tell me will be that.

"He drugged a girl from that nightclub near the alley, and when

I caught him and chased after him, he threatened me. Said he worked for some dangerous people and that if he didn't take the girl to them, we'd all be dead."

"Who was he working for?" My nostrils expand.

Fucking Bryce. What the fuck did he get mixed up in?

"I don't know. But I looked through his phone after I shot him, and there were some cryptic texts to someone named P. He was sending them photos of naked girls, Gio, and they'd reply with prices."

I force my eyes closed. "Fuck!"

I back away, slamming a fist into the wall beside her. She takes in my rage quietly, placing a hand on my shoulder.

"You didn't know."

"Of course I didn't know!" I curl a palm around her nape. "Is that what you thought? That I'd allow him to do that? God damn it, Iseult! I'm not perfect, but I'm not a fucking monster."

Her shoulders drop and a crease forms between her brows. "I wasn't sure what you knew. At first, I worried you did know, but the more time I spent with you..." Her eyes bore into mine. "The more I realized there's no way you could've."

The edges of my vision blur, my temples throbbing with a dull ache.

She pauses and looks me dead in the eyes. "I have no regrets, Gio. I'm sorry it had to be your friend, but he wasn't worth your friendship."

"Do you still have his phone?"

I need to see this for myself. I need to know who the fuck he was.

"My father does. I'm sure after he's done hating you, you can convince him to show you."

I snicker. "Yeah, I'm sure he'll be very cooperative." I grip the back of my head. "Why the hell didn't you tell me as soon as you found out who I was looking for?"

"Because I didn't want to tell you in case you didn't believe me."

My heartbeats echo in the chamber of my heart, and in an instant, I erase the gap between us and pull her body against mine.

"I would've understood, bambina." My fingers stroke down her cheek, and her lips part as I do.

"And the man Walter saw that day? Who was he?" I ask, remembering what the homeless man told us.

On that day, I had a feeling she might have known something, and maybe a part of me suspected this, but hearing it is a whole different beast.

She roughs a breath. "He's someone who works for my father. He took the fall when the hungry detective who wasn't paid by my family wanted to pin this on someone. Devlin, who you know as Donny—"

"What?" I jolt my head back.

"Yeah…" She grimaces. "I knew about him too. Sorry?"

I regard her with slow, uneven inhales. "Go on."

"Donny is his first name. Devlin is his middle. To protect me, Devlin made sure his fingerprints were all over the gun they found in the garbage right next to Bryce's body."

I shake my head. "I always suspected that gun was left there for a reason. No idiot would leave evidence behind that would be so easy to find."

She nods. "I'm sorry, Gio. I really am. I wish I wasn't involved in any of it, but it's what happened."

"I don't even know what to say…" I grind my molars.

Anger toward my friend, the situation, the fact that she omitted the truth from me…it all piles on.

"I'm sure you want this back now, and I understand."

My eyes jump to her hand as she tries to take the ring off.

My palm fastens around her fingers before she can utter her next word. "Don't you dare take that off, Red." I give her a quick, hard kiss, my heated gaze fixated on her. "Nice try, though. Too bad for you, I'm still marrying you. You *will* be my wife, Iseult Marino…" My lips brush over hers. "Best friend killer or not."

She breaks with a tearful laugh. "I'm never getting rid of you, am I?"

"Not in this lifetime, and not even in the one after that. And it's best you remember that."

ISEULT

His fingers stroke my bare back while I'm tucked on his chest. I would be lying if I said I wasn't worried about him learning that my family was involved in Bryce's death. It's probably one of the top reasons I never told him. Even when it was difficult for me to admit it to myself.

But Gio being Gio, he didn't leave. He stayed, and then he made love to me, reminding me what I mean to him. After that, of course, he fucked me to all hell, reminding me that he owns me too.

"I'm really worried about Eriu," I say. "What if something really happened to her? No one knows where she is, Gio."

Tynan called half an hour ago, saying that there has been no news. They spotted her car on some cameras within a twenty-mile radius from the house, but then it just disappeared.

My sister doesn't know how to disappear. Something isn't right. I just hope I'm wrong.

Sergey appears in my mind, as though taunting me, reminding me that he has the upper hand. He knows where I am, but I still don't know where he is. I don't even know where to look. I don't have access to my father's men or their tech equipment.

I'm on my own, which really sucks.

I should tell Gio, but I don't want to involve him. Maybe I can talk to Tynan about it, because this isn't about me anymore. It's about Eriu now.

"We'll find her," he attempts to reassure me. "I have Grant looking too."

My chest tightens, and I smile easily. The fact that he asked his friend to help means so much to me.

"He's good at finding people. He did find you," he teases, causing me to glance up and run the tip of a finger across his full, firm lips.

"You're so handsome," I say, warmth coursing through my veins as he grins, his eyes hooded.

He grabs a handful of my ass. "Did you just give me a compliment, or was I imagining it?"

I huff out a laugh. "Don't get too excited. It won't happen too often."

"I'll take whatever scraps you give me, bambina."

"I don't want to give you scraps," I confess earnestly. "You deserve more than that."

I drop my lips to his, kissing him forcefully, causing him to groan. He arches his semi-hard cock into my core while his tongue runs across the seam of my mouth. How he's already hard after what we just did amazes me.

"And what do I deserve?" he asks gruffly.

"You deserve to be told that you're handsome, strong, comforting." I snuggle against him, a smile clasped to both sides of my lips. "That you are everything I didn't know I needed. That you make me feel like it's okay to be me. You're kinda becoming my person, Giovanni Marino, so maybe you're stuck with me too."

"Your person, huh?" He kisses the tip of my nose. "And what does that mean?"

"It means I can depend on you to be there. That I can be myself around you, feel safe in the knowledge that you'll never willingly leave me, no matter how many times I have told you I'd leave you."

His eyes gleam with adoration as I go on.

"It means I want to stay here in your arms more than anything, even when staying feels like the scariest thing in the world. But I want to be afraid, because being afraid means you're someone worth fighting for."

His chest expands, and his eyes go round.

"Did I say something wrong?" I ask, my heart racing like mad.

"No, baby." He swallows thickly, his voice raw. "You said everything right."

And with a hard breath, he grabs the back of my head and kisses me. And I feel it—all those intense emotions, all the things he feels for me. I feel it in our kiss and in my heart. And in this moment, I know for certain that Gio will be my husband and I will be his wife.

His guttural groans vibrate between us, needing and wanting each other like no two people ever have.

"I've never wanted to be called by my full name more than I do right now," he rasps, his mouth sucking my jaw, teeth grazing down my throat as he flips me under him.

"Is that so, Giovanni Marino?" I tease, arching myself into him.

He's thick and hard, my legs parted for him, needing him inside me, to remind me how right we are together.

"Fuck, baby…" A hand strokes me between my thighs.

I moan as he runs one digit in between my wet slit, forcing the tip of his finger inside me, right before my phone goes off.

Of course it does. But it could be news on Eriu.

"I have to get that." I push him off and he lets me grab my phone from the nightstand. He flips onto his back while I find Kora's name on the screen.

A huge grin falls to my mouth as I answer. "Miss me already, huh?"

But instead of hearing her happy voice, I hear a pant and a cry. "Kora?"

Gio instantly recognizes the alarm in my voice and sits up.

"Kora are you there?"

"Iz?" she cries. "He's got me…Sergey. They grabbed me on the way from lunch, and—"

An icy current runs down my entire body until I'm bathed in arctic fear.

"Zamalshi, suka!" The moment I hear that bastard's voice, my fist clenches. A bang registers in the background and she screams, like he just hit her.

"Don't you fucking touch her!" I shout.

Gio's already on his feet, cursing violently, a gun in his hand.

"Privet, dorogaya, how have you been?"

My insides roil the second his thick Russian accent addresses me. I inhale sharply, trying to control the wave of panic that comes swooping through my body.

"Fuck you, Sergey!" I explode, unable to contain the years of pent-up rage.

"You've still got a sharp tongue, I see, huh? Maybe I should've burned that off first."

"How's your eye?" I snicker, grinding my teeth.

"You think this is funny?!" He howls. "Ya ih ubyu. You understand me? I will kill them!"

"Who's *them*?" My gut churns.

"Say hello, krasavitsa," he tells someone.

And it's then I hear her, recognizing her weeping.

"Is-Iseult?" Eriu cries. "Please don't come—"

"Shut up, you stupid bitch!"

She wails harder as he slaps her. Or hits her. Fuck, I don't even know.

"Don't you touch my sister!" My breaths barrage out of me. "Tell me where you are. You can have me instead. Just let them go! This is between us."

"I could do that…but I could just kill them both, no? Then I can come after you and finish you off too." His laughter is pure evil.

"If you can manage to kill me. Because in case you forgot, you couldn't kill me at seventeen. What do you think you'd be able to do to me now?"

His breath is noisy, and I'm glad I'm getting to him. I want him angry. I want him to come for me.

"You're so full of yourself, aren't you?" he seethes. "Well, we'll see how strong you are against my men."

"Your men?" I laugh. "Can't handle fighting me on your own, huh?"

"I'm not stupid. I know my own limitations. I know what you do and how well you do it."

"I'm glad you do, old man. Because I *will* kill you, Sergey. This *will* end."

"So then how about you stop wasting my time and come see me for old times' sake?"

"Name the time and place, you bastard."

"Look at your phone. And whatever you do, come alone. I will know if you're not, and I will kill the girls if you don't obey."

Then the phone goes dead, and I see the text from Kora's cell. And when I read the address, every hair on my body rises.

I know the place well. A place that still haunts me. The same one he kept me in.

This means I have to head back home without anyone finding out and following me there.

Gio is suddenly beside me while my head spins.

"I called Tynan," he says with a reassuring arm around my shoulders. "I told him Sergey has Eriu."

Fuck. I have to think of a way to go there without any of them playing hero and getting my sister and my best friend killed.

"You shouldn't have done that." I pivot to face him. "I have to go alone. He said he'd kill them if someone else shows up with me."

"Like hell you are." He takes my hand in his, face twisting with worry.

"I have to. It's the only way to ensure Eriu and Kora don't die."

"God damn it!" He runs a frustrated hand through his hair.

"You make sure no one follows me, okay?" I try to control my racing heart.

Time is running out. Sergey is unhinged. I don't even know if he'll keep his word. He could be killing them right now.

"Once I have them, I will let you know."

"You need backup. Just fucking give me the address, Iseult," he pleads. "I won't show up unless you need me. Promise."

I know he'd never keep that oath. I may not know everything about him yet, but I know that.

"Let me text it to you."

But instead, I give him a false address, about forty miles off from the target location. By the time he drives back to Massachusetts or tells my brothers where I am and they all realize I lied, I'll hopefully have Eriu and Kora.

I quickly shoot off a text, and he looks at his phone with a nod.

Suddenly, he grabs both sides of my face, pounding raw emotions spilling out of his gaze. He edges his face closer, looking me deep in my eyes.

"I can't lose you, Iseult. Do you understand me?"

"I can't lose you either." I sigh, holding his cheek in my palm. "But this is something I have to do."

Thirty-Nine

ISEULT

The bulletproof vest is heavy around my chest, my combat boots thudding against the concrete. I always carry the proper gear in my car in case of emergencies, and this is one big fucking emergency.

With a gun in hand, I slowly creep in the darkness of the abandoned warehouse I once called home for a week.

I never wanted my sister to know what it was like. The fear. The powerlessness. The panic. But here I am, back where it all began.

My skin crawls when I recall how he burned me, how I begged for him to stop. How I cried. My heart rate accelerates, but I fight the first instance of panic. Taking deep breaths—in, then out—I control it. I ease it.

I can't lose my composure. My focus has to be on saving Eriu and Kora.

"Show your face, Sergey!" I yell out.

Laughter greets me—a villainous laugh.

This is my time to finish him off. To reclaim my life. Because while he was out there, I couldn't rest. I couldn't breathe without thinking about what he did.

"I'm so happy to see you, malen'kaya."

His voice climbs from somewhere above, but I can't see a damn thing. The flashlight I'm holding on to isn't big enough to illuminate the entire space. I point it upward, finding him standing at the top of the stairs.

Something animalistic twists inside me when I stare at him after all this time. A snarl fights its way out, and I rush for the stairs, needing to get to him, to end his life once and for all.

The years haven't been kind to Sergey. His face has aged quite a bit, and he seems shorter than I remember, or maybe it's because I'm not a little kid anymore. He wears a black eye patch around his left eye, and despite the three-piece suit he wears, he still looks like a damn pirate.

I bet Gio has already told my whole family where I supposedly went, and they're all definitely looking for me. Unless he decided to go rogue—which, knowing him, is a strong possibility. I just couldn't afford any of them fucking this up. He's going to be pissed, but once I'm alive and the girls are safe, it won't matter.

"Where are they, asshole?" I start up, pointing my nine right at him.

"I must admit, I was very skeptical that you'd show up alone," he says. "But my men have informed me that you have kept your word."

"Unlike you, I actually know how to do that." I take two more steps up. "What is this about, Sergey? Want payback for your eye? Well, I'll give it to you."

I climb up further until I'm right in front of him, practically towering over his short frame.

"Just let them go."

"I'll take more than your eye, dorogoya. I'll take everything." His upper lip curls. "And just like your mother, I'll burn you alive and send your papochka the video present."

At the mention of my mother, my pulse beats like a drum in my ears and my hands itch to get to him. To kill him. But I have to save my sister and my friend. They're alive. They still have a chance. I can't let him take them too.

"You can do whatever you want to me. Just take me to them and let me see that they're okay."

"Let's go, then." He extends a hand for me to lead the way.

But I shake my head. "You go first."

He chuckles. "I won't hurt you. Not yet."

"Just walk, old man," I snap, and that has him scoffing.

"Funny girl."

He leads the way through a long, equally dark narrow pathway, a drip of water sounding off in the distance. We turn right, then left, then another right, and come to a black door.

"Open it," he demands, standing off to the side while my body pumps with adrenaline, a bout of anxiety hitting me in the chest.

I place the flashlight back in my pocket. My hand on the doorknob, I slowly turn it, pushing it all the way, coming into a large empty room.

It's then I see Eriu and Kora, all the way at the back. Gagged, hands tied up in front of them, while they're on the floor on their knees, two men behind them with guns pointed to their heads.

Anger pummels through my voice. "Get those weapons off of them!"

"Why would I do that?" Sergey challenges. "It's my insurance policy. You do something to me, and they shoot both girls."

Eriu wails while Kora holds her hand. My sister's eyes lock with mine, tears leaking from the edges.

I'm sorry, I mouth, and she only cries harder.

"They're innocent," I tell Sergey, as though that has ever made a fucking difference to the psychopath.

"Net dorogoya, there's no such thing as innocents in our world. You should know that by now." His fingers run down my arm, and I flinch his touch away.

"What I know is…" I bite down on my molars. "…that you killed my mother over territory and then took me as revenge, which cost you your son. Was it worth it?"

He stares at me through his one good eye, his dark brown gaze turning narrow. "To do what I did to your father, to take his wife… Of course it was worth it."

His leery grin doesn't help the quiet wrath that dances inside me, wanting blood.

"He was always so full of himself. I wanted him to hurt, and I did that."

He doesn't even care that his own son is dead, does he?

"Let's get this over with," I clip out, marching toward the girls.

When I get right in front and see my sister's bruised cheek and Kora's bloody nose, my blood rushes to my ears.

"You fucking hurt them!" I grab him by the collar of his blue pinstriped jacket and near my face to his, until there's barely anything between us.

"They were resisting." He chuckles. "That's what happens to bitches who don't behave." He looks me straight in the eyes. "Get off of me, or they die."

The men dig their muzzles into Eriu's and Kora's heads, giving me no choice but to release him.

"Tell your men to ease off of them." My inhales and exhales fight for space in my lungs. And I squeeze the weapon in my hand.

He inclines his chin at them, and they back off a little.

From the corner of my left eye, I find a few bricks just lying around, like someone forgot to finish a construction of some kind, dust and debris under my feet. Maybe I can figure out a way to distract them, then hit one of the men with a brick and shoot Sergey and the other one. But that would be risky. Either one could kill the girls.

What the hell can I do here?

As I'm thinking of ways to extinguish all three, something rattles in the distance, like someone hit or dropped something below us.

Sergey jerks his head toward the noise.

"Idi prover," he tells one of the men.

"Lodna." The guy rushes out of the room.

Within a minute, he lets out a scream. And soon enough, that scream dies, and we're left with nothing but silence.

"I swear…" Sergey tightens his jaw. "…if you sent someone, you will all die."

"I have no idea what's going on out there." I lower my face until I'm in his space. "Maybe it's your boys. Last I spoke to them, they wanted you dead."

He laughs, throwing his head back. "They will get what's coming to them for turning on me."

The rattling sound returns, taunting us in a steady rhythm.

Sergey peers over at the other man, like he's not sure if he should tell him to go and see what's happening.

"What's wrong, Sergey?" I mock. "Scared to be alone with me?"

My devious grin makes his whole face go red.

"I'm not afraid of any woman." He looks me up and down with disgust. "I remember how loud you screamed. How much you begged."

His laughter grates up my insides while the rattling grows louder.

"Not begging anymore, am I?"

"Go see what happened," he tells the other man, who silently walks away, taking his weapon with him.

We're finally alone, and I don't worry about who's out there—who's hurting his men—because as the second one screams, I rush for Sergey and throw him on the ground with a round kick. He falls hard with a grunt, the gun in his hand slipping. I grab it immediately, whacking him hard on the head, before I drop it and use my fists, over and over until he groans, until blood seeps from his forehead, his cheek, his brow. It's everywhere.

Kora screams to get my attention, shimmying closer, and I realize their ankles are bound too.

Leaving the bastard behind, I slip both guns into my waistband and rush toward Kora, undoing her binds first, knowing if I need help, she'll be the first to be able to give it to me.

She rips off her gag and throws her arms around me for a quick embrace while I free my sister.

Once Eriu's gag is free, she snivels and throws her thin arms around me, tucking her head into my shoulder as she cries.

"You're okay. It's okay. I'm sorry." My hand clasps the back of her head. "I'm so sorry about everything." My voice cracks, relief washing over me.

She's okay. He didn't hurt her.

"It's not your fault." She sniffles. "I left because I didn't want to marry him. Because I knew he cared about you."

"What?"

Before she can say anything else, a gunshot rings out.

"Fuck! We have to go. Get Eriu out of here while I deal with him," I tell Kora, who jumps to her feet.

"I need a weapon." She reaches out a hand. "Just in case those assholes come back."

I nod, handing her Sergey's gun while I tighten my grip on mine.

"Take your sister and go." She glares down at my tormentor with revulsion. "Let me take care of him."

"Make it hurt," I toss out crudely, no longer caring if I'm the one to kill him.

Getting my sister to safety is the priority now. Taking Eriu's hand, I plow toward the door, and as I do, a gunshot rings out.

Eriu lets out a guttural scream, and it takes me a second to realize why.

Because that bullet didn't come from the outside.

No. It came from here.

A river of crimson rolls down my arm, and I register the burn at my shoulder as I turn around.

Slowly pivoting.

And as I do, my best friend's demonic eyes greet me. The gun I gave her is pointed at my chest while she wears a vicious grin I've never quite seen her wear before.

GIO

The amount of fury I have within me right now, knowing she lied to me about where she's going, is insurmountable.

Of course, I had every intention of following her. And she knew that. My little Red knows me well. I tried tailing her after she left, but she must've caught on, driving like she was in a drag race before I lost her.

When I finally arrived at the location she gave me, it was an empty, abandoned lot. No trace of Sergey or Iseult.

I called Tynan and told him everything, and he wanted me to come to Patrick's home so I could help them with intel.

As soon as I saw Patrick, I knew I still wasn't his favorite person. But I also knew we had to talk. I owed it to Iseult and to our future.

While the Quinn boys are grabbing weapons and equipment before we go scouring all possible locations, I walk into Patrick's office without knocking.

He's got his face in his palms, a glass of clear liquor beside him. He's lost two daughters, and my mother is still pissed at him. He's got a lot of reasons to drink.

He looks up, a tight glare crossing his face.

"We need to talk," I say, pulling up a chair in front of his desk, not giving a fuck if he wants me here or not.

"What the hell do you want? Not enough you got one of my daughters running away and another doing God knows what."

"When I get her back, I'm marrying her. Iseult *will* be my wife. And the way I see it, you have two options."

His nostrils expand, but he lets me go on.

"You either accept it or live a life without her. Because there's nothing you can do to me to make me give her up."

"Who the hell do you think you're talking to?" He rises slowly, eyes expanding.

My features tighten. "We're both men. I'm just telling you what's going to happen. I thought, of all people, you'd understand, seeing as how you didn't get to be with my mother. How you two were sneaking around while she was engaged to my father.

I thought you'd see through your bullshit and let us be together."

"That is *not* the same." His chest rapidly rises and falls. "I loved her."

"And I love *her*."

"What?" His brows rise, and speechlessly, he nestles back down, the hardness vanishing from his face little by little. "You love my daughter?"

"Hell…" I run a hand down my face with a laugh. "I may have never been in love before, but I think I am. Because I don't know what else this feeling would be." I press my fingers to the center of my chest. "That heaviness here that makes you feel like if she's not with you, you may as well die."

"I know that feeling quite well," he snickers. "And you've been in love with her how long now?"

"Sometimes it feels like I've been in love with her forever and just didn't know it until I met her."

He chuckles faintly. "Oh, son, yer fecked, aren't ya?"

"Yeah." I shrug. "She's worth it, though."

"Aye, she is." He nods. "So when did it start?"

"I met her way before I knew she was your daughter. We were both on the same job a little over a year ago. Then she ran off. And I found her. And once I did, I couldn't keep myself away."

"A year, and I'm only hearing of this now?"

"She disappeared on me for four days the first time and a year the second time. I couldn't find her until that day I walked into your house and saw her again, standing next to her sister."

"Jesus Christ." He drowns his drink and pours himself another. "If you two would've explained this, we could've avoided all the theatrics."

"I tried. She didn't want to, telling me she'd never marry me and that's what you wanted. Then too much time passed, and she got nervous."

He nods. "And she wants to marry you now?"

"She does."

He smiles. I can tell he really loves her.

"She's tough, my girl. As tough as they come. But she's also fragile, and she doesn't like for people to know that. So if I agree to this, you've gotta promise me you're going to take care of her, even when she fights you on it." His eyes are stern as he waits for my answer.

"I'm used to her fighting me." I smirk.

"Feckin' hell. I've gotta talk to her. I was too harsh. I didn't know… I was worried about Eriu, and I said things." He shakes his head, picks up the glass of liquor, and downs it in one quick gulp. He places the glass back down and stares at me. "You ask her already?"

"I have." I nod. "The day before you threw her out."

"And what did she say?"

"Well, she didn't toss the ring at me." I chuckle.

"I guess we're going to have ourselves a wedding."

There's a knock on the door, and Cillian appears, his green eyes bouncing between us. "We got a location on Iseult. We've gotta hurry."

"Where?" Patrick and I jump to our feet simultaneously.

"The same place that fucking bastard held her back then."

"How the hell didn't we think of that?!"

Patrick storms toward the door, and I follow.

"No time for that now, Dad. We've gotta go before he takes them all somewhere we can't find them."

Forty

ISEULT

"**K**ora!" I cry. "What the hell are you doing?" It had to be an accident. Maybe Sergey hit her, and her arm jerked and she shot me.

But as I stare down at Sergey's barely moving body, still groaning from the beating I gave him, I know I'm feeding myself lies.

She laughs, a heinous laugh. I don't even recognize her.

"Iseult?" Eriu whispers, dashing behind my back. "What's happening?" Fear trickles between her words as she trembles against me.

"I don't know," I breathe. "But stay behind me. You understand?"

"Okay. But you're bleeding," she adds.

"I don't care right now."

Aiming the weapon at me, Kora kneels beside Sergey, checking his wounds. "Hang in there, Papa. I'll get you out."

"Papa?" I whisper, my heart racing.

My stomach churns. But that makes no sense, because Paolo is her father. My father has known that family since she was born.

An eerie feeling creeps into my gut.

"Kora, what the hell is going on? What are you doing? You fucking shot me!"

Her attention zaps to me, eyes narrowed, her upper lip curling. "You don't know how long I've waited for this." She straightens herself, the gun aimed at me. "He told me that we'd be together. That I could go to Russia with him. And all I had to do was find enough intel about what you guys were planning against him."

Eriu gasps.

"Shh, it's okay," I tell her, my own head spinning, my brain unable to catch up with the treachery of her words.

Her eyes are distant and demonic as she continues.

"But it's been years since I infiltrated the academy! And I'm so sick of it!" she snarls, the muzzle once again aiming in my direction.

Drops of my blood drip on the floor beside my foot. I ignore it, not having a choice. I have to figure out how to get us out of here.

She paces back and forth as she laughs coldly. "See, he wanted revenge for what you did to him, and he was tired of waiting, so the last part of his plan for me was to help him get exactly that. And when I saw Eriu leaving, I called him, and he sent his men to get her."

"You fucking bitch!" My heart rams in my ribs.

She betrayed us right before my eyes. I trusted her. I loved her, and she was nothing but a mole. How could I have been so blind?

She giggles, biting into her bottom lip, flinging her blonde hair back behind her shoulder. "I outsmarted you. Can you believe it? I outsmarted *Iseult Quinn*." She scoffs. "That must *kill* you."

Enraged, my pulse thrashing, a hand on the gun at my waistband, I rush toward her. But as I do, she raises the weapon to the ceiling and fires.

A warning shot.

"Get any closer and I'll kill your sister." She grins. "I know how little you value your life, but her…" She jerks the weapon behind me at Eriu. "I know you care about her."

"How could you do this!" I shake my head. "We were friends. I welcomed you into my life, my family's life, and you betray us?"

Recalling all the talks we had, all the times we had fun and laughed, I feel even more betrayed. She was pretending the entire time?

"My allegiance is to my father. He's my blood. Paolo was never my dad. He adopted me from an orphanage in Russia after my mother died. Can't remember her." She shrugs indifferently.

Adopted? They never said a fucking word to anyone. I remember seeing photos of Paolo's wife at the hospital with Kora in her arms. They lied?

"But they brought me here and pretended I was theirs. Until I discovered the truth about where I came from by doing one of those blood ancestry things. All of a sudden, I had Russian blood, and I knew neither of my so-called parents were Russian. So I went digging."

She paces again, lost in her own thoughts, a crude smile fastened to her mouth.

"I found family members online, called them, spoke to them, until I found Sergey. He didn't want me at first, denied it, but then he admitted the truth." She glances down at him adoringly. "I was his daughter. Of course he regretted not claiming me, right, Papa?" She grins at him in a sadistic way. "But I've forgiven him. We're going to be a real family. And you…" She glares, pointing accusatorily at me with the gun. "You will not take that away from me."

"You don't want to do this, Kora. You don't want to kill me."

"I'll kill anyone who hurts my father. Do you understand?!" she shouts.

Out of nowhere, something explodes, and a heavy fog erupts, blinding us all.

"Eriu!" I cough, rubbing my eyes. "Eriu!"

I feel for her, finding air, as male shouting goes off. Stomping… heavy stomping.

"I'm here!" Eriu calls, grabbing my hand. "I'm right here."

I breathe a sigh of relief.

"Vazmi yeyo," someone says in a heavy Russian accent, and then more voices.

The smoke starts to dissipate, and I make out multiple men in all black, weapons in their waistbands.

"Who's here?" I call.

"Ah, Iseult…" Konstantin's voice rings out as calm as ever as he appears right before me, eyes practically black. "I'm glad to see you have fared well."

"Let me go!" Kora screams as two men hold her arms from each side, while Sergey is still on the ground, trying to get up.

"What the hell are you doing here?" I cough, while Eriu does the same, sticking to my side like glue.

"I tracked him down. He thought he was clever, eluding us, but he was never very smart."

"They're mine," I snap with a heavy inhale. "Both of them. I will never forgive you if you take that from me."

He stares at me, his concentrated gaze considering my words. "He's my father. It should be on me to end his life. But I will give you Katarina."

"That's her name?" My eyes widen.

"That's the name her mother gave her, yes." His lips jerk. "I had wondered where our sister disappeared to after your mother died."

"How the hell did no one know you have a sister? And how did she end up with Paolo?"

He sighs. "Well, you see, my father had an affair with a whore back in Russia. One of many, of course, but only one of them got pregnant. She had a child."

He gestures behind him with a jerk of his head.

"The woman died when Katarina was a baby, and my father did not want her, so she went into foster care until she was adopted. But once Katarina found out who her real father was, she never let him forget that he abandoned her." He laughs, as though lost to his memories. "She was a feisty young woman, and my father took a liking to her savagery, especially when she killed two of his men to get to him, then on another occasion burned down his car. All to get his attention. And that she did."

He turns to look at her, shaking his head, while she narrows her eyes and fights to escape the clutches binding her.

"He could have killed her," he goes on. "But my father felt a kinship to that fire inside her. She was every bit like him. So he made her a promise after he found out who adopted her. He told her if she spied for him for a while until he was satisfied, he'd let her live with him."

"And you just let this all happen without telling my father?" I raise my voice, completely consumed with rage. "He's going to have your head for this."

His mouth curls like a serpent. "I would not threaten me if I were you. I hold no allegiance to your family. If you were duped by some girl, that is on you."

He's right. He didn't owe us a goddamn thing. And it's never been Konstantin's M.O. to be an honorable man.

"Did she see him often before the war between our sides began?" I ask, staring at her while her face pulls with a cunning grin.

"He didn't share all the precise details, but I do, in fact, know she'd sneak out of high school to see him. That's when they were first reunited, when she was around fifteen."

"How the fuck did I not know?!" My voice carries. "I told her everything. I *trusted* her with everything."

"It's really not your fault. She was a very good liar." He grins at her. "Like father, like daughter."

"Don't look at me like that, Konstantin," Kora grits. "You have never helped me. You had everything. His attention. His love. While I had to live with people who weren't even blood."

"Like that was so fucking difficult!" I snigger. "Paolo was a great father, and Cynthia was a wonderful mother, you fucking ungrateful bitch! Do you know what I would've done to have my mother back, biological or not?"

I take a step forward, but Konstantin sticks out his arm, blocking me. I shove it away, and he doesn't stop me.

"Your father took her away." I pause, staring at the woman I no longer recognize. "He never cared about you." I laugh wryly, disgust chained to my voice while rage marks her features. "He never wanted you. He was using you to get to us. And you just fell for it. Like the starved, pathetic girl you are." I shake my head. "Now you're going to die, Kora. And as you do, you're going to know I'm the one who killed you."

Eriu gasps, and I forgot she was standing off the side with one of Konstantin's men.

"Could you tell them to take her out for this?" I ask him.

"Of course."

"No, I don't want to go!" Eriu cries.

"Please just wait outside, okay? I don't want you to see this. I'll be done soon, and we can go home, okay?"

Tears leak out of the corners of her eyes, but she nods and is ushered out.

Once she's gone, my attention returns to my former best friend.

"Such a coward." She spits in my face, and I wipe it with the back of my arm while the men tighten their grasps on her. "Going to kill me without a fair fight?"

I remove the nine-mil at my waistband.

"You don't deserve anything but that. Believe it or not, I cared about you," I confess while my heart breaks. I didn't mean anything to her, while she meant everything to me. "You were pretending the whole time, weren't you? Sneaking off to tell him everything about the academy, about my family."

"That's right." She wags a brow, a contemptuous grin on her mouth. "He knew everything. It was his idea for me to join Caellach. So I begged Paolo. Begged him until he allowed it."

I drill her with a cutting look. "I hope it was worth it, Kora. I hope wherever you go, you're finally happy." As I raise the gun in the air and aim right between the eyes, I stare at her one final time. "Goodbye, Kora."

"Wait!" she shouts, her expression softer.

A glimpse of the friend I once thought I knew appears. But her mask flips, and the devil is exposed yet again.

"I'll see you in hell, Iz." She chuckles.

Pop.

Her laughter dies with my bullet. Her head slumps forward, and I watch as the men carry her out of sight.

"Feel any better?" Konstantin appears beside me, towering

over me.

He's at least a good six-seven. A damn giant.

"No," I admit, placing my gun back. "Not at all."

"Yeah…" He throws an arm around my shoulders. "That's one thing about revenge. It doesn't really make you feel any better. Maybe even worse."

"Get your fucking hands off my wife!"

Gio!

My heart warms at the sound of his voice and, turning around, I find him there, staring affectionately at me. But also with a whole lot of anger.

His eyes take me in with Konstantin, and he looks about ready to break his arm off…or worse. I push off Konstantin just as Gio prowls toward me and grabs my jaw as soon as he's near.

He searches my eyes, his brows snapping, and then he kisses me, nipping and groaning as he pulls back breathlessly. "Never do that shit to me again, you hear me?"

I nod, filled with my own untamable emotions.

Konstantin chuckles. "Welcome."

"Boss…" one of Konstantin's men calls, running up behind Gio. "He almost killed us to get up here."

Konstantin breaks with heavy laughter. "That's alright. We were just about done here. Just one final thing left."

He removes a knife from a case in a holster around his waist. Staring at me, he extends his palm and nods. Eyes widened, I pick up the knife.

"Thank you," I breathe, accepting his gift, which is what this is.

"Make him hurt, baby." Gio clasps my nape and pins his forehead to mine. "I love you."

I nod, feeling the weight of his love, but unable to say those words. Not here, not now, not in this maddening chaos. Squeezing his hand, I make my way to the man who ruined my life.

Sergey's face is barely recognizable from the beating. I didn't realize how badly I had hurt him until this moment. And my throbbing knuckles are definitely paying the price.

I settle on top of him, straddling his body. "You are going to lose your other eye before you lose your life."

A sardonic chuckle fights its way out, blood dripping down the corner of his mouth as he slowly props himself on his shoulders.

"Malinkiya suka, like your mama." He grins, crimson lining between his teeth.

And with a quick twist of my hand, I stab him straight through the eye and watch gleefully as he screams, over and over, until my ears bleed.

I yank out the blade, and this time, I stab him right in the center of his throat. His mouth parts on a silent scream. With a groan, I drag out the knife and stab him again and again, until my hands are coated in his blood, until some of it splatters onto my face.

"He's gone, baby." Arms fold around me from behind, my fiancé's voice lulling me out of the rage-filled fog.

The fight in me slowly scatters, and when he gently takes the knife from me and lifts me into his arms, I cry, letting it all go. The pain, the horror I endured, the years of suppressed anger and sadness… I let it all go right here in his arms.

Because I'm finally home, and he gave me that.

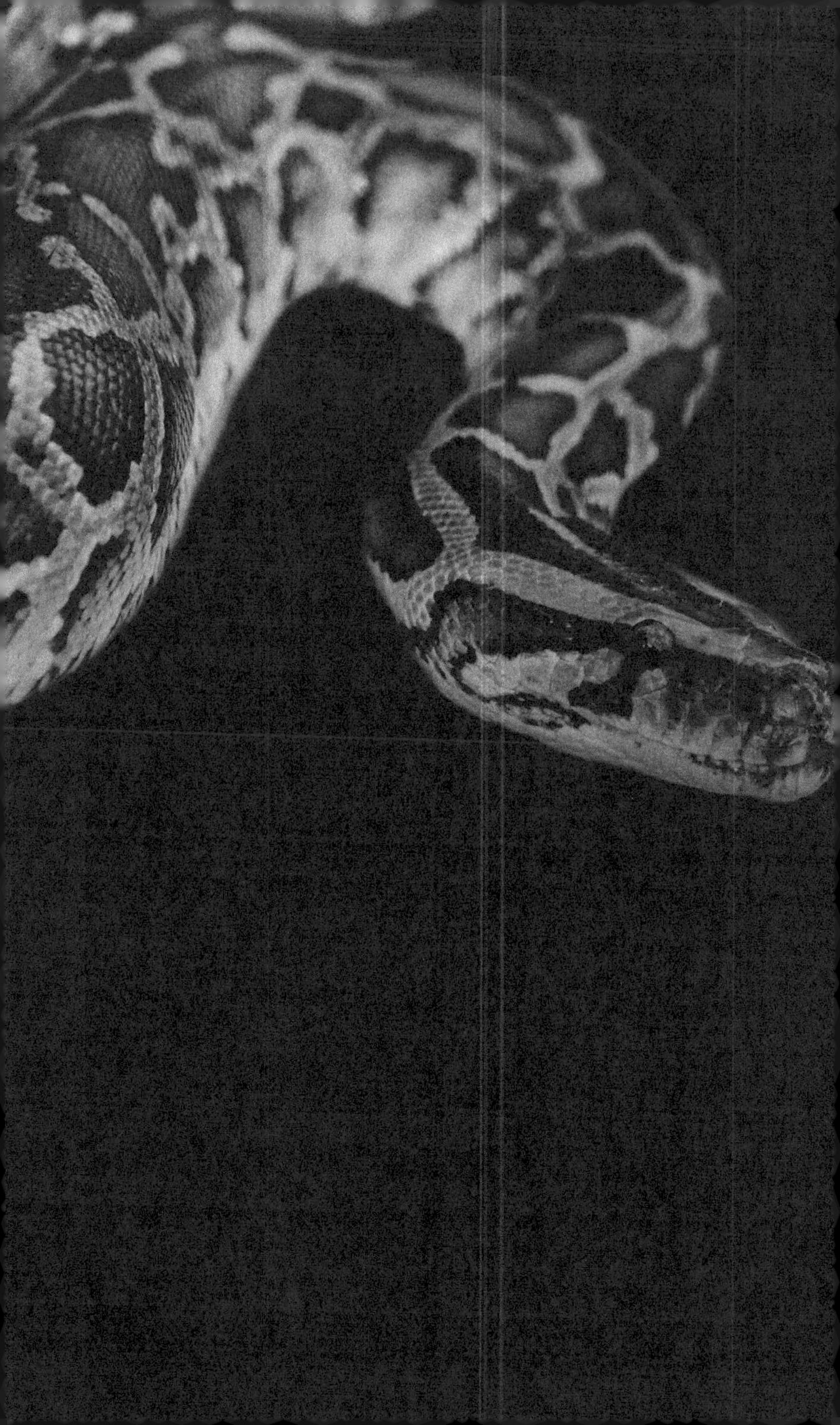

Forty-One

GIO

While Iseult is back in her home in Cherry Grove, taking a bath with her arm stitched and bandaged, I pace back and forth in her bedroom, attempting to contain the pummeling of my pulse.

We barely said a word to one another on the way back. She was content with my arms around her, and I didn't want to ruin the moment by telling her how angry I am at her for lying to me. She could've gotten herself killed.

I could've lost her. I could've lost the only woman I've ever loved, and that fear hasn't left me.

She got herself shot, and fuck, it could've been much worse. But at least it was only a graze on her shoulder. One of Patrick's docs patched her up and said she should be good as new in a few weeks. Red, of course, acts like it's no big deal. But to me, it is. She's mine. Mine to worry about. Always.

The water of the adjacent shower turns off, and a few minutes later, she's coming out, wearing a loose-fitted black t-shirt and black leggings. Her hair is damp, pulled up into a messy bun, and her gorgeous face has not an ounce of makeup on. I could stare at her for my entire life and never get bored.

As soon as I lay eyes on her, every ounce of anger simply vanishes. And in its place is just a man who's completely obsessed with his woman. All I want to do right in this moment is hold her and tell her how much I really love her.

"Hi," she says as she closes the door. "We should talk."

Inhaling a fiery breath, I erase the distance between us, my gaze sweeping over every inch of her face.

"Don't ever put yourself in danger like that," I whisper, cupping her cheek, my forehead bowing against hers. "I didn't realize how badly I was worried about you until I found you. My heart felt like it was ripping right out of my chest, bambina." I dart back to look at her, her brows drawn, her own emotions evident. "The thought of losing you makes me insane."

"We already established that you're crazy." A faint smile falls to her lips.

"Of course I'm crazy." I brush my mouth with hers. "Crazy about you."

She sighs. She fucking sighs like in those damn romantic movies that I'll never admit I watch.

"You could've told me where you were. I would've given you space," I say.

She chuckles. "Oh, come on, Gio." She throws her good arm over my shoulder. "Let's be honest. You never would've done that. You would've stormed in, and who knows what would've happened." Her eyes press to a brief close. "I had no idea Kora was going to betray us, and neither did you. Maybe the outcome would've been worse had you gone in." She palms my cheek. "I told you I could handle myself."

"This has nothing to do with your ability to keep yourself safe, baby." I lower my mouth to her forehead and leave a tender kiss behind. "I know you can. Believe me, I know… But as your future husband, could you maybe *not* make me worry like that from time to time? That's all I'm asking for."

Her eyes caress me, lingering on mine for so long, I don't even know if she'll say something in return. But then her lips spread into a wide grin, and that smile… It brings my soul to life.

"I love you so much, Gio."

My heart pummels, and I almost have to wonder if I heard right. Because that was the first time she ever said it.

"I'm sorry, could you repeat that, because it almost sounded like…"

She fights a laugh. "It was a slip of the tongue."

I inhale, my chest swelling. And I close my eyes, feeling like a damn giant on top of a mountain.

"Say it again," I whisper. "Please, baby, say it again."

"I love you." She kisses the corner of my mouth, and I groan, my palm gripping the back of her head.

"Again."

"I love you," she whispers, and this time as she does, I kiss her with all the mustered-up passion, our love filling the void I've lived with for so long.

Never realizing what it meant to truly have everything.

ISEULT

"You wanted to speak to me?" I walk into my father's study the following day as he places a book on his floor-to-ceiling bookshelf.

I used to read a lot when I was a kid, but I stopped after Mom died. She loved to read. It was her favorite thing, so of course, it became mine. She'd sit in the outdoor gazebo and curl around a good romance novel. She'd get lost in the world, and we'd talk about it too. About good men and how they should treat women. I know she'd approve of Gio if she met him. That fulfills me somehow, to have her approval without actually having it.

My father had gotten the bookshelf for her. I guess that was one of the ways he showed her he loved her.

"Sit." He gestures toward his chair and glances down at my shoulder with a strain of his features. "How are you feeling?" He takes a seat across from me.

"I'll be fine, Dad." I shrug. "You know I've had worse."

He nods. "I know, but as your father, that doesn't make me feel any better. I never wanted this life for you, Iseult." He blows out a breath. "I wanted you married, happy with some kids. But I ruined that for you, didn't I?"

"Of course not. Being married doesn't guarantee happiness, Dad."

He chuckles, shaking his head. "You're not wrong. But still, I wanted you to be happy and that's what I saw for you."

"Maybe it's not too late."

"Yes, Gio… That's why I wanted to talk to you." He pauses, his eyes rapt on my face. "About what I said to you last time…" He clears his throat and straightens his spine.

Apologizing isn't my father's strong suit. He reacts before thinking sometimes. And after what happened to my sister after having to kill someone I thought was my best friend, I don't even need an apology. I just want to be welcomed back.

"It's fine." I give him a smile to ease the tension on his face.

"As long as you're not throwing me out again, we're good."

"Shite, darling, you know I couldn't last a day without you. I'm old and stubborn and I felt you violated a code of honor I hold dear. But I know now, that wasn't true."

"He told you?"

Gio hadn't talked to me about having a discussion with my father, so this is all news to me.

"He did, and I'm glad. He really loves you."

"How could he not?" I raise my chin.

He chuckles. "Your mother would've loved to see you smiling like that again. I have no doubt she's been watching over you, over all you kids, from up there." He points to the heavens.

I don't believe in God myself, but I can respect his belief. I do hope she's watching me, though, and I hope I made her proud.

"So, you love him, then?" My father leans into his chair.

"Unfortunately." I roll my eyes.

"Well, that sounds like marriage to me." His laughter fills the room, and I laugh with him. "I wish you'd felt comfortable enough telling me all of this so we could've avoided my heatedness."

I scoff. "Really? Come on. You would've brushed it off and told me to find someone else."

"Not if I thought it was serious."

"It wasn't then. It is now."

"Well, then I will support your union. But I want the marriage done fast. Will that be a problem?"

"Not if Fernanda has anything to say about it."

That woman can plan a wedding in a day.

"Poor lad. I don't know how he's going to tolerate you," he teases.

"I'm not so bad. After the first few years, he'll get used to me." A grin spreads across my face.

"You don't know what it does to me to see your face shining like that." He huffs out a burdened breath. "I never really told you how sorry I was for what he did to you."

His eyes grow sad, and my heart clutches in a tight fist, knowing exactly who *he* is.

"No." I shake my head, slanting forward to grab his hand. "What happened wasn't on you. Sergey was insane. You didn't do anything to provoke it." I squeeze his knuckles. "I'm okay, Dad. You don't have to worry about me."

He nods and closes his eyes for a quick moment.

"I have something for you." He lets go of my hand and rummages inside his desk drawer. "Your mother made me promise to give this to you for when you have your first real love."

My heart skips a beat. "What?"

"She left you a letter, darling."

"She did?" I pant and sniffle back tears that come storming in like a gale brewing on the horizon, waiting its turn to erupt.

To have her words, to have a piece of her… It would mean everything to me.

"She had this thing she did," he explains, handing me a closed envelope, my name scribbled in fancy cursive. "She wrote you all a letter for important times in your adult life."

"Mom," I whisper with a cry, running my fingertips over each curve.

"I hated that she did it because it meant she was planning for the chance she would die before me, but she kept on doing it, regardless of what I said. And I'm really glad she did." His voice grows tender.

It's then I really see it in his eyes. His love for her. In his own way, he loved my mother too.

"Why didn't you tell me?" I ask, afraid to open it, my heart ramming in my rib cage.

"She was specific. Only give it to you on certain occasions. And I'd never break her trust."

"Thank you," I whisper.

"Yeah." He scrubs his face with a palm. "Enough heavy stuff. How about we go and get some food and drinks? The cooks have prepared a feast for everyone. The Marinos all should be here shortly."

"I just need a minute with Mom," I tell him.

"Of course you do, darling. You come down when you're ready. Oh, before I forget, there's one last thing. Hadleigh called. Hudson is missing."

"What? What do you mean, missing?"

He shrugs. "He went to work the other day and never came home."

"Are we helping her find him?"

"We will, but we can't let her know how we do it."

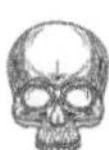

As I settle beside Gio in one of the spare rooms at my father's house, my hands tremble around the letter, afraid I'll burst into tears at the very first line.

My vision clouds while his hand gently caresses my back.

"It's okay, baby. I'm right here. Not going anywhere. Unless you want me to." He gazes softly, and I shake my head.

"No. I want you to stay. It's just a lot for me. I never thought I'd hear from her again, you know?"

"Of course."

This is going to be something I cherish, waiting for all the letters she has written.

"Can you open it?" I grimace. "Because I'll just sit here all night staring at it."

He chuckles. "Sure, bambina. I'd do anything for you."

His words, the way he stares longingly into my eyes… I feel his emotions reflected back. Never thought a man like him could ever love a broken woman like me. But he loves me with his whole heart. I can just see it right there in his eyes.

I've spent so many days telling myself I was okay, that the scars on my body and the wounds I carried in my heart in silence didn't bother me. That my anxiety was just the way it was.

But I was wrong.

Hopefully, I can gather the courage to talk to someone, a shrink or something. It's worth a shot. I never believed in therapists, and honestly, I don't think they work for everyone. But I can't say that until I actually try it for myself.

Gently, with every care in the world, he opens the envelope and hands it back to me. With a woosh of a breath and a final glance at him, I remove the letter and start to read.

My Dearest Iseult,

If you're reading this, I'm probably not here OR you snuck into your father's study and found this. If that's the case, I'm grounding you.

I let out a bout of laughter even as the tears claim my emotions.

But if that's not the case and your father gave you this letter after I'm gone, then I hope you're not crying. Because I'm not sad knowing you found true love.

I know sometimes you thought the books I read were cliché, but I truly believe that some people are meant to find that kind of love, that level of commitment and self-sacrifice. And if you have found that in someone, then you're richer than most of the people in this world.

Whoever he is, I hope he takes care of you. And I hope you take care of him too. That's what makes love work: a mutual devotion and constant work. Keep working. Because love is worth it.

I'm so proud of you, my darling girl. I don't have to be here to know that. You're special, Iseult, and I never want you to forget your light and that warrior heart, no matter who tries to take it.

Knowing you, you'll walk right up to them and snatch it right back.

Until my next letter.

I love you forever.

Love,
Mom

The tears have pooled in my eyes as I start the letter all over again, memorizing each word, knowing how much it must've hurt her to write this.

I wonder when the next letter will come. I can't wait for it.

His arms circle around me, and I slant my head on his shoulder and cry.

And with Gio, I know it's okay to cry. Because being in love means being who you are, and I can be that way with him.

Forty-Two

ISEULT

Hand in hand, we make it downstairs to the dinner my father arranged for both sides of the family.

It's a way to celebrate Gio and me, and it was something everyone needed. Between what happened with Gio's father and his betrayal of Raph and what happened with Sergey and Kora, we needed to unwind.

I spot Eriu sitting by herself on the sofa, watching Sophia twirl in her pink tutu, her brown hair up in a ballerina bun while she dances to Taylor Swift's "We Are Never Ever Getting Back Together."

I give Gio a kiss on his cheek, telling him I need a moment with my sister. His lips drop to the top of my hand before he rushes toward Sophia and throws her over his shoulder.

She giggles. "Put me down, you crazy man!" Her little fists pound on his back.

It makes my heart swell to see how good he is with his niece. He'd make a good father. Maybe we'd balance each other out.

"Hey…" I sit beside Eriu, not having spoken to her since what happened yesterday.

She slept most of the day and seemed quiet once she woke up. Not that I can blame her. It was a lot, especially for someone who hasn't been around violence.

She's lived a pretty sheltered life, and I'm glad for that. I'd take her place every time. I want my sister to be like a normal girl her age—attending college, having boyfriends, going to parties. Not get kidnapped by my tormentor and bitch of a best friend, who turned out to be an evil cunt.

"Hey." She returns a faint smile. "Sophia is so darn cute, isn't she?"

"Yeah…" I stare fondly at the little girl. "She's alright."

Eriu glances at my arm. "Does it hurt?"

"Nah, I'll be fine." My lips pinch with a smile. "Nothing to worry about. Doc said I'll be good as new in no time."

Other than a scar, I'll be healed in a few weeks. Just a flesh wound, like I thought.

She nods, staring silently at everyone.

"Look at me," I tell her.

When she does, I take her hand in mine.

"I'm sorry, Eriu. I'm so sorry if you left because of me. It's been eating at me, and I can't help but think what could've happened to you if I hadn't found you."

"Why would you be sorry? You didn't do anything wrong." Her brows lower. "I told Dad the same. The only reason I left was because I didn't want to marry Gio. And after Dad's wedding— after I realized how much Gio cares about you—I figured if I left, Dad would have no choice but to make you marry Gio."

My laugh fills me with warmth. "That was pretty ballsy."

She shrugs. "Sometimes I have it in me."

"You have it all in you, Eriu. You're strong. Beautiful. Capable." I drag a long inhale into my lungs. "I love you."

"And I love you." She slants her head. "You deserve this, Iseult. You've always been so worried about taking care of me. Running away was my way of taking care of you."

"Hit me right in the feels, why don't you?" I twist my face and snicker.

"I mean it." Her eyes stare sharply at me. "I still can't believe Kora did that. I can't get it out of my head. I thought she was our friend."

I clasp an arm around her. "I know. This world is made up of people who are capable of hurting us in unimaginable ways. But we have to remember that there are just as many people who would give us the world without us even asking."

My eyes go to Gio, and his find mine.

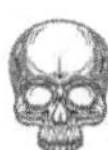

I hold Sophia's hands as we spin around my father's living room, waiting to see which one of us becomes dizzy first.

I didn't make the rules. The kid did. And she's one stiff competitor.

"Are you ready to give up yet?" she joshes, while everyone else chuckles.

"Gonna get bested by the wee one," Fionn teases.

"Not in this life," I mutter, my head literally spinning.

How the fuck is she not done yet?

"Are you sure you're not dizzy?" I ask her.

"Nope." She goes even faster. "Daddy says I have superpowers. I used to spin like this when I was three, and he would worry, but

I never got dizzy. Right, Daddy?"

Michael chuckles. "Yes, princess. But maybe you should stop now and go have ice cream."

"The ice cream will still be there, Daddy. I have to win."

"Oh my God. You're a little devil," I huff, slowing down, until I stop completely because I'm about to fall on my ass and really embarrass myself. "You win!"

The entire room spins like a merry-go-round and the damn bullet wound throbs like a mother. I drop my palms on my knees and take some deep breaths.

"You owe me twenty dollars, please," the tiny devil declares, sticking out her hand, standing in front of me.

Well, more like five of her is standing in front of me while I try not to heave.

"How about Uncle Gio gives you that money?" He loops an arm around me from behind and kisses the back of my head. "I could've told you to never go head-to-head with Sophia in this game," he whispers to me. "She's going to win every time."

I groan. "Could've led with that before I suffered at the hands of this tiny human."

"Kinda wanted to see you get beaten by a six-year-old."

I turn and glare, his face appearing wobbly before my eyes.

"Let me get Iseult on the couch," he tells Sophia with amusement flanking his tone. "Then I'll give you a fifty."

He shifts to my side and still has his arm planted around me.

Sophia's eyes grow wide, and her mouth widens with joy. "I can buy so much gum with fifty dollars. Thanks, Uncle Gio!" She throws herself at him and hugs him tightly.

As I settle on the sofa, he takes out his wallet and hands her the cash.

"Thank you!" She grins and waves the cash around, dancing all silly, while Elsie comes to sit by my side.

"I heard what happened with Kora…and Sergey," she speaks low in my ear. "If you ever need to talk, I know someone."

"I may take you up on that."

I don't know if she was told about my past with Sergey or just the present, but I intend to talk to her about it when I'm ready. Because I know, of all people, she would understand.

"Of course," she adds. "You know my demons, and you know therapy helped a little. So has Jade. She can help you too."

Elsie lived a horror of a life before she found Michael. She and her two friends, Jade and Kayla, were kidnapped and trafficked by the Palermo crime family before the Cavaleri brothers extinguished them. Faro Bianchi, who once ran the family, killed the brothers' father when they were kids, and that caused them to go on the run. Until fifteen years later, when they grew a massive empire and took their revenge. From what Gio told me, Jade married Enzo Cavaleri, who saved her from that life.

So I know Elsie means well when she says she wants to help me, and I'm grateful for that.

I return to watching Gio and Sophia dance together, him goofing around with her, and it makes me smile.

She glances over at me and quietly says, "You'd be a great mother someday."

"I don't think that's true."

"It is." Her penetrating gaze probes mine like she's sure.

"How do you do it?" I ask her, staring at Sophia. "How are you so good at being her mother?"

Her large brown eyes gleam. "It all comes from here." She places a palm against the center of her chest, then picks up my wrist and places my palm over my beating heart. "I promise you have it too."

"How do you know?"

"Call it intuition." Her mouth jerks. "Plus, who else would spin around the room the way you did with her just because she asked?"

"Call me competitive."

"No." She scrunches her nose. "It was more than that. You like her."

"I kinda do."

GIO

"So, you got the woman you wanted after all, huh?" Raph bumps my shoulder, watching Nicolette and Elsie talking while Iseult and Eriu chat with their father.

"So did you," I tell him just as Michael strides up with a glass of whiskey in hand.

"What are you two talking about?"

"About how fucking pissed I still am that you arranged an engagement to Eriu behind my back."

I'm not mad anymore. I'm just messing with him, and he knows it too, with the way his mouth jerks.

"Seems it all worked out in the end, didn't it?" he muses.

"It did. Thank God, or I would've killed you."

He chuckles dryly. "Sure, you would've."

Just as we're about to walk over to our women, chaos erupts, and someone bursts through the room. And as soon as I take in his dark hair and blue eyes…

Devlin—or Donny. Whatever the fuck his name is.

"Where is she?" His eyes scan the room. "Where in the bloody hell is Eriu?"

The man looks like he's on the brink of losing his sanity.

"I'm right here," she whispers, walking up to him slowly.

His eyes probe her from top to bottom. "Are you alright?"

His arms reach for her, but when he registers Patrick marching up behind her, he lowers them.

"Where's Sergey?" Devlin seethes. "I'm gonna kill him."

His tone is brisk, ready for war, and by his bloody knuckles, I can tell he has been battling, most likely out looking for her like we were.

"Seems like you're late to the party." Cillian throws an arm around him. "Come, have a drink. It's been too long."

"Not yet. We need to talk about something I found about that arsehole Bryce." He stares me dead in the face. "We should do it in private, though."

"Come on, Sophia." Mom takes her hand. "Let's go raid the kitchen and find all the candy."

She wags her brows while Sophia's widened gaze darts to everyone, even as Mom drags her away.

My pulse slams in my head.

"What did you say?" I march up to him.

"Ah, you again?" His cold expression greets me.

I fist my hands, wanting to pummel his face.

Iseult curls an arm around me. "Relax. Both of you. We're all on the same side."

"Same side?" Devlin snickers. "I'm not on the same bloody side as someone who's friends with a low-life trafficker."

"He had no idea," Iseult informs him and takes a single step toward him, her eyes narrowing. "So you'd better watch your tongue when you're talking about my fiancé."

She grabs my hand and holds it tight.

"I see." Devlin eyes me hard. He pauses before he finds his next words. "So you're saying you had no idea he was helping smuggle hundreds of girls for six months before he died?"

"Fuck no. We'd never approve of that."

I peer over at my brothers, their expressions deadly at the news. They knew Bryce. Maybe not as well as I did. But we find this kind of thing reprehensible.

"You may speak freely here," Patrick advises. "You're amongst friends. So tell us everything you know."

"That gold card we found on him, with a number on the back that wasn't traceable. I tra—"

"Did you say a gold card?" Michael advances forward. "Do you have a photo of it?"

"Aye." He reaches for his phone and swipes before he shows the screen to Michael.

"Fuck… I know that card."

When I stare over at the screen, the color drains from my face.

"It's not possible," I say. "They're dead."

"Who are you referrin' to?" Devlin asks, giving us a curious look.

The room has grown quiet, all eyes on us.

"The Palermo crime family," I explain.

"What?" Elsie's words fall below a whisper. Fear slams into her horrified gaze.

"Don't worry, little dove. No one will touch you." Michael clasps her cheek as she shudders. "No one, Elsie. I swear it."

She nods, but tears line her eyes.

"How do you know it's them?" Devlin asks.

"That's their card. The one they used to run their sex club. Members would call the number on the back, and someone with a mask would pick them up, blindfold them, and bring them to a secret location."

"Bloody hell," Devlin mutters. "If you're saying they're dead, how the hell was Bryce working for them?"

"I don't know," Michael retorts. "But we'll find out. Is there anything else? What were you saying about tracing the number?"

"I did trace it, but it was disconnected. Bryce was calling someone named P right before he drugged Eriu's friend that night. Now we know who P is."

"Wait…" I raise a palm in the air. "What do you mean, he drugged Eriu's friend?" I turn my sharp gaze at Iseult and she lets go of my hand. "I thought it was you there that night saving a woman from Bryce. You told me you killed him."

"What?" Eriu interrupts, and my attention jumps to her. "She didn't…" She stares intensely at her sister.

"Eriu! No!" Iseult scolds, rushing for her.

But Eriu shakes her head. "You're done protecting me." Her gaze darts between Devlin and Iseult. "You both have done enough. I don't need anyone protecting me anymore."

She turns her attention my way.

"I shot him. I killed Bryce."

Shock punches me in the gut.

"You? Really?" I press my fingers into my eyes. "Why?"

"He tried to take my friend, and when he wouldn't let her go, I shot him."

Jesus Christ.

But Bryce deserved it.

"After he was lying there, I called Devlin and my sister. Iseult took us away, but Devlin got caught by the cops when someone reported the gunshot. So instead of letting me take the blame, he did. He kept me out of prison." Her eyes grow soft as she looks at him.

His features strain, jaw clenching as he stares at her. "I'd do it all over again, lass."

"You shouldn't have." She shakes her head, and her expression pulls with anguish. "It was on me. You shouldn't have had to endure that because I messed up and left without you and went to that club."

"You mean you shouldn't have drugged him and snuck out?" Patrick offers. "Aye, you're right about that. But that's all forgotten now. Devlin is out. We can celebrate that. But we must also find out who has taken over for the four dead Bianchi brothers. Because if they're not in charge, someone else is."

"I think it's time to call Dom Cavaleri," Michael declares, getting his phone out of his pocket. "They need to know that their war may not be over just yet."

He dials Dom's number and puts him on speaker, the cell ringing until he answers.

"Michael," Dom greets. "What the hell do you want?"

"This is not a social call," my brother explains. "I have some news on the Palermos, and you're not going to like it."

Thick, heavy silence greets us, followed by a muttered curse. "What do you know?"

"Found someone who has resurrected their trafficking business."

"Not possible. We would've heard something."

"Except they may have started it outside of New York," Michael adds. "The man who was working for them was doing it in Boston."

Something shatters, and Dom's breaths come loud through the line. "Send me all the information. We'll do some digging, get the feelers out."

"Alright."

"Can't fucking believe this is happening again." He shuffles around.

I can imagine the kind of shit he's going through at the moment. To hate a family as much as they hated the Bianchis, and to find out someone may be trying to start that again, it must be killing him.

The Cavaleris were the ones who not only brought down that family, but got all those involved in the club arrested. At least that's the rumor. It made national news. The images of the many celebrities and politicians were plastered on TV screens.

"I will call for a meeting with the Azienda tomorrow," Michael says. "To find out what each of the families have heard."

The Azienda is the alliance between the now four families of the Cosa Nostra. The Palermo crime family, of which the Bianchis were in charge, was once a part of the alliance. So the only ones standing other than us are the Rosolinos, the Cambrias, and the Grazias.

"Make sure you let me know what they say," Dom says curtly, his tone accusatory, like he doesn't believe Michael would.

"I will," my brother replies. "Same goes for you. I want open channels between us about this."

"Fine." Dom doesn't sound like he likes it.

But he doesn't have to like us to carry out a mutual goal, and that is to extinguish whoever Bryce was working for.

Forty-Three

GIO
TWO WEEKS LATER

My estate has been decked out for a wedding. Mom took care of everything, of course.

About one hundred of our closest friends and family are in attendance to witness the most stubborn woman wed the luckiest man in the world.

I haven't seen her for two days. Two long, aching days without her in my bed.

She took the whole "can't see the bride the night before the wedding" thing way too seriously. And I've missed her like crazy. Can't wait to get my hands on her.

But mostly, I can't wait to see her walk down the aisle and pledge her life to me. I never thought she'd go through with this. I had money on her running away again, leaving me alone at the altar.

But she's here somewhere, getting ready with Eriu, Elsie, and Nicolette.

Waiting at the end of the aisle with my brothers, I fidget with my cufflinks, the tux making me feel too constricted. Fucking bowties.

I loosen it a little.

Is it hot in here?

"Nervous?" Raph asks with a chuckle.

"No. Just want this shit over. I need that damn priest to officially say she's my wife so she can't ever fight me on it."

Just then, the music changes to the wedding march and everyone gets to their feet.

My heart races. My eyes remain glued straight ahead. Tall, clear vases with blood-red candles line each end of the aisle runner, where she's about to walk down from.

I don't see her yet. My gut is knotting, the nerves building, until…

"Holy shit," I whisper.

Fucking tears slam into the back of my eyes.

I've never felt this amount of…everything before. Not until this very moment.

Everyone else disappears as my eyes lock with a grinning Iseult, her red strapless ball gown fitting tightly around her waist, a bouquet of white lilies in her grasp. Patrick looks proud as he leads her toward me.

She doesn't have on a veil, and I love that I can see her clearly, see the brightness of her eyes as she looks at me. And in them, I don't see any doubt or fear. She's giving herself over to me completely, and I'll cherish that—cherish her—for as long as I'm alive.

Only a few steps remain, and then she's there and I'm finally about to hold her.

Her father kisses both sides of her face, then walks up to me. "You do good by her, you hear?"

"It'd be my honor."

He nods and places her hand in mine. And before I can think better of it, I grab her face in my hands and kiss her so damn hard, my heart's ready to fucking explode.

Laughter breaks out, and I reluctantly pull back, while she smiles widely at me.

"Missed me?"

"You have no idea how much, bambina. Never leave me for that long again."

"Always so dramatic." She locks her hand with mine, gazing affectionately, and together we face the priest.

He recites his lines, and when it's my turn, I do the same.

He then says to her, "Do you, Iseult Gwendolynn Quinn—"

"Gwendolynn?" I whisper in mock horror.

She narrows a teasing stare. "If you want this wedding to happen, I would shut up about it if I were you."

When I chuckle, she looks to the priest and lifts up her chin. "Go on. Please."

He clears his throat, his thick gray mustache jerking. "Do you, Iseult Gwendolynn Quinn, promise to take Giovanni Roberto Marino to be your husband, to have and to hold from this day forward, for better, for worse, for richer, for poorer, in sickness and in health, to love and to cherish, 'til death do you part?"

At that last line, she looks at me with a mischievous glint in her eyes, and I know just what she's thinking: the first time we met.

"What will it be?" the priest asks sternly, and we fight the urge not to laugh, staring into each other's eyes.

"I do," she promises. "I really do."

And before the priest has a chance to announce us as husband and wife, she leans closer, her feathery lips against my ear.

"Just so you know, husband, I always sleep with a knife under my pillow."

"That's okay, my little bambina, because I sleep with a gun under mine."

The dance floor is filled with people, while I spin Iseult around the center of it.

"This marriage thing isn't so bad so far." She grinds her ass on me while I groan, snaking my hand around her stomach.

"You keep that up, and I'm gonna get you pregnant by tonight."

She stills, her body growing tense.

"I want that, Iseult. I want a family with you, baby." My mouth drops to the space between her neck and shoulder, kissing her, my teeth grazing her skin.

"What if I ruin our child and make them hate me?" She whirls around, and in her eyes, I find fear—so much of it, it's like she's buried in it. "What if I'm the worst mother? Would you even love me then?"

My hand clasps her nape. "You never have to worry about my love for you. It can carry us through anything, Red. I promise you that. And as far as kids, we'll figure it out together." My gaze penetrates hers. "But I know that you will be one hell of a mother. You'll see."

"Well, if I'm not, I'm blaming you for it."

I laugh. "That's fine by me, as long as I have your permission to start tonight."

"Maybe if you play your cards right…" Her eyes turn hooded, and she discreetly slinks a hand between our bodies and wraps her hand around my semi-hard cock.

"You'd better get that hand off my dick or I will find the nearest room and fuck you in it."

"Promise?"

Just as I'm about to answer, about ten of my men rush into the tent, heading straight for me.

I instantly tense.

Something is wrong.

Iseult becomes equally nervous.

"Sir," one of them says. "We have a situation outside by one of the gates. There's been a breach."

"What kind of breach?"

"It's best if you come with us." He glances at Iseult. "And it may be best to come alone."

"Absolutely not!" Iseult grinds her jaw.

I grab her hand. "My wife is to be kept in the loop of everything that goes on in our home, do you understand?"

"Yes, sir." He nods.

"Make sure all the men know that."

"Of course."

"Now, let's go see what's going on," I demand.

As we're about to head out, Michael and Raph, along with Patrick and Mom, tread toward us.

"What's going on?" Michael asks, noticing the seriousness of the situation.

"Something happened by one of the gates."

"We're all going, then," Patrick announces.

And at this point, I don't care who comes as long as someone fucking tells me what's going on.

"Let's just go," I tell my men, and we follow them out to the southernmost gate.

He opens it and stops, looking intensely at me, his eyes filling with quiet disdain.

"He killed three of our men and left a present," he reveals.

My pulse slams in my ear. "What the hell are you talking about?"

He exhales a short breath as he rounds past the gate entrance, and I'm the first to follow him out.

"What the…" I whip my head back, and my heart rate quickens.

"Oh my God!" Mom cries and hides her face in Patrick's chest.

"Who did this!" Michael bellows, while Raph mutters a curse.

I take in the sight before me, three of my men with their throats sliced open, one missing a hand, as though sawed off.

"We don't know," my guy offers. "But…"

His eyes swivel toward the gate, and it's then I see it.

The missing hand. A knife through it.

But that's not all, because pierced with a knife is a piece of paper, and it has my mother's name on it.

My gut pummels with a heavy feeling as I yank the knife out, taking the note in my hand as the severed hand falls to the ground.

"The note is addressed to you, Ma," I tell her.

That has her tearing her face away from Patrick and looking at me questioningly. "W-w-what?"

I turn the paper around, and she tracks her name clearly written in blood.

Fernanda

"Open the fucking thing!" Patrick hollers. "Tell me who it's from, so I can find the bloody arsehole and kill him."

"Oh my God…" Mom gasps. "It can't…I…no…" She swallows thickly and backs away, almost tripping on one of the dead bodies.

Patrick grabs her forearm and steadies her. "Do you know who did this, darling?"

"I…uh…maybe? Oh, God," she cries. "Please, just open it."

Quickly, I unfold it, but when I actually read the typed-out words, I jerk my head back, a cold rush of disbelief launching through my blood.

"Ma? Tell me this isn't true."

She cries.

Oh, fuck. Fuck!

"What the hell does it say?" Raph asks.

And with a grinding of my jaw, I read the words out loud.

Dear Mother,

I hope this letter finds you well. I'm so glad to see the beautiful life you've built for yourself. But I must admit, I am a little hurt that life didn't include me. I see you kept my twin, Raphael, but I guess I was disposable. Thrown away like trash.

But don't worry. I know where you live. I've known for a long time. Waiting in the shadows. But I'm done waiting. And I'm coming for you. For all of you.

—A

"Holy shit," Iseult mutters, while everyone else appears shellshocked.

"Ma." Raph's voice hardens. "Tell me this isn't true."

With a heavy sob, she covers her face with a palm. "I'm sorry." She sniffles. "But I can't do that."

"Bloody fucking hell!" Patrick explodes. "You had another one of my sons and never told me?"

"Oh, God, I'm s-s-so sorry." She can't stop crying, trying to get the rest of the words out.

"Just tell us, Ma," Michael boils. "What the hell is going on?!"

"It was so long ago." She swipes under her eyes. "I gave birth to two fraternal twins that day, but was only allowed to keep one."

"Why the hell is that?" Patrick's face grows redder by the second.

"You see, that boy… He had your eyes, Patrick." She scowls, her face crumbling. "One look into them, and my mother knew. I knew. And so would Giancarlo." She pauses to collect herself. "So my mother told me I had to give him up, or else our plan to make Gian believe the baby was his would backfire."

"So you just let her take our baby?!"

"No! Of course not. I fought. I begged. But she threatened to take both of my babies. And I had just given birth, Pat. I was disoriented, bleeding, my heart aching. But she took him and told me he would go to a good home. Then she bundled him up and left with him. I never saw him again!" she wails. "Oh my God." She falls to the ground and sobs. "What have I done?"

Patrick lowers beside her and holds her. "It's okay, darling. I know. It's okay."

"What was his name?" Raph asks, his face crestfallen.

"I don't know. I never even signed a birth certificate. My mother must've paid the staff at the hospital to keep it quiet once they realized I now had only one child in that room."

"So we have nothing to fucking go on." Michael runs an aggravated hand through his hair. "Get this cleaned up," he tells the men. "Now. And if any of you breathes a word of this to anyone, you will die."

"Yes, sir."

Patrick picks Mom up, and with the letter in my hand, we head back to the wedding, pretending our world hasn't just turned upside down.

ISEULT

My head is still reeling at the news that Raph has a twin. And after the wedding wound down, Gio and I escaped to our bedroom. He needed time away from the noise, because that news hit all of us.

That crazy lunatic who fought off Gio's foot soldiers and managed to cut off one of their hands is my half brother. I mean, he clearly belongs in the family, no doubt about that.

"Are you okay?" I ask him as he removes the rest of his clothes, his eyes roving down my bare body.

"I will be in just a minute." His hungered stare has me aching, but I worry about him.

"Are you sure?" I ask, sitting up.

"I just need to get lost in my wife right now."

The bed dips with his weight as he pushes me flat on my back and curves his body to mine just right.

He wasted no time moving all of my belongings into his home before the wedding. I have never witnessed someone's stuff getting moved as quickly as mine did. The man hired over ten people to make sure I had all my things arranged before we became husband and wife.

His eyes bore into mine as he fits a hand between our bodies, his fingers slowly strumming my clit.

"Slow," he grunts. "I wanna savor you slow."

I moan softly at the familiar warmth cruising through my body, his cock rock hard against my core. He works me gradually, relishing in this moment, and I never want it to end either.

"Spread those thighs wider for me, wife. Let me feel what I do to you."

As I do, he thrusts his fingers deep inside me until my back arches, my eyes seeing stars when he massages my G-spot.

"That's it. That's my good girl. Give me one before you come around my cock."

With his thumb, he continues to fondle my clit while his fingers piston inside me, until the pressure mounts and stars erupt before my eyes.

I scream out his name, staring into the eyes of the man I love with such fevered desperation, I ache in my soul.

He's my perfect equal, my partner in crime, my everything. I'd die for him. But most of all, I want to live for him.

I want to be the best version of myself, because he deserves that. Because he gives me that too.

He growls as my pussy continues to ripple in waves, giving him everything before he slips out his fingers and sucks them into his mouth without looking away from my eyes.

"What do I taste like?" I ask him, my lips feathering over his as I rock myself against his rigid length.

"Mine," he says with a heartfelt oath, the power of that single word echoing through my heart. "You taste like you're mine, the way you were the moment I met you."

With one last look into my eyes, he kisses me hard, lining the crown of his cock against my entrance and slamming home.

And I know without a doubt that this love is forever, and it's only just the start.

<h1>Forty-Four</h1>

<h2>ADRIEL</h2>

<h3>FERNANDA & PATRICK'S WEDDING</h3>

My mother looks happy, laughing with my father. They don't appear as though they ever even missed me.

I chuckle to myself. But my chest tightens.

Why would they? I was given up like I meant nothing. Left alone in a dark world without anyone who cared what happened.

A fist curls at my side as I grab a drink from the waiter who passes a tray. Tipping it to my mouth, I swallow the entire thing, savoring the burn as it goes down. I don't even know what the drink was, nor do I care. But I need more if I'm to survive it here with all of them.

My line of attention zeroes in on my twin.

Raphael.

The lucky one. The one who never had to endure the things I

did just to survive. He was with our mother. He was loved. While I was anything but.

The need to kill him unfurls in my gut until all I see is red.

I needed to come here. To see them before I leave my surprise. To watch the way they are with one another.

The pain cuts like a knife. But I'm used to that, aren't I?

It was easy to slip into their wedding.

Find out who's attending. Murder one of them and pretend I was him. And bam, I'm in. Had to create a fake ID using the dead guy's name first, of course. But that wasn't too difficult either.

My family has no idea who I am or what I've become. Nor how long I've been watching them all. Waiting to make them pay, especially *her*.

My mother.

The woman who gave me up.

All evidence points to her. She never married my father. She married some other asshole, who's now dead. But maybe my father did know. Maybe he didn't care either. It wouldn't surprise me. It's one thing I was never sure about when I went digging.

So many bodies piled up at my hand. The ones from the orphanage. The nuns who hurt me. Lied to me. One of them talked. She was there when Granny handed me to her, wailing in her arms. Probably crying for the same mother who wanted nothing to do with me.

But did she ever bother to find out if I was safe? If I was cared for?

The answer to all those questions is NO!

Mommy never came looking for her abandoned son.

My life started in the gutter, and I lived there my entire childhood.

I was a foster kid. Beaten. Bruised. Wholly disregarded.

But things changed when I was in my teens. A couple adopted me. And no, it wasn't some happily ever after. It was worse. So much worse than I could've imagined.

My chest rises and falls with anxious breaths.

No. Not here. Not now. Control yourself. You're not a child anymore. You're a thirty-eight-year-old man.

They're gone now. Thanks to me. It's my job to take out the trash, and they were my first. My parents ended up with their throats slit in their kitchen. And me? I ended up with all their money.

And my other parents, the ones laughing right now? They'll suffer the same end.

"Excuse me," a woman says, bumping into me from behind.

A little girl who I know is my niece, Sophia, is beside her. The girl stops, looking up at me through inquisitive brown eyes, her brows tugged.

"Do I know you?" Sophia asks.

"No, young lady." My mouth snakes up at the corner. "I don't think so."

"Are you sure you're not one of my daddy's friends?"

"I am definitely not," I laugh. *More like enemy.*

"Sorry about that," Elsie remarks, grinning as she pulls the girl away. "We have to go take some family photos."

Why the hell did that sting so fucking badly?

As she pulls the child away, Sophia continues to stare at me from behind her shoulder.

It's a shame I'll have to kill her father too. None of them will survive.

I'm coming for them. *All* of them.

They can try to run, but there's no hiding from me.

I'm ready to play.

GIO
ONE WEEK LATER

I didn't know what to expect when Patrick told me there was a letter waiting for me from his late wife.

I have no idea what she could've written to me as I hold it in my hands. There's unexplained fear battering in my chest, like I'm afraid of her words from beyond, like I'll somehow not live up to whatever she has written.

Settling on the edge of the sofa, I open the flap and reach inside, retrieving the perfectly folded letter.

I wanted to read it alone. And when Iseult said she was going shopping with Elsie, Nicolette, and her sister, I figured it was now or never.

Unfolding it carefully, I start to read the words from the woman who gave me my wife.

To the man who'll marry my daughter,

I know we haven't met, but somehow, I feel like we have. Because if you love my daughter as much as I do, then we're connected that way. Through our shared devotion to one of the most important people to me.

So, as a mom who's no longer here to watch out for my baby girl, I ask you to do that for me. Love her. Really love her. Tell her she's beautiful and special. Let her know you'll always be there through the good and the bad.

Because let me tell you, the bad comes when you least expect it. And it's the strongest who survive through the wave that swears to swallow you.

Don't let it.

Just swim together until you reach the shore, stronger than before, and I promise the fight will be worth it.

I hope to meet you one day, maybe in another life, because I know that if my daughter chose you, you must be someone special.

Thank you for loving my Iseult, because I know she'll love you with all her heart.

Love,
Mom

I clench my jaw. And as I look skyward, I close my eyes and send that woman a message, swearing to do right by her daughter, because loving her is all I know how to do.

ISEULT
SEVEN YEARS LATER

"Rowan! Laina!" I call from the kitchen. "Breakfast!"

I flip the scrambled eggs around, hoping no one notices that I may have burned them a little. Okay, fine. More than a little.

I grimace as I start adding a hefty amount onto the plates for my two kids.

Yes, that happened. I'm a mom. And I can't say I've regretted a second of it.

My six-year-old fraternal twins were the best thing to have happened to Gio and me. And that man, the way he loves them is something to witness.

He's been every bit the perfect partner, not just at home, but outside of it. Right now, he's getting the kids ready for school while I make breakfast. Which was my idea. I wanted to redeem myself from last week when I made pancakes and burned them. Apparently burnt food is all I'm capable of. I'm just hoping no one realizes this time…

"Coming, Mommy!" Rowan yells from the top of the stairs in our home in New York.

I decided to stop teaching at Caellach, though I still do what I did. I'm still an enforcer, and I don't see myself ever quitting that.

But stepping away from Caellach was my idea. Gio would've moved to Cherry Grove if that's what I wanted. He would've moved to Mars for me if he knew that was my dream, but I needed to step into my shoes. I needed to live away from my father's constant eye. But I do miss seeing my sister all the time. I guess my brothers too. Sometimes.

I hear the pounding of footsteps and voices rushing down.

"Be careful, guys," Gio scolds. "If you crack your necks, your mother is gonna kill me."

I laugh as I make him a plate too. It looks semi-edible. Ish.

Picking up the kids' plates, I bring them to the table, then gather up ours and place them down.

"She can't kill you, Daddy," Laina sasses. "You're her husband."

This child may send me into an early grave way before a bullet ever does.

He snickers.

"You don't know your mother as well as I do," he mutters lowly just as they make it down.

I pop a brow, staring right at my gorgeous husband just as both kids rush to me for morning hugs. Kissing them both on the top of their heads, I strut over to him and throw both arms around his shoulders.

"I heard that," I whisper across his ear.

He growls, grabbing a handful of my ass through my jeans, tugging me closer as the kids rush for the table.

"You're so beautiful, bambina. Especially when you've got those killer eyes pointed at me." His smirk deepens.

The back of my hand strokes across the curve of his jaw, the stubble prickling my skin. "Maybe after they get on the bus, we can have a little fun."

His eyes turn hooded, his other hand riding up my spine, and he grabs my hair, kissing me hard. As he pulls back, his jaw clenches, and he looks to his right, toward our children.

"Okay, kids, hustle up and eat. Mommy and Daddy have important business to attend to."

I laugh at his serious expression.

Laina giggles, her eyes twinkling for her father, because this man is her whole world.

"You touched Mommy's butt," Rowan giggles.

"Hopefully that's not the only thing I'll be touching," he whispers for my ears only with a wink before he's heading to the table, tugging my hand.

We settle across from each other, and when Laina pops some eggs into her mouth, she gags.

"Mom, this is so disgusting." She grimaces.

"Laina!" Gio scolds. "That's not polite. Your mother worked very hard on this breakfast…" He dips his fork into the plate. "…so you should say thank you."

He brings the eggs to his mouth, and as soon as he starts to chew, his face almost pales.

Our eyes clash as he forces himself to swallow that down.

I glare. "It can't be that bad."

Forcefully, I stab my own fork into my breakfast and throw some egg into my mouth.

"Oh, God!" I grab a napkin and spit it out. "Why did no one tell me how awful that was?"

"Uh, Mommy, I kinda did." Laina scowls, her bright green eyes popped wide at my horrified expression.

"Okay, new rule," I offer. "From now on, Daddy cooks breakfast. Or anything, actually."

"Yay!" both kids bellow as I roll my eyes.

"How about cereal this morning?" he asks them, while their faces fill with the sheer joy of having a bowl full of marshmallows for breakfast.

Once he pours them each a bowl, he makes us bagels with cream cheese.

And with the kids talking over one another, we eat together—a family. It's something that once upon a time felt like only a dream that someone else was having.

I never thought that I was capable of being a decent mother or a decent wife, but somehow, I became both, and I thank the man who's currently unable to peel his eyes off of me for that.

His constant reassurance, devotion, and love knew no bounds. In his eyes, I was both beautiful and special, and after all that I went through, it took a while for me to believe it too.

"Okay, kids, school bus time." Gio takes their plates to the sink as they jump to their feet.

"Grab your lunch bags," I remind them, pointing to the counter.

Both of the kids freeze, their eyes growing horrified with each passing second.

"You didn't make the lunch, did you, Mommy?" Rowan asks, his hazel eyes full of affection, yet fear.

"No," I huff through a pinched expression. "Your daddy did. I only packed it."

"Oh, thank God." Laina releases a big breath.

"Wow, guys, real nice. Really feeling the love this morning," I tease while the kids grab their backpacks and lunch bags, giggling at me.

Gio slides up to me, his big strong hands cupping my hips. "Don't worry, Red. I'm gonna make you feel real loved in just a little bit."

"Promises, promises." I draw my lips to his and kiss him slow, my tongue rolling with his.

"Mmm," he groans.

"Eww! They're kissing!" Laina gags.

As we draw back, the room swells with our laughter.

"Okay, hugs, you two," I tell them, stretching out my arms.

"The bus will be here any minute."

They both rush to me, squeezing each one of my legs.

"I love you guys," I remind them, kissing their cheeks, my heart warming.

"Love you too, Mommy," they echo.

And with each one holding their father's hand, they sprint out the door while I rinse the plates and toss them into the dishwasher.

Minutes later, I hear the roar of the school bus, and when I turn around, Gio's already walking back inside.

"Now, where were we?" His eyes rove down my body from across the room before he marches toward me slowly, his black button-down stretching across his muscular chest.

But as soon as he reaches me, my phone rings. His hands curve around my hips, thick fingers stretching around my behind.

"Who is it?" he asks when I pick up the phone and find my father's name there.

"Hi, Dad."

My lips twine up when Gio's mouth peppers rough kisses up my neck, his grunting reverberating through my body.

"Iseult, I have a job for you, and it's time-sensitive. As in right now."

I groan to myself, dropping my head back. "Okay. Give me the details."

Once he does, I say, "I'll get it done."

When he disconnects the call, my fingers sink into Gio's hair, and I yank him back. "Going to have to take a rain check on the orgasms, husband. He needs me immediately."

"Oh, come on." He grits his teeth. "How the hell does that man manage to call every time I'm about to fuck you?"

"Sorry." I shrug a single shoulder, my toes curling at the thought of him inside me.

Grabbing his cock, I stroke his already-hard erection.

"Gonna have to wait," I say, our eyes connected as one before I let go and head backward for the stairs. "Maybe you can use those cuffs on me tonight."

"You bet your pretty ass, I will." He follows me, his eyes narrowed like he's famished for a taste of me.

I run up the stairs while he chases me, the both of us laughing as I enter our bedroom. He leans back against the wall, watching me get the safe from under the bed, enter the code, and retrieve two of my knives and a nine-mil.

Lifting a leg over the bed, I pull up my jeans and slip a blade into the ankle holster already there, while I place the gun in my waistband.

His gaze is sinful and intense. "Fuck, baby, that gets me every time."

Biting on my bottom lip, I lower my leg, strutting over to him, the other knife still in my grasp. When I'm near, I line the blade up against his throat, my lips brushing over his.

"I love the way you love," I breathe, rocking my hips into his, my heartbeats pounding for the way I feel for him.

This man is eternally mine.

"I'll never stop," he promises.

And I believe him.

With a quick jerk, he flips me around, pressing my body up against the wall, pinning my wrist with the knife in it as he kisses me with all the passion that is still there between us, reminding me that a love like ours comes once in a lifetime, and I'm forever glad that it's mine.

Thanks for Reading!

Want to know what happened to Hudson Mackay and why he's missing? Pre-Order *SHATTERED SECRETS*, coming September 7, 2023!

This one is a twisty, angsty amnesia romance about a man who is presumed dead only to resurface years later with no memory of his wife or his past life.

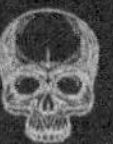

Surprised about Adriel? Me too! He wasn't supposed to happen. But thanks to a conversation I had with Shania Trujillo, my reader and friend, we have a fourth book! For those who've asked if Kayla, Elsie's friend, will ever get a story, well she is! This will be hers.

Find out what happens with Adriel & Kayla in *SAVAGE WOUNDS*, the last book in the Messina Crime Family series, coming January 8, 2024!

Playlist

- "Murder" by Mako
- "Get Out Alive" by Andrea Russett
- "Dirtier Thoughts" by Nation Haven
- "Breathe" by Mako
- "Addict of Magic" by Picture This
- "Leave Me in the Dark" by Alexander Stewart
- "Howling" by SYML feat. Lucius
- "I Didn't Know" by Sofia Carson
- "Better" by Billy Raffoul
- "Scars" by James Bay
- "Born Alone Die Alone" by Madalen Duke
- "Where Are You?" by Elvis Drew feat. Avivian
- "Wannabe" by Austin Giorgio
- "Love Into a Weapon" by Madalen Duke
- "Bang Bang (Remember My Name)" by BELLSAINT
- "What's Left of You" by Chord Overstreet
- "Part Goddess Part Gangster" by Madalen Duke
- "Lost" by Dermot Kennedy
- "Never Til Now" by Ashley Cooke feat. Brett Young
- "Blame's on Me" by Alexander Stewart
- "Too Late to Love You" by Ex Habit
- "PLEASE" by Omido feat. Ex Habit
- "You're the One" by Luca Fogale
- "Breathe Again" by Harrison Storm
- "Pieces (Hushed)" by Andrew Belle

- "Small Disasters" by Dean Lewis
- "What Makes You Sad" by Nicotine Dolls
- "Hide and Seek" by Klergy feat. Mindy Jones
- "Kind of Love" by Natalie Jane
- "Bad Dreams – Stripped" by Faouzia
- "What You Do to Me" by John Legend
- "You Put a Spell on Me" by Austin Giorgio
- "Single Part of You" by Jamie Grey
- "What You're Running From" by Jamie Grey
- "All for You" by Dean Lewis
- "Shackles (Pitched Down)" by Steven Rodriguez
- "Lovely" by Billie Eilish feat. Khalid
- "BULLET" by NF
- "Parachute" by Kyndal Inskeep feat. Song House
- "Joy Ride" by Hueston

Also By Lilian Harris

Fragile Hearts Series

1. _Fragile Scars_
2. _Fragile Lies_
3. _Fragile Truths_
4. _Fragile Pieces_

Cavaleri Brothers Series

1. _The Devil's Deal_
2. _The Devil's Pawn_
3. _The Devil's Secret_
4. _The Devil's Den_
5. _The Devil's Demise_

Messina Crime Family Series

1. _Sinful Vows_
2. _Cruel Lies_
3. _Twisted Promises_
4. _Savage Wounds_ (Coming January 8th, 2024)

Standalone

1. _Shattered Secrets_ (Coming September 7th, 2023)

For Lilian, a love of writing began with a love of books. From *Goosebumps* to romance novels with sexy men on the cover, she loved them all. It's no surprise that at the age of eight she started writing poetry and lyrics and hasn't stopped writing since.

She was born in Azerbaijan, and currently resides in Long Island, N.Y. with her husband, three kids, and a dog named Gatorade. Even though she has a law degree, she isn't currently practicing. When she isn't writing or reading, Lilian is baking or cooking up a storm. And once the kids are in bed, there's usually a glass of red in her hand. Can't just survive on coffee alone!

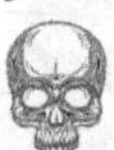

Lilian would love to connect with you!
Email: lilanharrisauthor@gmail.com
Website: www.lilanharris.com
Newsletter: https://subscribepage.io/LilianHarris
Signed Paperbacks: https://bit.ly/LHSignedPB
Facebook: www.facebook.com/LilianHarrisBooks
Reader Group: www.facebook.com/groups/lilianslovlies
Instagram: www.instagram.com/lilianharrisauthor
TikTok: www.tiktok.com/@lilianharrisauthor
Twitter: www.twitter.com/authorlilian
Goodreads: https://bit.ly/LilianHarrisGR
Amazon: www.amazon.com/author/lilianharris